NO CURE FOR MURDER

Led by Koznicki and Harris, Koesler and the officers rushed from the room in search of the sound. The screams were coming not from the adjoining office but from the one adjoining that.

It was Sister Eileen's office. It was her secretary, Dolly, who was screaming.

Koznicki, unexpectedly agile for his size, was first to enter Sister's office. He saw Dolly standing near the large executive desk. At sight of him, she ceased screaming, but stood badly trembling.

Koznicki followed her riveted gaze to the knees and feet of a prostrate figure half hidden by the desk. It was a nun. He could see the white habit extending to sensible black shoes. . . .

Also by William X. Kienzle
Published by Ballantine Books:

ASSAULT WITH INTENT

DEATHBED

KILL AND TELL

SHADOW OF DEATH

SUDDEN DEATH

DEATHBED

William X. Kienzle

BALLANTINE BOOKS • NEW YORK

Copyright © 1986 by GOPITS, Inc.

Library of Congress Catalog Card Number: 86-1184

ISBN 0-345-33189-3

This edition published by arrangement with Andrews, McMeel & Parker

Printed in Canada

First Ballantine Books Edition: April 1987

For Javan

Acknowledgments

Gratitude for technical advice to:

Sgt. Roy Awe, Homicide, Detroit Police Department
Ramon Betanzos, Professor of Humanities, Wayne State University
Patricia Chargot, Staff Writer, *Detroit Free Press*
Jim Grace, Detective, Kalamazoo Police Department
Mary Ann Hayes, R.N.
Timothy Kenny, Deputy Chief of the Criminal Division, Wayne County
  Prosecutor's Office
Patrick McAlinden, Director of Treatment, Western Wayne County
  Correctional Facility
Sgt. Daniel McCarty, Police Arson Unit, Detroit Police Department
Neal Shine, Senior Managing Editor, *Detroit Free Press*
Samaritan Health Care Center, Detroit:
  Sister Bernadelle Grimm, R.S.M.
  Sister Rose Petruzzo, O.P., Director, Department of Pastoral Care Service
  Sister Genevieve Shea, S.L.W., Chaplain
  Sister Marie Thielen, R.S.M., Vice President for Sponsorship
  The Reverend Roland Schaedig, Chaplain
  James Culver, Pharm. D., Director of Pharmacy
  Donald Grimes, Quality Assurance Coordinator, Pharmacy
  Dolly Wasik, Secretary, Pastoral Care Department
  Barbara Wineka, Director, Department of Volunteer Services
Mt. Carmel Mercy Hospital, Detroit:
  Thomas J. Petinga, Jr., D.O., FACEP, Chairman, Department of
    Emergency Medicine
  Rosemary Clisdal, R.N., Assistant Charge Nurse, Department of
    Emergency Medicine
  William M. Collins, CRNA, Staff Anesthetist, Department of Anesthesia
  Vivien Dishmon, R.N., Assistant Head Nurse, Department of Surgery
  Scott T. Harris, M.D., Chief Surgical Resident, Department of
    Emergency Medicine
  Willard S. Holt, Jr., M.D., FCCP, Chairman, Department of Anesthesia
  Gloria Kuhn, D.O., FACEP, Director of Residency, Department of
    Emergency Medicine
  Maureen Loose, R.N., Staff Nurse, Department of Surgery
  Bob Mahanti, Surgical Assistant, Department of Surgery
  James Patton, Biomedical Engineering Technician
  Robert Roussin, R.N., Assistant Charge Nurse, Department of
    Emergency Medicine

1

SISTER! CAN YOU HEAR ME? CAN YOU HEAR
me even though you are dead?

*I am the one who killed you. But you must know that. By
now, you must know all the answers.*

*It was a mistake. It was a mistake ever to have set
myself on this course. But that is of little consolation to
you. It is too late for consolation. And I must confess I am
sorry. But what good does that do you? It is too late for
sorrow.*

*You are dead and this unbearable pain in my head goes
on.*

It was all so useless.

*With all my heart I wish I could change the course of
these events. I wish I could change what has already
happened. But of course no one can do that. No one can
bring you back to life.*

*If I were to tell this story to someone—and I may very
well be forced to do so—where would I start?*

I suppose I would start where so many hospital stories begin. In the emergency room . . .

"There is no heartbeat."

"Uh-huh."

"I do not get any pulse." Dr. Lee Kim pressed his fingers against the patient's carotid artery.

"Uh-huh." Kim need not have made the statement. Dr. Fred Scott could hear the long pauses between the monitor's blips.

Nurses and other doctors were methodically cutting away the woman's clothing. None of it had much value. As the last of her underclothes dropped to the floor, one of the EMS crew who had just delivered her to St. Vincent's emergency department began external massage of her heart.

Scott aimed a small pocket flashlight into her unblinking eyes. "Pupils are dilated and fixed." Delicately, he flicked his index finger along her eyelash. No response. He knew it was hopeless.

Kim jammed a needle just below the clavicle to establish a subclavian line. He inserted a catheter and began the flow of chemicals intended to stimulate the heart. "Nothing," he said, noting the absence of cardiac activity on the monitor. "No response."

Still the uniformed man, one hand cupped over the other, continued to pump against her chest.

Kim removed the catheter and snapped off his rubber gloves. "Do you suppose the medical examiner will pass on this one?"

Scott smiled broadly. "Willie Moellmann is up to his ears with probable homicides. I can't think he'll want a little old lady with a likely cardiac arrest." He removed his gloves.

The discarding of the gloves led the others in Trauma Room One to assume, correctly, that efforts to resuscitate the patient were ended. She would be registered "Dead on Arrival" and preserved in the hospital's morgue until paperwork was completed and a mortician called for the body. Meanwhile, a nurse would inform the immediate family of her death.

"What's goin' on next door?" Scott stood tiptoe to see over the crowd in Trauma Two. Most of those in Trauma One, once their patient had been declared DOA, had moved to the adjoining room, partly to help and partly from curiosity. By now, slightly more than twenty staff members were crowded into the room.

Scott was tall enough to see most of the action. Which was fortunate, as there was no room for him inside the arena.

"What is it?" Scott asked of anyone willing to answer.

"Gunshot," replied a nurse. "To the chest."

Scott could see it. Just under the left breast: A small, neat hole; only a slight trickle of blood from the wound. They had cut away her clothing and were covering her with a hospital gown. She was conscious, able to communicate, and apparently young. That was the good news. But she was enormous. That was the bad news. If they had to go in after the bullet, those layers of fat would be of no help to the surgeon nor to her heart.

Scott became aware of someone standing beside him. It wasn't one of the regular staff; the newcomer was too intent. He seemed to be scarcely breathing, as if viewing such a scene for the first time. Approximately Scott's height, perhaps an inch or two taller, he wore a long white hospital-issue jacket, on the sleeve of which was a badge reading, "Pastoral Care Department." Scott tilted his head to look through the bottom portion of his bifocals and make out the man's identification tag.

"You're Father Koesler, eh?" Scott offered his hand.

3

He could not extend it. They were pressed too closely together.

"Yes," Father Robert Koesler replied. "And you're . . ." He tried to make out the other man's ID, but the card had flipped over and only clear plastic was showing.

"Scott. Fred Scott."

"You're a doctor?"

Scott nodded and smiled. "Bless me, Father, for I have sinned. I'm in charge of this loony bin."

"The entire hospital?"

"No, no. Thank God. Just Emergency."

"Oh."

"And you're the new chaplain."

"Well, temporary."

"I know. You're taking Father Thompson's place while he goes on a well-deserved vacation."

Koesler smiled. "News travels fast."

"You bet. This is just a little Catholic hospital and everybody pretty well knows everybody else's business."

They were silent for a few moments, watching, as doctors, nurses, and technicians carried out their various responsibilities with a professional air.

"Your first time in Emergency?"

"Yes," Koesler admitted. "Fascinating."

"Did you see the bullet hole?"

"Yes."

"Probably a small caliber. No telling yet where the slug went, where it is, or how much damage it's done."

With considerable effort, several doctors turned the woman on her side while one examined her back.

"They're making sure that's the only wound and that it's the entry. When I was starting out in this business I had a gunshot victim with a wound just about where hers is. And with just as little blood. So I treated the wound. We were getting ready to take him to surgery when I

4

noticed a considerable amount of blood had dripped from the cart to the floor. We turned him over and found four more wounds.

"You don't want to make a mistake like that more than once—if that often."

Suddenly, there was a rush of people out of Trauma Two. Koesler, taken by surprise, was carried back by the human tide.

"They're going to take X-rays," Scott explained. "We have to do that. It's tough to find out exactly where the slug is with one X-ray. See, X-rays are two-dimensional and the body is three-dimensional. We've got to find out whether the bullet is near a vital structure."

"But there was only a trickle of blood. Doesn't that mean the injury isn't too serious?"

"Not necessarily. It may have done a lot of internal damage. She may be exsanguinating internally."

Exsanguinating, Koesler thought. *Sanguis:* Latin for blood. *Ex sanguine:* bleeding out. It probably means she may be bleeding internally. He hadn't expected to call on his recollection of Latin to get him through his three-week hospital stint.

After the X-rays were taken, the crowd returned to the room, with Scott and Koesler still at the outer fringe.

"They've catheterized her." Scott continued his commentary for Koesler's benefit. "See the bag at the foot of the cart? Bright yellow. That's good; no blood in the urine. And see the bag hanging up there with the IV? That's decompressing the air in her stomach. You make an abdominal incision without doing that and her whole stomach could pop out at you."

Koesler did not want to think about that. In fact, he had approached this whole venture with a good measure of trepidation. Father Ed Thompson, a classmate, had needed a substitute in order to take a vacation. He might have

5

asked another chaplain to cover, but the Archdiocese of Detroit was getting a bit thin on chaplains—a bit thin on priests in general. So Thompson had let his need be known through the priests' newsletter.

Koesler had wrestled with the request for several days. Thompson would be gone during the first few weeks of January. Normally, so closely following Christmas, this was a slow time in the parish. It would not be terribly difficult to find a religious-order priest to cover for Koesler's daily Mass schedule at St. Anselm's. And Koesler ascertained that he would be able to fit the hospital's single Sunday Mass into St. Anselm's weekend schedule.

He wanted to help his friend and classmate. Yet he hesitated. Koesler knew himself well enough to question his effectiveness in a hospital setting. It was one thing to visit patients occasionally, stay awhile, and then leave. Quite another thing to be ultimately responsible for their spiritual welfare throughout their hospital stay.

Furthermore, Koesler was unsure how he would react to this very situation—a hospital emergency. He had no history of being especially cool and calm in the face of blood and death. And that, by and large, was his image of a hospital: a place where people, especially on admission, bled a lot. And of course a healthy percentage of them died there. No one was about to kid him; he'd read about carts with bodies and DOA tags dangling from toes.

In the end a combination of charity and curiosity won the day. He wanted to help his friend and at the same time he thought this experience might add a dimension to his parochial ministry.

So here he was, standing in the emergency unit of St. Vincent's Hospital, awaiting the arrival of the family of an elderly woman who had just been pronounced dead in Trauma One. While waiting, he was witnessing the treatment of a frightened woman who had been shot. Well, at least there wasn't a lot of blood. Thank God.

"See those X-rays mounted on the viewer over there?" Scott resumed his explication.

Koesler nodded.

"See the frontal view? See the slug on the right side? It looks like it's resting right next to the spine. Now, see the side view? It's actually nowhere near the spine. But they're going to have to dig through a lot of layers to get it."

Koesler gave thanks that he would not be doing the digging.

A doctor began explaining to the patient where the bullet was and what they proposed to do about it. He was interrupted by a nurse who related the patient's blood pressure.

"Uh-oh," said Scott. "The pressure fell. They'll take her to surgery stat."

He proved prophetic. Attendants unhooked bottles trailing tubes inserted in various orifices, the cart's brakes were released, and the patient was whisked away.

Scott intercepted an exiting doctor. "Who did it? Anybody find out?"

"Complete stranger," the doctor answered. "She was coming out of the bank. Some kid shot her and grabbed her purse."

"Good Lord! They used to just knock people down. What's this world coming to!"

A loud barking was heard.

"Now, dammit, who let a dog get in here?" Scott was angry.

At that moment, a laughing nurse entered the trauma area from the main emergency section. "It's not a dog. It's a man who think he's a dog!"

"What!"

7

Koesler followed Scott, who moved at a brisk pace, determined to get to the bottom of this nonsense.

They entered a long, narrow space with a totally white decor, partitioned on one side into ten curtained stalls. At the far end of the room was a naked man, indeed barking in fine imitation of a dog. Several attendants were slowly closing in on him. When the man lifted one leg to urinate, Scott could take it no longer. He turned away, breaking up in laughter.

Koesler followed suit. When he looked up again, three very elderly nuns in most traditional habit came into view. All three were chattering like magpies. Catching sight of the naked man, as one they covered their eyes and turned away. But they continued talking without missing a beat. The middle nun, easily the oldest, appeared to be injured.

"You certainly have a lively pond here," Koesler observed to Scott.

"You ain't seen nothin' yet. It's still morning, and a Monday to boot. It usually gets more interesting as the day progresses."

Koesler decided he could wait for the buildup. Waiting, in fact, was what he was doing. For the family of the deceased.

Forewarned, St. Vincent's emergency unit was preparing for the imminent delivery of one male and one female, both Caucasian, who had been involved in an auto accident at Cass and Lafayette. The EMS crew had called in with their estimated time of arrival and condition of the injured.

St. Vincent's emergency staff calmly began laying out the equipment their experience told them would be needed. There was no tension. Time enough for that when the

8

victims arrived. If anything, the atmosphere was one of bantering.

"Who were those three nuns?"

"The three old ones?"

"Come on! Were there three young ones?"

"Carmelites."

"Discalced Carmelites?"

"Yeah."

"I thought they weren't supposed to talk."

"They aren't."

"What is this? They wouldn't shut up."

"In a situation like this, when there's an accident, that's an exception. Then they are allowed to talk."

"What was the problem, anyway?"

"The oldest one fell down a flight of stairs."

"You mean because she fell down the stairs, the other ones could talk?"

"I guess that's it."

There was a slight pause.

"Do you suppose the two younger ones pushed the older one?"

Koesler smiled. The relatives of the dead woman still had not arrived.

There was a flurry of action at the admitting doors. Two stretchers were removed from the EMS van and placed on gurneys, which were then hurried into Trauma Rooms One and Two respectively.

Doctors Scott and Kim in One began working on the man.

This seemed to be the sort of case Father Koesler had been anticipating. Not the DOA, who had resembled a limp mannequin. Not the woman with a small, neat bullet hole in her chest. This man was a mess. His face had been badly damaged and there was blood all over him. Nevertheless, Father Koesler was holding up quite well. He

9

didn't know if it ever got much worse than this. But, so far so good.

Dr. Scott worked on the patient's head area while Dr. Kim checked for vital signs. Meanwhile, others were cutting clothing away and briskly performing their respective tasks.

"Watch it! Watch it! Watch it!" Scott fairly shouted. "Watch his neck. We could easily have a break there."

"Blood pressure's normal."

"He's unconscious."

"I'm getting a rapid heart rate."

"He's sweaty and kind of clammy."

"Respiration is twenty-six per minute."

"That's a little bit fast."

"Can you see his pupils?" Dr. Kim asked.

"Uhh . . . no," Scott answered. "Too much facial swelling. I can't get his eyes open."

"Look at that blood draining from his ear," Kim said. "It may be severe brain injury. I think it is. What say we send him up for a CAT scan as quickly as we can?"

"Uhh . . . OK—wait a minute . . . I'm getting a faint odor of alcohol." Scott's nose was just above the victim's mouth. "Let's do a blood test."

Blood was taken and the dipstick inserted. Scott quickly scanned it. "Uh-huh. It looks hypoglycemic. The paper isn't registering anything. I don't think he's got any sugar left. Let's have two amps of D-50 stat."

Scott snatched the ampule from the nurse and immediately injected the contents directly through the IV line.

Modestly smug, Scott's eyes darted from the sweep second hand of his watch to the inert patient. In seemingly no time, the patient stirred, stretched his extremities, then tried to open his eyes. He couldn't, due to the swelling.

"Fifteen seconds," Scott announced. "He's conscious. Let's go from here."

As though fleeing a plague, all save the X-ray technician cleared the room. It was X-ray time.

Koesler again found himself pressed alongside Dr. Scott.

"That was close," Scott said.

"What would have happened?" Koesler asked. "I mean, what would have happened if the man had been taken up for a . . . uh . . . CAT scan?"

"What would have happened?" Scott repeated the question, taking time to consider the likely outcome. "His blood sugar was way low. Without that shot of dextrose, and with the amount of time needed for the CAT scan . . . he probably would've had a seizure on the table—or even a cardiac arrest."

"You mean—"

"He could have died. The brain needs sugar."

"Holy mackerel! You saved that man's life."

Scott shrugged. "You win some, you lose some. But if we hadn't done that blood sugar test, we should have had our rumps kicked all over downtown Detroit. It's one of those simple tests you should do routinely in a case like this. Sometimes you forget."

Koesler could not get over the almost miraculous recovery he had just witnessed. "That was fantastic. That man will probably never know how close he came to dying. One medical procedure saved him. But it's just as possible another medical procedure could have killed him."

"That's the way it goes in the hospital, Father. Most all the people who come here are in trouble—some of them serious trouble. Oftentimes their physical condition hangs by the proverbial thread. It doesn't take much—nature, their own attitude, or a mistake—for their condition to worsen or even become terminal. Yep, life here hangs by a thread."

X-rays were completed. The medical team swarmed

back into the room, leaving Father Koesler still awaiting a family that would be grieving.

For some time, a rather nondescript man had been standing behind Koesler. No one had paid him much attention. In part because he was nondescript, and in part because he was wearing an appropriate uniform—a long white hospital coat. An ID dangled from the lapel. The top line identified him as Bruce Whitaker. The second line identified him as a hospital volunteer. Thus identified, and given St. Vincent's rather casual internal security, he was virtually free to roam the hospital at will.

Whitaker had been a volunteer at St. Vincent's for several weeks. Besides performing helpful if menial services for various units and departments, he had been carefully observing hospital procedures, with emphasis on such volatile and high-risk areas as emergency, intensive care, intensive cardiac care, and the clinic.

He could not have agreed more with Dr. Scott: Life here hung by a thread. That thread was Whitaker's principal concern. But he had observed enough. He was ready to act.

2

EITHER OUT OF INCIPIENT FRIENDSHIP,
compassion, pity, or some combination thereof, Dr. Scott
seemed to have taken Father Koesler under his wing.
Having completed what was expected of them in the
emergency unit, Scott and Koesler were immersed in a
coffee break in the hospital's small, ancient cafeteria.

It likely was friendship, thought Koesler, since they
were able to endure long stretches of silence without forcing meaningless conversation. That pleased Koesler, for he
had had positive feelings toward Scott since their meeting
just a few hours before, although, given the in-built stress
and sudden demands of Scott's work, Koesler thought it
odd that the doctor appeared so lighthearted.

Scott's receding hairline and clipped beard framed a
rather cherubic face set off by a neatly trimmed mustache.
The hair was a salt-and-pepper mix. Scott carried a bit of
unwanted weight. He probably would have been considerably
more overweight if his work did not demand so much time
on his feet and so much physical activity.

"Remarkable looking woman, isn't she?" Scott ran a hand through his beard.

Koesler started. He realized he had been idly regarding a woman who had been making her way slowly through the cafeteria, stopping to chat at almost every occupied table.

Though he had never met her, Koesler well knew who she was. During the years he had been editor of the archdiocesan newspaper, he had published her picture many times. She was the highly regarded Sister Eileen Monahan, OSVDP (Order of St. Vincent de Paul), chief executive officer of St. Vincent's Hospital for as long as anyone could remember.

Yes, she was a remarkable looking woman. There was a saying as well as a general agreement that nuns were ageless. That had been more generally true in the recent past before most religious orders of women had changed their minds, their rules, and their habits. The traditional habits covered everything but a woman's hands and face. Facial wrinkles often were pulled smooth by a tightly fitting coif. The casual onlooker could never tell whether a nun had any hair at all, let alone whether it was gray or white.

But now was the day of the modified habit. Usually consisting of an off-the-face veil and a modest dress or suit whose only relationship to the former habit was its color. It was, for religious women, a day of truth in advertising.

The truth was . . . Sister Eileen had kept her figure. Granted it was a mature figure—Koesler guessed she must be in her mid- to late-sixties—but she was a grand looking woman. A very attractive, interesting face, and eyes that had endured a lot of suffering, her own and others'

Both Koesler and Scott detected a pattern to her tablehopping. She was working her way toward them.

Sister Eileen seated herself across from Koesler and

smiled warmly, extending her hand across the table. "Well, if it isn't Father Koesler. I haven't had the opportunity to welcome you to St. Vincent's."

"Thank you. I guess now I'm official." Koesler noted she had a very firm handshake. "Although I have been welcomed."

"The pastoral care team?"

Koesler nodded.

"What did they tell you?"

"Well, Father Thompson bequeathed me his beeper. He said it was the kindest thing he could do for me. He said it would free me from being lashed to a telephone."

"By and large, that's correct," Scott agreed.

"Sister Mary Kevin introduced me—or rather, reintroduced me—to the theories of Kübler-Ross on the process of dying. And she described the chaplain's routine when there's a death in the hospital. And Sister Rosamunda—well, briefly, she urged that I spend most of my time being quiet and listening. Come to think of it, that's pretty much what all three of them advised."

Eileen sipped her coffee. "Not bad advice, at least for a start. This may seem like a very strange enterprise at first. Most beginning chaplains, especially after undergoing the orientation you've just had, are apt to be a bit nervous about what to say to sick or, particularly, to dying people. The best advice anyone can give at this point is that which you received.

"But it would be a serious mistake to overlook all the experience you've had in the priesthood. How long have you been a priest, Father?"

He paused to figure. "It'll be thirty-two years in June."

"Yes, and you'll always be drawing on those years. In no time, you will feel very much at ease. In the meantime, 'shut up and listen' is not bad advice."

15

"Actually, it's at least the second time I've gotten precisely that advice."

"Oh?"

"Yes. The first time was just after Cardinal Boyle—he was a mere archbishop at the time—appointed me editor of the *Detroit Catholic*. My one-time pastor, Monsignor Stitt, was presiding over a formal dinner. I guess I was making too many comments to suit him. Anyway, he said, 'Father Koesler, if you're going to be an editor, you had better learn to shut up and listen.' I've never been able to figure out what that had to do with being an editor. But I thought in general it was good advice. I've just never been able to follow it very well. I must confess I am not a very good listener."

"Well," she finished her coffee, "if you're not, you're not. We're both kind of old dogs to learn new tricks."

Her frankness in admitting the difficulty of change surprised Koesler. He did not want their discussion to end just yet. "May I get you another cup of coffee?"

"Why, yes. That would be nice."

"How about you, Doctor?"

"No. I've got to get back." Scott excused himself and left. He was odd-man-out in this conversation between two people who had dedicated their lives to religion. It had happened to him many times in this Catholic hospital. He knew the signs.

Koesler returned with two steaming cups.

"What have they had you do so far, Father?" Young nuns and priests would have begun on a first-name basis. These two were of an older school. They would use each other's title.

"Earlier this morning, I took Communion calls to my floors. Later, I covered a death in the emergency unit."

"What do you think so far?"

"I'm not sure. Maybe it's too early to tell. I've certainly

brought Communion to the sick often enough. But there was something different about this. In a parish situation the sick are in their own homes. The people here seemed a bit more . . . uh . . . vulnerable.''

''That's very true, Father. At home most of the activity revolves around the sick member of the family, who remains in familiar surroundings. Here the sick person is part of a broader system. He wakes up, is fed, is medicated, and retires when the system tells him to. And often he is not even wearing his own bedclothes.''

''That's going to take a little time to get used to. But the death scene will take even longer to get into.''

Sister Eileen smiled. ''Problems?''

''Well, first I learned that in a code blue, everyone except the chaplain breaks his or her neck to get to the scene.''

''That's right.'' She grinned. ''The chaplain's just in the way until the patient either makes it or doesn't.''

''Well, I waited for the family to arrive. When they did, Dr. Scott met them, explained what had happened to the deceased, answered their questions, then left them to me. And all hell broke loose.

''I took them to what you jokingly call a quiet room and I got a look at the abyss where there will be the weeping and gnashing of teeth.''

''So what did you do?''

''Remembered what I'd been told and shut up and listened.''

Eileen leaned forward and put her hand on his arm. ''That's all they wanted you to do. They wanted to vent their grief, and your silence as well as your presence allowed them to do that. I think as you follow up with this family, you'll find them thanking you for being there and letting them express their emotions.''

''I hope you're right. But then, you probably are; you've

17

been at this so long—oh, pardon me; I didn't mean to imply anything about your age."

She laughed. "Don't apologize. I *have* been at it a long time. Though not quite as long as this hospital's been here."

Koesler had been aware, vaguely, that St. Vincent's was an antique. Everything testified to that: the worn hardwood floors, the high ceilings, the creaks and squeaks, the smell of the place—somewhere between mustiness and the odor of sanctity. But he was unaware of its exact age. "How old is it?"

"Almost 150 years."

"Wow!"

Sister Eileen chuckled. "Sometime between then and now, I came upon the scene. Fresh out of the convent, I came here as a nurse, then moved up to supervisor, then briefly a vice-president, and finally, chief executive officer."

"You've paid your dues. But this brings up another question . . . if you've got the time?"

"What could be more important than satisfying the curiosity of our temporary chaplain?"

"Well, I've asked this question of others, both before I came here and during my orientation. But I have yet to get an answer I can understand."

"Yes?" She smiled.

"Why go on with it? Why perpetuate St. Vincent's Hospital?"

Sister Eileen turned quite serious. She did not immediately reply.

"There are municipal hospitals here in downtown Detroit," Koesler persisted. "And from all I know, they lose money regularly. It must be far worse for St. Vincent's. Yet there's no reason you have to stay here. Almost all the other Catholic and private hospitals have either closed or moved out to the more financially secure suburbs. And no one counts them cowardly for doing so. It just makes good financial sense to get out to a place where you can survive."

She chewed her lip. Koesler was mildly surprised at her hesitancy to answer. She must have faced this question, internally and externally, many times.

"The answer is not involved, Father. We are here because this is where the poor are. Of course we could move to another area in the core city. But why should we? We'd only be seeking another poor area. And the poor we have with us right here.

"Oh, yes, we could move out to the suburbs. Mind you, I am not in any way speaking pejoratively of the other Catholic hospitals that have done so. They use much of their profit for the benefit of the poor." She fell silent.

"Then, why?" Koesler pressed. "Is it some sort of death wish?"

She searched the priest's face, seeming to assess his ability to understand.

"We do it—no, I should accept the responsibility . . . this supremely impractical decision is almost totally mine—I do it because our founder told us to. If St. Vincent de Paul is identified with anyone, it is the poor. According to our order's constitution, we were founded to serve the poor. That is our primary purpose. Some may interpret that to mean that if they are going to serve the poor, they must first themselves survive. There certainly is something to be said for that. It is extremely practical. It's just that I don't see it quite that way."

The little coffee left in Koesler's cup was cold. He pushed the cup aside. "From your explanation, I must assume that you represent a minority viewpoint?"

"Decidedly."

"One woman against the world."

"Just about."

"But how do you manage to keep the place open? I

mean, even with the best of intentions, there's all that red ink at the end of the fiscal year. That's reality.''

"Indeed it is. I wouldn't argue the point. Fortunately, a majority of the board of directors of the Vincent de Paul Health Corporation are members of my order, and dear friends. But even a couple of them are wavering. In fact, in four years we must begin to break even or there simply will no longer be enough support for us to stay open.''

"Any plans? On how to break even?''

"Some . . . oh, don't worry; we won't go down without a fight. But''—she checked her watch—''I'd better saddle up and make some rounds or we won't last the day.''

They rose and took their cups toward the counter area.

"What have they got you doing this afternoon, Father?''

"I'm going to check the new patients on my floors. Then I'm supposed to see if the other chaplains come up with anyone who wants confession or needs the Sacrament of the Sick.''

"Sounds like a busy afternoon. And don't forget—''

"I know: Shut up and listen.''

Sister Eileen pointed an index finger at him and used her thumb as a facsimile of a gun hammer.

Smiling, they parted.

They had told him that security was lax and that he probably could get around the hospital pretty much at will. He hadn't believed them. But he had been willing to try it. And now he was simply amazed.

It hadn't been difficult getting past the lady who screened prospective volunteers. As rehearsed, he claimed that he worked part-time as a janitor for a nearby community theater and that he wanted to spend as much time as he could spare helping those less fortunate than himself. Yes, he understood that his acceptance as a volunteer was no promise of regular employment; if it happened, that would be nice, but he was in no way counting on it.

A few more questions and a few simple forms to fill out and he was issued a long white hospital coat. His picture was taken and the print affixed to his identification badge: Bruce Whitaker, Volunteer.

On the face of it, the coat and ID were indistinguishable from those of most of the other hospital personnel. Nurses, aides, even many of the doctors, wore the same. Of course the identification differed. But few people did more than scan the ID tag. At most, some looked at it just long enough to get his name.

Things were going far better than he could have hoped.

Of course there had been that unfortunate collision in the corridor with the aide who was carrying a food tray. That had been a bit of a mess. But it had been her fault as much as his. She should have looked before she picked up a full tray from the cart. Anybody could have been coming down the hallway at that precise moment. The fact that he'd been studying room numbers as he walked quickly and distractedly down the corridor was his excuse. What was hers? Besides, he *had* stopped and helped clean up the mess.

And then there was the specimen bottle. He had been thrilled when the nurse asked him to take it down to the lab. They trusted him! It was a good feeling—a good feeling that lasted until he reached the basement corridor. That was when he had dropped the bottle. Damned terrazzo floor! The bottle had bounced, then hit and shattered. Oh, well; the nurse would never remember who she had entrusted the bottle to. As for the specimen, there was plenty more where that had come from. He smiled. How clever! He would have to tell the others about that.

For better than an hour, no one had bothered him. He tried to appear purposeful, as if on some mission, as he familiarized himself with the various departments of St. Vincent's.

So far, he had been most impressed with the emergency unit. So much seemed to be going on there that his head had been figuratively spinning from watching all that activity. He must tell the others of the near catastrophe he had observed. The one where the unconscious man might have died if the one doctor's orders had been followed. But the other doctor had ordered an additional test and, as a result, the patient's life was saved. Whitaker had been even more impressed than the others present at how easily a fatality could be caused by a simple mistake. Yes, he must tell the others about that.

Hello! What's this? A section of the hospital he had not been shown on his orientation tour. Or had he? He couldn't quite recall. In any case, the sign identified it: Clinic.

He wandered in casually, cautiously. His first impression was that it was a combination of the emergency unit and a pharmacy. The facility contained a huge store of medical supplies as well as many separate cubicles where patients could be seen and treated. About all it lacked of the emergency unit were the trauma rooms and the exotic equipment they held.

He'd better investigate and see what went on here. There was some activity behind the curtain in cubicle two. As authoritatively as possible, he walked to a spot just opposite the cubicle. He pretended to study a chart lying on the long, curved counter. Though he didn't know who was speaking, he could hear quite clearly.

"How many times has this been for you?" a male voice asked.

"I d'know," an indifferent female voice replied. She sounded black.

"You don't know how many times you've been pregnant?" An unmistakable tone of incredulity.

"I don't rightly know that I'm pregnant now, y'see."
She sounded strangely disinterested.

"You said that you haven't had a period for two months!"

"I said that because you axed me how long it's been."

"You said you're suffering abdominal pain."

"Stomach ache."

"But your abdomen isn't particularly tender."

"It still hurts."

There was a pause. "Okay," the male voice continued,
"you wait here for a few minutes. There'll be a nurse in to
see you in a little while."

The curtain was whipped back, then closed behind the
man as he left the cubicle. Whitaker was able to see inside
for only a second. The patient was seated on a gurney. She
wore a print hospital gown, much the same as those used
in the emergency room. And she was, indeed, black.

The man's garb was similar to Whitaker's. White shirt
and blue tie; dark trousers topped by a white frock coat.
There was an identification badge, but Whitaker could not
read it. Draped around the man's neck was a stethoscope.
Whitaker assumed, correctly, that he was a doctor.

The doctor glanced briefly and quizzically at Whitaker.
But the white hospital coat and ID seemed to assuage his
curiosity. Whitaker busied himself at the desk.

"Maggie," the doctor addressed a nurse, "get a specimen from the gal in two. I want a urinalysis done."

"Okay."

The nurse squeezed by Whitaker on her way to and from
getting a bottle. Yet she didn't seem to notice him. He
couldn't get over it: it was almost as if he were invisible.

The nurse obtained the specimen from the patient in
cubicle two and departed. Some twenty minutes passed
before she returned. Meanwhile, Whitaker concentrated
diligently on remaining as still and inconspicuous as possible. He didn't notice that one edge of his sleeve had fallen

23

into an open stock bottle cap containing a concentration of Gentian Violet. The dark blue-purple solution was slowly seeping up his sleeve.

The nurse handed the doctor the test results. With the chart under his arm, the doctor reentered the cubicle. Once again, Whitaker could see the patient only momentarily. She seemed quite young. Again he could hear their voices clearly. It helped a little now that he knew what they looked like.

The thought crossed his mind that it would be better for the patient if there were more privacy. But he dismissed that thought quickly in favor of the advantage it gave him to be able to overhear their conversation. It did not occur to him that few, if any, in the clinic would ever bother to eavesdrop.

"Well, Ms. Tyler, according to our records, you've been at St. Vincent's quite a few times. Though usually in emergency or maternity."

Whitaker assumed the doctor had referred to the chart. Ms. Tyler did not reply.

"You've been pregnant five times and you have four living children; is that correct?"

"Not 'zactly. I been pregnant more like six, seven times."

"The others were abortions?"

"I didn't have nothin' done." Somewhat truculently.

"Spontaneous abortions, then. Well, you're not pregnant this time."

"Thank the Lord."

"Thank the Lord, indeed. You've just got a stomach upset. And I'll give you something for that. But you could have been pregnant, couldn't you?"

"How's that?"

"You're sexually active now? You have a boyfriend?"

"Oh, yeah."

24

"But, Ms. Tyler, you're a diabetic. The last two times you were here for delivery of a child, you almost died. Didn't the doctor or a counselor give you any information on family planning? On how not to get pregnant again?"

"Oh, yeah, they done that."

"What did you decide on? What form of contraceptive did you agree on?"

"Oh, they fitted me with a wire."

"An IUD? Then what happened? It's certainly not in place now."

"It come out."

"And you didn't come in to have it replaced? Don't you know that without it you could get pregnant again?"

"I guess."

"Look, Ms. Tyler"—his tone grew conciliatory—"this is very serious. Your diabetes—your illness—very much complicates matters when you become pregnant. You could die. As a matter of fact, if you get pregnant again, you probably will die. And you might have been pregnant this time. It's just luck—and no more than luck—that you aren't.

"Ms. Tyler, you've got four children. You don't need any more, do you?"

"No, sir."

"You don't even want any more, do you?" He sounded hopeful.

There was a pause. "But I can't lose my man. If I don't give out, Tyrone be gone." She sounded worried.

"There's a way we can fix this all up."

"There is?"

"Yes. It's called a tubal ligation."

"A what?" Nervous.

"We could tie your Fallopian tubes."

"My what?"

25

"It's a simple operation. We can do it right here in the clinic. We can even do it right now."

"It's an operation?" A touch of panic.

"Yes. But it's such a simple operation, we can do it right here in the clinic."

"What do it do?"

"It'll make it impossible for you to get pregnant ever again."

"And I don't have to wear anything or do anything more?"

"No. The operation will take care of everything."

"And I can give out to Tyrone?"

"Tyrone will never have been happier."

"Then I guess it's okay."

Whitaker had been listening to their conversation so intently that he hadn't noticed the nurse's aide who had been standing next to him, studying him. "Bruce"—she'd read his ID—"if I were you, I'd take my sleeve out of that Gentian Violet."

Startled, Whitaker glanced first at her, then at his sleeve. The solution had crept upwards until now it had darkened a significant portion of his cuff. And the aide—she was the same girl he had literally run into earlier when they had spilled the lunch tray.

"It's all right . . . it's all right," he repeated inanely as he squeezed the cuff. He succeeded only in staining his fingers.

Bruce left the scene in rather total confusion. But he'd heard enough. He must get to the others as soon as possible and tell them what he'd learned. And he would have to do something about that nurse's aide. She had noticed him. She had read his ID. She knew his name.

Whitaker had assailed his duties that day confident he was unnoticed. But someone else, due initially to nothing but a series of coincidences, had noted, then taken some interest in this ill-omened man. There had been the food tray collision; the dropped specimen tube; the patient bent almost into pretzel shape when Bruce had tried to adjust her electronically-powered bed; the cracked stained-glass window in the chapel where he had tripped over a prie-dieu.

At that, the silent observer hadn't noted the nurse who was still searching for the chart Bruce had accidentally set afire; the patient who would never find her dentures that Bruce had accidentally flushed down the toilet; or the medical library where books were now out of order because Bruce had tried to look up some information. Not to mention a variety of other mishaps.

But merely from what had been noted, the observer was impressed. Never had the observer seen such a star-crossed creature. However, on the one hand, volunteers were not in great supply, and, on the other, one never knew when information about such a person might come in handy.

3

IT SEEMED MANY HOURS SINCE THE COFFEE break. Actually, it was only a little more than four. But, by his lights, Father Koesler had spent a busy afternoon.

He had visited with nine newly admitted patients; heard three confessions; anointed five, three of whom would go to surgery tomorrow; and offered Mass at 5:30 P.M.

It was now 6:15 P.M. Tray in hand, he was making his way through the cafeteria line. He was hungry, but too tired to eat much. From a fairly generous offering of ingredients, he put together a salad. That and coffee should do it.

The cafeteria was sparsely occupied. It was between visiting hours and much of the day staff had gone home.

Koesler took a seat at a long, empty table, said a silent grace, and started on the salad. He noticed Dr. Scott going through the food line. Scott appeared to be unaccompanied. As he settled with the cashier, he scanned the scattered diners, spotted Father Koesler, and headed in his direction.

That pleased the priest. He had liked Scott from the beginning and was sure he could learn much from him.

Scott sat down heavily, letting out his exhaustion. Koesler glanced at the doctor's tray. Apparently, tiredness did not affect all men equally. In addition to a salad, there was an ample piece of pizza, sliced roast beef, potatoes and gravy, and a mixture of carrots and peas. No wonder the doctor's frame, despite the stress and physical demands of his work, carried excess fat.

"I'm glad you happened on this time to eat," Koesler opened. "Nice coincidence."

"It was no coincidence," Scott replied. "I figured you'd eat right after you said Mass, so I timed my break for now."

"Oh?" There was something more. There had to be. Koesler waited.

"So, then, how did your first day go?"

"Busily. This is a very demanding place. I can see where you could burn out in a hurry here."

Scott smiled and ran a hand through his beard. "Wait awhile. It gets easier. The newness does take its toll. But about the time you're ready to leave us, you will have fallen into a routine. It's the routine that insulates you. Just wait and see; I'll bet in a very short time things will change for you."

Koesler picked at his salad while Scott plowed into his meal. Several minutes passed. Still no hint as to why the doctor had selected a dining time that included Koesler's company.

"Okay, Doctor," the priest said at length, "I give up. Why did you decide to dine with me?"

"Scotty. Everybody calls me Scotty."

Koesler would not return the dispensation. Only his relatives, fellow priests, and a few close friends used his given name with his implicit permission. Otherwise, he preferred his title. He was not discountenanced in any way by those who presumed to call him Bob. What others called him was their problem, not his. It was just that he felt he functioned on a professional level better if he was perceived by those he served as a priest rather than a buddy.

"Very well, then, Scotty, why did you schedule your dinner break to be with me?"

Scott was mixing a few vegetables with a small piece of the pizza and a forkful of potatoes and gravy. Evidently, he blended his food as he ate. Koesler did not want to look.

"I didn't want you to eat alone."

"Come on." Koesler smiled.

"Okay." Scott blended his food into an indescribable blob. "It's this way: Even though your stay here will be brief, we're going to be working together a lot, often quite closely. All the patients here are sick, almost by very definition. But you'll find the sickest by far in the OR—operating room—and the ER—emergency. And those two are my bailiwick.

"Now, there are code blues all over this place. Shoot, people have been known to arrest out in the lobby while they're waiting to register. But you'll find you're going to be summoned for codes down to the OR and ER more often than anywhere else. So I thought it would be good if we got to know each other better. And if you got to know this place and some of its personnel better."

"But I've already had orientation—"

"To be a chaplain—a temporary one at that. There are things going on here besides the care of souls that are going to concern you—ready or not. Are you game to learn in the school of hard knocks?"

Koesler nodded. He felt the question was rhetorical.

"Right," Scott affirmed. "First, how about some dessert?"

"No, thanks." Koesler found it difficult to believe that Scott had finished all the food on his tray. But he had.

"Coffee?"

"Sure."

When Scott returned, his tray contained two cups of coffee and one huge banana split. Koesler felt awe at Scott's appetite.

"Okay," Scott said, "let's start with the boss lady."

"Sister Eileen Monahan."

"The same. She is unique—and I do not use the term lightly. She, and she alone, is the reason St. Vincent's continues to sputter along. It long ago passed the point at which it should have been shut down. It is a financial disaster that is getting worse rather than better.

"Even in the brief time you've been here you must have noticed there are very few well-to-do, well-educated patients—white or black—occupying our beds. They're mostly indigent blacks. And precious few Catholics."

Koesler nodded. Making his rounds this day, he had not met a single patient, white or black, who would have fit socially or financially into Koesler's Dearborn Heights parish.

Scott continued. "Lots of patients who come here not only can't pay anything, they're not covered by anyone—neither their own resources nor medical insurance. But by decree of Sister Eileen, not one of them is turned away. Somehow the hospital is expected to swallow their costs. As you can imagine, the hospital regularly gags on their expenses.

"Then, there are a goodly number who can't pay their own costs—well, who can?—but, while they have no private insurance, they are covered by Medicare, Medicaid. Then things get complicated. What with DRGs—that's diagnostically related groups—we can have the patient hospitalized for only a limited time and we can collect from the government only a set minimum fee. Not only is that extremely restrictive to the patient, the hospital is not going to get rich. Indeed, since the hospital cannot tuck administrative costs or any future planning in the bill, it begins a slow fiscal retreat.

"These are the kinds of odds facing Sister Eileen."

"I see." Koesler shook his head. "But then even more so now than when I asked Sister this afternoon, I find it difficult to understand why she bothers trying to keep St. Vincent's afloat. Especially here in the core city." Koesler's hands were wrapped around the cup with its untasted coffee. He preferred warm hands to a warm stomach.

"She's trying to bring the ideals of service of St. Vincent de Paul to Detroit's inner city," Scott explained. "And I'll be damned if she doesn't almost carry it off. And it's all her, too. No doubt about it, St. Vincent's Hospital and Sister Eileen Monahan are almost identical. They've been together so long they have become inseparable. She's always here. She's always available to everyone. She inspires a special spirit in everyone, from the orderlies to the volunteers to the head nurses."

"Do I detect an omission of the doctors?"

"Oh, yes, you do. But as far as the doctors go, Sister Eileen has written the book on the care and feeding of doctors. It's not that she can't be firm with them when necessary. It's more that she has a magical touch when it comes to the little things, the infinitesimal perks that are so dear to doctors. Things like—you know—'Dr. So-and-So wants this special instrument in the OR' or, 'Dr. So-and-So wants the charts kept in this special way.' Then, along comes Sister Eileen to say that Dr. So-and-So really ought to have that instrument. Or, without offending the nurse in charge, Eileen will see to it that an exception is made for Dr. So-and-So and that the floor nurses will keep his charts in his own peculiar way.

"But those doctors, generally, are the ones who have made a conscious and rather generous decision to stick with the core city. And in doing so they have made the not inconsiderable sacrifice of giving up great wealth and prestige patients. Outside of these, many of the other doctors on staff here simply could not ever be accredited to the swankier hospitals. But . . . they are all we've got."

"I see."

"Take for example Dr. Lee Kim."

"The one who was working with you in the emergency unit."

"Right."

"He's not a good doctor?"

"On the contrary, he's quite good. He just can't quite figure out what he's doing here at St. Vincent's. This is not in his timetable at all."

"I don't understand." Koesler tasted the coffee. It was tepid. He shuddered and set it aside.

"He came here from Korea. Not unlike many other doctors. And, like many other foreign doctors, his progress has been arrested at an innercity hospital. He makes no bones about it: He wants to be affiliated with the affluent suburbs."

"And in this, I take it, he is not alone."

"No, that's true. But his ambition causes him to take a rather casual attitude toward some of his work here."

"Casual?"

"Uh . . . for instance, suppose we have a terminal case. Somebody whose life system can be supported by mechanical means alone. Well, rather than waste half an hour of his valuable time, he will go to the family and say, 'Do you want us to do everything?' "

" 'Everything'?"

"It becomes a rhetorical question. The point is, he could spend some time with the relatives, the next of kin, and talk about the quality of life this patient is not going to have in a coma and plugged into machines that will breathe for him, keep his heart going, filter his waste. Dr. Kim doesn't want to spend a lot of time explaining the choices the family has. And the easiest way of getting out of that chore in a hurry is to ask the family simply, 'Do you want us to do everything?' Few families will have the gumption or the knowledge to ask about alternatives. They will say, 'Of course, do everything.' At that point, Dr. Kim will put in an order to plug in the life-support systems, and leave the patient to vegetate."

"I see." Koesler thought he did. "But what does conduct like that have to do with the hospital—or Sister Eileen?"

"For one thing, it drives costs up, most of the time needlessly. Instead of spending a lot of money on systems that keep essential body functions going, the patient should be allowed to die with some dignity. But doctors like Kim never quite give dignity a chance. So it's that much more difficult to balance a budget."

"I see."

"Now, Dr. Kim is by no means alone in his approach to terminal patients. Where he could have a problem, that could cause the rest of us to have a concomitant problem, is in the clinic. Has anyone told you much about the clinic?"

"I know where it is. You treat outpatients there. You even have outpatient surgery."

"Right. It's also where we have some of our more pressing ethics problems."

"Oh?"

"Normally, they're not problems for most doctors. Certainly they're not problems for other hospitals. But they're very definitely problems for Catholic hospitals.''

"Let me guess: family planning."

"Right."

Koesler looked slightly puzzled. "Well, as far as the 'official' Catholic teaching goes, there are only two approved means of family planning. One is complete abstinence from sexual activity, and the other, under set circumstances, is the rhythm method." Absolutely nothing had changed in the Church's attitude toward family planning in the thirty-odd years Koesler had been a priest. Church approval of the rhythm system had occurred shortly before he had been ordained in 1954. "But very few pay much attention to that view any longer. Just the bishops, some priests, and a few very conservative lay Catholics."

"But you see, Father, the bishops like to exercise a good measure of control over Catholic hospitals."

"That makes sense. They'd exercise complete control across the board if they could. But family planning is a private matter between each couple. At most it might enter the confessional as a question or as a matter for some discussion. But I can see where in a hospital you're in the external forum and the bishops might be able to control—or try to control—the hospital's teaching and practices."

"Exactly. And that's where a place like St. Vincent's is in a lot of trouble. If we don't dispense information and devices for all medically approved methods of birth control, we lose government funding. That, in itself, I think, would not discourage Sister Eileen. But she knows our patients have a right to this information and service. And she is determined to make it available to them. The peculiar twist in all this is that most of our poor patients couldn't care less about birth control. They figure the more babies the better."

"So," Koesler clarified for himself, "St. Vincent's

35

provides the information and means of artificial birth control under the threat of losing government financing—but against the bishops' directives—and because the CEO believes it's the medically and ethically correct thing to do, even though most patients don't want the information in the first place.''

"That's about it."

"A dilemma. A real dilemma. But where does Dr. Kim fit into this?"

"As usual, Dr. Kim is involved in shortcuts. But, in this instance, they are rather significant shortcuts.''

"Oh?"

"I don't have this firsthand, but from some of the clinic personnel I trust. Dr. Kim, when faced with any sort of problem pregnancy, will routinely perform a D & C—at least he will call it a D & C."

"D & C?" Koesler asked.

"Dilatation and curettage. You dilate the cervix and scrape the womb's lining. It's standard treatment for any number of gynecological problems. But not for a problem pregnancy. Then it's a euphemism for abortion. And that's where St. Vincent's draws the line. Our policy permits teaching methods of contraception, the implantation of IUDs, prescribing birth control pills, even sterilization . . . but not abortion. Not abortion."

"I see."

"It would be lots harder to prove, but according to some, Dr. Kim also schedules hysterectomies with some abandon."

"He does?"

"Yes. Even when the woman's condition does not warrant it, a hysterectomy is sometimes the easiest and at the same time the most lucrative therapy."

"What a crime to perform such radical surgery if a woman doesn't really need it!"

"Indeed. But it is convenient. However, if these charges can be proven, Dr. Kim will be out on his ear."

"Oh, my. But"—Koesler's brow furrowed—"there's still a shortage of doctors. Wouldn't he be able to tie in with another hospital?"

"Perhaps. But remember where St. Vincent's is on the desirability list. It's something like a baseball player being unconditionally released from a last-place team. And remember where Dr. Kim wants to go. Very definitely up from St. Vincent's. Not down. Not even a lateral arabesque."

"So," Koesler concluded, "I would guess that would be motivation enough for Dr. Kim to clean up his act."

"Maybe. Maybe. Unless he had an alternative."

"An alternative?"

"He might try to hurry the closing of St. Vincent's. If the hospital closed shop before he was dismissed . . ." Scott's gesture signified a satisfactory conclusion, at least by Dr. Kim's lights.

They picked up their trays and headed for the counter area. En route to the conveyor belt that would carry their trays to the dishwasher, they encountered a man who had just settled with the cashier and was scanning the cafeteria preliminary to selecting his dining place.

"Hello there, John," Scott greeted him. "Have you met our substitute chaplain yet?"

"I haven't had the pleasure."

Scott introduced John Haroldson, chief operating officer of St. Vincent's. Haroldson, of medium height, appeared to be in his mid-sixties. His heavily lined face was framed by wispy, wavy white hair. His eyes were a very light blue and when he smiled, as he was doing now, all the lines of his face moved in an upward direction. Koesler's impression was of a rather nice-looking, friendly gentleman.

"So you're going to be with us until Father Thompson returns, eh?" Haroldson observed.

"That's right. This was my first day on the job and I must admit I've learned a lot, with a lot more to learn."

"Don't worry, Father, the hospital won't jump up and bite you. You'll get along fine. If there's anything I can do to help, don't hesitate to call on me."

Haroldson headed for a table. Scott and Koesler deposited their dinner trays on the conveyor. They stopped together just outside the cafeteria. For the moment, they were alone in the corridor.

"That's another one," Scott said.

"Another one what?"

"Another problem area."

"Oh?"

"Haroldson goes back in this hospital almost as long as Eileen."

"That's a problem?"

"Not in itself. It's just that John has a bit of a persecution complex. He's always moved up a notch behind Eileen, until, of course, her final appointment. When she became a supervisor, he was named assistant comptroller. She moved into a vice-presidency; he became a supervisor. Then he became COO with the likelihood of eventually becoming CEO. But Eileen leapfrogged him into the top job.

"It doesn't show, but John Haroldson is a bitter man, and the principal target of his bitterness is Eileen. It's really manifested when they're together, especially in a meeting."

"I've been here only a day," Koesler said, "and I've just met Sister Eileen this once, but it does seem to me she'd be able to handle someone's bitterness. I mean, she's already juggling any number of problems—most of them far more serious than envy."

"It's not that she can't handle any sort of frontal attack that Haroldson might launch. It's that the longer he stays here, the more he covets Eileen's position. It's a need, as he sees it, to balance the scales of justice. But he hasn't long to go till mandatory retirement—a few months at most. And I get the feeling he wants to set matters straight before he has to leave here."

"How could he do that?"

"I'm not sure. I just think that might be his aim."

They began walking toward the elevators.

Almost facetiously, Koesler commented, "Well, there's Dr. Kim and now Mr. Haroldson. Anyone else to be concerned about?"

"Sure. But once you know what's at stake here and the lay of the land, you'll be able to figure things out for yourself with no additional help from me."

"I doubt that."

"There is one more person you ought to be aware of who just might slip by."

"Who's that?"

"Sister Rosamunda."

"Sister Rosamunda!" Koesler exclaimed. "Why, she's the embodiment of the grandmother most people would want if they were able to invent their own!"

"No argument. It's just that Rosey should have been retired years ago. But her ultimate fear is being put on the shelf. And Eileen is simply too kind to insist on her retirement. On the contrary, each year that it comes up— and it does come up each and every year—Eileen goes to bat with the corporation on behalf of Rosey. And in deference to Eileen, they allow Rosamunda to stay."

"That sounds sort of nice. Very considerate of Sister Eileen."

"Except that Rosey is left dependent on Eileen's continued good will. As long as Eileen is in charge, the corporation will continue to defer to her on this. But eventually, inevitably, Eileen will be forced to pull the active plug on Rosey. And that will be the end of Rosey's professional life.

"Add to which, Rosey—although officially she is listed as the sacristan and still has access to the patients—is getting senile. And on top of all that, she's got a bit of a drinking problem. Not much, mind you, but enough to upset the applecart."

"A drinking problem! You've got to be kidding!"

"I don't kid. Not about that kind of thing. Now, Father, you know that's not unheard-of. Although most Catholics—and I suppose that includes priests—like to think that someone like the aged and venerable Sister Rosamunda is above every human failing, above every human condition. But that's just not realistic. With Rosey, it began years ago when arthritis joined her long list of medical problems. There was a lot of pain and a reluctance to depend on medication. Which, with an accumulation of ills like those that hit Rosey, wouldn't have done all that much to relieve the suffering. Like many elderly people in pain, she turned to alcohol for some relief. She's still on it."

"Okay, suppose she is . . . what has that got to do with anything else?"

"Only this: that while there are some people—like the two I've mentioned—who might deliberately plan to undermine Eileen in running this hospital, somebody like Rosey could deep-six Eileen's operation very effectively, if unintentionally. Or, she could even be used by someone who wanted to get at Eileen."

A small bell sounded and the "up" button lit. Up was their only option. They were in the basement. They entered the elevator, silent during the one-story ride.

The lobby was vacant, with the exception of the receptionist, who was busy at her switchboard. The two men paused again.

"Let's sit down for a moment," Scott said.

Since no one else was in the lobby, the two men had a wide selection. They chose a two-person couch against the wall near the elevator.

"A group of us here at St. Vincent's happen to appreciate what Eileen is trying to do," Scott commenced. "We try as best we can to make it work—because of the way we feel about her. You're going to be here only a few weeks. But in that time God knows what might happen.

"I used to read your stuff in the *Detroit Catholic* when you were editor. You struck me as the kind of person who would understand what Eileen is trying to do—that is, if you knew about it—as well as recognize some of the roadblocks along the way. So, for the duration of your stay in Father Thompson's absence, and on behalf of those who are backing Sister Eileen—including Father Thompson—I guess I'm asking for your support."

"Well, you have it. Very definitely. Just one question: How long do you think you all can hold things together?"

Scott ran a hand through his beard for a few moments. "Not long enough, I fear. Like all hospitals, the bottom line on St. Vincent's is a deficit budget. The ledger for this hospital looks like a gigantic nosebleed. But for Eileen's sake, we want it to last as long as it possibly can.

"Eileen is dedicated to serving the poor. And, inspired by her sacrifice, we join her. So we stay here as some sort of sign to whoever wants to recognize what we're doing.

"Almost everyone else in the health care business is in it to make a living, if not a damn good profit, while we watch the money trickle away. It would be nice if someone bailed us out. But, then, there's almost no way anyone could do that. Our deficit is a bottomless pit. So we say, 'what the hell,' and dive into the folly that is Christianity.'' Scott paused and looked significantly at Koesler. "With all of that, are you still with us?"

"Gladly. But you have given me lots to think about." He smiled. "I'll see you tomorrow."

They parted. After hanging his chaplain's uniform in the closet of the pastoral care department, Koesler made his way to his car in the nearby parking lot. All the way back to his parish, St. Anselm's in Dearborn Heights, he continued to ponder all that Dr. Scott had told him.

Without doubt, there was more to St. Vincent's Hospital than met the casual eye. He would have to be alert to every nuance, especially those that affected Sister Eileen or her program.

At St. Anselm's, he checked the desk in his office. There were only a few phone calls to be returned. He could do that in the morning.

I wonder what it will be like to kill a nun. Why should it be any different from killing anyone else? Is there some circle in hell reserved for murderers of nuns?

The whole business is ludicrous. I would laugh if I could. But I cannot. The pain—the pain in my head is killing me. It feels as if the top of my head is about to blow apart.

It is not as though death is foreign to this place. A hospital almost 150 years old! Thousands of people have died here. What is one more!

The good nun's soul would be assumed into heaven. Why not? She probably is not aware that she is torturing me. That she is twisting a band of stress ever tighter until my head is ready to explode! The hounds of hell are screaming in my brain!

Will no one rid me of this troublesome nun? No one? No one! Then I must do it myself.

42

She must die. And I must do it. At the right moment. But soon—it must be soon!

The expression "As different as the night the day" could not find a truer embodiment than in a hospital. St. Vincent's was no exception. Nor was there any doubt that schedules were established for the convenience of hospital personnel.

Day began when the day staff arrived at approximately 6:00 A.M. Day began slowly. Both staff and patients were trying to wake up. Patients' conditions were checked. Cheery words spoken. Grunts returned. Sponge baths given. Medications administered. The action and commotion intensified as the day progressed.

Some patients did nothing; some were healing, some dying. Some were wheeled down to surgery. Some to therapy. Some to postoperative intensive care. Some returned to their rooms. Some received visitors. Some, if they could afford the rental, watched the mindless games and soaps of daytime commercial TV. Some who could not afford it watched one of the two "free" channels. One of these showed ancient slapstick movies. The other was the chapel channel, which, most of the time, showed a large, empty ornate chapel. Patients were fed three meals a day plus an evening snack, according to doctors' orders.

A kind of climax was reached in late afternoon. After which came a gradual decrescendo.

Dinner was followed by prime-time TV and/or visitors. At 8:00 P.M., visiting hours ended and night prayers were broadcast.

Most employees had gone home, thus the hospital tempo slowed. There was a last-ditch effort to supply patient needs. After 10:00 P.M., in effect, the patients would not be needed until morning.

It was now just a few minutes after ten. All corridor overhead lights were off. Floor-level night-lights gave only scant illumination to hallways.

George Snell, a burly security guard, was on duty.

There was no reason anyone should have rested easily on that account. Though widely recognized for his prowess as a ladies' man, George was by no means the most reliable member of a security force that was hardly top-flight. It was, when all was said and done, the best security service St. Vincent's could afford.

George, supported by both arms, was leaning against a wall on floor 3-D. Between him and the wall was a nurse's aide, also theoretically, on duty, but who George knew could be talked into a short break.

"How about it, baby? How's about a little?"

"I'll say this for you, George," replied the virtually imprisoned aide, "you sure have a way about you."

"Yeah."

"Why, you could charm a girl right out of her better judgment."

"That's the idea."

"I know what the idea is, George. But we are on duty."

"Duty, rootie. Everybody's asleep."

"No, they're not, George. And if one of them rings that little bell at the nurses' station, the charge nurse is gonna start wonderin' where I am."

"Don't worry, baby, I'll cover for you." He winked elaborately.

"And you're supposed to be on duty, too. What if something happens?"

"What's gonna happen at old St. Vinnie's? The hospital's asleep and this end of downtown's deserted. We're the only ones awake." He leaned closer.

"Well . . . ," she vacillated, "where can we go?"

44

"I got that all figured out, baby. Room 3009 is a single and it's vacant."

"A single! For you? And me, too?"

"We will be as one."

"A pretty big one."

"Baby, we can stand here and talk about it all night. Or we can get it on."

"Okay. But I got a hunch we're gonna be sorry."

"Baby, one thing I can promise you, you ain't gonna be sorry."

They made their way, she leading, down the hall to 3009. As she entered the room, she heard a dull plop behind her. She couldn't believe her eyes. His clothing was in a heap on the floor. He must've been loosening everything on their way down the hall. If it were an Olympic event, George would win a gold medal for disrobing.

So there it was.

Two things seemed evident: He was ready and she was not likely to be sorry.

Lay on, George Snell.

Late evening—a quarter past ten—her time of day.

Sister Eileen had finished her paperwork. No one had disturbed her since night prayers at eight o'clock. Slowly, gradually, gratefully, her body chemistry was tapering off.

It's funny, she thought, how, over the years, she had become so attuned to hospital routine that she and St. Vincent's had become as one. Something like a couple who have been married a great number of years. The hospital's ebb and flow was matched by her own emotional highs and lows.

As the patients and, in a sense, the hospital also, began to drift into quiescence, so did she.

As was her custom, Eileen would take one final tour of the various floors before bedtime. The pattern conformed to all the routines she had built up over the years. This was her time of silent prayer and reflection as she figuratively tucked the hospital in.

The night-lights gave an eerie glow to the otherwise darkened hallways. As she walked down the corridors she could hear the old building. Each evening it seemed that St. Vincent's was settling further into the ground. It wasn't true, of course; it simply was the sort of sound an old, well-constructed building makes.

The sound of deep, restful breathing emanated from most of the darkened rooms. Sleep, induced or natural, but a peaceful sound. A few patients still had their TV sets on. It was against the rules at this hour. But Sister would do nothing unless the noises were loud enough to disturb other patients.

There was something different about this evening. Eileen could not put her finger on it. But something was different. Was it a foreboding? She couldn't tell. Just that tonight was different. Shivering, she pulled her shawl tighter around her shoulders.

From time to time, she passed by a window to the outside world. A solid coating of snow covered everything but the sidewalks around the hospital. The long-standing snow contributed its unreal glow to the dimly lit surroundings.

And the sirens. Always the sirens. Emergency vehicles delivering frightened, ill, or injured people to St. Vincent's or one of the neighboring hospitals. Or a police car delivering someone in handcuffs to police headquarters.

"Hello, Sister."

"Oh!" It was so unexpected. She had thought she was alone. But she'd been so deep in reverie, she had been unaware that the charge nurse had caught up and joined her.

"I'm sorry. I didn't mean to frighten you."

"You didn't frighten me." Eileen would not admit that anything in her hospital could frighten her. "I just didn't hear you."

"It's these shoes. Plus I get in the habit of creeping around at night. How's everything?"

Such a big question. "Okay, I guess. Just making some rounds before bedtime."

The nurse was well acquainted with this routine, as was the rest of the staff. The joke had it that wristwatches could be confidently set depending on where Sister Eileen was in her nocturnal rounds.

"By the way, Sister, you haven't seen Helen around, have you?"

"Helen?"

"Helen Brown, one of my aides. You know her."

"Of course. No, I haven't seen Helen. As a matter of fact, now that you mention it, I haven't seen anyone but you so far. And I should have passed one of the guards by now."

"The guards!" The nurse threw up her hands. "What next? I think the hospital should hire some agency to protect the guards."

"Could Helen be in one of the patients' rooms?"

"I suppose that's where she must be. But she's been gone longer than usual. I just wondered. I guess there's nothing to worry about."

"I don't think so either. But I'll keep an eye out."

"Oops! There goes the phone." The nurse hurried back toward her station where the phone was buzzing softly.

The guards! Eileen could make all the resolutions she wished and nothing would happen. This service, while it left very much to be desired, was the best St. Vincent's could afford. Perhaps it was fortunate that police head-quarters was on the next block.

Nevertheless, she would speak to John Haroldson, the COO, tomorrow. Perhaps he could get some favorable response from the service.

Dear God, how much longer could she keep this institution going? Sometimes she dreamed that she was literally Scotch-taping and tying string around St. Vincent's to keep it together.

And always the nagging question, Is it worth it? Seemingly, it was the question on everyone else's mind. She couldn't afford to let her mind dwell on it. At least not overtly. Her attitude had to be steadfast, uncompromising. She was convinced that the moment she faltered, St. Vincent's would come tumbling down. In this, she was not much mistaken.

"Oh!"

In her startled outcry, she scared both herself and the elderly gentleman who had just exited his room at her left.

She recovered quickly. "I'm sorry I startled you. Are you all right?"

"Whatinhell!" the old man muttered. "Goddam women! Gotta scream all the time! Scare a guy shitless, you let 'em. All the time gotta scream. Goddam women!"

"I said I was sorry. May I help you with something?"

"Goin' to the bathroom. Can do that without you. Did it for years. Just don't scream no more. Or I won't have to go to the bathroom no more. Goddam women! Gotta scream all the time!" Muttering, he proceeded down the hall.

Eileen couldn't suppress a smile. In the good old days, she would have been wearing a traditional religious habit. The old man had not recognized her as a nun. Undoubtedly, he would have been mortified if she had identified herself.

48

But it was odd. Twice tonight she had been frightened. That never happened.

She offered herself the simple excuse that both the nurse and the elderly patient had come out of nowhere suddenly, unexpectedly. It was the element of surprise that had frightened her. Nothing to worry about.

Though she was able to rationalize the episodes of fright, Eileen could not shake the feeling that something was different here tonight.

She shrugged the apprehension away. You could not function in a hospital in this part of town if you allowed yourself to be the victim of panic. It was either be brave and face this reality with confidence in God, or strike one's tent and move on.

It was odd that she had encountered only the charge nurse and the bathroom-bound patient. True, she had not yet seen the missing aide, Helen Brown. That was not untoward; Helen might very well be occupied in another wing. But the absence of a security guard bothered her. She certainly should have passed one by now.

"Uh—!" Eileen had not screamed since she was a teenager. She tried to scream now. But no sound escaped through the large muscular hand that covered her mouth. His other arm slid under her chin, pressing hard into her neck.

She felt her body being lifted. She squirmed and struggled, but could not break free. Had she ever imagined such a thing might happen, she would have thought she'd be brave. But she was terrified.

It was ungainly, but she kicked and flailed. The more she struggled, the tighter grew the grip on her neck. An opaque pall dimmed her vision, intensifying her panic. Her heart pounded. A mounting sense of dizziness enveloped her.

Fearing she would never awake, she fought the lowering

darkness. Yet she welcomed it as an escape from the pain and terror.

She gagged and lost consciousness as her assailant dragged her into room 3009.

✦ ✦ ✦

Things have to be very serious before the sacred routine of a hospital is demolished. This, then, could be described as a very serious situation.

The CEO had been all but murdered. By a deranged, chemically dependent escapee from the detox unit. Sister Eileen had been saved, at the last moment, by George Snell, one of the hospital's security officers.

The corridor lights had been turned up throughout 3-D. Many of the patients had awakened; several were wandering about the rooms and hallways. As many of the staff as could be assembled were present. Chief Martin, head of security, was presiding.

Once the resident on duty determined that Sister Eileen, beyond a few bruises and some diminishing fear, was all right, she had been placed in a bed and mildly sedated.

"Now, you wanna run that by me again? From the top?" Martin was pardonably skeptical at the tale of Snell's singular skill, bravery, and efficiency.

"Well"—Snell basked in the figurative spotlight—"I turned the corner down there"—pointing toward the corridor's dead end—"and I seen this guy grab Sister and start to drag her into this room."

"Uh-huh. Then?"

"Then I got down here fast as I could. When I got in the room, he was chokin' her. So I hit him. And he fell. And when he did, he let go of her. Then he hit his head on the bed and he was out cold. Then I called you. And you know what happened from then."

"Uh-huh. Where did you hit the guy?"

"In the mouth . . . the face, I guess."

Chief Martin studied the unconscious patient who was being attended by the resident. "Hey, doc, there any marks on that guy's face? Like he's been hit or somethin'?"

"No . . . no," the resident said, "I don't see any. Just this big bump on the back of his head where he hit the bed frame."

"So," Martin turned back to Snell, "if you hit him, how come he got no marks on his face?"

Pause. "Maybe I pushed him . . . it all happened so fast."

"Uh-huh." Martin continued to ponder the scene. None of Snell's story jibed with Snell's previous proclivity to uninvolvement. But Martin was unable to come up with any alternative to Snell's story.

There was one present who could come up with a different story. However, for many reasons, not the least of which was a personal interest in not having the facts revealed, Helen Brown wasn't talking. But, barely able to stifle a smile, Ms. Brown recalled those events very clearly.

After his award-winning performance in disrobing both himself and her, Snell had propelled them onto the mattress with such enthusiasm that the bed slid several inches closer to the window.

Minutes passed as seconds. Snell seemed insatiable. No sooner was one episode concluded than another began. Ms. Brown had no way of telling how long that had gone on when she heard an unexpected and inexplicable sound in the corridor.

"George," she stage-whispered, "somebody's out there!"

"Shh! This is no time for small talk."

"Come on, George!" Struggling to get out from under. "George! Somebody's out there!"

Snicker.

"George, somebody's fighting out in the hall!"

"And I'm fightin' in here. I'm fightin' to keep goin' for you, baby."

"George, don't you think you ought to investigate?"

"I am, baby. And I like what I find!"

"George! George! They're coming in here! George, they're fighting! George, it's a man, and he's choking somebody! George!"

"Now, baby, get ready: Here comes the Snell Maneuver!"

Snell appeared to be going through a procedure not unlike a cowboy mounting a horse. Halfway through that maneuver, Helen Brown pushed him. She shoved with all her strength. It was enough.

Caught unaware, he toppled out of bed and, with momentum building, rolled across the floor. In rolling, he made contact. In effect, Snell took the man's legs right out from under him, much the same as a roll block in football.

The man dropped Sister Eileen's body and, tumbling over Snell, fell, hitting his head against the metal bed frame.

George Snell got to his feet and surveyed the scene. A detox patient, in pajamas and robe, unconscious. The CEO, unconscious. A nurse's aide, conscious and naked, in bed.

This was the part from which Helen Brown never completely recovered. Snell wanted to get back in bed and continue with what he promised was the storied Snell Maneuver.

It was all Ms. Brown could do to dissuade him from his maneuver and persuade him to: get dressed and allow her to do the same, fabricate a believable explanation for what had happened—without ever coming close to the truth—and, finally, call his superior.

Sister Eileen would regain consciousness and apparently be none the worse for her ordeal. She would have a new, if guarded, regard for the hospital's security.

And George Snell would become almost a folk hero to St. Vincent's staff.

For another reason entirely, he would be enshrined in Helen Brown's memory and imagination.

Father Koesler's dreams were busy. In several of them, Sister Eileen was under attack, sometimes by the Nestorians of unhappy memory, sometimes by the modernists, sometimes by the Holy Inquisition. Koesler had a difficult night defending her.

It was one of those times when he was glad to see the dawn. Even if it was one of those dark, frigid, snow-caked mornings typical of a Michigan January.

4

THE EUGENE I. VAN ANTWERP CORREC-
tional Facility was a recent addition to Detroit's penal
system. At one time, the city had owned only one jail—
the Detroit House of Correction, more familiarly know as
DeHoCo. But, at the insistence of the state legislature,
the city had been forced to expand its penal facilities.

The expansion did not necessarily involve change. The
buildings, of course, were new, modern, and clean. The
consensus, however, was that it would be difficult to
improve on the philosophy that governed DeHoCo. So, the
new facility housed a tried-and-true approach to penology
in a new setting.

The facility was christened after a one-term (1948–49)
mayor of Detroit. Mr. Van Antwerp, a Catholic, was the
father of eleven, among them two priests and two nuns.
Mrs. Van Antwerp candidly explained that she had planned
an even dozen until she learned that every twelfth child
born into the world was Chinese. Mr. Van Antwerp's
fertility, both in quantity and quality, might have won a

Catholic Family of the Year Award. Unfortunately, Mr. Van Antwerp passed away on the very same day Marilyn Monroe died. Consequently, Mr. Van Antwerp's obituary was buried in Detroit's metropolitan newspapers.

Those who remembered and valued Mr. Van Antwerp's many contributions to the city in a long life of civic service, were gratified when an important edifice was named in his honor. No Detroit buildings bore the name of Miss Monroe.

Just as the Detroit House of Correction was more familiarly known as DeHoCo, so the Eugene I. Van Antwerp Correctional Facility was becoming more popularly know as Van's Can.

Three of the inmates of Van's Can had begun their terms several years before, at Jackson, then moved up to DeHoCo, and were now serving their final years at Van's Can. The three had been found guilty of conspiracy to commit manslaughter.

As with many murderers, these three convicts were among the least dangerous inmates in the prison. The reasons for, and objects of, their erstwhile homicidal attempts were outside the prison walls. Inside the prison they were obedient, even docile.

In fact, if one could ignore the reality that they had attempted to kill—and, at least in one instance, almost did kill—they were rather resolutely law-abiding citizens. Their one area of bitterness sprang from the treatment they had received while studying for the priesthood in a Catholic seminary many years before. They had gotten into trouble as a result of their attempt to, in their view, balance the scales of justice.

In the beginning of their incarceration, they had been four, not three. But one, having been judged less culpable than the others, had received a lesser sentence. What with serving ''good time'' (five days per month credited against the sentence) and a parole, he had been released from Van's Can some six months ago.

With these six months behind him, he was now permitted to visit his still-incarcerated companions. And this is what he was doing now. Carrying a small white index card setting forth his identity, the identities of the three prisoners he wanted to visit, and their prison numbers and terms, he approached the guard. Somehow, he had never been able to bring himself to call the guards "screws" as the other prisoners did.

The uniformed but unarmed guard studied the request for visitation. "Okay, but you gotta wait. They're over in the Big Top at lunch."

The lobby was virtually deserted. Whitaker seated himself on a long, hard bench, near the far wall. He sat quietly and studied the prison reception area as only one who had once been incarcerated there could. It brought back memories, few pleasant.

He sat, staring at the blank, whitewashed wall. He could hear the faint but unmistakable prison sounds. Barred doors being slammed. The shuffling of feet moving but going always only a brief distance. Several TV sets tuned into different channels, loud in the various blocks, muffled at this distance.

How could he ever have thought that Van's Can was "not so bad"? It was the comparison, of course. Jacktown had been so severe, forbidding, threatening. So old, with the lingering odors of urine, feces, perspiration. Filled with desperate men.

Jacktown had made DeHoCo seem almost like a resort. In the beginning of their stay at DeHoCo, all four had initially been confined in the dog ward because their crime had been murder, or at least conspiracy to murder.

The dog ward had been a mistake, an almost fatal mistake. Only the most violent killers were confined in that ward. Strangely, it was the most peaceful ward in the block—only because its inmates respected the viciousness of their colleagues. None would raise a hand to another— because of the certainty of savage, hair-trigger retribution.

Almost immediately, it became all too obvious that "the four" were completely out of place in the dog ward.

They were removed at once and placed in medium security with Outside Placement. In this category, they were able to work on the farm and attend the various trade school classes.

From that time, prison officials became aware of the special character of these men. Despite their crime, none of them had a distinctly aggressive, violent nature. They had been angry at treatment they had received from their Church years before. They were angry now at what they considered the dangerous liberal trend of their Church. But beyond that, they were rather peaceful, respectful, obedient, reverent men. Almost like Boy Scouts. Their most disconcerting behavior was a bizarre tendency to be consistently clumsy. And while that could be extremely annoying, it was not a crime.

Because of the exemplary behavior of these four, they were among the first to be sent to Van's Can.

It was their transfer from DeHoCo to Van's Can that Bruce Whitaker was now recalling. At first it had seemed to them a large leap toward eventual freedom. But soon they realized that this impression was due entirely to the freshness of the new facility. Here there were no leftover odors, memories, or ghosts. Those would come later.

Some of the sounds were growing louder. The shift that had been eating in the Big Top, the central refectory, was done.

A guard summoned him. Whitaker knew the way from the reception area to the combination auditorium/gymnasium well. He had walked it many, many times. But he obediently followed the guard through the various cell-block doors. There was no alternative. As he often reflected, this procedure was like passing a ship through the locks of a waterway. No door unlocked before the previous one had been relocked.

Whitaker and the guard entered the vaulted room. Trustees and medium-security prisoners were allowed to receive their visitors in the gym. Those in maximum security were confined to a long, narrow, screened-off room in the basement where they could communicate with visitors only by phone.

Whitaker immediately found his three friends. They were seated at a picnic table, on a long bench whose uneven legs made balance precarious at best. They seemed pleased at his visit. He had no trouble believing they were pleased.

The guard left Whitaker at the table, then moved to a nearby wall where he kept them, as well as other inmates and visitors, under casual surveillance.

"So, how are things in the world?" the First Man asked.

"You shouldn't ask," Whitaker, the Second Man, said. "I can see now why some of the guys here don't want to leave. And why when they do leave they want to get back in."

"You're forgetting what it's like in here," the Third Man said. "You always did have a convenient memory."

"Now, now," the Fourth Man said in a conciliatory tone, "There's no use our getting off on the wrong foot. Let's hear what he has to say. How did it go in the hospital? Were you able to get in?"

"It was easier than any of us imagined," Whitaker replied. "I just applied to become a volunteer and they took me."

"No questions?"

"Oh, yes, there were some . . . but we anticipated everything the interviewer wanted to know. I'm not even sure whether she checked my story about part-time janitorial work at the Back Porch Theatre. But if she did, she found out that's true. There were just a few papers to fill out. But, again, we anticipated everything they wanted to know."

"No one recognized you?" asked the First Man.

"No, not that I know of. I try to stay aware of being recognized. But I don't think anyone has."

"I'm not surprised," said the Fourth Man. "It was a long time ago that our pictures were in the papers."

"Yes. And nothing was published about my parole. So, no one expected to see me."

"Besides," said the Fourth Man, "your disguise is very good. Those horn-rimmed glasses and your toupee make it difficult for even me to recognize you."

"Couldn't you afford a better rug?" the Third Man asked. "It looks cruddy. It looks like a small dog died and you had to decide whether to bury it or wear it. And you made the wrong decision."

"It's not my fault." Whitaker seemed genuinely aggrieved. "They gave me only a pittance when I got out of here. And do you think an amateur theater group pays a part-time janitor a princely sum?"

"It's all right," the Fourth Man assured them. "It doesn't matter what its quality is. The important thing is that it's a good disguise . . . it *is* a good disguise, don't you think?"

The First and Third Man concurred, the Third rather grudgingly.

"All right," the Fourth Man continued, "you've penetrated the hospital's security. That's very good. Are you able to move about at all?"

"That's the best part. . . ." Whitaker sniffed about

fastidiously; there was some odor. . . . "I've tested that identification badge in almost every section of St. Vincent's. No one questions it. Hardly anyone even looks at it. Sometimes people walk around the hospital with their ID badge flipped over and no one questions it even then."

"Do you think you'll need that theology diploma so they will accept you as a Protestant chaplain?" asked the First Man.

"Not necessary."

"What about our plan to have you carry around a stethoscope so you can masquerade as a doctor?" the Third Man asked.

"I thought about that. But, no, not yet anyway. That might cause more problems than it cures."

"All right," the Fourth Man said. "Then what have you learned? Is it as bad as we feared?"

"Oh, yes. It is very, very bad. God knows what-all they're doing. But just in one day I located their clinic. And I can only tell you the place is a veritable cesspool."

"No!"

"Yes!"

"Such as . . .?"

"Birth control!"

"Artificial?"

"Very!"

"No!"

"Yes!"

"How do you know?" the Fourth Man was barely controlling himself. In this, he was doing much better than his companions.

"I saw with my own eyes the pamphlets they're handing out for distribution to women. Indiscriminately!"

"No!"

"With pictures?"

"Yes! Illustrated!"

"Did you bring any?"

"No. I was afraid I'd be searched."

"Of course."

"But that's not all!"

"There's more?"

"Oh, yes. They even have devices they give out free of charge!"

"Devices?"

"Yes. What do you call them, prophylactics?"

"Condoms?"

"Rubbers?"

"No! Prophylactics!"

"Same thing!"

"Oh."

"How about abortions?"

"What about them?"

"Do they do them?"

"Abortions?" Whitaker repeated.

"Yes, dummy, abortions!" The Third Man never had possessed a long fuse.

"Not to the best of my knowledge. I mean, I didn't actually see anything like that. But I'll keep looking."

"Anything else?"

"Well, yes. I don't know exactly what was going on . . . but from the way the doctor was handling it, it seemed like it probably was wrong."

"Whatinhell are you talking about?" the Third Man demanded.

"Watch your language," the First Man admonished.

"My God, we've been in prison for years," said the Third Man. "You'd think your vocabulary would expand a little."

"Just because we're in the mud doesn't mean we have to wallow in it," the First Man retorted.

61

"Will you two calm down," the Fourth Man said. "Now, tell us, what was it you saw?"

"It was a woman—I'm pretty sure she wasn't married—who's had lots of kids, I suppose out of wedlock. Anyway, the doctor tested her and said she wasn't pregnant. But he wanted to make sure she never got pregnant again."

"What did he do?"

"Fitted her with one of those devices, I'll bet."

"A device?"

"An Inner Uterine Device! An IUD!"

"They've got them. The doctor mentioned that. For one reason or another, the IUD—whatever—didn't work for this woman. No, this was going to be a foolproof way of avoiding pregnancy again."

"What was it, for the love of God!"

"I didn't understand the doctor very well. It sounded something like a 'tutu migration.' I tried to look it up in their medical library, but I couldn't find it."

"A tutu migration? A tutu migration! My God!" exclaimed the Third Man. "He's talking about a tubal ligation!"

"What's that?"

"When they tie off the woman's Fallopian tubes. Then neither an egg or the sperm can get through," the Third Man explained. "Why do we have to depend on this idiot to do our work for us?"

"Because he's the only one of us who's free."

"It's not fair."

"But what about the tubal ligation?"

"As far as I'm concerned," said the Fourth Man, "it's the straw that breaks the camel's back."

"What do you mean?"

"All these things—birth control information, devices, and now sterilization—all of them are in direct violation of Church teaching. We've got to do something about this!"

62

"Are you sure?" Whitaker was almost pleading. "The last time we were trying to come to the defense of Holy Mother Church and look what it got us: prison!"

"Look back over history, brother," the Fourth Man admonished. "It was always the same. Peter imprisoned, then crucified—upside down, mind you. Paul imprisoned and executed. All the Apostles except John. And they certainly tried hard enough with John. Anyway, martyrdom down through the centuries has been the lot of true Catholics. Nothing has changed."

"I've been wondering about that," the First Man said. "I don't know that I'm really cut out for martyrdom. I think, all things considered, I'd rather be a confessor or a virgin or something. Martyrdom hurts."

"I can't say I disagree with that," Whitaker said.

"Yellow-bellied sapsuckers!" the Third Man spat.

"Now, now," the Fourth Man cautioned, "we've got to stick together. We're surely not doing this for ourselves. We're doing it for God's Holy Church. We're doing it for the Holy Pope of God! Besides, we aren't courting martyrdom. We've got to make very clever plans so that this hypocrisy that's masquerading as a Catholic hospital will be exposed."

"What do you mean?"

"I mean, the only reason these mortal sins are going on in a Catholic hospital is because the authorities are not aware of what's going on."

"Are you sure of that?"

"Of course! Cardinal Boyle is just not informed of what some of his pinko priests and nuns are up to. If he were informed, he'd do something to clear up the situation."

"Are you sure?" asked the First Man. "Sometimes I get the impression that Cardinal Boyle doesn't want to know what's going on in the inner city."

"It doesn't matter, really," the Fourth Man explained.

"Even if you're right, once it is made known, what's really going on in St. Vincent's Hospital, whether Cardinal Boyle wants to do something about it or not, he has no choice. The pressure from the universal Church, from the Vatican, will force him to make things right."

"You mean the Vatican will know what we've done?"

"You mean we'll be that famous!"

"Absolutely!"

"But what in hell are we going to do?" the Third Man wanted to know.

"How about blowing up the clinic?" the First Man suggested.

"Sounds good to me," the Third Man agreed.

"No, no," the Fourth Man protested. "That would just win sympathy for them."

"Well, then, what?"

"It's a matter of doing something that will get St. Vincent's Hospital into the news. And not in any complimentary way, either. Something that will get their evil practices publicized."

"But how can we do that?"

"I have a plan," said the Fourth Man, to the relief of the others.

"Before you get into your plan," Whitaker said, "I just thought of something else."

"What?"

"When you asked if I'd been recognized by anyone—"

"Yes?"

"Well, no, not really. The disguise seems to be effective. But there is one girl . . . she didn't recognize me, but she noticed me."

"Noticed you?"

"Well, we met earlier in the day." Whitaker neglected to mention that their meeting had involved a collision that resulted in someone's lunch ending up all over the floor and wall. "And then we met again later in the pharmacy." He didn't mention that this meeting was occasioned because his white coat was slowly being dyed blue. "She used my name. But I'm pretty sure she read it off the identification tag."

"Was she the only person you met?"

"Yes, just the girl—twice."

"You'd better check up on her," the Fourth Man advised. "If she does know who you are it could ruin what we're trying to do."

"How do I do that?"

"Get to know her a little bit better. Find out what she knows."

"All right. I'll do it. Now, what's your plan?"

"Wait a minute," the Third Man said. "I smell something."

"Yeah," Whitaker agreed, "so do I. As a matter of fact, I've been smelling something peculiar for a long time now."

"What is it?" the Fourth Man asked.

There was a moment of silence as each of the men looked at one another.

"I guess it must be me," the First Man confessed.

"You!"

"Well, you know we're not supposed to take any food out of the Big Top. . . ."

"Yeah, we all know that."

"Well, I did."

"What in God's name did you take?"

"Some cheese."

"Cheese! My God, man, you might just as well have left an Indian trail to follow. Where is it?"

"Under my armpit."

"On second thought," said the Third Man, "that's just

about the best place you could have hidden it. There won't be that much difference in the smell.''

"What are you going to do?"

"I don't know."

"Listen, it won't be long before one of the guards notices it's beginning to smell like a cheese factory in here. You've got to do something."

"But what?"

"I've got an idea," the Fourth Man said. "There are only three guards in here so far. And there's only one anywhere near us. I'll go over and talk to him . . . distract him. Meanwhile, see that heat register near the floor there? You go over, slip the cheese out of your shirt and stick it behind the grate. See? The thing's loose; you won't have any trouble. You'd better come with me," he said to the Third Man.

"But what about my cheese?" the First Man protested.

"Never mind the cheese!" said the Third Man. "You'll be lucky not to lose any good time. Let's do it. Now!"

It must be some law of physics, thought Whitaker. Probably the Seesaw Principle. Some sort of natural law that states that when a weight is abruptly removed from one end of a plank that is unevenly balanced, the other end of the plank goes down. In any case, as the Third and Fourth Men stood up, the First Man hit the floor hard, with the bench clattering down with him.

The guards tensed. But when they recognized who was responsible for the commotion, they relaxed. It was by no means unusual for that bunch. Then, while the Third and Fourth Man engaged the nearby guard in conversation, the First Man did manage to slide his slab of cheese behind the heating grate. Following that, the Fourth Man barely had time to explain his plan for the hospital before the gym was evacuated while the guards searched for an errant skunk.

The *Detroit News* was rare if not unique among big-city newspapers. The present building was erected in 1917 and had not been substantially altered in the intervening years. If, in the spirit of a young Mickey Rooney and Judy Garland, some kids had wanted to stage the 1928 classic, *The Front Page,* they could have credibly used the city room of the *News* as their set. Not that much would have to be changed.

The ceilings were anachronistically high. Genuine wood paneled the walls. There were no cubicles, no partitions separating one desk from another. Not one desk was decorated with a word processor terminal.

Install some outdated phones, restore some of the old oak furnishings, bring back a few of the old-fashioned desks and one could be in the Roaring Twenties.

Adjacent to the city room was the sports department and the news room, with desks positioned in claustrophobic proximity. In an outside row that provided a bit more breathing room, was seated Patricia Lennon. On her desk were several open files she seemed to be studying. Actually, the files were no more than props, permitting her active mind the luxury of wandering over a number of potential stories she might develop.

Gradually, Pat became aware of someone standing beside her. She looked up. It was Leon London, city editor of the *News*. He was smiling at her. It was difficult not to.

"Pat, if you're not working on anything else right now, we could use some help developing that story on the disturbance at Cobo Hall last night."

"As a matter of fact, I am, Leon." Her mind raced through the stories she'd been considering. Any one would be better than covering the Cobo Hall incident. That story could write itself. Bring in a top rock group, provide less than adequate law enforcement personnel, and you're likely to get a riot. That was about the size of what had occurred the previous night at Cobo Hall.

London was now genuinely interested. "Oh? What've you got going?"

It was the moment of truth. She would have to pick one of the many possibilities she'd been considering. "I'm developing a piece for the Sunday magazine."

"Oh?"

Which one? "Old St. Vincent's Hospital, downtown." The die was cast. "It's coming up on its one-hundred fiftieth anniversary, and it's a really interesting place with a fascinating history. It was the original hospital in the city and, of course, the first Catholic hospital. And it's one of only two Catholic hospitals remaining in the city."

• "That old! I hadn't realized."

"And it may not be there an awful lot longer. As far as I've been able to tell, it's on really hard times. Without some more research, I couldn't tell you how it's managed to stay alive as long as it has."

"Really!"

"I think it must have something to do with that nun who runs it. We've done a few stories on her over the past few years. But nothing in any kind of depth. I think she may very well be the story of St. Vincent's survival."

"Interesting."

Lennon was hoping London would soon run out of one-line comments. She had just about exhausted the small amount of research she had done on St. Vincent's. In fact, she was already skating on factually thin ice. She could only hope, on the one hand, that the few small details she had ad-libbed would prove accurate and, on the other, that London would find her narrative convincing. The alternative would be wasting a lot of time dredging up the same old quotes from the same old sources ending in the same old story.

"Who are you working with on this one?"

"Bob Ankenazy." She would have to tell Bob about that. But she needed an editor/rabbi to justify her developing this or practically any other story.

"Sounds good. Keep me informed." London moved on to find another reporter who would tell metro Detroit readers that the area's youth was going to hell in a handbasket.

Seldom had she begun a feature story on such a whim. Either St. Vincent's and its unsinkable chief executive officer would prove an adequate subject for the in-depth style of a magazine article or Lennon had glommed on to one of her rare lemons.

In any case, now that London had brought the matter to a head, she had only one direction in which to go. First, she would have to engage Ankenazy in her story. Without a sponsor editor, she would be up the proverbial creek. She already had the standing offer of space from the magazine editor. Then she would have to get a move on research and then, of course, write the story.

5

BRUCE WHITAKER HAD BEEN NERVOUS.
He had had that feeling—all to usual for him—of being
very much alone in attempting to accomplish something
for which he was inadequate.

And he was not even anywhere near carrying out the
group's goal yet. First he was supposed to find the nurse's
aide with whom he'd come in contact yesterday. Then he
was to discover how much, if anything, she knew about
him. It had not occurred to him that there weren't that
many nurses' aides in this relativaly small hospital. And
that she very probably would be assigned to the same floor
she'd been on yesterday.

As was so often the case, his fears were out of proportion to reality. Finding her had not been nearly as difficult
as he had anticipated.

He had found her on the floor. At just about the same
spot he'd first met her. She was cleaning up after dropping
a breakfast tray. At least he hadn't been the cause of this
spill. While she scraped the egg and cereal off the carpet,

he was able to scrutinize her ID. Her name was Ethel Laidlaw and she was, indeed, a nurse's aide.

He had just delivered a tray of medications to the nurses' station. Thus he was between assignments. He volunteered to assist Ethel. Together, they managed to spill only three more breakfasts, disconnect two telephones, tip over a bedpan, and unplug a patient's oxygen supply. They had had the presence of mind to call a nurse to reconnect the oxygen tube.

Over a coffee break, Bruce informed Ethel, in response to her question, that he worked part-time as a janitor at the nearby Back Porch Theatre. Ethel had never known anyone in show business. She was impressed.

Fortuitously, she had the afternoon off and there was a matinee at the theater. Bruce, being an employee, could get tickets at a moment's notice.

Actually, with the average size of the audience at the Back Porch, anyone could get any number of tickets to any performance. In any case, Bruce took Ethel to the 2:00 P.M. performance of *The Manic Sperm*, an avant-garde drama by one of Detroit's fledgling playwrights.

Perhaps it would have been wiser if they had not bought popcorn. But then, as janitor, he would clean it up later.

Ethel told Bruce she'd never been to theater-in-the-round before. He confessed that neither had he. In fact, this was the first performance he'd ever attended at the Back Porch Theatre, even though he worked here.

The Manic Sperm opened with an irregular, frenetic beat of bongos and the resonance of loud snoring from the nearly vacant back row.

It did not take long for Bruce and Ethel to decide this play was not for them. The drama contained virtually all the usual four-letter words, repetitiously.

The final straw fell when the female lead whipped off her blouse, revealing small, very firm breasts. This was closely followed by the male lead's removing his trousers and slinking briskly across the stage, serpentine fashion, toward the leading lady. He resembled a . . . well . . . a manic sperm.

The departure of Bruce and Ethel was underscored by the abrasive sound of popcorn being crunched underfoot. Several catcalls were directed at them. Some by members of the cast.

Bruce took Ethel to one of downtown's famous Coney Island eateries. They were seated at a table for two.

"I'm terribly sorry about that play." Bruce dropped his wallet to the floor.

"That's okay. You hadn't seen it before. You didn't know." In trying to be helpful and retrieve the wallet, she hit her head on the table.

"Oh, I'm sorry." Bruce's gesture to touch her hand was aborted. He was not sure how a relationship between a man and woman should begin. But his intuition told him Ethel was not the sort of girl one touched on the first date.

"It's okay. I only wish I had a nickel for each time I've bumped my head."

This was a no-nonsense place whose intent was to move customers in and move them out. Bruce and Ethel ordered Coney Islands and coffee.

They shared an awkward silence until the coffee was served. Both added cream and sugar to their coffee. Both slopped some coffee on the table. The spilled coffee mingled in the middle of the table. It seemed significant. Both blushed.

"Ethel, I've been meaning to ask you. I mean . . . well, this may be impolite. I'm not sure how to put this, but . . . well . . . are you married?" He stirred his coffee vigorously, spilling more of it.

"Why no, of course not. You don't think I'd go out

with you if I was a married woman, do you? What do you take me for?"

"Oh, I'm so sorry! I didn't mean to insult you. I shouldn't have asked."

"No, no, it's okay. We don't know each other at all. Or we don't know very much about each other, at least. I guess questions are okay. Else we'll never get to know each other. How about you? You married?"

"Me? Oh, no. No."

"Not never?"

"No, oh, ha-ha, no. Never."

"C'mon! A good-lookin' guy like you? I'll bet you've had your share of girls. Haven't you?"

He knew he was blushing violently. "No, not really. Would you believe this is the first honest-to-glory date I've ever had."

"Would I believe that? I'd have a hard time, I'll tell you that."

"Well, it is. Honest. How about you? I don't want to embarrass you, but you're pretty good-looking yourself. I'll bet you've had lots of dates."

"Well, you'd lose. Oh, I've had a few. But usually only one per fellow. I'm really not all that good-looking. And besides, I tend to be a little on the . . . uh . . . clumsy side."

"You too! Did you notice the first time we met we ran into each other and spilled someone's supper?"

"Yeah, I did notice that." She couldn't help being self-conscious.

Bruce felt a strong urge to be as honest as possible with this woman. "Actually, this is not exactly how I look. I don't need these . . ." He removed his eyeglasses. ". . . and this hair is not mine." He removed his toupee and stuffed it in his pocket. He felt naked, but relieved that at least part of the truth was known.

She seemed surprised but not shocked. "Well, you do look different, I must say. But . . . well, I mean . . . I did know that wasn't your real hair. But I had no idea what you might look like without it. Well, you look great. I think you look better without the hairpiece than you do with it. I really do."

He was extremely pleased. He hoped they'd be able to strike up a real friendship. And that never would happen if he could not be honest with her.

"Now, there's one question I've got to ask, and it's very important." He leaned across the small table. "You've got to be completely honest with me, Ethel."

"Yes?"

"Now that you've seen me with and without a disguise, have you ever seen me before? Do you know me from anywhere?"

She looked at him thoughtfully. "Why, no, Bruce. I never set eyes on you before. Not never!"

"Good. Very good."

"But why didja ask a question like that for?"

"No real good reason. Only that you seemed to be following me around. I mean, after we bumped into each other, then the next time I looked up—in the clinic—there you were, telling me my sleeve was in a solution."

She wouldn't look at him. "Well, I kinda likedja. You didn't yell at me when we bumped into each other. And then you stayed and helped me clean up the mess. And all the time, you seemed so apologetic. Nobody ever treated me so swell before. I guess I kinda likedja at first bump. I was so hoping and praying that you'd come look me up today. I guess this is one time when my prayers really got answered."

Bruce could scarcely be happier. There was only one more possible fly in his ointment; he'd better get that cleared up immediately. "Speaking of prayers getting answered . . . well, this is a delicate area, but, well, you work at a Catholic hospital, and I was wondering . . ."

"Am I a Catholic?"

"Well, yes."

"Oh, yes, I'm a Catholic. That's for sure. How about you?"

"Oh, yes. Yes, indeed." Bruce realized he was still only halfway there. These days it was by no means enough merely to be Catholic. One was either a liberal or a conservative Catholic or, if one were neither but still claimed the designation, such a person hardly deserved to claim any religion. And if one were a liberal Catholic, he or she might just as well be a Protestant. That left only one acceptable category.

Which slot was Ethel in? The answer, Bruce knew, was crucial to their continued friendship. But how to discover . . .?

The waiter brought their Coney Islands, basically large hot dogs heaped with chili sauce. In lifting the chock-full bun from her plate, Ethel spilled some sauce into her coffee.

"Waiter!" Bruce found himself speaking more forcefully than was his custom. "There's been an accident. Bring this lady another cup of coffee!"

The waiter, with a look and a gesture that said it's easier doing it than arguing with this turkey, did as Bruce had commanded.

Ethel was most impressed.

"Ethel . . ."—Bruce tried very hard not to ruin his sandwich—"are you aware of what goes on in that hospital? In St. Vincent's?"

Ethel considered that question, evidently for the first time. "Well . . . operations, treatments, therapy, uh . . . health care—was there something else?"

"I mean, in the clinic, for example."

"The clinic?"

"Yes. Giving information, counseling, devices for the practice of artificial birth control. Like that!"

"Oh, policy! No, I never pay any attention to policy. I got enough problems with bedpans and the food trays and keeping the patients in water. Things like that."

"But, now that I brought it up, Ethel, what do you think of that kind of thing?"

"What?"

"Artificial birth control."

"It's wrong, ain't it? Ain't it against the Church? I mean, there was a lot of talk about it some years ago. And didn't the Church settle it? Didn't they say it was a sin? Seems that's how it came out. I guess I didn't pay much attention. I mean," she blushed, "it didn't have much to do with me. If you know what I mean."

"Sure. But that means that you accept the official teaching of the Church? The ordinary magisterium?"

"The ordinary what?"

"Never mind. If the Pope says it, you believe it?"

"You'd better believe that! Good heavens, if you can't trust the Pope, who can you trust? I mean!"

"You don't know how happy that makes me!"

"Really! I wouldn't have guessed."

Bruce was elated. In his excitement, he fumbled his Coney Island. He saved the sandwich, but his napkin fluttered off the table. Ethel dove to save it before it hit the floor. In doing so, she again banged her head against the table. She sat up a bit dazed. She rubbed her forehead. They both laughed.

Bruce was more and more convinced he had found a kindred klutz. Talk about relationships formed in heaven!

Contentedly, they finished their Coney Islands and coffee. The check the waiter had left was saturated with coffee and stained with chili sauce. Nevertheless, Bruce was able to make out the total. He left payment plus a small tip.

As the couple left, the owner breathed a silent prayer that they would forget his location and never return.

Ethel lived in a downtown apartment complex owned and operated by the League of Catholic Women. Bruce accompanied her home. As no male visitors were allowed beyond the lobby, they parted with a hearty handshake just inside the front door.

Ethel went immediately to her efficiency apartment. It was still early. She turned on the television. It was either game shows, soap operas, or an old movie. Ethel did not watch much daytime television. When she did, it was usually the soaps. Most of them featured a healthy measure of romance, even if it did tend to be a bit heavyhanded.

While the old black-and-white set was warming up, Ethel decided to shower.

Naked, she stood before the full-length mirror. She had only a few minutes before the shower steam would fog it.

Ethel tended to be ruthlessly objective, which could be—and frequently was—discouraging. Face: very plain. Her dishwater blonde hair was adequate, though it tended to be a bit stringy. Her eyebrows matched the coloration of her hair. Thus, they were almost invisible, adding little character to her nondescript oval face.

As for the rest of her, what could she say? It was a thirty-seven-year-old body that had never been pampered. The skin was no longer tight. Things were starting to sag. On the plus side, her frame contained not too many extra pounds. So she still possessed curves. But, standing there unclothed, she did not remind herself of a Hollywood starlet or even a go-go dancer. If anything came to mind, it was those pictures of women—naked and shamed—marched off to an open grave by a bunch of Nazi animals.

Steam obscured the mirror. End of speculation.

Hot showers felt particularly welcome on cold winter days. God, she hoped she would see Bruce again. It was the truth. She had never had a second date with a boy, or with a man for that matter. Once they discovered her essential clumsiness—the discovery never took long—they could not end the relationship quickly enough.

Maybe Bruce was different. He certainly was not Mr. Suave. But, more important, he was patient and understanding. She hoped against hope that she was not mistaken. That something could be developing between them.

But then what would come of it? There was a moment of panic. She had never been . . . intimate with a man. How would that work?

She decided to hurry her shower and get down to those soaps with a more active interest. Maybe she could learn something from them. Maybe she could get a book or two from the library that might prove helpful.

Of one thing she was certain: If the opportunity for romance and love presented itself, she would not muff it. She might fumble everything else in life. But by God, she was not going to fumble this.

On the way to the garret he called home, Bruce was stopped by the general manager/owner/producer/director/ male lead of the Back Porch Theatre. The man did not allude to Bruce's job as janitor, mostly because he knew they could not get a dog to clean up for what they were paying Bruce. However, Bruce was advised that he would never again be welcome in the audience; the Back Porch's presentations were intended for mature adults, not for easily shocked children, and Bruce had better not forget it!

Bruce absorbed the abuse as he always did—in silence. He was convinced that if things did not always go as they should in this life, there would be another life wherein wrongs would be corrected and justice done. Slime who would stage an immoral drama and then excoriate someone who walked out on it, well, according to Bruce's theodicy, they would be dealt with by a harsh and avenging God.

Until then, as his leader had pointed out, the lot of the just was martyrdom, in one form or another.

He made his way to the partially furnished attic that was home. While changing into his denim shirt and overalls, he studied himself briefly in the mirror.

It didn't really matter whether he was wearing his glasses and toupee; he was a cipher. Sort of round. A round head and a round body. An awkward gait. He wondered why he bothered with a disguise. From long experience he knew that no one ever noticed him.

One exception to this rule of oblivion was Ethel. Or was she too good to be true? Only time would tell. But he felt good around her. More surprising than that, he felt comfortable with her. She was the first female he'd ever met who did not make fun of his clumsiness.

But what if it did work? What if they . . . fell in love? His concern became apprehension. He'd never loved a woman. Not romantically. Here he was, thirty-two years old, and he'd never even had a conscious orgasm. Oh, sure, there'd been nocturnal pollutions. But nothing awake. He subscribed to that theological persuasion that held, for all practical purposes, that sex was dirty and so one should save it for a loved one.

In any case, Bruce could not afford the luxury of daydreaming about romance. He had a task to perform. He had a mission. It was God's work against an evil empire of sin. That came first. It had to. After that—and only after that—could he see if something might develop between him and Ethel.

He could, of course, pray over it. And he would. While he cleaned up the popcorn.

✦ ✦ ✦

Sister Eileen Monahan sat idly at her desk. Since the attack, she'd had dufficulty concentrating, particularly when alone. There was a tendency to relive in memory the panic that had overcome her when she was grabbed from behind and choked—the feeling that she was about to die.

Her struggle to remain conscious and stay alive had surprised her somehow. She had always assumed that when the time came to face death she would be able to abandon herself to the will of God and go with a sense of peace. And when she was attacked, she'd had no doubt that she was about to die. Now, as a result of that incident, she was trying to better prepare herself for death under any eventuality.

As for the hospital staff, fortunately the turmoil over the incident was quieting down. After the initial brouhaha, everyone recognized that it had been no more than a freak occurrence. The assailant had been suffering the early symptoms of withdrawal from a drug overdose. He'd had no real idea of what he was doing. He would have attacked anyone walking down that corridor at that time. That she had been the victim had been her bad luck, but no more than a coincidence. The main benefit of the episode was that security had been tightened in the detox unit.

"There's someone to see you, Sister."

Sister Eileen glanced up at her secretary. Then she squinted through her half-glasses at her appointment calendar. She had a meeting in half an hour. Blindly she could have bet there'd be a meeting in a short while from anytime. But there was no appointment scheduled for this time.

"She doesn't have an appointment." There were times when Dolly came close to reading Sister's mind.

"Who is it, Dolly?"

"A Miss Patricia Lennon."

Patricia Lennon. Patricia Lennon. The name rang a very definite but ill-defined bell.

"From the *Detroit News*."

"Oh." Pause. "Give me a couple of minutes, Dolly, then show her in, will you?"

"Yes, Sister." The door closed behind her.

Pat Lennon.

The full given name had fooled her. With Patricia Lennon she was unfamiliar. With Pat Lennon she was right at home. Sister had been reading Pat Lennon's byline for what seemed like ages. First in the *Detroit Free Press*, where she'd been a reporter for several years before moving down West Lafayette to the "Old Gray Lady," as the *News* was known.

But what was Pat Lennon doing at St. Vincent's? From all Sister could recall, Pat was one of the city's top reporters. What did they call them . . . investigative reporters. Yes, from all Sister had heard and read, Pat Lennon was one of the best investigative reporters around. Which brought Sister back to the beginning: Why would a top investigative reporter be calling at St. Vincent's? To investigate? What?

That, thought Sister, is all we need. Here we are, hanging on by a thread and here comes someone to unravel that thread.

St. Vincent's existence was so increasingly precarious that Sister Eileen had lived through its death in anticipation many times. It was anyone's guess how much longer the institution might endure. But she had poured so much of herself into it that she had figuratively joined her life to that of the hospital. She guessed she might die a little if St. Vincent's were to close.

She could not see the presence and interest of Pat Lennon

81

as anything but a threat. But, like all the other threatening realities of life, this one too must be faced.

Pat Lennon entered Sister's office, smiled and, hand outstretched, approached the desk. Sister Eileen stood and they shook hands. Briefly but thoroughly the two appraised each other.

Lennon was surprised. Newspaper photos did not do Sister Eileen justice. She seemed a warmly attractive woman. Lennon had been through parochial school, even a Catholic college. She was used to nuns in traditional habits. She reflected on what a waste it would be to wrap this woman in yards and yards of wool. Any woman who could keep her figure into late middle age deserved to let others know.

Sister Eileen was surprised. While she had seen Pat's byline many times, as was so often the case with reporters there was never an accompanying photo. Columnists were well recognized, because their photos usually ran with their columns. But reporters, who were easily of equal or greater importance, lived lives of personal anonymity. Over the years, Sister had seen her share of reporters, but this one was different. Why, she could easily have been a motion picture or stage star.

Beyond appearance, each woman realized and acknowledged that the other was both expert and extremely competent in her field. They respected each other.

Sister gestured to Lennon to be seated. "So, what brings you to St. Vincent's, Miss Lennon?"

"Pat." Lennon invited the use of her first name.

Sister Eileen nodded. However, as was the case with Father Koesler, she herself would be more at home with her title.

"For the longest time, I've sort of had St. Vincent's in the back of my mind," Lennon opened. "I mean, here it sits in the middle of downtown Detroit. And yet, in a way, it isn't here. With no disrespect, Sister, St. Vincent's is one of the last refuges anybody thinks about. There are so many big hospitals, like Receiving or Harper or Grace—and some, like Children's, that specialize—that not too many people think very often of St. Vincent's.''

"So, you've come here just to think about St. Vincent's?" It was more a voicing of incredulity than a question.

"I want to do a feature on St. Vincent's for our Sunday magazine."

"Oh."

"Is there a problem?"

"I hope not. What do you intend to do?"

"Start by interviewing you. Then, tour the hospital. Sort of get the feel of it. Talk to some of the staff. If it's okay, spend some time in various departments like the emergency room, the X-ray lab; maybe talk to some patients. I'm not sure where this will lead. But it's supposed to be a feature article, so it should be fairly comprehensive. It can't do St. Vincent's any harm. Most hospitals have gotten into advertising. An article in the *Michigan Magazine* could prove to be a better ad than money can buy."

She doesn't know where this will lead, but it can't hurt, thought Sister. We'll just have to see about that. "We'll do our best to cooperate," she said. Realistically, there wasn't any alternative.

"Can we start with your interview?"

Eileen checked her watch. "I'm afraid I haven't much time. I've got to attend a meeting in about fifteen minutes."

"Let's see how far we can get." Without being able to structure her story before all the interviews were completed, Lennon thought of making Sister Eileen the article's centerpiece. Only time would tell. "Would you mind if my photographer joins us?"

"Photographer?" Eileen had not counted on pictures.

This thing was escalating. "Oh, you must have some photos of me in your files at the paper."

"Nothing up-to-date. We'll want fresh shots of you and the hospital. We can contrast the way the building looks now with some of those ancient stills we've got in our library."

Sister chuckled. "You're not going to contrast my present appearance with some of those ancient stills of me that you've got in your morgue, are you?"

"Not likely. You probably don't look a lot different."

"That was a long time ago." Just the suggestion of days gone by brought a flood of memories. She forced herself back to the present. "Very well. What's your photographer's name?"

"William Arnold. He prefers William, not Bill."

She spoke into the intercom. "Dolly, there should be a photographer named William Arnold out there. Would you send him in, please."

A moment later, a young black man entered. Eileen did not count the cameras suspended from his neck and shoulders, but there seemed to be many.

Introductions were exchanged. Then, "Don't pay any attention to William, Sister. Just talk to me naturally. William will get some candid shots of you."

Eileen was not happy with this arrangement. She did not photograph well under the best of circumstances. And with a candid shot, the likelihood was great that her mouth or eyes might be opened too wide, or she might be grimacing. But, as with the interview, there was nothing much to do but cooperate. A lack of collaboration would only antagonize. And in a feature article, St. Vincent's needed all the help it could get.

Lennon opened her notepad as William began checking the lighting and moving things around. He was distracting; no two ways about that.

"So, Sister, when did you come to St. Vincent's?"

She needed ouly a moment to recall the date. "In 1936, I was just out of the convent with temporary vows."

Lennon's pen stopped, poised over the pad. She was figuring.

Eileen laughed. "I was eighteen at the time." Pause. "Which means I'm now sixty-eight."

Lennon looked at her. Incredible. For Pat, in her early thirties, the late sixties spelled "old." She would never have imagined anyone would look so good at sixty-eight. "Then you have been here . . . fifty years!"

Eileen smiled. She knew what Lennon was thinking. That she had been at St. Vincent's longer than Pat had been alive. "Well, off and on. There was some time taken out for further training, some degrees. But, it's true, St. Vincent's has been my one mission."

William was moving around behind and on either side of Lennon, snapping pictures madly. Sister Eileen found this quite disconcerting. But . . . there was no help for it.

"Isn't that a bit unusual, Sister? I mean, don't nuns and priests—especially nuns, get moved around a lot?" Lennon was remembering the nuns who had been her teachers. One of the most difficult challenges in tracking down one's former religious teachers was locating their present assignment.

"I guess that's true of most Sisters. It's hard to say how it happened that I've been here all these years. Timing has a lot to do with it. Some might say it was providence. I just happened to be here and ready to assume it each time a new position opened up. Now," Eileen shook her head, "I don't know that anyone wants the job."

"That brings us down to the bottom line, Sister. Something I want to explore in some depth. I know it will be the question uppermost in my readers' minds: Why? There doesn't seem to be any earthly reason why St. Vincent's should still be here. Why?''

"That is, indeed, a very big question, Pat.'' Eileen glanced at her watch. "Far too big for us to get into just now, since I've got a meeting to attend. Maybe we can pick it up later.'' She stood, as did Lennon. William mercifully stopped shooting.

"You did say you wanted to tour the hospital, didn't you, Pat?''

"Very much so.''

"It will be a bit delicate. You'll have to be most careful when it comes to our patients. They are likely to be frightened of you. And we can't have anyone disturbing the routine.''

"Trust us, Sister. We won't take anyone's picture without his or her permission. We'll be very circumspect. Maybe it'll be possible for us to talk again after we've been around the hospital and you've finished with your meeting.''

"That will be quite late in the day. But, we'll see.''

Eileen arranged with Dolly to have credentials made up for Lennon and Arnold. An aide was summoned to escort the two newspeople to the various nurses' stations and the various hospital departments.

As she left them, Eileen breathed a prayer that all would go well. For things to go well, particularly if they visited the clinic, would require a miracle. But then, Sister Eileen believed in miracles.

Because she knew how to cut through red tape, and because she was secretary to the CEO, Dolly was able to get credentials and an ID pass for Lennon and Arnold in record time.

Bruce Whitaker, who had just come back on duty, noticed Lennon and Arnold immediately. In this, he was not alone. The two made an odd couple even in the hospital setting. Lennon's striking beauty alone was enough to turn heads, female as well as male. And it was definitely noteworthy to see in the corridors a young black man with cameras hanging all over him.

Although he was scheduled to check in and receive an assignment, Bruce had not yet done so. Clad in hospital coat and ID badge, he now trailed the touring group at what he considered a discreet distance.

With Whitaker in tow, the trio visited for varying lengths of time: the noninvasive diagnostic lab, where EMG, EKG and EEG tests were evaluated; the renal unit; art therapy; the mental health unit; the open and closed psychiatric wards; the alcohol and detoxification units; the protective services department, and the respiratory therapy unit.

During the visit to each unit, Whitaker tried to get close enough to hear what was going on without having his presence noted. But invisibility eluded him. Especially when, while walking down the hallway on 2-B, he kicked over the IV stand, pulling down the patient attached to the IV. Then there was the nasty incident when Whitaker knocked the plug out of the wall socket in the renal dialysis unit.

At the scene of the first commotion, Lennon had assumed that Whitaker was a doctor. She also assumed that the patient, weak or awkward, had crashed into him. But at the second imbroglio, she began to doubt her earlier assessment. Why would a doctor be following them? And how could one so clumsy be a doctor? In a whisper, she asked William to keep an eye on the singular man, try to find out who he was and what he was doing.

Lennon had the vague impression that she had seen the man before. Something about him reminded her of some story she had covered. Other things about him argued against any previous meeting with or knowledge of him. Odd.

"So, how's it goin', uh . . . Bruce?" Arnold got close enough to read Whitaker's ID.

"Oh!" Whitaker was startled. He was sure he hadn't been noticed. The recent catastrophes that had been visited upon him were, in his frame of reference, quite ordinary occurrences. But, having been addressed, Whitaker squinted to make out the other's ID. "Things are okay, I guess . . . uh . . . Bill."

"William."

"Oh, excuse me . . . I thought . . ."

"William."

"Yes, of course. Whatever. William."

"You work here, Bruce?"

"Well, sort of. Not work, really. Well, not employment. Actually, I'm employed at the Back Porch Theatre."

"No shit! Whaddya do there, Bruce, Baby?"

"Well, it's part-time work, really. I'm the janitor."

"Ha! The kind of crazy stuff they do there, they'll probably write a whole goddam play around your broom. But whaddya do here, Bruce?"

"I'm a volunteer. But I'm sort of between duties right now. And I was kind of interested in you and the lady. Did I hear her say she's with the *Detroit News*?"

"Oh, yeah. That's Pat Lennon. A really neat lady."

"And you, Bill—er, William?"

"Staffer with the *News*."

"Staffer?"

"Staff photographer. I drew this assignment to go with Pat. My lucky day. She's a real pro. Fun to do a job with."

"So. What is she doing here? What are both of you doing here?"

"She's doing a feature on the place for *Michigan Magazine*. An' I'm taking a zillion shots so some editor can pick out the ones he wants to use with the article."

"You're going to do a feature article for the *News'* Sunday magazine on this hospital? On St. Vincent's?"

"That's about the size of it."

It was a miracle. The answer to prayer. Their entire plan had been to somehow get the news media interested in this hospital so that the authorities would be forced to confront the violations of Church law that were going on here.

Now here were a reporter and a photographer from one of Detroit's major newspapers. It was an answer to prayer. God was good.

But so far, nobody had shown these *News* people anything. Just routine stuff . . . treatment centers, machines, busy staff people, and sick patients. None of the evil stuff.

It figured. The nurse's aide had probably been warned not to show them any violation of Church law.

Now that he thought of it, Whitaker wondered if this reporter would recognize a sin if she saw it. He had no idea whether she was Catholic. Oh, God, this golden opportunity mustn't slip through his fingers.

Wait! The clinic! It was his best shot.

"How about the clinic?" Whitaker asked Arnold.

"I give up. How about it?"

"Don't you want to see it?"

"Not particularly." Arnold was growing bored.

"I think you should see it."

"Oh? Why?"

A good question. Not because they were advocating contraception. Although that was, indeed, the underlying reason Whitaker sought to interest them in the clinic.

"Because it's an integral part of the hospital . . . and you've seen just about everything else." It was the logical reason. Whitaker was grateful to the Holy Ghost for that inspiration.

"Makes sense. Hey, Pat, this guy says we should see the clinic."

"That's where we're going now"—Lennon looked at the aide-guide for confirmation—"isn't it?" The aide nodded.

That's odd, thought Whitaker. The aide had apparently planned to take them to that cesspool regardless.

As they made their way to the clinic, the aide continued her explanation of those sections of the hospital through which they were passing. Lennon took notes and occasionally asked questions. For the most part, Arnold let his cameras dangle. Tagging along behind the threesome was Whitaker.

Evidently, Arnold found the clinic interesting. He took light readings and began snapping pictures. The aide flagged a nurse, made introductions and stepped back to allow the nurse to take over explanations.

The nurse guided Lennon and Arnold through the clinic. Fortunately, it held few patients at the moment.

There had been no ostensible purpose for Whitaker to accompany them through the clinic. His presence was in no way called for. Nor could he think of any pretext to stay. So, reluctantly, he left the group and went to volunteer his services elsewhere.

Later, he overheard the clinic nurse tell someone that Lennon had taken particular notice of the family planning services. All was well as far as Bruce Whitaker was concerned.

Meanwhile Arnold had gone through almost two rolls of film and had decided that was about all he'd need. He started to pack his gear.

Lennon, too, felt she had heard enough and closed her notepad. She noticed several pamphlets displayed on a counter. She picked one up and paged through it. Clearly, she found it interesting. She began reading in earnest.

"Excuse me," she addressed the nurse, "but these

pamphlets—are they available to the patients? The clients who come to the clinic?''

The nurse scanned the pamphlets. ''Why, yes, of course. Is there something wrong?''

''They've got family planning information.''

''We get quite a few pregnancies in here. Not as many as some hospitals. But that's because we're in the core city. Lots of older people. Still, we do get our share of preggies.''

''Do all pregnant women get this material?''

''Routinely, yes. You'd be surprised at how little some of these women know about getting pregnant. Even some who are already mothers. Oh, they know enough about coitus. But when it comes to sperm and ova and menstruation, more often than not you can forget it.''

''But these pamphlets have information on . . . uh . . . 'artificial' contraception.''

''Yes?'' The nurse was surprised that a contemporary woman—let alone an urbane reporter—would take issue with contraception. Of course, the lady was from the News, which was a rather conservative paper. But, really!

''Well, unless I am seriously mistaken,'' Lennon said, ''the Catholic Church still condemns contraception.'' Pause. ''And this is a Catholic hospital!''

''Lady, I don't make policy here; I just follow it. But I can tell you one thing: It's like shoveling sand against the tide.''

''Oh?''

''Well, like I said before, most of the girls who come in here pregnant don't know how they got that way. They just know they're pregnant. And even after counseling and literature like this, or even after giving them anything from the Pill to an IUD, they still come back pregnant again. About the only time it ends is when they get a tubal ligation.''

"You do that here?"

"Uh-huh. Actually it's simple out-patient surgery now. Usually there aren't any complications."

"But that's sterilization."

"Well, it's not as if we did it as a regular practice. Only in some extreme cases."

"Such as?"

"There was a typical one the other day. A lady who'd been here before. Thought she was pregnant again. Turned out to be a false alarm. But she's a diabetic. And that condition seriously complicates pregnancy. So the doctor did a tubal. Really, it was the only humane thing to do."

"How about vasectomies?"

"No. Not usually. Something like that can be done in the physician's office."

"How about abortions?"

"Oh, no. That's where the hospital draws the line."

"None of your doctors perform abortions?"

"Not here. But most of them are accredited at other hospitals—all of which permit abortions. Of course, some of our doctors simply don't perform abortions, period. But those on our staff who do just take their patients across the street."

"But you do provide contraceptive counseling and devices . . . and you do perform sterilizations?"

"Oh, yes. But keep in mind that as far as the counseling is concerned, we are just supplying information these women should have received somewhere else—school or home or someplace. The devices are supplied only with the patient's knowledge and consent. And that, of course, holds true for sterilizations. We don't even recommend tubal ligations unless there are some additional extenuating circumstances. Like the diabetic I told you about."

Lennon packed her notepad and pen away. "Well, thank you. You've been very helpful. Very."

She concurred that William Arnold's job was done, at least for the moment. He returned to the *News* where he would submit his film for development.

A reporter! And a photographer! News travels fast in this little hospital.

Why would the Detroit News *be interested in St. Vincent's? No matter. If what is going on here is reported, all hell will break loose. I will be able to share my private hell with the rest of the world.*

Most of all, it will be the end for that damnable nun. The light of day can destroy her as thoroughly as I ever could.

And, if it doesn't . . .?

I still can act.

That poor, miserable acid-head! He almost did my job for me. If it had not been for that stupid guard, it would be all over now. Dumb luck. She would be dead. It would be no one's fault. And it would be over.

All right. I will give the Detroit News *its chance to bring her down. That way, once again, it will be no one's fault. No one's fault but hers.*

All right. We'll see about the power of the press.

But God, it can't take long. The pain in my head! It is driving me mad!

If someone does not get rid of her soon, I will! By God, I will! One way or another, I will bring her down.

In the meantime, smile, clown! No one must know. No one!

Lennon retraced her steps to Sister Eileen's office to await the nun's return. She paged through several magazines, but was unable to concentrate.

93

Eventually, Eileen returned. She seemed startled to find Pat there. "Waiting long?"

"Not really."

"Sorry. Meetings have a way of dragging on."

They entered her inner office and sat where they had hours earlier. Eileen looked intently at Lennon. Something was troubling the reporter. "Have an interesting tour?"

"Very. Basically, it seems you have a rather smooth-running operation here. I think I noticed an extra something in the personnel. I'm not sure what it is—more sensitivity, more personalized care, Christianity—something. *That* I will have to check out more thoroughly. But I'll get right to what interests me the most—your clinic."

"Ah, yes, the clinic." She was not a crack reporter for nothing.

"Admittedly, it's been a long time since I've had any formal training in Catholicism. But I try to keep up with reading and some study. Some of the stories I work on require some specialized knowledge. For instance, I did a story not too long ago on Casa Anna out in Dearborn Heights. It's a home for adolescent girls who are in trouble. Usually a lot of trouble."

"Yes. I know it well."

"The average inmate is unmarried and pregnant. I interviewed the psychologist-social worker about their pregnancy counseling."

"You don't have to go any further, Pat. I know what you're driving at: The girls get no contraceptive information whatsoever."

"That's what I learned. And that, as the social worker explained, is because Casa Anna is a Catholic institution."

Eileen continued to gaze at Lennon, but merely nodded.

"But that's not the case in your clinic. Of course, I don't have to tell you that. My question may be a little complex, but . . . what's going on here?"

Even though Sister Eileen had feared that Lennon would ferret out some of St. Vincent's less kosher secrets, the nun was unsure how best to explain it all.

She silently welcomed any help the Holy Spirit might send.

"The first thing you ought to know," she said, finally, "is that a considerable amount of the clinic's budget is underwritten by federal money. And I tell you quite frankly that if we did not offer the full spectrum of family planning, that money would be withdrawn."

"Oh?" Lennon had not expected such a candid statement. She flipped open her notepad and began writing.

Eileen sighed. But it was inevitable. "Having said this, I can only hope you will trust that I am being totally honest with you."

Lennon nodded. She continued writing.

"The second thing, and, I believe, the more important thing you should know, is that the policies of this hospital are set quite independently of any financial consideration. In the case of our clinic, it just so happens that government funding is available for that operation only as long as clients are given information and counseling on family planning without any reservation. And, since it is our policy to provide the full scope of family planning information, we gratefully accept the much needed government funding."

She paused. Lennon looked up from her writing. Her countenance betrayed her thoughts.

"You find this rather hard to believe?"

"Frankly, uh-huh."

"Frankly, I must admit I don't blame you."

"Look, Sister, reporters—sportswriters mostly—still once in a while talk about little St. Ambrose High back in the fifties and sixties, winning all those city football championships. Beating big public-school teams like Cooley and

Chadsey. There was no earthly way a little Catholic school could just happen upon so many huge young boys who were so good at football and all conveniently living within parish boundaries. No way, that is, unless the school was shamelessly and illegally recruiting.

"So, an enterprising reporter one day went over to interview the principal. When asked if the school recruited its players, the nun said, 'Of course not.' Well, because a nun said it, the reporter dropped the story. But most of the rest of us believe that in her next confession, that nun confessed that she had stretched the truth a bit—once—in a good cause.

"I want to believe you, Sister. But I can't just because 'Sister said . . .' Especially when what you say doesn't seem to add up.

"Let me put it to you the way I see it. Casa Anna has girls who get pregnant with the frequency other people catch colds. But the social worker tells me the girls can't be given counseling in contraception because this is against the rules of the Catholic Church. Okay. I think this is a pretty dumb rule—but a rule is a rule. And they're following it.

"Now we come to St. Vincent's . . . a Catholic hospital. As far as I can see, you are bound to the same rules as Casa Anna. Yet you offer counseling in contraception. If you didn't, government funding would be cut off. But you do offer it and you get the funding. Finally, you tell me you're not doing this for the money. Does this add up, Sister?"

Eileen smiled. "You say it doesn't add up, Pat. But that's because you've left out one very important number."

"What's that?"

"We've gone further than the government demands. If we were offering this service solely to get government funds, there would be no earthly reason why we would not provide contraceptive counseling and leave it at that. That's all the government requires. But, as you have undoubtedly learned, we supply contraceptives and even perform sterilizations. That's considerably more than the government requires. So, if we are adopting a policy on family planning for the sole purpose of being funded, why do we go well beyond what is required for that funding?''

Lennon stopped writing and was perfectly still as she considered what Sister had said.

"Okay," Lennon said, "you win that round. But it leaves the basic question: Why are you offering contraceptives and performing sterilizations?''

"A good question. An honest question. And a difficult question. I suppose the only responsible answer is that it was my decision. It was a prayerful, conscientious and hard-fought decision.

"St. Vincent's has been in this area of Detroit since 1845. It has changed with the city and it has changed with the neighborhood. It started on the corner of Larned and Randolph, moved to Clinton, and finally here on St. Antoine.

"Pat, some people believe in luck, chance, coincidence. I believe in all those. I also believe in divine providence. I think it was providential for St. Vincent's to have been created in Detroit. I think God intends it to be here, now, for this community.

"But, Pat, this community, among many other things, does not understand self-control or abstinence or rhythm as a means of family planning. Such concepts are utterly foreign to the culture of most of the people we serve.

"And I know the question that's on your mind. How can we bend our principles, compromise our standards to conform to the morality we find around us? Two wrongs do not make a right. And all that. Well, we cannot compromise the teachings of Christ for any reason whatsoever. And here it gets a bit difficult. I don't know that I can explain everything to your satisfaction. But there are some of us who do not believe the Church is entirely correct in each and every one of its teachings. We believe it is at least possible that the teaching of Christ and the teaching of the Church are not identical in each and every case.

"You must know that this is not a conclusion lightly reached. It is achieved only through much prayer and much consultation. And even then it is a conclusion painfully reached. But when reached, it must be followed."

"Must be followed . . ." Lennon laid the pen on her pad and sat back in her chair. "Must be followed . . . it rings a bell. Someplace back in high school or college. Of course! Your conscience . . . one's conscience . . . you have to follow your conscience." Pause. "But there was a hook in that . . . wasn't there?"

Eileen smiled. "I guess you could call it a hook. You have to have what was called 'a normal conscience.' "

"That's right!" Lennon seemed to be enjoying recalling ancient rules and regulations that she had at one time been expected to memorize. "There were different kinds of consciences, weren't there?"

"Yes." Eileen, considerably earlier than Lennon, also had memorized rules and doctrines. The difference was that Eileen never forgot what she'd learned. "There were scrupulous, lax, normal, correct, and erroneous consciences."

"That's right!"

Eileen felt as if she were passing a test.

"And," Lennon continued, "you figure you have a normal conscience in this and so you find you have to follow that conscience."

"That's exactly correct."

Lennon was lost in thought for several silent moments. "But what about Casa Anna?"

"What about it?"

"No contraceptive counseling there. Does that mean the nun in charge of Casa Anna doesn't agree with your assessment of Church law?"

"Pat, I've always found it a mistake to judge others. There's no way of telling all the circumstances that go into a person's decision. It's possible that Sister Ludmilla simply goes along with official Church policy in this matter. I don't know. We've never discussed the matter.

"But I would suggest one very conceivable, if not plausible, possibility. You said it yourself just a few minutes ago when you mentioned that Casa Anna is in Dearborn Heights."

"What has that to do with it?"

"Most of the local Church authorities prefer not to want to be informed of what's going on in the core city as far as things Catholic go. Certainly that's true of Cardinal Boyle. He understands that if we are to be relevant to the communities we serve, we cannot do things the way they are done in the suburbs.

"A suburban parish, for instance, conducts the Sunday liturgy just exactly as Rome has specified. The local liturgical commission insists that the parochial Mass be celebrated exactly as the liturgical texts direct. But, far more importantly, suburban Catholics want everything to be done correctly.

"However, St. Hugo's in Bloomfield Hills is not St. Patrick's in Detroit. What relatively few parishioners St. Patrick's has are mainly blacks, most of whose tradition is Baptist. And if St. Patrick's were to offer Sunday liturgy precisely as St. Hugo's does, St. Patrick's would be left with virtually no congregation. So that if someone were to phone on a Sunday morning and ask, 'What time is Mass?' the priest probably would reply, 'What time can you get here?'

"So, St. Patrick's has one of the better blends of a

Catholic-Baptist service on Sundays. The parishioners of St. Patrick's greatly enjoy this liturgy. It makes sense to them. It touches them. No one takes any offense. On the contrary, they are very much at home with that blend of the known and the unfamiliar. Or, the unfamiliar ritual of the Catholic Church is understood and recognized in the blend with the Baptist expression.

"So, it is certain that some parishioners of St. Hugo's would be very much disturbed if they were aware of what was going on at St. Patrick's Parish. And if they were disturbed enough, they would undoubtedly have recourse to Cardinal Boyle. And then he would have no choice but to take some action against what is going on at St. Patrick's Parish."

Sister Eileen fell silent. The impression was that it was not a silence during which she was thinking of something else to say. It was an invitation for some sort of comment.

"Wait a minute," Lennon said, at length, "I think I see what you're driving at. You're saying that you don't want the authorities to know what's going on in this hospital. And you're also claiming that the authorities don't want to know. And who's likely to break the news to everyone? I am.

"Is that it?"

Eileen sighed. "That's it."

"You want me to sit on this story! Do you know what you're asking me to do?"

"I think so."

"I don't think you do. Hunters wait for a deer. Kirk Gibson waits for a fast ball. Priests wait for a repentant sinner. Reporters wait for a good story. And believe me, this is a good story. The story I came here to get was a puff piece—a good story, but not a news story. But what I've got here could take this out of the *Michigan Magazine* and put it on the front page with lots more news to come as people react to the story.

"Sister, this is my job! If my editor found out that I was sitting on a story like this, he'd have my scalp. And he'd have every right to. It would be downright unprofessional."

"I suppose that's all true." Eileen's eyes were downcast.

"You can't ask me to do this!" Lennon's resolve was showing a chink.

"No, I suppose not."

"It's my job!"

"So you've explained."

After a lengthy pause. "What would happen after we published this story?"

"Probably just what I suggested. Cardinal Boyle would have to take some sort of action."

"Like what?"

"That's difficult to predict. He might demand that I change the policies of St. Vincent's to conform with Church directives. Although I doubt that some influential Catholics would be satisfied with that."

"Would you change the policies if he—they—demanded it?"

"No. I couldn't. Not in good conscience."

"If you didn't, then what?"

"I might be asked to leave the order."

"Leave the order?"

"Leave religious life. Stop being a nun."

"He'd do that?"

"I don't see how he could avoid it. No matter how he felt about it."

"And what would happen to St. Vincent's?"

"That's a prognosis I can't make with any certainty. In its present state, with the clientele that come here now, I suppose eventually it would close. I know that we are having a difficult time staying open now. But we're surviving. This is just not a facility for white middle-class suburbanites. No more than is St. Patrick's a parish for the affluent. That's not our community. We are doing our best now to relate to our community, such as it is. We are trying to bring a distinctly Christian attitude to this health care facility. And Christianity knows no color, no class, no restrictions in its Christlike love.''

Lennon shrugged and packed away her pen and notepad. ''I shouldn't have asked you any of these hypothetical questions. That was not professional of me. I can't afford to consider consequences of a legitimate story. If I did, I'd be a basket case in no time. And the public would be denied its right to know.''

Lennon rose and smoothed her skirt. ''I hope you understand, Sister. But whether you understand or not, it is my job.''

''I understand, Pat. It's not going to make my day. But that has nothing to do with your job. You've got to be faithful to that. Just as I must be faithful to mine. No matter what happens, know that I will not hold you responsible. The decisions were mine. I made them. Now I must live with the consequences. Maybe it will not be as bad as I anticipate.''

''I certainly hope not.''

Lennon left the office. She did not look back. She couldn't.

6

FATHER ROBERT CAME HOME TO FATHER Harold.

Where else in the world, thought Koesler, as he parked in the garage adjoining St. Anselm's rectory, would you hear anything like that except in the celibate world of the Roman Catholic priesthood?

A Catholic rectory, mused Koesler; a home for unmarried fathers.

This association between him and Father Harold was somewhat less than a marriage of convenience. It was more a union stemming from desperation.

Definitely, it was not a marriage made in heaven. But few rectory matchups were. In the good old days—in the sixties and before—when there were comparatively lots of priests, men were teamed at the whim of the bishop. Or, more likely, as the result of personnel juggling by the men of the Chancery, with a perfunctory blessing by the bishop.

Now, as the Church was running out of priests, all too

frequently parishes were forced to shift for themselves when it came to priests who would assist the pastor.

Thus it was by a combination of fidelity and luck that Koesler had managed to secure the parish-sitting services of Father Harold while Koesler played chaplain at St. Vincent's. Fidelity in that Koesler faithfully led a group of St. Anselmites to an annual retreat at the Passionist Monastery. And luck, since the Passionists happened to have a surplus Father Harold for the first few weeks of the new year.

From frequent association, Koesler knew Harold quite well. He was a large man in his sixties, only slightly balding, and always, when on call, garbed in the religious habit of the Passionist order.

The Passionists had been founded in the early eighteenth century by St. Paul of the Cross for the purpose of preaching retreats and missions. The Passionists remained faithful to their roots as well as, and frequently considerably better than, any of the other old religious orders. But once in a while a Passionist could be cut from the herd to pastor a parish or, in this case, baby-sit one.

Friendly and reservedly gregarious, Harold hailed from somewhere out west—Oklahoma or Texas. It was never clear exactly whence. His theology was anchored squarely in the pre-Vatican II Church. A fact that left him a bit nervous, a condition betrayed by his darting eyes. He never quite knew when what was to him an innocent dogmatic statement might draw anything from good-natured laughter to derision to, at rare moments, agreement. So he seldom volunteered conversation. Mostly, he reacted to questions from others.

Koesler entered the kitchen from the connected garage. He heard some at first unidentifiable noise. It was television, the local evening news. He remembered now: Father Harold watched television a lot.

"Hello!" Koesler called above the TV noise. He placed on the dining room table the burger and fries he had picked up on the way home.

"Hello there, Father." Harold greeted him warmly and moved from the living room to the dining area. Thus, as usual, he would be able to watch TV and keep Koesler company while he ate.

"What do we have on the evening news?" Koesler placed his hat and briefcase on the seat of a chair, draping his coat and scarf on the back of the chair.

"What?" Harold was able to focus on only snatches from both Koesler and the TV. But he was able to recall from his subconscious what he had missed from each medium. From experience, Koesler knew all he had to do was wait. "Oh," Harold predictably continued, "it's that skirmish they had the other night over at Cobo Hall. They're just beginning to identify some of the people they arrested. Mostly kids."

"I guess that's who you'd expect to find at a rock concert."

"What? Oh, yeah. I suppose so. Ought to be home. Only trouble when they're out that late. Unsupervised."

"I suppose." It wasn't worth arguing over. Koesler opened the foil that protected his steaming burger. Others came home to a prepared meal, he thought. Oh, well, this is considerably better than nothing.

From his briefcase he took a soft-cover booklet entitled, *Ethics Committees: A Challenge for Catholic Health Care*. Sister Eileen had lent it to him. He had paged through it earlier. He wanted to read a couple of sections more carefully.

"How'd things go at the hospital today?"

"Pretty good. I think I'm getting the hang of it."

"Huh? Oh, yeah. It can't be much different than making sick calls in the parish, eh, Father?"

"No, not much different." It was wildly different. Koesler did not care to seriously interrupt Harold's evening news.

The ethics brochure contained a brief history as well as an explanation of the ethical directives. Koesler felt a twinge of parochial pride to learn that the first U.S. Catholic code of medical ethics, in 1920, was a reprint of the *Surgical Code for Catholic Hospitals for the Diocese of Detroit*. This basic code had been revised, in effect, only twice: in 1954 and again in 1971.

Briefly he wondered about updating such an important document only twice in more than sixty years. Especially since those years spanned a unique knowledge and information explosion, particularly in the field of medicine. The wheels of the Church grind exceedingly slow, he thought, but really!

He continued reading.

"Harold," Koesler said at length, "do you know why doctors don't tie a woman's tubes in a Catholic hospital?"

"What?" Once he reran the tape, Harold blushed. He always got a bit flustered when confronted with anything even remotely sexual. "Uh . . . oh. It's against the law. Isn't it?"

Actually, Harold was quite certain it was against the law. At least it had been the last time he'd looked. But for all he knew, it might have been changed this morning. No telling what these hairy young whippersnappers were going to do next.

"Well, according to this, and I think it's correct, it's not so much laws that govern medical ethics as it is Church teaching."

"Church teaching?" Harold's mind might be partially tuned to a conversation with Koesler, but his eyes were riveted to the TV set. "Oh, the ordinary magisterium, you mean."

"Precisely. The good old ordinary magisterium—the ordinary teaching authority of the Church."

"That's when the Church isn't teaching infallibly." Harold was just making sure that hadn't changed either.

"That's right. And there are those who claim there's been only one infallible statement since the doctrine of infallibility was defined a little more than a hundred years ago at the First Vatican Council."

"The doctrine of the Assumption of the Blessed Virgin Mary into heaven, wasn't it?"

"Right. So everything else—and that's a lot—falls under the ordinary magisterium. And do you know how they came up with this medical code?"

"Just look at this, Father. This was the only goal the Red Wings scored last night."

Koesler craned sufficiently to see the TV screen. He was just in time to see a red-suited skater sweep across the ice, receive the puck in a pass from his wing man, fake the goalie, and slide the puck inside the crease.

"They're not doing very well, are they?" Koesler did not follow sports as faithfully as he once had.

Harold shook his head sadly. "Not like the good old days with the Production Line—Lindsay, Abel and Howe. Man, that Gordie Howe—what a player!"

"Those were the good old days, all right." If he was no longer an avid jock, Koesler could at least remember. "And those blood-and-guts games against the Maple Leafs and the Canadiens!"

"Umm—excuse me, Father, what did you ask me about?"

"The Code of Medical Ethics. Know how they arrived at it?"

Harold shook his head. "Not rightly." He returned to the TV.

"They asked for it."

"Eh?"

"Catholic hospitals kept bugging the bishops to spell out medical moral ethics. Can you imagine that, Harold? Talk about the good old days! Nowadays we hope the bishops and the pope will keep quiet and not muddle things any more than they already have. Back then they wanted *the word*. And they surely got it. The bishops even sent the question of tubal ligation and material cooperation to the Vatican. And they got their answer. Now we have to live with it."

Harold clenched his jaws. He didn't care for talk that made light of the bishops and the Holy Father. But he was a guest in this rectory. And his parents had raised him to be well-mannered.

"So," Koesler continued, "to return to my original question about why Fallopian tubes aren't tied in a Catholic hospital: The reason is because the Vatican said so. That's it."

Harold felt compelled to say a word for Holy Mother Church. "But Father, that is the ordinary magisterium!"

"I know that, Father Harold. But to demur from the ordinary magisterium is not to be branded a heretic."

"No, you're not a heretic if you deny the ordinary magisterium. But you're wrong."

"That's one view."

"Oh, really, Father!" TV was disregarded. "I must object. I believe that Catholics may not dissent from Church teaching. And—not that I mean for a moment to presume to tell you your obligation—but pastors may not accept dissenting views in their parochial ministry. And finally, Catholics who have any doubt about Church teaching may suspend or withhold assent while they take every opportunity to resolve their doubt through study, consultation, and prayer."

108

"In other words, Harold, Catholics who don't agree with Church teaching may pray until they do agree."

"You're oversimplifying, Father."

"Am I? What about our obligation to form our own conscience and follow it?"

"That's true, Father. But the Church helps us form a true conscience."

"Sure, Harold, the Church is supposed to help us. But in your explanation, the Church is not so much helping as it has taken over the whole job. Instead of working to inform our conscience and help form it, the Church simply invites us to pour our conscience in her mold and all the Catholics come marching out believing in, and judging everything in, identical ways."

"Do you have another explanation?"

"I think so. Try this, Harold. Suppose, to begin, that we have an obligation to recognize the Church's teaching role. And we also have an obligation to know what the Church is actually teaching. I mean, Harold, how many times have you had a discussion or an argument with someone only to eventually realize that the other person doesn't really know what he's talking about—that he doesn't know what the Church actually teaches about a given point."

"That's true."

"Okay, so we're together so far. We recognize that the Church is an authentic teacher. And we must know correctly what the Church is teaching. Okay?"

"Okay."

"Next step: If we're uncertain or in doubt about a teaching of the Church, we give the presumption of truth to the magisterium. I think you'll agree to that, too."

"Right."

"Okay, now for the final step. If it happens that our own experience and conviction—which we carefully and prayerfully reflect on—tells us that the Church's teaching on a specific matter is inadequate, incomplete or inapplicable to our personal life, then we have the right—the *responsibility*—to depart from the Church's teaching and follow our own well-formed convictions and conscience.

"What do you say to that?"

"Depart from the Church's teachings! Oh, Father, I could never believe that!"

"How else could we possibly form our own conscience if we don't have the freedom to do so?"

"But Father, the power of the keys! Christ said, 'Thou art Peter and upon this rock I will build my church . . . and I will give you the keys of the kingdom of heaven. Whatever you bind upon earth will be bound in heaven. And whatever you loose upon earth will be loosed also in heaven.' "

"We're all familiar with the *'Tu es Petrus'* . . . text, Harold. But, like everything else in Scripture, you've got to put it in context. How did Peter conduct himself in the early Church?" Koesler continued, answering his own question. "Read the first twelve chapters of Acts with the idea of checking out St. Peter's role in the Church. He does not have anything close to the power and authority of the Popes of recent memory. Peter is challenged not only by Paul in their famous confrontation; the entire Christian community—which was then entirely Jewish—calls Peter to task for admitting Gentiles into the Church. And later, Peter doesn't just decide to take a trip as a missionary; the whole group sends him off.

"Peter's role in the Church is not that of an infallible potentate, but a coordinator, a leader. And that's what I think we mean when we call the Pope the successor of Peter. So, the 'power of the keys' maybe isn't as absolute as we've been led to believe."

"I don't know, Father. I just couldn't bring myself to disagree with Church teaching."

"And nobody's asking you to, Harold. My point is, there is more than one view of the teaching Church. And our separate views represent the thinnest line between a liberal and a conservative attitude toward the Church. There are, for instance, Catholics who would not grant the amount of time you so generously concede to conform one's conscience to Church teaching. As far as these people are concerned, if you doubt, you're out.

"On the other hand, there are liberal Catholics who would not offer the magisterium the benefit of the doubt, as I would. These people are convinced that at least most of the bishops are far more concerned about preserving the institution than searching out evangelical truth.

"Then there are liberals who are so liberal they themselves admit they simply have left the Church altogether. Just as there are conservatives who have fashioned their own rigid Church that is far more Catholic than the Catholic Church.

"Then there are people like you and me, Harold, who differ minimally if radically." Koesler smiled. "I'll let you be a Catholic if you'll let me be one too."

Harold returned the smile. It seemed a happy compromise. Then he grew concerned. "But how will this look to outsiders, Father? Won't this give scandal if we Catholics openly disagree with each other? If we're not united?"

"It's already happened. Pope Paul insisted that his encyclical, 'Humanae Vitae,' was not an infallible statement, but it certainly was the ordinary magisterium of the highest order. And in that document, he spelled out the traditionally approved methods of family planning: rhythm or abstinence. But Catholics, at least in the First World countries, have maturely and prayerfully decided that this particular

Vatican decision is not for them. Has anybody confessed practicing artificial birth control to you lately?"

"No."

"Remember how it used to be?"

"Yes." Harold winced. "Almost all the marrieds either were expecting, or practicing birth control—and confessing it."

"So family planning remains a moral problem for a few lay Catholics, some priests, most bishops. And of course the Pope. As a matter of fact, in the field we've been talking about—medical moral ethics—there is a bit of divergence."

"There is?" Harold was surprised.

"The Code of Medical Ethics has been approved by the U.S. Conference of Bishops and supplemented by and blessed by the Holy See, but it is not enforced by any national conference of bishops. It is implemented by each individual bishop in his own diocese."

"It is?"

"Uh-huh. So there is a bit of divergence. Generally, they try to overlook the differences within the good-old-boy network. But differences there are."

"Really! I had no idea! Father, will you look at that cloud pattern on the weather map. Looks like we're in for some more snow."

"I guess so." Koesler went into the kitchen to make some instant coffee. As far as he knew, he was the only one left in the world who would attempt to drink the coffee he made. The taste never offended him. And he was at a loss to know why others refused his coffee. He had forgotten that years in the seminary had made him an omnivore. And that if not for bread and peanut butter, he very probably would have starved long before ordination.

As he stirred his usual overabundant spoonful of instant coffee granules into the steaming water, he wondered what he had accomplished by his disputation with Father Harold. Probably not much. Harold would continue to let the Church Xerox his mind and conscience. At most, perhaps he would understand how others might responsibly differ with the ordinary magisterium. That alone was a not inconsiderable achievement.

In the brief time since his inadvertent rescue of Sister Eileen, George Snell had achieved the status of in-house hero. Singlehandedly he had raised the image of a ragtag protective service to a level of respectability. Nor had he himself been unaffected by the new image that had been created.

He had long considered himself God's gift to womankind. Now he saw himself as fearless guardian of St. Vincent's Hospital and all its personnel as well.

He had conveniently managed to blot out the stark reality of that fateful evening. If aide Helen Brown had not upset his balance while he was entering into the famed Snell Maneuver, Sister Eileen undoubtedly would have been strangled. As it was, she had come all too close to death. And she would have been murdered in the same room with him. He would have risen satisfied and sated from his unique maneuver to discover the corpse of the CEO he was supposed to protect.

As it was, he was a hero. And that was plenty good enough for him. So good, indeed, that since l'affaire Eileen he had taken to actually patrolling his beat. Who could ask for anything more? Certainly not his supervisor.

"Checkin' in a little early, ain't you?" Chief Martin asked.

"Early? Didn't realize I was early," Snell said virtuously.

"Yeah, early."

"Better early than sorry. I made that up."

"Yeah? Well, you ain't gonna be paid overtime just 'cause you came in early. I made that up."

"You don't have to pay me overtime. I'm just here to do my job."

The chief scratched his head. "What is it with you? Ever since you kayoed that detox guy, you act like a cross between Superman and Mother Teresa."

"Oh, no sir, Chief. I'm just little old ordinary George Snell, doin' my job."

"Another thing, Snell. I paced off the distance down that hallway you said you covered when you seen that guy drag the nun into the room. I paced it off maybe a dozen times. No way I can see how you covered that distance in the time it had to take you to get to him in time to save the nun. You just ain't in no way, shape, or form that fast."

"You know how it is, Chief: In moments of stress you don't know your own strength or speed."

"I dunno. I guess you had to do it. But I'll be damned if I can figure out how you did."

"Chief, my strength is as the strength of ten because my heart is pure."

It definitely bolstered Snell's inward and outward credibility that he himself had come to believe this fairy tale.

"And now," Snell said, "if you'll excuse me, Chief, I'll start on my rounds."

"Go ahead." Martin turned toward the closed-circuit television monitor. "But you ain't gettin' any overtime."

Snell sauntered off. After all, he was early. He began his patrol in the hospital's basement. At this hour, it was the eeriest section of the plant. Housekeeping, the kitchen, and general cafeteria were all closed and the people who worked there were long gone home. No one else should be in the basement. No one else was.

That was slight disappointment. George had been rather looking forward to another confrontation. Unarmed though

114

he was, he was convinced he could handle any disturbance. So much had he come to believe in his own misbe-
gotten reputation.

From the basement, he took the elevator to the fourth
floor, which was completely residential. A skeleton staff
of nurses and aides fluttered about answering patients'
summonses, delivering medication, in general being busy.

"Evening, Officer Snell," one passing aide greeted.

It surprised him. He hadn't expected to be greeted. In
fact, he had never before been greeted by anyone on the
hospital staff. He had been convinced that, on the one
hand, no one knew his name and, on the other, that no one
wanted to.

Evening, Officer Snell. It had a nice ring. He could
grow to like it.

She was a pretty little thing, too. For a split second, he
toyed with the idea that he might bestow God's greatest
gift to women upon her. But in that second she was gone,
disappeared into one of the rooms. He might have pursued
her. But he wasn't going to do that any more. He was a
celebrity now. If someone wanted his favors, she could at
least inquire, if not beg.

He boarded the elevator to the first floor. Now he would
work himself up to the third floor, the scene of his triumph
both over the assailant of Sister Eileen and, literally, over
nurse's aide Helen Brown. As he recalled, and this he
clearly recalled, the crescendo and climax of God's gift
had been denied Ms. Brown. That, he felt, should be
remedied.

First floor, through the day busier than most downtown
streets, was now deserted. And all the more creepy for its
comparative silence and emptiness. Even though Snell felt
slightly more invulnerable than Achilles, he moved through
these corridors somewhat more cautiously.

What was that? Something had moved up ahead. It

wasn't just the movement. Anyone might have been walking in this hallway. It might have been a late departer from the day shift. It could have been someone going from one department to another. From, say, one of the residence halls to the emergency room. But, somehow, he was certain it was not. Whoever it was had been moving furtively, stealthily.

Snell's only consolation was that the furtive figure had seemed very small. In a confrontation, he would have every advantage of size. If the figure were human.

Snell began to perspire freely. But if he were going to take this job seriously, he would have to investigate. He really would.

Warily, he quickened his pace, trying to close the distance between himself and the mysterious figure.

Once again, the figure stepped out of the shadows. By now, Snell had advanced to within a few feet. "All right!" he commanded. "That's far enough! Stop where you are!"

Sister Rosamunda collapsed against the wall, clutching at her heart. Snell was overwhelmed with confusion. "Sister! S . . . S . . . Sister," he stammered. "What . . . I had no idea . . . are you okay?"

"Whew!" She could say no more. Her eyes, as she looked up at him, exuded a mixture of fear and fury.

"S . . . S . . . S . . . Sister, are you all right?"

"I think so. No thanks to you! Who are you, *in nomine Domini*?" She squinted through her bifocals. "George Snell, is it? Well, George, where did you get your training? With the Gestapo?"

"I . . . I'm sorry, Sister. I didn't know who you were—I just saw you sneaking down the hall—"

"Sneaking! Sneaking, is it? I was not sneaking! Nuns don't sneak! How dare you!"

"Like I said, Sister, I'm sorry. I didn't know who you

were. I had to find out. For the safety of the patients. I just had to find out. You could have been anybody.''

"No, I couldn't be anyone but me, you ninny!''

"Well, I couldn't tell that, Sister. All I saw was someone sneaking down the hall.''

"There you go again!''

"God, I'm sorry. I didn't mean sneaking.''

"Then stop saying it, *in nomine Domini*.''

"Yes, Sister.''

"That's better.''

"Well, anyway, where were you going? I mean, it was odd that you were snea—going down the hallway—so . . . uh . . . cautiously.''

"What business is it of yours, young man, where I'm going? I've been a part of this hospital since long before you were born. Can't I go somewhere in the evening, down to the chapel to say some night prayers, without being scared half out of my wits by some ape!''

"Oh, to chapel, that's different.''

"What's different about it, young man? Is there any place in this hospital that is out-of-bounds to me? Has anyone given you any orders regarding my behavior in this hospital?''

"Well, no, ma'am . . .''

"What is this 'no, ma'am'? I am a Religious Sister of the Order of St. Vincent de Paul.''

"Yes, ma'am, I mean, yes, Sister.'' By this time, Snell would have been hard pressed to give the proper spelling of his own name. He just wanted out of this confrontation.

"Well, then, am I free to go, young man? Or do you have some more bizarre surprises for me?''

"Oh, no, Sister. I just . . . can I do anything to help you?''

"Get out of my way! And while you're at it, get out of my life!''

Snell backed away. He had never attended parochial school. But in just a few moments, Sister Rosamunda had taught him all the abject terror and humiliation ever experienced by a nice little Catholic boy or girl in the good old days.

He was beginning to doubt himself and his newfound resolve. He needed something. Something to rekindle his confidence. If he had been a religious person, he might have said a prayer. As it was, though employed by a Catholic hospital, he was less an agnostic or atheist than simply a backsliding Baptist.

Yet, almost in answer to his unoffered prayer, he heard a sound. A metallic object striking the terrazzo floor. A sound that should not have been made at this hour. Who'd be carrying something metallic? Maintenance? If it were someone from maintenance, why didn't he show himself? Someone was lurking in the shadows. Snell's opportunity for self-redemption.

Turning on his powerful flashlight, Snell began to retrace his steps. Hugging the wall, he directed the beam all around, into corners and behind columns. The trouble with these old buildings, there were too many places a person could hide.

Pressed tightly against the opposite wall and partially hidden by a pillar, Bruce Whitaker cursed his luck. Why had he dropped the pliers? Everything had been going so smoothly. The plan laid out by his comrades had been working flawlessly until he'd dropped the damned pliers. The racket, enhanced by the night's quiet, had alerted the guard. Now Whitaker had become fair game. He was being hunted down. The guard was only a few yards away.

What kind of explanation could he give when inevitably he was found out? A volunteer roaming the corridors at night? With a pair of pliers? What for? This could get nasty. Could he be thrown back in jail for something like this? Probably not. But he undoubtedly would be dismissed from the hospital as a volunteer. All their plans would be washed away. How would he be able to face his friends? Failed again! And all because he had dropped the pliers!

Well, there was no sense in continuing to try to hide. In a few seconds he would be found out. He might as well step out and surrender. One good thing, as far as he could recall, the guards were not armed.

Whitaker was just about to step out into the soft indirect light of the hallway when he heard a sound behind him, further up the corridor. He could not identify it, but it was a very specific sound. He was not the ouly one who had heard it. The guard's flashlight beam swept by and focused further back up the hall.

"Who is that? Who's there?" the guard called out.

No response. But there had been a sound. No doubt of that.

The guard walked past the column where Whitaker cowered, heading toward where the sound had come from.

Exhaling relief, Whitaker slipped down the hallway as the guard and he passed as ships in the night. What luck! What outrageous luck! This, very definitely, was not the way it usually worked out for Whitaker. Could it be that things would turn about for him? Whatever. He must get on with his task.

"Who is it, I said! Who's there?" Snell tried to focus the beam in the general area whence he thought the sound had originated.

A young woman stepped out of the shadows. She was dressed as a nurse's aide. She seemed embarrassed. Whitaker was too far down the corridor to see who it was. Nor did he care. He was intent alone on his mission.

Snell relaxed. She presented no physical challenge. Still, he was puzzled. Who was she? What had she dropped?

And what was she doing there, in the shadows, on the main floor at this hour? All questions that had answers. And he would have them.

Snell focused the beam on her identification tag. "Ethel Laidlaw." He noted that she was small-breasted. But young enough so that they were still fairly firm. Firm little breasts. One could make a case for them, too.

"So," he said, "Ethel Laidlaw. What is Ethel Laidlaw doing here now?" Snell stood close to her, emphasizing the disparity in their sizes. He was so big while she was so small. He liked to impress people with his bulk.

"Oh, I'm so embarrassed."

"Now, why's that, little lady?" Snell's male-chauvinist-pig tendencies were beginning to blossom again.

"Well, I just wanted to meet you. And when you were on my floor, you walked by so quickly . . ."

"Wanted to meet me, eh?" Snell leaned forward, putting one hand against the wall and, in a way, trapping her. "Whatever would you want to do that for?"

"Well . . . because you're a hero. I mean . . . you rescued Sister Eileen the other night . . ."

"Well, little honey, you don't have to hide in the shadows to meet me. I'm just like everybody else. Put my pants on one leg at a time. Take 'em off the same way." Snell tried to insert extra meaning in the statement. "Why, I wouldn't even known you were here if you hadn't dropped something. What was it you dropped, anyway?"

"Oh . . ." Ethel hadn't dropped anything; she didn't know what had been dropped. "My pen . . . I dropped my pen." She held it up to prove that, if nothing else, she did indeed have a pen.

"It didn't sound like a pen. "But, what the hell; who cared? It might just be possible that Ethel Laidlaw was in need of God's greatest gift to women. "But, never mind.

Well, here I am. Now you've met me, what do you think?"

"Well, there's this reputation you got."

"Yeah? No kiddin'."

"Well, people talk. You know."

"Yeah? What're they sayin'?"

"Oh, I couldn't repeat it." She blushed.

"You can tell me. I mean, my God, it's my reputation." Is it possible she's a virgin, he wondered.

"Well, there's talk . . ."

"Yeah . . .?"

"Something about . . . a maneuver . . .?"

Damn! I haven't even been able to demonstrate it fully to anyone here yet. And already they're talkin' about it. "So, what have you heard about it?"

"Only that it's . . . uh . . . unique."

"Well, you know, it is. I only . . . uh . . . do it with very special people."

"Oh." Blush.

"Would . . . uh . . . you be . . . uh . . . interested?"

"Oh, Mr. Snell! Me?"

"George."

"George."

"Once we get it together, baby, you will never be formal again."

"Oh, George!"

"Oh, Ethel!" Snell began fumbling, rather expertly, with the buttons of her uniform.

"Wait!"

"Wait?"

"Yes, wait! I have an idea."

"An idea? Ethel, this is no time for thinking."

"Well, yes. As a matter of fact, it is, George."

"Well, what?"

"Don't you think we ought to find a bed?"

"A bed."

"Don't you need something like a bed for your . . . maneuver?"

"Now that you mention it . . ."

"The pastoral care department."

"Pastoral care?"

"They've got an empty bed. In an empty room."

"No."

"Yes."

"Let's get there."

Pastoral care was only a short distance down the hall. They got there in world-record time.

Snell returned his concentration to Ethel's buttons.

As he reached bra depth, Ethel said urgently, "Wait!"

"Again!"

"I've got another idea."

"Ethel, has anyone told you you think too much?"

"It's just something to make it better."

"Baby, nothing make it better than I do!"

"I think it might."

Snell considered the possibility that this simple matter was getting entirely too cluttered. "Well, what is it?"

"I can't say it."

"You can't—!" On the other hand, this might be interesting. If Ethel were, as he suspected, a virgin, she may have been harboring fantasies. Snell always fancied fantasies and indulged them whenever possible. "But, if you can't . . ."

"Let me whisper it to you."

"Okay."

Snell lowered his massive head to Ethel's rosebud mouth and listened.

"Yeah . . . okay . . ." A smile began to form. "Well, why not . . . why the hell not?"

Snell stepped back from Ethel and began to disrobe

himself, slowly, sensuously. It was a male striptease. Ethel appeared to be enjoying it immensely. But she sat there watching him without removing a stitch of her own clothing.

At last, George stood stark-naked. "Baby, I'm ready!" There was no doubting that truth. "Let's go!"

"No! No! The rest of it too!"

"Oh . . . God . . . okay."

After all, her suggestion seemed to be working so far. George found that his striptease, while she remained completely clothed, was a real and rare stimulant. Why not go along with the rest of her fantasy?

Leaving his uniform—indeed, all his clothing—on the chair next to the bed, Snell retreated to the bathroom and turned on the shower. He'd never tried anything like this before. The plan called for him to return soaking wet. She would be clad in her under clothing, which he would rip from her body. He, a Beast from the Ocean's depths, taking her—the Earth Woman.

And, of course added to all this, like a preternatural gift, would be . . . the maneuver.

He completed the shower, stepped out, and was about to dry himself when he recalled he was supposed to present himself fresh from the Ocean. Kinky. He liked that in a woman.

"Aha!" He bounded into the room in a mikadoesque stance. By anyone's standards, he was ready.

"Aha! Ethel! Prepare to meet your fate . . . Ethel? Ethel?"

She hadn't mentioned anything about hiding. Besides, that was carrying this thing just a bit too far, dammit! There was such a thing as too much foreplay.

"Ethel?" He looked in the closet. He looked in the two adjoining offices. "Ethel?" He looked under the bed. That was it. There was no place left to hide.

She was not there. Could you believe it? After all, she

was the one at whose initiative this whole thing had begun. Now she was nowhere to be found.

And that was by no means all.

His clothing was gone. All his clothing.

Whatinhell am I gonna do now? There's nothing left. And I didn't get to use the maneuver. In fact, I haven't used it since I got to this rotten place. Use it or lose it.

But for the present, he had to get out of here, saving as much face as possible.

Reacting as much from panic as anything alse, he stripped the bed of its brown blanket, which he wrapped around himself. Cautiously, he let himself out of the room. Step by step, he inched along the welcome shadows of the corridor. When he reached the seemingly empty lobby, he knew he would have to make a dash for it. The switchboard operator was the sole inhabitant of the brightly lit foyer. She seemed absorbed in a paperback romance.

He made a break for it, bare feet hardly making a sound as he pitter-pattered over the terrazzo floor. No sooner was he outside the building than the bone-chilling cold of a January night hit his basically bare body with Arctic force. Cursing Ethel, he danced his way across the pavement and through the parking lot as if proving his faith over hot coals.

George Snell, macho man that he was, never locked his car. So it was no problem for him to hot-wire the vehicle and get the heat going. For the first time in many minutes he could now relax slightly. He would drive home, don his other uniform, and get back here to try to retrieve the missing uniform at least in time to check out.

As for Ethel, that crazy broad, he was unsure whether he never wanted to see that unmitigated pain again, or whether, to ease his dark night of the soul, he wanted just enough time with her to dissect her. Sufficient for later thoughts of revenge. Right now, he had to salvage what he could of his reputation as defender of the hospital and God's gift to women.

✦ ✦ ✦

Bruce Whitaker continued to make his way through the corridors as quietly and unobtrusively as possible. He had dropped the pliers only three more times. Fortunately, having eluded that guard, he was challenged by no one else.

From time to time he caught a glimpse of someone who seemed to be preceding him down the hallways. A small figure hugging the walls and courting the shadows, much as was he. Now that was puzzling. But, whatever; he had his mission, which happened to coincide with God's holy will, and he must carry it out.

At long last, he reached the clinic. All along the way, he had wondered what had happened to the guard who had nearly discovered him. Strange. The man must have become preoccupied with whoever had made that distracting sound. Whitaker attributed it to providence. He had a tendency to attribute most of his luck to providence. Except that, in most instances, his luck was bad. This was an exception.

Which made him wonder why, with a run of good luck going for him, something was going on in the clinic. No one should be in there at this hour. Given the infamous security of St. Vincent's, it had been relatively easy to get a duplicate key made. But now he didn't need it. The door was unlocked. Someone was in there. He detected a wavering flashlight beam. Someone was moving about, surreptitiously.

Carefully placing the pliers inside his jacket pocket—a decidedly good move—Whitaker quietly eased his way into the clinic. He found a position from which he could

125

see what was going on, yet be far enough removed so he would not, in turn, be seen.

Once his eyes grew accustomed to the dark, he could see rather well. The dim glow from the streetlight glinting off the fresh snow cover added to the small illumination of the flashlight, making it possible to identify the person who had preceded him into the clinic.

Sister Rosamunda. What in the world could she be doing here? She was rummaging about in a section that contained many bottles. She seemed to know what she was looking for and where to find it. She removed two bottles from a shelf and placed them within the folds of her ample traditional habit. Then she turned out the flashlight and moved toward the door.

As she departed, she walked within ten feet of him. Seemingly, she did not notice him. He stood stockstill and made no noise. That in itself was a small miracle. Under ordinary circumstances, in a situation like this, he would have sneezed, coughed or, in his very intention not to move a muscle, knocked something off a shelf.

This time, he did not. Providence. His good luck continued.

Sister was gone. Whitaker stayed motionless for a short while, letting the peace, quiet, and emptiness of the place wash over him. Of course there were those institutional noises that old buildings make—squeaks and groans. But, in time, they took on a lulling character.

He grew quiet within himself. He felt his pulse. It seemed regular, and slow enough. He guessed that his blood pressure might be close to normal—which, in itself, was a bit abnormal.

It was time. He must carry out the mission with which his colleagues had entrusted him.

He moved forward. Carefully, he picked his way among the cabinets filled with fragile containers. He could not believe he was doing all this, especially in relative darkness, without breaking anything or causing any commotion.

His narrow penlight beam fell on it. There it was. The drawer with the label reading, "IUDs." He opened it. There were several boxes inside. He removed the first box, put it on a nearby counter, and opened it.

So this was what it was all about. Even so he was not sure what it was all about. Not only had he never seen an IUD, he was pretty much unfamiliar with female anatomy. But, putting two and two together, he came up with what he hoped was four.

This form of contraception, according to the best lights of Bruce Whitaker, took place in the following manner:

Through intercourse, the male deposited the germ of human life in the female's womb (as in ". . . blessed is the fruit of thy womb, Jesus"). This germ, or seed, grew in the womb for nine months. However, if an IUD were inserted, there would not be room enough for both the device and the baby. Thus, since the device was metallic and the baby mere flesh and blood, eventually the device would push the baby out before due time. There was no danger to the woman. She just let the baby and the device fight it out.

But all that was about to be changed.

Whitaker removed the first device from the box. So this was it. This was the tool of the devil that interrupted pregnancies against the teachings of the Holy Pope of God and his bishops.

With his pliers, Whitaker twisted one end of the device slightly out of shape, then with the side cutter pinched off one blunted end, creating a cruelly sharp point.

He deeply regretted the need to do this. But it was his mission. He must do it over and over—to each of these devices. It would take him the better part of this night. But never again, in this clinic at least, would women get away with forcing their babies out of their wombs with impunity. Now they would begin to pay for their crimes as the sharp, twisted edge of the device would tear at their wombs.

Actually, he and his colleagues were certain this bloody procedure would not be repeated that frequently. It wouldn't take many perforated wombs before the attention of the medical and police establishments would be focused on St. Vincent's. The hospital's immoral practice of contraception would be publicized by newspapers, TV, and radio.

The local Church authorities would not have the luxury of looking the other way. They would be forced to take action against the sins of this hospital.

Then would he and his colleagues be vindicated. Of course their identity would have to remain secret. But the important thing would be that they had served God and the true Church. That would be reward enough.

Besides, the cloak of anonymity would protect them for further work for the Church. Then would their martyrdom of imprisonment be avenged.

He found it difficult to believe he was actually carrying this off. It was a smooth operation. As he went through box after box, altering the IUDs, he found it arduous, monotonous work. But, in his hands, it was a labor of love.

✛ ✛ ✛

"I been tryin' to raise you for 'bout an hour. Where you been?" Chief Martin seemed more amused than angry.

"Oh, around." Guard George Snell gave every indication that he would not go out of his way to communicate.

"Been quite a while since you started your tour of duty."

"I guess."

"Have any trouble?"

"Can't say that I did."

128

"Anything unusual happen?"

"Just the usual. Place's pretty quiet now."

"Uh."

"Any calls?"

"Nope. Say, I see you're not wearing your beeper. That must be why I couldn't contact you."

"Oh"—as if noticing for the first time—"I must have left it home."

"Strange; I thought I saw it on you earlier . . . when you first got in tonight."

"No . . . I musta forgot it."

"Mmmmm." Martin reached under his desk, fished about, and came up with a small black electronic device. "Could this be yours?"

Snell's jaw dropped. He felt as if he had stepped into a pit and was sinking deeper by the minute. "I don't think so . . . couldn't be: I forgot mine at home."

"Oh, then this isn't yours either." Martin edged a carton out from under his desk. It contained a uniform. Identical to that which George Snell was wearing.

Snell stared at the box, speechless.

"This is yours." It was more a statement than a question.

". . . uh . . . what makes you think so?" Snell tried to defer inevitability as long as possible.

"For one thing, it's an extra-large that's been let out. You're my only guy who wears anything that big. For another, the jacket's got a food stain—which I noticed when you showed up for work tonight and which the jacket you're wearing hasn't got. For another thing, your beeper was attached to the belt.

"And finally, you're the only guy I know who would wear bikini undershorts with red hearts all over 'em."

During the ensuing pause, Snell assessed the evidence. "That's my uniform," he finally concluded.

"I know it's your goddam uniform! What I want to

know is how you happened to lose a whole goddam uniform on duty—including your shoes, socks, and underwear!"

". . . uh . . . where did you find it?"

"I didn't. One of the other guys checked out the laundry. Somebody threw the whole goddam mess down the chute.

"I repeat: How'd you lose every stitch you were wearing—while you were on duty?"

". . . uh . . . I'd rather not say."

Martin leaned back in his chair. "Rather not say, eh? Well, I'm certain sure you'll get bugged by the other guys, so, eventually you'll talk."

". . . uh . . . the guy who found it: Does he know it's mine?"

Martin shook his head. "So far, only me—and you."

"What's it gonna cost for you to sit on this?"

"I thought we'd get to that. One: From now on, you show up on time and don't leave early. Two: You keep a log on where you are when you're on duty. Three: No more loafing around. Keep movin' all the time you're on. And that, of course, means no more nookie.

"I may think of some more later on . . . but that'll do for the moment. Deal?"

Snell, shifting from one foot to the other, gave it some thought. "Okay, deal."

"Good. Might just as well start now. Get your ass moving; you're still on duty. You can pick up your . . . spare . . . uniform after your shift."

Snell resumed his patrol. He knew—there was no doubt—he'd never be able to live up to that agreement. He'd have to figure out how to explain tonight's embarrassing episode or how to deal with unemployment. Neither alternative was attractive. But one had to plan for one's future.

As soon as Snell left the office, Chief Martin began to

chuckle. Then he began to laugh. He spent the rest of the night either chuckling or guffawing as he pictured Snell tiptoeing down the corridors, then dashing through the cold and having to drive home, all while virtually naked. Given Snell's history and reputation, there was little doubt what had occasioned his nakedness. The only missing part of the puzzle was the identity of the broad who had turned the tables on Snell and screwed him. All in good time. All in good time.

✦ ✦ ✦

"So what's got you so preoccupied?" Joe Cox asked.

"What?" Pat Lennon had, indeed, been lost in thought. "Oh, sorry."

"Nothing to be sorry about . . . you've just been mighty quiet this evening."

"Oh, a problem I've been trying to work out."

"Want to talk about it?"

"Nothing much to talk about . . . it's a decision I've got to make."

"Okay."

The television was on, but neither was paying much attention. Cox had been alternating between mild attentiveness to PBS's offerings and the latest *USA Today*.

Lennon had been paying even less attention to TV. Mostly, she'd been staring out of the window both meditatively and absently. Reclining on the sectional couch, it was easy to be mesmerized by the view from their apartment high atop Lafayette Towers.

Only the main thoroughfares had been plowed and/or salted. Most of the side streets in Detroit had only one hope of snow removal: spring. From this perch, one certainly had an overview. One fascination was to watch two cars traveling toward each other on the same side street. Each had little opportunity but to follow the ruts carved out of the hardened snow. Eventually, that would lead the cars on a literal collision course. When that inevitably happened, it was interesting to see which driver would back off and how.

While watching the sparse traffic flow, Lennon was trying to reach a decision on how she should treat her St. Vincent's story.

As far as she could judge, the raison d'etre of the hospital had become quixotic. More than a century ago, St. Vincent's had been a necessity for the city—the region, for that matter. It had once been the only hospital in the Northwest Territory. But over the decades things had drastically changed.

Where once St. Vincent's was Detroit's necessity, now, arguably, the city could get along without the hospital. Particularly in the core city, the municipally owned hospitals were adequate—roughly—for the patient load. The well-to-do to the downright wealthy who inhabited downtown's warn high-rises and townhouses would, outside of the most pressing emergency, never see the inside of any of the area's hospitals. Their doctors were affiliated with ouly the better suburban health-care facilities.

As for the poor who were trapped in the inner city, they made few if any elective visits. Governmental charity addressed only the most crucial medical problems, and then only for the briefest periods.

Her original slant on this had been, she was convinced, an honest feature piece for the magazine. What she had stumbled on was quite another story. A Catholic hospital giving broad birth control counseling, providing contraceptives, even performing sterilizations, was front-page news. No doubt of it. She was too good a journalist not to recognize that.

The problem was the probable consequence following publication.

Could she blow the whistle on this operation? Certainly end the career of Sister Eileen Monahan? Likely cause the closure of this if nothing else historically important hospital?

Many nonjournalists would have little difficulty making the decision not to publish. Possibly only another journalist could understand her inner turmoil. As defense attorneys are expected to defend no matter how they feel about or what they know about their clients, reporters are expected to report. Editors and publishers are expected to be concerned about what to publish. Reporters report and frequently must struggle and scramble in order to do so.

That tendency to report is simply more finely tuned in the case of a staff writer of the caliber of a Pat Lennon.

At this moment, she was trying to reach a less drastic, but possibly contributory, decision: whether to let Joe Cox in on her problem.

Lennon and Cox were an interesting study. Few would argue that the two were among the best, if not actually the best, investigative reporters in the city. At one time both had worked out of the *Detroit Free Press*. Lennon had moved to the *News* several years ago. So now, while they competed for stories, they also worked for genuinely competitive publications.

In this, Detroit was among the dwindling number of fortunate major cities whose metropolitan newspapers were in sharp contrast with one another in almost every conceivable facet.

During the time both had been at the *Free Press,* Lennon and Cox had begun living together without benefit of clergy. Each had a previous marriage; neither had children. Both felt they had chanced upon something rare and fine: a relationship that found them loving each other and growing in that love. It was the epitome of what one might hope to find in an exemplary marriage. Neither wished to chance mucking up what they had by getting the certificate that society expected them to acquire stating they were married.

In addition, their sex was great.

The obvious pitfall, of course, was that their jobs frequently placed them in direct competition. By now, they had worked out some ground rules. Each recognized that if their self-made rules were not scrupulously observed, it could easily mean the end of their personal relationship. So the rules were scrupulously kept.

One of these rules would have to be invoked should Lennon choose to solicit Cox's help in making her decision on how to treat what she'd uncovered at St. Vincent's.

The rule was Confidentiality. And it was tricky.

Getting to know each other as well as they had, it was next to impossible to keep secrets. It was only natural that Lennon had mentioned to him that she was taking on St. Vincent's as a feature piece for *Michigan Magazine*. And she had. So Cox knew what she was currently working on.

Then, being as upset over this decision on how to handle the story as she was, and having grown as familiar with him as she had, it was impossible to hide her distress from him.

For Cox, it would be simple to add this up and conclude that there was something bigger than met the expectation about this hospital story. At which point he might wander over to the hospital. It would take him no longer than it had her to find the piece that didn't fit in the puzzle.

That must not happen. If it did, it would mean that one of them, by virtue of their personal relationship, had taken professional advantage of the other. And if that happened even once, it would spell the end for them.

So, in this supremely delicate matter of confidentiality, their attitude had to be comparable to the priest's with regard to the seal of confession. There could be no exceptions. Each absolutely had to respect the other's confidences.

134

Of course, again analogous to the priest's treatment of the confessional, if either Lennon or Cox were to come into knowledge of something like this from another source, such as a snitch, or while on an unrelated editorial assignment, there would be no violation of the other's confidence.

Reflecting on all this, Lennon determined she had little alternative but to include Cox in her decision-making process.

So she told him what she had discovered in the hospital's clinic.

Cox whistled low and sincerely. "Wow! That's a multi-installment story that could hover around page one for a long time."

"I know."

"And it's been awhile since we've had the local Catholic Church embroiled in a hot little controversy."

"And that makes it all the more sensational."

"The only problem I find is that I don't see your problem. Go with it! Right?"

"That's the problem: I'm not sure."

"What! It's a legitimate news story, isn't it?"

"Oh, sure."

"You came upon it honestly. I mean, you didn't even use any deception in uncovering it."

"As a matter of fact, they just showed it to me. It was part of the tour."

"Their tough luck, then."

"I still don't know."

Cox moved to the couch and sat at her feet. "Look, I'd like to be able to play devil's advocate. But I'd find that kind of hard. It's a good story, a legitimate story. The kind of story you're in this business for. Is it because the hospital's Catholic, and your background—"

"No. Well, maybe yes. No, not because it's Catholic. Maybe because it's Christian."

"Huh?"

"Broader than Catholic. The little place is there trying to do what Christ would do if he were here. To do that, according to their lights, they have to go against some of the official teachings of the Catholic Church. It's . . . it's more Christ-like."

"The more you explain, the less I understand."

"It would be almost like crucifying Christ again." She was talking more to herself than to him. "No, I won't do it. There are some things I cannot compromise, even for a good story."

"You're not going to use it?"

"And neither are you!" She looked him squarely in the eye.

"I know our agreement. No, I won't use it. But, by God, I'm glad I'm not Catholic."

"You don't understand, Joe. It's got almost nothing to do with being Catholic."

"It's certainly got nothing to do with being a journalist."

"It's what I've got to do."

Cox shrugged. "That's what you've got to do. There are things we just have to do. And times we have to do them." Slowly he peeled off one of her stockings. Then the other.

She smiled. "It's bedtime, isn't it?"

7

THIS WAS ONE OF THOSE DAYS. ONE OF those days you'd rather throw away. But, on the other hand, Sister Eileen did not favor wishing away any of her remaining days. There simply were a number of unpleasant things that needed doing. And she was the only one who could do them.

Already she had had to address a meeting of the nurses and nurses' aides relating to some of the slipshod work going on in the hospital. Special mention had to be made regarding breakage. A great deal of that had been going on. The report given Sister Eileen identified the specific aide responsible for most of that, one Ethel Laidlaw. A notation had been added that aide Laidlaw apparently was not willfully careless or guilty of malicious destruction. It seemed to be a case of congenital clumsiness. Nonetheless, the damage was considerable.

In her lecture, Eileen went out of her way to, on te one hand, inform all present that the identity of the principal offender was known, and, on the other, not to mention her by name. Everyone there, including Ethel, knew exactly who Sister Eileen was talking about.

To cap the climax, during the session, Ethel managed to tip over the coffee urn. There was an unscheduled fifteen-minute break while the mess was cleaned up.

Sister Eileen was seated at the desk in her office sorting the mail, separating those matters that demanded immediate attention from those that allowed some procrastination. She also was awaiting the next bit of unpleasantness on today's agenda.

Her secretary spoke through the intercom: "Sister, Dr. Kim is here to see you."

That was it.

"Send him in, Dolly,"

Kim entered and went immediately to the chair at the visitor's side of Eileen's desk.

Trim and tall, Kim was cursed—as far as Sister Eileen was concerned—with more than the average Oriental inscrutability. He had come to Detroit and St. Vincent's from Chicago, where he had interned at an even poorer hospital than St. Vincent's. Chicago had been his first step after leaving his native South Korea.

Chicago had recommended him as having impeccable credentials and as specializing in general surgery. At St. Vincent's he was expected to softpedal his specialty in favor of doing a bit of everything. Interns and residents all were expected to do a bit of everything.

There was no doubt in anyone's mind that Dr. Lee Kim had definite plans and a timetable in which to accomplish his objectives.

One of those objectives most definitely was to not linger overly long at St. Vincent's. Kim planned to move up and out of Detroit. In which direction, initially, was not of prime importance.

Kim crossed his legs. He exuded confidence. His performance deserved an award; in reality, he was not all that confident. Inside, he was a nervous wreck. He was well aware of his problem. His enemy was time. He had too little of it.

By his timetable, he should have been long gone from St. Vincent's. Every time he walked its ancient halls, he was reminded that this institution had gobbled up any number of doctors in its time. It could too easily happen to him.

Look what had happened to Fred Scott, Kim's superior in Emergency. Kim both admired and despised Scott. Scott was the most amazing technician Kim had ever experienced in emergency situations. At the same time, Scott had let his remarkable skills take root at St. Vincent's. Kim's greatest fear was that the same thing would happen to him. That years from now, he would be mired in Detroit's core city in a health-care facility that should have closed its doors decades ago. He would still be patching stab wounds and removing slugs from people who'd been fighting over the final swallow of cheap wine. Still be exposed to their vomit and feces.

So, he tended to hurry things along. He really couldn't help himself. It was late. Late in his ball game.

He hurried things along. Sure he didn't spend a lot of time with the immediate families of terminal patients. It was, after all, up to them to inform themselves of their options. Surely they'd seen enough movies and television to know what life-support systems were all about. If they wanted their kin to be maintained in a vegetative state, what concern was it of his?

Same with the whores who were forever getting pregnant. Too dumb to stay on the Pill. Just as likely to pull out their IUDs as their tampons. Counseling was a waste of time. Far easier to scrape out their prematurely tired uteruses, and the fetuses in there as well. The dumber ones you could always badger into agreeing to a hysterectomy. And while that could be time-consuming, it was good practice.

Time was better spent being in the right places, being seen by the right people, talking to the movers and shakers of the local medicine scene, brown-nosing them. The big thing is to get St. Vincent's behind you. Get into the real world of the Caddies, country clubs, influential patients. And get there yesterday. Time was an enemy.

The other enemy, perhaps even more threatening than time, was sitting across from him. Sister Eileen Monahan. He knew she had her suspicions. He was also pretty sure that she had no proof. Without proof, she would never bring him up on charges. Which didn't mean she didn't want to get him. Only that, for now, she couldn't.

But he also knew that the very instant she could, she would get rid of him. And then where would he be? Dismissed from St. Vincent's! Who would consider him after such degradation?

That was why he was in such inner turmoil. He had no way of telling what she knew. He would soon find out. Meanwhile, it was crucial that he present a calm and tranquil exterior.

They sat across from each other for several moments in silence, each measuring the other.

Eileen opened a file folder and began paging through it. Kim shifted in his chair. It was increasingly difficult to retain an unruffled exterior.

"Dr. Kim," she said at length, "is all going well for you here at St. Vincent's?"

"As well as can be expected." He was pleased to use the bromide response traditionally given in hospitals to almost any question.

Eileen smiled tightly. "And how 'well' may we expect that to be?"

"I have no complaints." Pause. "Have you?"

Pause. "Doctor, when you came here from Chicago last year, we had a long talk."

"I remember it well."

"Good. Then you'll recall that I spoke at considerable length about the spirit here at St. Vincent's."

He did remember it well. At the time, he had thought her a bit overage to be a cheerleader. "May I again remind you," Eileen continued, "that this is only a small health-care facility, in precarious financial balance at best. So much so that, in order to survive, we must work together in a spirit of trust unequaled in most similar institutions. We lack the numerical strength to carve out a niche for ourselves and bury ourselves in some specialty. But, most of all, among the capabilities we lack—and I wish we could afford—is we have no 'watchdog' committee to police our operation. So, to a greater extent than most health-care facilities, we must function on an honor system. We must police ourselves."

"I remember all of that very well, Sister."

"As you complete your first year of residency, Doctor, I thought it would be good to evaluate your position here."

"Have there been complaints? Has not my work been satisfactory?"

"Satisfactory? Technically, yes. Every evaluation of your work has been more than satisfactory. In emergency situations and particularly in the OR, you are reported to be calm under fire and a gifted surgeon."

"Then all is well."

"Not quite. And this is not merely hearsay. It's your attitude toward people. Toward patients and their families."

"Attitude?"

"I know that's difficult to define. For one thing, among

our patients, an unusually high percentage of those on life-support systems are yours."

"Without the systems, they'd be dead now."

"With the systems, they are already dead now, for all practical purposes."

"If it is the cost of maintenance—"

"Of course it isn't the cost. No more than it would be in any other hospital. If someone's life can be prolonged for any positive purpose, then of course we must do everything we can. But many of your patients are vegetating. Many have reached a terminal state even as you order procedures to begin."

"If the wishes of the family—"

"I know all about the wishes of the family. And I've heard about your routine in getting their consent to put the patients on the machines."

"Is there anything medically improper in all this?"

"Not technically. But one tends to wonder why so high a percentage of the families you talk to decide that we must, in your phrase, 'do everything.' One wonders if you are doing this just to save yourself the time it would take to sit down with the families and explain the options available to them."

"Sister, do you not think your conclusion is a bit far-fetched and rather unsubstantiated?"

"All by itself, perhaps. But then we have your rather cavalier attitude towards D & Cs."

"What do you mean by that?" He knew she was coming close to pay dirt.

"The word I get—"

"From whom, may I ask?"

"We won't get into that just now. These are not formal charges."

He breathed a bit more easily.

"I've heard that you frequently don't even order a

142

pregnancy test when it is called for, before going right into a D & C," she continued, "and there are times that you've removed a fetus."

"That is not unique."

"It isn't unique unless it happens again and again. Then it's another name for abortion."

"Do you not think that is a bit strong, Sister?"

"No, I don't. And you well know our policy on abortion at St. Vincent's."

"I see."

"Is there anything else on your mind, Sister, before I reply to all this?"

"No. And I am eager to hear your reply."

Kim relaxed measurably. She hadn't mentioned all those unnecessary hysterectomies. Was it possible she hadn't heard about them? In any case, she wasn't going to bring them up. So much the better.

"Since you want to know what I think," Kim began, "I think it is easy for you as a Caucasian American to apply a racial stereotype to one such as I."

"Racial stereotype!"

"Yes. It is very easy for you Americans to group us Asians into one category and claim that we have no respect for life."

"That has nothing to do with this!"

"Is that so? Do you have any documentation for the charge that I perform a D & C merely in order to abort?"

"I told you I am not concerned at this time with formal charges or documentation. I can only tell you that I have heard about it from more than one source. Sources, I might add, who are most trustworthy."

"I cannot allow my life, my professional conduct, to be affected by innuendo and rumor—and that is what I consider these unsubstantiated charges to be based on." Kim realized he was moving into dangerous ground, almost challenging Eileen to bring formal charges. He decided to turn the tables. "And, as to the allegations regarding my handling of the terminally ill, does that not argue just the reverse of the first charge—that I have no regard for life? How very *un*Asian of me to want to prolong someone's life, do you not think?"

"Dr. Kim, one look at your patients while they are being mechanically sustained will tell anyone worlds about the quality of life to which they've been relegated.

"Besides, you have twisted and jumbled everything I've said with your gratuitous reference to an Asian prejudice. There may be some in our society who feel that Asians prize life less than do we in the West. But I am very definitely not in that number. I am too well aware that we in the United States have less than an enviable record when it comes to racism. So I am conscious of our own failings. But being conscious of racism does not necessarily mean being guilty of it.

"No, Dr. Kim, I am not dealing in stereotypes. I am talking about one doctor—yourself—who has determined to disregard the cautions I gave when you joined us." She closed the file folder, indicating their meeting was drawing to a close. "Dr. Kim, my purpose in meeting with you is simply this: I want you to consider this a formal warning. You are perilously close to facing dismissal from the staff of this hospital. If I were forced to the point where I must bring formal charges against you, I have every confidence that I could do so effectively.

"Doctor, I don't want to be forced to affect your career adversely. But I may have no choice in the matter. And this may happen very soon. It would be wise for you to prepare yourself for the worst.

"I'm sorry. That will be all for now."

Wordlessly, Kim rose and left the room. His departure was one fluid motion. There was no betrayal of nervous-

144

ness or embarrassment. There was no show of emotion whatsoever.

However, after he exited the secretary's office, Dr. Lee Kim leaned back against the wall and forced himself to breathe deeply and slowly. His emotions, held in such excellent check while with Sister Eileen, were in turmoil.

In his mind's eye, he could see the fissures forming in the plan he had laid out for his life. This damned nun held the hammer and chisel that could bring him down. That must not happen. It would mean the end of his dream, the end of the good life he envisioned.

Earlier, he had known there was trouble—a lot of trouble. He had known, more in the abstract than in the concrete, that something would have to happen—something drastic. Now there was no question. He would have to think this out to the last detail. And then act.

Sister Eileen shifted papers on her desk without paying them much attention. She felt drained, not completely, but substantially. She could not afford a thorough draining. She had yet at least two more extremely taxing encounters to handle.

The necessity of scheduling unpleasant meetings was what she most abhorred about any effective leadership role. But such meetings were inescapable. She owed it to poor old St. Vincent's to do all she could to keep her baby alive and well. But no consideration could keep these meetings from being unpleasant.

She opened the file folder of the next person on her schedule. She didn't need to study this person's background. She knew it almost completely by heart. She closed the file, folded her hands, and lowered her head in prayer. She had just begun to lose herself in meditation when the intercom brought the message that her next visitor was waiting.

John Haroldson, chief operating officer of St. Vincent's,

entered. A broad smile broke his heavily creased face. But his eyes betrayed a worried mind.

They exchanged hearty greetings. It was ever thus, thought Eileen. John, the hail fellow well met. But only on the surface. Underneath, there were always troubled layers in John's life. Layers that would be revealed in good time. Inevitably.

"Your summons surprised me, Sister. It isn't time for our monthly meeting."

It made Haroldson nervous not to be in control of any situation. And since he had little inkling as to Eileen's purpose in calling this meeting, this situation was, at least initially, not in his control.

"It wasn't a summons, John," Eileen sighed. "It was an invitation."

"Whatever"—still the confident smile, the worried eyes—"it didn't seem like an invitation I ought to refuse."

"John, John . . . can we never stop playing games?"

A flash of anger. "I don't play games, Sister. I know a summons when I get one."

"Have it your way, then."

Haroldson nodded curtly. The smile was gone.

"I want to talk to you about the future, John."

"The future?"

"Yes, yours and St. Vincent's."

"Oh?" He was withdrawing.

"You're getting close to the Michigan Catholic Conference retirement age, John. It's just four months down the line. Are you giving any thought to your retirement?"

"Retirement? Why, no. No reason to. I'm fit. You've got the results of my latest physical. I'm in fine shape, even leaving my age out of it. Why should I think of retirement?"

"Because you're nearing the compulsory age for it, John."

"But . . . but you can waive that . . . as . . . my superior." He seemed loath to acknowledge her position.

"I can. But there's no reason I should."

"My health—"

"Exactly. Your health. It's fine. Where did you ever get the idea one must be at death's door in order to qualify for retirement?"

"Sister . . ." His tone came close to pleading; only with effort did he stay in control of himself. ". . . this hospital has been part of my existence. After Elizabeth died, in time, this place has gradually replaced her in my life. I can't leave here."

"John, you're not the first person who felt there was no life after retirement. But you know as well as I that most people get over that feeling and really come to enjoy retirement. You can, too."

Haroldson was silent. Head lowered, he seemed to be studying his clasped hands. "You're serious, aren't you?" There was a touch of panic in his voice.

"Yes. I am. But it's not going to happen overnight, John. There are months between now and then. Months when you can continue your contributions to St. Vincent's and, at the same time, do a little planning for retirement."

Silence.

"With your background, John, there are lots of things you might do in very productive fields. With your education and experience, you could teach. You could teach part-time in the seminary, or in a business school. You could teach a medical morals course in one of our colleges. There are so many opportunities for a man with your talent.

"Or, on the other hand . . ." She found herself reaching to fill the vacuum left by Haroldson's lack of response. ". . . you might just want to relax for a while . . . get accustomed to being out of this routine of getting up and out every morning and spending so many demanding hours on the job. Just leaving the routine might put an entirely new perspective on your whole future.''

There was a prolonged silence. Eileen decided she would not try to fill it. All it could have been was idle chatter.

''You don't like me, do you? You never did, did you?''

Good God. The same as with Lee Kim. Neither man would stay with the subject. She was not prejuiced against Kim because of his race. And her feelings toward Haroldson had nothing to do with his retirement. If Kim and Haroldson had been women, some man undoubtedly would've blamed the digressions on their hormones.

''John,'' Eileen said rather firmly, ''we're talking about retirement because you are nearing the age of compulsory retirement. That makes sense to me!''

''I knew it shortly after I came here to work. You and I never had the same vision for St. Vincent's. And it's gotten worse over the years. It's not secret. Everybody in the hospital knows it.''

''John!''

Haroldson lowered and shook his head. He was almost talking to himself. ''We climbed the ladder together here at St. Vincent's. Except you were always a rung ahead of me. Always my 'superior.' Even when I became chief operating officer, you were chief executive officer. Always above me. Always over me. Always opposing me.'' He looked up, directly at Eileen. ''And now the coup de grace. Forcing me into retirement.''

''John . . .'' Eileen shook her head in frustration. ''I'm not forcing you. You've reached retirement age. That can't come as any surprise to you.''

''The fact is, you could waive that requirement.''

''The fact is, I happen to believe that, under ordinary circumstances, retirement is a good idea.''

"Oh, do you? Then what about your retirement, dear Sister? Are you going to follow me on this lovely path you've outlined for me? Will you retire?"

Eileen felt herself reddening. "That's a different matter, John. And you know it."

"Because you're a dedicated religious and I am a mere layman?"

"Of course not, John. You know as well as I that the powers that be are eager to close down St. Vincent's for good and all. If I were to retire, that would be their green light. I'd like to leave the hospital in viable enough shape so that it could continue under its own steam. And that may be possible one day if my plans work out. But it certainly is not the case now. If I were to leave here now or in the foreseeable future, it would be the end."

"Not necessarily."

"What? What can you mean, John?"

"I could keep it open. I've been here nearly as long as you. I know this place as well as you. Maybe better. My policies would be as good as, or better, than yours. I could win over more of the board members." The tone of flustered panic was evident. "You wouldn't even have to retire. We could work together. We complement each other. If we were to work together, we could unite the board. We could make the hospital what it once was!"

"John, John," she said softly, "don't. Don't do this to yourself. Although you're making this resemble death, it's not. And you're not dying. Think about it. You're a spiritual man; pray over it. Give yourself some time to consider it seriously. You'll come to terms with the notion of retirement. You'll have to," she concluded firmly, "because, in the final analysis, you are going to retire. Do it well. You can, you know."

He seemed drained. But in a few moments of quiet, he appeared to have regained control of himself. "Yes, yes, of course. There is no alternative. I just need a little time.''

There was another pause. Eileen had no inclination to hurry him. Better that he take a few moments to compose himself.

"Sorry about my behavior back there," he said. "It shouldn't have taken me by surprise. Just as you said. I know what the retirement age is. And I certainly know how old I am." He smiled, but it was forced. "If there's nothing else . . ."

"No, John, that's all."

He rose to leave, but almost stumbled. Eileen half stood to go to his aid, but he waved her back.

"Just a bit disoriented, I guess. I'll be okay." He departed.

Haroldson had planned to go over some of the accounts payable this morning. To him fell the regular burden of deciding which bills must be paid and which could be delayed. Cash flow was a near-mortal problem at St. Vincent's.

But now he was too shaken to be able to concentrate on business. He went directly to the chapel, knelt in the back pew, and buried his face in his hands. In no time he was lost in reflection.

Leave St. Vincent's. Leave St. Vincent's under his own power. He smiled. He rarely thought of leaving his hospital. But when he did, he always pictured himself being carried out, probably dead.

The anger rose again. He tried to hold it in check. Anger was a sin. And sin was a failure Haroldson steadfastly tried to avoid.

But, wait a minute . . . . anger wasn't always a sin. It couldn't be. Jesus had been angry at the moneychangers in the temple. Moses had been so angry with the chosen people and their golden idol that he smashed the Commandment tablets.

These thoughts he'd been having lately, these emotions he'd been experiencing, perhaps they were not as sinful as he had feared. What was it Eileen had just said . . . with his background . . . with his background he might be able to work it all out. All it required was some thought, some definitive plan. And then, put it all into action. Certainly. He could expect to be able to do that.

Eileen had barely had time to compose herself after meeting with Haroldson when her secretary entered Sister's office.

"I don't know what to do with this one, Sister."

"What is it, Dolly?"

"Sister Rose is here for her appointment. But Pat Lennon, that newspaper lady, is here too. And she hasn't got an appointment. And you know how Rosie gets when her schedule is upset."

Despite the way she felt, Eileen smiled. "Rosamunda will keep. She has all these years. Ask her to come by right after lunch. And show Ms. Lennon in."

Dolly winced. It was she who would receive the brunt of Rosamunda's cantankerous disapproval of a fractured appointment. But she would, of course, carry out her assignment.

Lennon entered and was seated.

The nun was impressed. Lennon was wearing an entirely different ensemble from yesterday's. But like yesterday's, today's outfit was functional, while at the same time extremely attractive. And expensive. Pat Lennon must buy her clothing at one or another of the super-swank suburban boutiques. Heretofore, the nun had given little thought to the wages of journalism. Now that the consideration occurred naturally, Eileen supposed a reporter's salary must be handsome. She also supposed that Pat's fine wardrobe was extensive. This supposition was valid.

At their previous meeting, Pat had explained why she felt it her duty to do what would amount to an exposé on the family-planning service offered at St. Vincent's. Eileen had not expected to see the reporter again. She had assumed Pat would go about completing her research and, one day soon, Detroiters would be reading all about it. So she was unprepared for Lennon's present unscheduled appearance.

"Yesterday," Lennon began, "I dropped one shoe, as it were. And it's just not fair not to let you know that I'm going to hold on to the other shoe . . . at least for the time being."

"I don't understand."

"Yesterday, I told you all the reasons why I couldn't overlook this story on contraception in a Catholic hospital. But last night, I got to thinking it over and, well, to cut it short, I decided I couldn't do it. I couldn't chance derailing the service this hospital is trying to provide. It gets complicated . . . but there are just some things I'm not prepared to compromise for the sake of this job."

"Well, I must say that is easily the best news I've had today."

"At the same time," Lennon continued, "I don't want to create any false impression. I'm not . . . I can't make any promises down the line. I can't foresee what may happen. There may be complications later; circumstances could change. I can't even be specific. Something could happen. Another reporter, say, could stumble onto the story. I couldn't allow him or her to beat me. You see?

"But, for now," Pat took out her note pad, "let's forget your family planning policies and get back to the original thrust of this story—the hospital, its past, its present, its future, and you."

Eileen sighed in relief. "Fair enough. I must admit that the possibility of your doing that story has been like a

152

cloud hovering over me ever since we talked about it. This is welcome news!"

"But . . ."

"Yes, I understand your reservation. And if another reporter were going to develop the story, I would make certain you got every bit of cooperation we could provide. It would be the least we could do in return for the favor you're doing us. Now," Eileen checked her watch, "how about joining me for a little lunch?"

"Could we talk during lunch?"

"Better. You can meet more of the staff."

"It's a deal."

✛ ✛ ✛

"What were you doing here last night?"

"Huh?"

"I mean, It was the evening shift. And you never volunteer for that. We don't even have volunteers for that shift." Ethel Laidlaw lifted her cup and allowed the excess coffee to drip back into the saucer. There had been a spill.

"What makes you think I was here last night?" Bruce Whitaker moved his glass about, making thin white circles on the table. He'd had a spill.

" 'Cause I seen you."

"You did?" Pause. "Are you sure?"

"Certainly! I know who you are. I seen you on the main floor after visiting hours."

Trepidation welled up in Whitaker. She had seen him. Of that there was little doubt. But where had he been when she saw him? How much had she seen? How much did she know? Could she, as his colleagues had warned, prove to be a serious barrier to his goal? And what would he do—what could he do—if she became an obstacle in his path?

"So . . ." A little more milk slopped over and he began

making new thin white circles on the table. ". . . you think you saw me, eh? Well, then, smartie, where was I when you saw me?"

"Down around pastoral care. What's such a big deal anyway? So you were here after hours. So what? What I couldn't figure out was why you were slinking around. Why was that?"

"What?" He was stalling, shamelessly stalling, to figure a clever way out of this without having to do something drastic.

"Sneaking around! Why were you sneaking around?"

"I . . . I was on a special mission, Ethel. I can't go into it in any kind of detail. But I was on a special mission. A secret mission."

"Okay."

She bought it! He couldn't believe it. Maybe he had missed his calling. Perhaps he should have been a spy. Or maybe ambassador to the U.N. He had never before tried his hand at subtle equivocation. It wasn't so difficult.

"So, Ethel . . ." He ceased creating circles; he had used up all the excess milk on his glass. ". . . what were you doing on the main floor at that hour, if I might turn the tables?"

"Saving you."

"What?"

"From the guard."

"What guard?"

"The one who was about to find you when you were hiding against the wall."

"Uh . . ."

"You remember: You were going along the wall, keeping in the shadows, on your secret mission. And that guard challenged you. He was about to shine his light on you."

"Uh . . . then what happened?"

"I coughed. Didn't you hear me?"

"No."

"Well, the guard did. Then he found me instead of you."

"No kidding? No kidding! Then what happened?"

"Then I . . . uh . . . distracted him."

"Why'd you do that?"

"To help you, Bruce. You looked like you needed help. I mean, I didn't know you were on a secret mission. But it did look like you didn't want that guard to find you. So I made sure he didn't."

"And you don't know where I went after that?"

"No, silly! I was distracting the guard. So your great big special mission is still a secret."

"Gee, Ethel, that was really great of you! That was a big help. And I didn't even know. Gosh, I wish there was something I could do for you. I mean, in return for what you did for me."

Ethel sighed elaborately. "Maybe there is." She bit into her sandwich and realized that she should not have ordered egg salad. She had been trying, not altogether successfully, to convince Bruce that she was not a congenital klutz. Now here she was with egg salad squeezed out the other side of her sandwich, dripping from her fingers to the plate. It was not a good show.

"You mean there's some way I can help you?" Bruce seemed not to notice Ethel's eggy predicament. He might have been preoccupied with renewing the white circles. He had had another spill.

"I need to get that nun out of my hair. But for the life of me, I can't think how to do it." She licked her fingers, but to little avail. The egg salad was now dripping from the other side of the sandwich.

"What nun?"

"Sister Eileen."

"You mean the head of this hospital?"

"Uh-huh."

His heart soared. Could they be in on the same mission? "But why?"

"Because if I don't get rid of her, she's going to get rid of me."

"But why?"

"There have been reports, entirely unproven, that I am . . . uh . . . clumsy. And that I've caused some damage."

"Ethel!"

"Yes. And at a meeting just this morning, she threatened to fire me if she heard any more of those unfounded rumors. And . . . and . . . Bruce, Bruce, what am I going to do if she fires me? I'll never be able to get another job. There just aren't that many jobs around now. And getting fired . . . and not having a recommendation . . . oh, Bruce, I don't know what to do!"

She was on the verge of tears. As she reached for her cup, a gob of egg salad dropped into the coffee, splashing some into the saucer. When she lifted the cup, there'd be another slop-over.

Bruce was confused. Which was bad news for the integrity of the food in front of him. He did not know how to handle a woman under the best of circumstances, let alone one on the verge of tears.

"That was cruel of her, Ethel." He tried to touch her arm reassuringly, but managed only to spill more coffee. "But I don't understand. What did you mean when you said something about getting rid of Sister? How do you mean 'get rid of'?"

"Oh, I'd just like to kill her!" She shook her head. "I've been having such terrible headaches. I even think I may be having one of those—what do you call them— personality changes. It scares me!"

"Ethel . . ." Bruce leaned forward, dragging his tie through the gravy. ". . . you don't mean . . . m . . . m . . . murder!"

"Oh, Bruce, I don't know," she almost wailed. "I just can't think."

"Ethel"—by now his tie was stirring the gravy—"I may be able to help you. To solve your problem. Not the way you have in mind. But just as good."

"It would get rid of her? Get her out of my hair? Before she could get rid of me? Oh, Bruce—"

"Leave it to me, Ethel." He noticed his tie. He pulled it free of the gravy. The tie fell against his white hospital jacket, mottling it.

Till now, Whitaker had been torturing himself thinking of the damage he would be causing women who would use the IUDs he had altered. But, he kept reminding himself, it was for a good cause. The greater honor and glory of God, for starters. Next, the triumph of the traditionalists' cause.

Now there was an added dimension. He could do it for Ethel. Which was a little odd, since he had already done it. Maybe he could dedicate it to Ethel. Or just let her in on it. That was it.

When the matter came to a boil, when women who'd been hurt by the IUDs—Whitaker had never been clear on just how the IUDs would damage women, but he had been assured it would happen—returned complaining, and the media would be eager to report this news, then would the administration of Sister Eileen topple. The hospital would be forced to abide by the laws of Holy Mother Church.

At that time, when it had become a fait accompli, he could tell Ethel what had happened and, modestly, who had caused it all.

It was not a bad scenario. He let it develop in his imagination while leisurely making more circles with the bottom of his glass.

Meanwhile, at a table just a few feet away, Father Koesler was captivated by the bizarre dining behavior of the bunglesome duo.

"Hey, Father, come back to earth," Dr. Fred Scott said. "Here poor Dr. Kim is telling us his troubles and you're a million miles away."

Koesler returned to awareness with a start. "Oh . . . I'm sorry."

"What in the world were you thinking of?"

"I was watching that odd couple at the next table destroy their lunches and ruin the table. Most remarkable. The man looks familiar. But I can't place him. Probably reminds me of some movie personality I can't recall. Does anyone know them?"

Seated with Koesler and Scott were Dr. Lee Kim and Sister Rosamunda. In response to Koesler's question, Scott and Kim shook their heads.

"Sister Rosamunda . . ." Scott tugged gently at her sleeve. Her aural senses were adequate. But, taking advantage of her advancing years, she chose to hear selectively. "Rosey!" Scott said more loudly.

"Eh?"

"Do you know those two at the next table? The guy with the two-bit toup and the girl sitting in all that mess?"

Rosamunda peered intently. "No . . . no, I don't think so. From her uniform, I'd say the woman is an aide. But I don't know about the man. Can't say I've ever seen him before. Probably a volunteer. They come and go."

"It doesn't matter," Koesler said. "I just thought I knew the gentleman from somewhere. I'm sorry . . ." He returned his attention to Scott. "You were saying . . .?"

"Lee was telling us about his meeting with Sister Eileen this morning. Disaster," Scott continued. "Lee feels he's on the verge of being dismissed from staff. He claims it's racial . . . thinks Eileen is prejudiced against Asians."

"Oh, do you think so?" Koesler said. "I really find that hard to believe. I get the impression Sister hasn't a prejudiced bone in her body."

"You don't know her," Kim said. "And she is not unique. Many Westerners presume that because someone comes from the East, he automatically has a lesser concern for life. I am only one of many Asian doctors on this staff whose position is threatened."

Scott looked askance as if he were hearing this indictment for the first time and not believing a word of it.

"And when you come to think of what it would mean to be dismissed from this hospital," Kim continued. "Just look at those two. . . ." He gestured toward the next table. "They appear to be a good example of people who could find a job nowhere. They are the kind of people your welfare state takes care of. But they are employed here. With that in mind—the sort of people who are permitted to continue working here—think of what would go through the mind of a prospective health-care employer when he heard that you had been dismissed by St. Vincent's! No other hospital would ever consider you."

"Kind of put a crimp in your career, eh, Lee?" Scott said.

"The end of my career."

Koesler hoped he would be ignored for a few moments so that he could reflect on this turn of events.

Undoubtedly, Dr. Kim's position at St. Vincent's was threatened. No one would have any reason to mislead anyone about that. The question was why.

Was it, as the doctor claimed, a matter of prejudice? Koesler supposed it possible. He himself had harbored some notions relating to the Asian concept regarding the sanctity of life. Notions that traced back to the event that had plunged America into World War II: the attack on Pearl Harbor and the wanton destruction of all those young servicemen. Notions that were reinforced during the Korean conflict when American soldiers testified to North Korean and Chinese troops attacking in wave after wave

159

until lethal machine guns became too hot to continue firing.

On the other hand, the U.S.A. was the only nation thus far that had actually used a nuclear weapon against humans. And almost singlehandedly devastated Vietnam and Cambodia.

Koesler guessed that something pejorative could be said about militaristic nations in general.

But he found it ludicrous to think of Sister Eileen as prejudiced. In her time at St. Vincent's she had been responsible for racially integrating the hospital, both patients and staff. That the patient population was now almost completely black was an accident of geography. But that there was a heavy percentage of Orientals and blacks on the staff was in good part the handiwork of Sister Eileen.

On the face of it, Koesler tended to give credence to the information Dr. Scott had offered earlier: that Dr. Kim was not relating generously to the patients and that there was some question of his performing clandestine abortions as well as unnecessary hysterectomies.

There was one other possible consideration. What if Dr. Scott were not on the up and up? After all, why should Scott have taken Koesler under his wing and shared all these secrets with him? Koesler had experienced the oversolicitous helper many times in the past. All too often such a person had an ulterior motive. Covering up for a personal involvement by focusing attention on others. Could this be the case with Scott? Or was Koesler being paranoid?

Once again, he became conscious of the table conversation. The thread had not developed much beyond the point at which he had dropped out of the verbal exchange.

"Well, I don't believe it for a moment, Lee," Scott said. "I don't see any problem with your career. But," he nodded, "there is somebody whose career definitely is coming to an end."

"Oh? Who?"

"That venerable gentleman just sitting down over there by himself."

"Haroldson? You must be joking!"

A very solemn-faced John Haroldson was seating himself at an adjacent empty table. His expression would discourage anyone from sharing the table.

"John Haroldson?" Kim said. "Why, he goes back almost to the beginning. Along with our beloved Sister Eileen."

"Not any more."

"Why not?"

"Retirement. Haroldson's reached the mandatory retirement age."

"How do you know?"

"Small hospital."

"One of the dinosaurs will live," Sister Rosamunda broke in, "the other must die."

"What do you mean by that?" Koesler asked.

"They're both retirement age." Rosamunda smiled innocently. "But only one of them will retire."

Scott nodded. "She's forcing Haroldson."

"You mean Haroldson doesn't want to retire?" asked Koesler.

Scott shook his head. "This place is his life. I wouldn't be at all surprised to read his obituary shortly after he's forced out of here. We've all seen it happen countless times. It's frequently a widow or widower, or a guy married to his job; take away what they're living for and they die."

"Do you really think so?"

Scott nodded. "Well, now, threatening Kim here, pushing Haroldson out, promising a crackdown in the nursing staff . . . one wonders where Sister's broom is going to stop."

"She is cracking down on the nurses?" Kim asked.

Scott nodded and ran his hand again and again through his beard.

"How do you know that?" Koesler asked.

A strange look came over Scott's face. "Small hospital." Koesler had never seen him look so . . . was it menacing?

It suddenly occurred to Koesler that, for someone who had seemingly gone out of his way to clue Koesler in under the guise of enlisting the priest's support of Sister Eileen, Scott was certainly muddying the waters.

What was his motive? Did he have something to gain from staff unrest? Were his comments designed to foment upheaval? Or was he merely playing the wry observer?

At best, concluded Koesler, Dr. Fred Scott was certainly being provocative.

Suddenly, Koesler became conscious of an undercurrent throughout the cafeteria. Sister Eileen had arrived.

That was not unusual and, clearly, it was not her presence that was causing the stir. With Eileen was Pat Lennon. She it was, who, outstandingly attractive and stylishly attired, was turning heads.

Koesler was reminded of his school days in the seminary when Detroit Red Wing Hockey Coach Jack Adams occasionally dined with the priest-faculty. As unusual as it was for the students to see a layman dining with their faculty, the single time Adams brought with him defensive star Red Kelly, the students were awed into near silence. The shock of red hair plus celebrity status did it. The momentary stunned silence had been broken by enthusiastic applause.

Those dining in St. Vincent's cafeteria did not applaud. But it was evident that they very definitely approved.

After helping themselves from the buffet counter, Eileen and Lennon threaded their way toward the far side of the

162

cafeteria. They stopped momentarily at the table where John Haroldson sat. The COO's customarily effusive greeting was muted this day.

The two women moved quickly to the next table, and Eileen introduced Lennon to Sister Rosamunda, Doctors Scott and Kim and Father Koesler.

Lennon had met only Koesler previously, and she showed some wonder at his presence. Occasionally in the past, Lennon had covered news stories that had involved Koesler. In addition, Koesler was a periodic source for her on religious stories, particularly those involving the Catholic Church. Now he briefly explained to her his substitute status at the hospital.

Table conversation was at first stilted. Neither Lennon nor Sister could know that Eileen had been the principal subject of dialogue only a few moments before.

But Lennon quickly became the cynosure, with questions coming from all sides about newspaper work and routine, stories she had covered, and the feature she was now developing on the hospital for *Michigan Magazine*.

This was acceptable to Lennon. She could not have interviewed these people in such a group in any case. Now, as they questioned her, she could make assessments and decide which of them might make better subjects for interviews.

Among the judgments she made was that Sister Rosamunda would make a smashing interviewee. She seemed the embodiment of that sweet little old nun of the past. The one who, in full religious garb, would be photographed swinging a bat, riding a roller coaster, or wearing a funny hat atop her headpiece.

Lunch was pretty much over for everyone when a rather round lady entered the cafeteria, glanced around obviously looking for someone specific, then headed purposefully toward Sister Eileen. As the expression has it, the lady wore the map of Ireland on her face. Wheezing up to the table, she stood facing Eileen. Held before her in both hands was a large rectangular box, apparently the cause of the lady's concern.

Bruce Whitaker recognized the box instantly. He would never forget it. It was one of the three boxes containing the IUDs he had altered! Somehow, someone had uncovered the plot.

Bruce had been wishing it would just be over by now . . . that the damage had been done and, he hoped, repaired. And that this hospital's policy had been exposed by the news media.

Instead, the plot had been discovered. He would be found out. At best, he would have to begin again. The blood drained from his head. He felt giddy and faint. Only with massive determination was he able to remain conscious.

"Sister," announced the lady holding the box, "and you too, Mr. Haroldson, would you ever be lookin' at this! Now, I'm well aware that the two of yez are lookin' to held down costs and manage the place's money as best ye can. But if anybody pays for these things, it'll be a crime callin' to heaven for vengeance. Just look at it, would ya!"

She took an object from the box and held it high for everyone's inspection. Clearly, she was seething.

The object she was holding suggested an S-shaped piece of metal, but one end appeared to have been clipped off and the new terminus was twisted out of shape.

"All right," Eileen said at length, "I give up. What is it?"

"What was it supposed to be is maybe the better question, Reverend Sister."

"All right then: What was it supposed to be?"

"This is one of a new shipment of curtain hooks. They came in just the other day. I didn't have a chance in

164

heaven of inspectin' the delivery what with everything else I had to be doin' at the time. So I took them three boxes and shoved them in the IUD drawer—we're running low on them too, wouldn't ya know. So today, I gets me first chance to get 'em up on the rods in the clinic—and what should I find? All three boxes of the blessed hooks is deformed!

"Now I ask yez, do they expect us to pay for them things? Why, if they'd fit in the curtains at all, they'd rip the poor things to shreds as well. What with their bent ends and all. It's a disgrace, it tis. And Mr. Haroldson, sir, if I was you, I'd stop payment on this. Honest to God, the workers today couldn't hold a candle to the good men and true of just a generation back!"

She was breathing heavily. It had been a long and impassioned speech for one struggling with a weight problem.

Bruce Whitaker could scarcely believe his hearing. Curtain hooks? Curtain hooks! Fate had been unkind to him for too long. Granted he had never seen an IUD and had only a vague notion of what its function might be. But dammit, that S-shaped device certainly looked as if it were what the doctor ordered, literally. And the damn things had been in the goddam IUD drawer.

Under ordinary circumstances, Whitaker was neither vulgar nor did he blaspheme. But this was one of those moments that tried men's souls. Now what was he to do? How could he ever tell his colleagues that he had penetrated St. Vincent's security systems, crept through the hospital after hours, and—with the unexpected help of Ethel—made it into the sin-wracked clinic, only to spend hours mutilating curtain hooks?

At this point, life was not pretty.

"Well, you're absolutely correct," Eileen said. "And it was good of you to find these things so promptly and bring them to our attention. We'll certainly not pay for such execrable workmanship. Please give all the details to Mr. Haroldson. He'll take care of it.'' Then, to the others at table, in effect dismissing the lady with the mutilated curtain hooks, ''Can you imagine! I've seen some shoddy work in my day, but that ranks with the worst I've ever seen.''

''Probably a disgruntled worker at the factor.'' Lennon was trying not to laugh. Likely it was not funny if one was fighting to contain costs with extremely limited funds as was surely the case with St. Vincent's Hospital.

But one person was taking this very seriously. No sooner had the lady drawn the connection between the curtain hooks and the IUD drawer, than did this person begin to draw another connection. It was most tenuous at first, but the longer this person thought about it, the more sense the hypothesis made.

This person had observed, over the past several days, with growing interest, the behavior of one Bruce Whitaker. There was an incredible series of disasters that seemed inevitably to follow in Whitaker's wake. Whitaker definitely seemed to march to a different drummer.

There was no telling where Whitaker might turn up next. His whereabouts in this institution had little, if anything, to do with his services as a volunteer. Of course there were times when he would be delivering or gathering or on some assignment. The sort of thing that a volunteer should do.

But most of the time, if one were paying careful note, Whitaker seemed to be on some inner-directed mission. Doing his own thing . . . whatever that might be.

Now, put it all together.

Who in his right mind would mutilate curtain hooks? No one at the factory. If someone at the factory-level, for whatever reason, wanted to sabotage a shipment of curtain

166

hooks, he wouldn't go to all the trouble of clipping off an end and bending the hook out of shape. Simply snapping it in two would serve the purpose better and more expeditiously. In addition to which, the qualty inspector would have caught it before it got out of the plant.

No, the boxes of curtain hooks had been placed—misplaced really—in the compartment reserved for IUDs and identified as such.

Supposing someone wanted to mutilate IUDs—whatever the person's reason for doing so would have to wait for additional revelation—but supposing that, for whatever reason, someone wanted to mutilate the IUDs. Botching the job as incredibly as this had been bungled would require an amazing degree of ineptitude. The kind exhibited by Bruce Whitaker.

If this hypothesis were correct, Bruce Whitaker had tampered with some harmless curtain hooks, mistaking them for IUDs. So far, that fit perfectly into his blundering method of operation.

But why would he want to monkey with the IUDs?

This would bear watching and Bruce Whitaker warranted a most careful surveillance. He might prove very useful indeed.

✦ ✦ ✦

Lunch was over. The case of the mutilated curtain hooks had been delegated to John Haroldson. Patricia Lennon, wearing the identification tag that had been prepared for her, had been sent off on her own—she preferred it that way—to develop her feature story.

Sister Eileen sat at her desk dictating into a machine replies to that mail she judged most urgent.

"Sister Rosamunda is here." Dolly's voice squeezed through the intercom. "Her appointment was before lunch, but you saw Ms. Lennon instead," Dolly reminded.

"Yes. Send her in, Dolly." Eileen had not forgotten. She wished she had. It promised to be one more unpleasant interview. If Pat Lennon had not come in with her announcement that she was not going to pursue the contraceptive story, it would have been well-nigh impossible to find a silver lining in this day.

Rosamunda entered and took a chair near the desk. Her face was inscrutable as always. She'd had years, lots of years, to perfect a stolid expression. More traditional years as a postulant, a novice and, finally, as she took her solemn perpetual vows. This, followed by almost sixty years as a religious. All these years, most of them in various hospitals, she'd been holding in her emotions and feelings. That's what she had been taught. That was the way in which she had been trained.

She was the sweet little old nun. People looked upon her as a curiosity, a relic of an irretrievable past. Some laughed at her. She did not much care. There wasn't a great deal of time left. Her vast hospital experience made her cognizant of the signs. Nothing of magnitude, like cancer. Just the slowing down of overworked organs and systems.

Sister Rosamunda now had but one goal: to stay in the saddle until the end.

It was a modest aim, but one in which she encountered determined opposition from divers quarters. Many in the administration of her religious order made reference annually to the fact that she was well-beyond retirement age. Not the least, Mother General herself. These were not mean-spirited women; they had her best interests in mind. They persistently mentioned that de Paul Center in suburban Farmington was a far better than average retirement facility. There she would be able to join sisters her own age and even older, friends of hers. With companionship, arts and crafts, and many other goings-on, she could remain as relatively active as she wished.

She fought them every step of the way.

So far, the only reason she had been able to win this annual battle was that Sister Eileen had been in her corner arguing that Rosamunda was a valuable contributor to the health care at St. Vincent's Hospital. Even the most determined religious superior was unwilling to take on Sister Eileen.

But lately, Eileen's support seemed to be wavering. It showed in the little things—attitude, a sharp word now and again, unaccustomed impatience.

Rosamunda prayed that Eileen would be able to persevere in supporting and defending the aging nun for at least a short while longer. That should be all she'd need. Rosamunda could feel herself letting go little by litile. She felt certain that one night she would go to sleep and simply never awaken. A good way to go. And not long more to wait. It was desperately necessary for her to greet that moment still active in service and not on the shelf.

Rosamunda had been dreading this meeting. She had a premonition it would be bad news. But she did not dread it any more than did Eileen. Because it was bad news.

"Sorry I couldn't see you before lunch, Sister," Eileen opened. "Ms. Lennon came unexpectedly and I couldn't postpone dealing with her."

"It happens."

"How've you been fealing?"

"Fine . . . Fine . . . No complaints."

"Oh . . ." Eileen had hoped the older Sister might have been more open and frank. They both knew she was not well. It would have put their dialogue on a more productive footing if she had admitted that.

"Is there something . . .?" Rosamunda wanted to avoid specifics if possible.

"Yes, there is." Eileen pushed the mail aside, folded her hands on the desk, and looked squarely at Rosamunda.

169

"Quite a few things, in fact. For example, you were scheduled to lead morning prayers this week. Two days you've been late and one day there were no prayers at all."

"Uh . . . perhaps it would be better if I were to be responsible for night prayers alone. It would be easier . . . I am sort of a night person."

"Come on, Sister, you have been a religious for more than half a century. What's more, you began back when we were all getting up practically in the middle of the night for prayers. And you've been doing it all these years. Now you tell me you're a night person?"

"People change. We're not as young as we used to be."

Eileen opened a file and studied it briefly. "How long has it been since you did intake interviews on your floor?"

"Uh . . . I don't know just offhand . . . not long."

"According to this record, two weeks. And that was one of the things you always said you most enjoyed. And you're good at it. Nobody, to my knowledge, was ever better than you at greeting new patients and making them feel welcome and at ease. But for some time, even before these past two weeks, your record has been very spotty on intakes."

"Uh . . . I'll pay more attention to that. I've slipped, I'll admit. But I've not been feeling all that well lately. Maybe the onset of a cold. Maybe the flu."

"I thought you said you were feeling fine . . . no complaints."

"Uh . . . well, nothing serious. A cold is not serious. Just takes a little starch out of a person."

Eileen shook her head. "It's more than a cold or even the flu, Sister. Your behavior has changed radically over the past year. It's not just morning prayers and intake interviews; it's your entire contribution to this hospital. You're not pulling your weight. And that's not like you.

170

Not like you at all. Over all the years we've been together, you've always faithfully performed all your duties. You are one of the few people whose work I've never had to be concerned about. Till now.''

Rosamunda studied her hands folded in her lap. Still there was no discernible expression on her face. Perhaps just a slight twitching at the corners of her mouth. ''It's not as easy anymore. You'll get there in due time. There comes a time when all the easy things get hard.

''But,'' she raised her head, ''I will do better. Just give me another chance. I'll be faithful to the morning prayers. And I'll do the intake interviews.''

''Sister . . . oh, Sister, don't do this to yourself. You are not the type who would neglect your duty through any fault of your own. If you could help it, you would. If it were physically possible for you, you would be doing your job. If you could still do your job, I would not be having this meeting with you or telling you the things I must say.''

''I can do it.''

''No, you can't.''

For the first time, Rosamunda met Eileen's eyes. Prescinding from humor or amusement, this was the first time Eileen had ever seen a clear emotion etched on the old nun's face. It was a barely controlled panic.

''Don't put me away.'' Rosamunda made it sound as if she were a candidate for euthanasia. ''I have so little time left. I want to spend my last days at St. Vincent's. I've never asked for anything before. I've always done what the Church—what our order—has directed. This is the first favor I've ever asked of a superior.'' Pause. ''Please.''

''You know you're making this much more difficult than it should be. The de Paul Center is a very nice place. Some of your contemporaries are out there. It's a beautiful setting. You can relax. There are no pressing duties. You won't have to greet newcomers. Life is leisurely. You won't have to get up early for morning prayers. You can rise pretty much when you feel like it.

"Sister, that is the life for you now. Your body and your spirit want it. Need it. Retirement is no disgrace. People do it all the time, routinely. You have done a magnificent job over a great number of years. You've held on longer than just about anyone else. You have a proud record. Take that umblemished record with you into a more relaxed life."

Rosamunda was rubbing her hands together as if she were working out a reluctant stain.

"Why can't you understand how desperate I am to stay active until the end? What must I do to stay here? What do I have to promise?"

"Go now, Rosamunda. Go now while there is still time."

"Time? What are you saying?"

"Sister, did you ruin those curtain hooks?"

"What? You must be joking. Why would I do a thing like that?"

"Because you were not yourself, perhaps. Because you were not in full possession of your faculties?"

"How can you say that? This is impertinence. You have no right to speak to me this way."

"I don't want to speak to you this way. You are giving me no alternative. Last night you took two more bottles of Elixir Terpin Hydrate from the pharmacy."

"I did what?"

"The pharmacist has been keeping track of them over the past few weeks. Recently, he became aware of a gradual loss of Elixirs. So he started keeping special track. They've been disappearing by twos and threes. And the other day, the pharmacist happened to see you take a couple. Did you become intoxicated and cut up the curtain hooks? Can you even remember what you did last night?"

"This is humiliating."

"I know it is. I wanted to avoid this."

"I only take a little. It helps me get to sleep."

"Sister, you're an alcoholic. You need help. You can get it at the Center, in retirement."

"An alcoholic! That's insulting! I just need a little help getting to sleep."

"No, you need 'help' all day long. That's why we changed the combination on the sacristy safe. We knew you were using the Mass wine all day long. It's very possible the Elixir is the reason you can't get up in time for morning prayers."

"How can you say such a thing? Why you've got a bottle of Terpin Hydrate right there on your shelf. What makes you so different from anyone else?"

"Sister, Terpin Hydrate is a medication. It is one thing to use it as medicine and quite another to become intoxicated by it."

Rosamunda seemed close to tears. Yet she continued to suppress any emotional demonstration. Eileen wished to God the old nun would—could—just once dissolve and be human.

"You've disgraced me, you know." Rosamunda barely whispered it.

"I'm sorry. I'm so sorry. But it doesn't have to be. What has been said here today, as far as I'm concerned, remains here. No one else need ever know. For my part, it simply had to be said. Sister, you are not only in need of retirement, but also in need of help with your . . . dependency. It has to be. It has to be. . . ."

Rosamunda appeared to have gotten a grip on herself. "How long do I have?" she murmured.

"I thought the end of this month." Eileen tried to sound positive and encouraging. "February is a good time to get out of the city, anyway. You'll be going to the Center at the very best time of the year. Nothing will be happening here except the snow will continue to fall and the ruts will get deeper. At the Center, you'll be able to renew acquaintances with so many of your friends. They have common prayer, you know. You'll be able to recite the Holy Office in common. And the Rosary. You're going to like it. I know.''

Eileen sensed that Rosamunda had tuned out and that these words were lost and wasted. She dismissed the older nun. As she did so, Eileen offered a brief silent prayer that Rosamunda would be able to reconcile herself to what had to be.

Eileen could not bring herself to say it, but the matter was no longer in her power in any case. For once, she had been overruled by the Provincial Council, which, after a long and sometimes almost acrimonious exchange, had ordered Rosamunda's retirement. And the Council did not even know about her chemical dependency. That would be a problem routinely dealt with once retirement had begun.

Eileen did not want Rosamunda to enter retirement bitter at her religious order to which she had devoted so many years. Bitterness directed at the order was likely to be renewed daily. Resentment directed at Eileen could be forgotten once Rosamunda had left the hospital scene. It would be better this way for all concerned.

It was, of course, depressing that Rosamunda would depart feeling animosity toward her. But, all things considered, it seemed the better course.

Rosamunda went directly to her room. She knelt at the prie-dieu before the small statue of Mary, the mother of God. But she wasn't thinking of statues or saints or God. She could think of nothing save the extinction of her final hope. She felt desolate. Beyond even the power of prayer.

And yet, it was not that she hadn't seen it coming. Eileen's attitude had changed markedly over the past several months. Rosamunda had known something was up. In fact, had known exactly what was up. She simply had not let herself admit it.

Now there was no hope. Her greatest fear would be realized. She would be put out to pasture with all those other nuns who were now of no value to anyone.

This is how one—at least one of her vintage—came to perceive oneself in religious life: One was of value in direct proportion to one's usefulness to the community. In the old days, no one had retired merely because of old age. Sickness, some sort of debilitating illness, was the only reason one was put on the shelf.

This was how she had been trained. This had been her attitude throughout her religious life. She was of value as long as she was of use.

Now she would be of no use and of no value.

She had fought it with every strength of her being. But to no avail. She was doomed to retirement in less than a month.

There was no avoiding it now. Not as long as Eileen was there.

The thought had crossed her mind before. Usually accompanied by a splitting headache and to be prayed away. But it was true: The force that was sending her into hated retirement was no more nor less than Sister Eileen.

What would happen if—but no, that was unthinkable! Or was it?

"It was kind of you to meet me, Inspector."

"Not at all, Father. We cannot have you working in downtown Detroit without our getting together occasionally."

Inspector Walter Koznicki headed the homicide division of the Detroit Police Department. Years ago, coincidence had brought Father Koesler and Inspector Koznicki together. As the police unraveled a series of killings that had become known in the media as "The Rosary Murders," Koesler had been helpful in the crime's solution. Since then, coincidence again had drawn the priest into the investigation of other murders with some regularity. And over these years, Koznicki and Koesler had become fast friends.

At Koesler's invitation, they had met and were dining in St. Vincent's cafeteria.

"Sorry about the ambience," Koesler said. "Not even any wine."

"Father, we cannot continue eating at the London Chop House every evening." A private joke; neither of them could afford to eat at that restaurant, among Detroit's most expensive. "This is good for the pocketbook if not the digestion."

Briefly, as they picked at their salads, Koesler explained his substitute status at the hospital.

As they conversed, they became the center of attention. This was entirely due to Koznicki's presence. Not that he was a celebrity; he shunned publicity. It was his size. He was a larger person in actuality as well as in bearing, creating the impression of being larger than life.

"So, Father, you are learning something new after all these years in the priesthood?"

"Well, yes. In a way. Ministering to the ill on a day-to-day basis is a lot different from visiting with them only occasionally as one does in a parish. Some of the clichés have to fall by the wayside when the person you're visiting is no better today than he was yesterday—maybe worse. It's different, it's rewarding . . . but it has also been draining. I don't know how people are able to do this as a career. But my hat's off to them."

"This is indeed a most important apostolate—to the sick."

176

"That's right. You don't see very many ill people, do you, Inspector? They're usually dead."

Koznicki smiled. "A bit of an oversimplification, Father. But, yes, most of my 'clients' are either dead or they are suspects. On the other hand, not all of your clients recover. Death plays a significant part in your work here too."

"You may not know the half of it, Inspector. Here, nobody dies alone."

"How is that?"

"If a chaplain is not with the patient when he or she dies, the chaplain will be along in a minute to try to comfort the survivors."

"I was not aware of that. At each death a chaplain is required?"

"Yes. It reminds me of what in effect is a second-class monsignor. It's been so long since we had a new monsignor named in the Archdiocese of Detroit that I'm not sure what the protocol is now. But there used to be two ranks. One had the title for life and was called a Right Reverend Monsignor. The other was a Very Reverend Monsignor and remained a monsignor only as long as the contemporary Pope lived. When the Pope died, the Very Reverend Monsignor ceased being a prelate. They used to call them shirttail monsignors. I was never clear whether the sobriquet came from the type of their ecclesiastical garb or because they were, in effect, hanging on to the Pope's shirttail.

"In any case, a bunch of us always thought it was rather consoling that no Pope ever died alone. As he drew his last breath, a whole bunch of prelates around the world were ceasing to be monsignors.

"And so it is in the hospital. Nobody dies alone. Always, in the wings at least, there's a chaplain."

"Leave it to you, Father, to find an ecclesiastical analogy for just about everything." Koznicki chuckled. "As a matter of fact, the chaplain is not the only nonmedical person who may be found with the dead and dying at this hospital."

"Oh?"

"I have no way of knowing whether you have noticed it, but frequently there will be a police officer present."

Koesler scratched his head. "Now that you mention it . . ."

"Some of our investigations begin right here in the hospital. In the emergency room."

"Of course they would. A fatal knifing or shooting would end up as a homicide investigation. As a matter of fact, we almost had one for you the other night."

"You mean one of the staff?"

"The Chief Executive Officer."

"Sister Eileen? What happened?"

Koesler recounted the story of the patient's attack on Eileen. "Of course no one was seriously hurt and since the assailant was a mental patient, the hospital handled it internally and the police weren't called. But if it hadn't been for that alert guard, Sister might have been seriously hurt or even killed."

"Any place these days can be dangerous," Koznicki commented. "But a hospital with its mental patients, and many other patients disoriented, has always been a dangerous place to one degree or another. It was fortunate for Sister Eileen that, as you say, the guard was alert. To be perfectly frank, Father, it surprises me more than somewhat that the security guard was that effectual. At least judging by its reputation, the security service at this hospital is not all that reliable."

"That's not very encouraging. Especially since I have the feeling that Sister Eileen may indeed be in some danger. And not just from unbalanced patients."

178

"Why do you say that, Father?"

"Actually, I shouldn't say anything. There is no hard evidence that something's wrong. It's just a feeling. Don't pay any attention to me, Inspector."

But Inspector Koznicki had far too much respect for Father Koesler's intuition to discount a matter about which the priest felt strongly. "No, Father, go on. Tell me what you think may be happening."

"Well, that's just it: Nothing is happening. It's just that I can't get rid of this feeling something is about to happen. It's like a dormant volcano that is rumbling: It may erupt; it may not."

"It has to do with Sister Eileen?"

"Well, yes. From some things I've been told and from what I've observed, there are a few people on this staff—I really have no idea how many—whose positions would be vastly improved if either this hospital closed or something happened to Eileen. Or both, since Eileen and St. Vincent's seem to be, in some sense, synonymous."

"Who might these people be, Father?"

"This is just between the two of us?"

"Of course."

"There's a Korean doctor, Lee Kim, who apparently has been playing fast and loose with hospital policy. Eileen has threatened to dismiss him from the staff. That seems to be kind of imminent. Evidently a dismissal from this institution would cripple his medical career. For the hospital to close, or for something to happen to Sister Eileen before any action were taken in his case, would be extremely helpful to him, to say the least.

"Then there's John Haroldson, the chief operating officer. He's at the age of compulsory retirement. And, while Eileen could waive that requirement, reportedly she will not do so. Haroldson lives for this place. But if Sister Eileen remains here for the foreseeable future, he'll be gone.

"And Sister Rosamunda. She is well beyond retirement age. She's still here because Eileen has waived the requirement in her case. But according to today's scuttlebutt, Eileen will do so no more. Something to do with Rosamunda's waning efficiency and also a bit of a drinking problem. Rosie, as nearly everybody calls her, is terrified of being tucked away in some home for ancient nuns. But if Eileen is still here and healthy at the end of this month, Sister Rosamunda will be forced into retirement.

"On top of that, rumor has it that some nurse's aide is going to be canned if she happens to break just one more thing in this hospital. And the poor girl apparently can't put on her shoes without breaking a lace. I mention her not as a particularly strong suspect—for what? . . . nothing's happened yet—but just to indicate the underlying threat of something that might befall Sister Eileen.

"And finally, there is Dr. Fred Scott, who has been a source for much of what I've just told you. He seems to be the 'good guy' in this drama. But I've never been completely comfortable with his having taken me into his confidence so completely and so soon after my arrival here. It's sort of a case of Dr. Scott's having protested too much.

"And there you have it, Inspector—for what it's worth. And it isn't worth very much. Sort of a scenario without a play. Or a murder without either a crime or a corpus delicti."

The Inspector did not reply immediately. When he did, he spoke slowly as if choosing his words carefully. "May I suggest, Father, that perhaps our past professional association—your involvement in some, shall we say 'lurid' murder investigations—has sensitized your perception to a degree where you have come to see a prospective homicide around every corner?"

Recognizing from the priest's expression that his friend

was not all that happy with his analysis, the Inspector hastened to add, "Nevertheless, it is good that you are aware of these possibilities. Sometimes merely the awareness of possible danger helps to avert it." He grew reflective. "All too often when a homicide does occur, friends, relatives, and acquaintances of those involved profess astonishment, with comments along the line of, 'I never would have dreamed . . .' Or they express amazement at what they consider the tenuousness of the killer's motivation." He shook his head. "One can never gauge the extremes to which a fellow human may be driven by what the rest of us would dismiss as a mere pinprick."

He smiled reassuringly. "If nothing else, Father, yours is an interesting conjecture. But," he added seriously, "it is quite possible, even probable, is it not, that all these things may happen—doctor dismissed, aide fired, elder couple retired—without any harm coming to either Sister Eileen or the hospital?"

"Perfectly possible, even probable," Koesler replied. He shook his head ruefully. "You're right of course. And I must say I feel more at ease just for having expressed my fears to you. This must work as confession sometimes does. The talking cure. Just saying it out loud, telling someone, takes a good deal of the onus from what's been bothering one.

"So, Inspector, I don't know whether anyone in this hospital is any safer for my telling you my concerns, but I feel better." Koesler laughed selfconsciously.

Koznicki joined in the laughter. "Well, then, Father, the evening has not been a total waste."

"I'll just get us some coffee and I'll shut up so you can tell me what's going on in your interesting life. We can drink a toast to the prospect of your not being called in here on any official business in the foreseeable future."

"Father, gladly will I drink to that."

Bruce Whitaker was surprised to find that the tacky marquee of the Back Porch Theatre announced a change in the bill of fare. *The Manic Sperm* had enjoyed one of the briefer runs in show-biz history. After less than a week, *The Manic Sperm* had been mothballed in favor of a new and equally experimental production of an original drama entitled, *The Roamin' Ovum*.

En route to his attic room, Bruce halted at the rear of the tiny theater. He could not see clearly through the dark and smoke, but there seemed to be no more than the usual handful of patrons, some noisily taunting the actors, who, between tying to remember their lines and their cues, returned the ridicule.

In the brief time Whitaker watched the performance, he had a devilish time trying to make some sense of what was going on. It appeared to be a two-character play. At least there were but two people on stage and no indication anyone else either had preceded or would follow them. He was unable to tell whether the actors were men, women, or one of each. Both had very long hair, both wore bulky and indiscriminate costumes, and both yelled so much their voices were hoarse.

The plot, as near as Whitaker could define it, seemed to be a contest of shouted insults and imprecations. If there was anything else of substance to the plot, it was the posed question of who was more important in lovemaking, the male or female. Or, as the actors themselves put it: Who had more fun, the sperm or the ovum? At this point, their clothing dropped to the floor rather astonishingly quickly. Thus selving one puzzle: It was a man and a woman onstage.

In no time at all, the woman clutched herself into a fetal position and began to roll toward the male. That, Whitaker reasoned, must be whence the play's title, *The Roamin' Ovum*, had originated. Though he had seen neither play from start to finish, it seemed to Bruce that there were great similarities between *The Manic Sperm* and *The Roamin' Ovum*. Now that he thought of it, the playwright's name on the billboard out front had seemed familiar. The same author had written both plays. Apparently the playwright's talent was limited to one thought. And that not a very advanced one.

Whitaker did not wait to learn whether the sperm or the egg had more fun. He didn't care. Besides, he was very depressed over those damned curtain hooks.

He continued up to his attic room, an extremely appropriate place in which to feel depressed.

If all this were not enough, after the performance of *The Roamin' Ovum*, Whitaker's landlord, who had portrayed the Sperm in the theater's previous and current productions, stormed up to the attic and pounded on the door until it almost came off the one hinge that held it to the frame.

Strangely, Whitaker never could recall the landlord's name. Bruce always thought of him as "The Sperm," though he was never brazen enough to address him as such.

In any case, The Sperm upbraided Whitaker mercilessly for everything from not sweeping the theater clean enough to not attending any of the performances. This after having ordered Whitaker not to return after he walked out on one of the very few performances of *The Manic Sperm!*

Bruce felt very low.

At the core of his dejection, of course, was his failure to mutilate the IUDs, having attacked instead boxes full of curtain hooks. Added to that was his frustration, fast on the heels of his promise to her, in not having aided Ethel in her quest for scurity.

Now he faced the painful necessity of telling all this to his colleagues tomorrow.

Bruce was strongly tempted to ship the whole thing. What could they do to him if he never again visited Van's Can? They were in. He was out. If he never returned, they could do nothing till they got out. By then, his parole would be completed and he could get out of town.

This was a more pleasant thought, so he dwelt on it. Leaving town, all the bad incidents behind him. Maybe—could he dare think it?—Ethel would go with him. He was utterly devoid of any experience in this field. Ethel was the first female, with the possible exception of his mother, who had ever seemed to take a real interest in him. He did not know how to handle this. But he was eager to learn.

First, he would have to justify Ethel's faith in him. And he did have more plans. Lots more. He had been studying, asking questions, and making some personal observations. It was quite possible that one or another of these plans could do the job.

He could see it now: The first of his clever plans that worked would bring the media down on St. Vincent's Hospital like dry sponges that needed news instead of water. As soon as the glare of publicity hit the hospital, the archdiocese would be forced to take action. And that, without doubt, would push Sister Eileen out of her position in the hospital. St. Vincent's would once again be a Catholic hospital loyal to the Pope and his teaching authority. And, added boon, he would fulfill his pledge to Ethel. Sister Eileen would be removed and Ethel's job would be unthreatened.

He wondered if it would be difficult to convince her to go somewhere else with him. She would have to leave a secure job. But it would be his success that would have secured that job. Given all this, would she see that he was her security and leave with him?

God, he hoped so.

This was such a pleasant thought he decided to go to sleep dreaming about it. The whole concept gave him strength to confront his colleagues on the morrow.

✦ ✦ ✦

Joe Cox lay on his side looking out the window. A light snow was falling. From the high-rise apartment at night, the city resembled a large, self-motivated toy.

There wasn't much traffic at this hour. One could watch headlights or taillights, depending on the cars' direction. Here and there in apartments and offices soft lights illuminated late labor or the winding-down after a day's work.

Most hypnotic were the traffic lights regularly signaling nonexistent traffic to stop or go. Cox, with a quiet wish that nothing exceptional would happen this night and that the *Free Press* would not summon him to report a fast-breaking story in a slow-moving city, had almost drifted off.

"Whatcha thinkin' 'bout?"

Called back from slumber, Cox looked over his shoulder. "For a change, not a thing. I was letting the city lights put me to sleep."

"Sorry."

"It's okay." Cox rolled over on his back. He looked appreciatively at Pat.

She was propped against a couple of pillows, working a crossword puzzle. She looked as if she were ready to attend a concert rather than retire for the night. Her hair was spread alluringly over the pillow as if it had been carefully arranged. It hadn't.

She was working the puzzle with a pen.

"I swear, someday I'll see you doing a puzzle on the typewriter."

"What was a typewriter?"

185

They both chuckled. Neither was sold on the word processor. As often as possible they would hammer out their stories on typewriters before transferring them to the compulsory processor.

"How was your day? I haven't gotten around to asking." She continued to fill in squares.

"The ordinary. They're dagging out that Cobo Hall incident. As usual, they're trying to nail the mayor on this one. Some on the city council are charging that Maynard Cobb should have insisted on more police protection for that rock concert."

Lennon gratefully recalled that if she hadn't in effect assigned herself to the hospital story, she would be covering the Cobo Hall incident. "*Was* it poorly policed?"

"Not really. But who can say? The usual contingents of cops and security guards. The problem is the muggers forgot to tell the cops that it was going to be their night to howl."

"At least nobody got killed. How many injured?"

"I forget. I think about thirty or forty—two or three rapes—less than ten still hospitalized. All in all, a bad show."

Lennon reflected that the whole nasty incident had occurred less than a couple of miles from this, their apartment. The sort of affair that contributed mightily to Detroit's less-than-savory reputation. But that reputation had become a self-fulfilling prophecy. Detroit wins the World Series, and the aftermath, due to a few flare-ups, is described by the nation's media as a riot. San Francisco wins the Super Bowl and the aftermath, despite a great number of flare-ups, is termed a celebration.

"Business as usual," she said. "Everybody wants all the cops in the city at the trouble spot. Yet when there's no one to respond to a 911, all hell breaks loose. How much longer you think this story'll run?"

"A few more days. Cobb will certainly respond to the council's criticism. Then that should pretty well be that. Unless some of the injured decide to sue this city." Cox rolled back facing the window. "How's your hospital story coming?"

Absently, Lennon touched Cox's shoulder and began lightly massaging it. "Okay. The nice thing about one of these magazine pieces is that nobody's in much of a hurry to get it. Compared with the average news story they want yesterday, there's a kind of eternal air to a magazine piece."

"That nun must've been grateful when you told her you weren't going to get into the contraceptive lead."

"Uh-huh."

"Probably the nicest present she's gotten since Christmas . . . wait a minute: They've got a vow of poverty, haven't they? Kill that and write: nicest present she's gotten since she was a kid."

"Uh-huh."

Lulled by the gentle massage on his shoulder, Cox began to once more drift toward sleep.

"Funny thing, though," Lennon said, "there's something going on in that hospital."

"Huh? Sure, sick people get better or they die."

"No, something to do with the nun—Sister Eileen."

"What?"

"I'm not sure. But I've got this feeling."

"Your spider-sense tingling, Spider Woman?"

Lennon chuckled. "No, seriously. Like when she took me to the cafeteria for lunch. She introduced me to some of the staff—by the way, I didn't tell you: Father Koesler is filling in for the regular hospital chaplain."

"Koesler . . . Koesler . . . where have I heard that name?"

"Friend of Walt Koznicki. We've covered him a few times in some homicide cases. Don't you remember?"

"Oh, yeah . . . chaplain to the homicide department."

"He is not."

"I know. It's my mnemonic for him."

"It doesn't work very well: You forgot him."

"Then I remembered him again. What about the staff you met?"

"Well . . ." Lennon set aside her puzzle and pen on the nightstand. ". . . it was in the atmosphere when we sat down to eat with them. Very stilted."

"What do you expect? You were the new guy on the block. Having you sit in killed their normal conversation."

"No, I expected that. It was something more. And if I'm right, it wasn't directed at me; it was aimed at the nun."

"So? Deference to a superior."

"You're not getting the drift, Joe. Please hear me out."

"Okay." Cox pulled the quilt up. This would have to be a pretty interesting story or he would soon be asleep.

"There was an air of hostility toward the nun. It was palpable. It was coming from several people. I don't know what they've got against her, but I'm going to find out."

"You're serious. You really think there's something going on?"

"Yeah. It's a physical thing. Like someone is out to get her."

"Get her? You mean harm her?"

"I think so."

"Okay. But if something like that should happen, it's open season on this story."

"I know."

"You know Nelson Kane—you should, you worked for him long enough. You know how he salivates when somebody comes up with a crying statue or the figure of Christ in a burning chicken coop. He is just not the type of city editor to overlook a hospital nun under attack."

"Nelson Ka—you didn't tell Nellie about the contraceptive angle of this story!"

"Of course I didn't. He'd have my ass in a sling if he knew about our nonaggression pact. Matter of fact, I think he kind of suspects. But if he knew for sure . . . wow!"

"Well, anyway, at the moment, it's just a feeling. I'll have to check it out. There may be nothing there."

"Backing away, are you? Just remember: If you come up with an injured or dead nun . . ."

"Heaven forbid."

"Okay, heaven forbid. But if you do, then it's open warfare, no holds barred."

"Joe, you wild and crazy guy, you never get it straight, do you?"

"Huh?"

"It's not when making war, it's when making love that there's no holds barred."

"I lie corrected."

Lennon smiled, turned off the lights, and slid beneath the quilt and Cox.

8

"YOU DID WHAT!"

"Easy!" the First Man cautioned. "You'll attract the guard."

"You did what?" the Third Man repeated, more quietly but just as furiously.

"We all heard him," the Fourth Man said. "He said he made a mistake. What kind of mistake, Bruce?"

"An honest mistake," Whitaker replied.

"What mistake?" the Third Man said through clenched teeth. "What the hell did you do, you idiot?"

"Now, now, there's no need to drop lugs on poor Bruce," the Fourth Man tempered. He turned to Whitaker. "Tell us what you did, Bruce."

"Well, I made a mistake . . . uh . . . instead of altering IUDs, it turns out I mutilated several boxes of curtain hooks."

"You what!" all three exclaimed simultaneously.

"Hey, what's goin' on here, anyway?" A burly guard rapped his knuckles on their table. "You wanna hold it down, or what? You get loud like that again and this visit's over. You'll get outta here, Whitaker. And the three of you'll go down with a recommend that y'll be put in the box and forgot. Do I make myself perfectly clear?''

"Perfectly clear, Captain," the Fourth Man said.

"Okay, then." The guard walked away and resumed his post against the wall not far from their table.

"Bruce," the Fourth Man said, "do I understand you to say that you mistook curtain hooks for IUDs? How in God's name did you do that?" His knuckles were white from gripping the table's edge.

"It was an honest mistake—"

"It was a stupid mistake."

"Honest."

"Stupid!" the Third Man insisted. "Incredibly, supremely, unforgivably stupid! IUDs look nothing like curtain hooks!"

"How was I to know? I've never seen an IUD. Besides, I'll bet these curtain hooks look like an IUD. They were S-shaped and made of strong metal."

"That doesn't make any difference. They were curtain hooks! Goddam curtain hooks!"

"Watch your language," the First Man cautioned.

"And," Whitaker continued, "they were in the drawer reserved for IUDs."

"That's different," the Fourth Man said. "That provides a logical explanation for why you might have confused them. Why didn't you tell us this in the beginning?"

"You didn't give me a chance. You jumped all over me when I told you I made an honest mistake. Now do you see how honest that mistake really was?"

"All right," the Fourth Man said in a conciliatory tone. "Tell us what happened so we'll be better able to plan for the future."

Whitaker began recounting the events of the night on

191

which he successfully attacked the curtain hooks. He reached the point where he was almost detected by the guard.

"You mean you were seen! You could be identified?" the First Man challenged.

"Well, no, not really. At that point something else happened."

"What?"

Whitaker's face broke into a beatific smile. "A miracle."

"A miracle!"

"A miracle. Remember that nurse's aide I told you about? Well, she helped me. She happened to be in the hospital at the same time. She saw me sort of sneaking down the main floor corridor and she noticed the guard was about to intercept me . . . and she . . . uh . . . intervened."

"Intervened?"

"She said she . . . distracted him."

"How?"

"I don't know. It doesn't matter. However she did it, she saved me from being discovered. That's the important part. Not how she did it."

"I don't like it," the Third Man said.

"Why not? Did you want me to get caught?"

"Frankly, I'm beginning to care less and less whether you get caught. Probably the worst that could happen is that you'd be thrown back in here, or DeHoCo, or Jacktown. I'm worried about *us*. We've only got a bit left. I don't want 'all day' time added to what we've got. Or to have to go back to Jacktown."

"What does Ethel have to do with all this?" Whitaker was getting defensive.

"Oh, it's *Ethel*, is it?" the Third Man said. "All right then, Ethel. I don't like the fact that she just 'happened' to be at the same place at the same time as you were when you were carrying out our mission. Or trying to carry it out. And I don't like that she knew you were sneaking around at night. And I don't like that she got involved. Just how much does she know about you? About us?''

"Okay, she doesn't know anything at all about you, about us. And she knows next to nothing about me. We've just eaten together a few times and went on a date. But she doesn't know anything about us or our mission.''

"Are you sure?'' the Fourth Man asked.

"Absolutely.''

"So you went on a date,'' the First Man said.

"You as much as told me to. You told me to get acquainted with her. And I did. And I have.''

"All right,'' the Fourth Man said. "But be careful. It's vitally important that she doesn't find out about us or our mission.''

Everyone nodded agreement.

The Fourth Man continued. "How about the rest of the people at the hospital? Do they know about the curtain hooks?''

"Yes.''

"Have they associated them with you?''

"No. They think it was a manufacturer's error.''

"All right, then,'' the Fourth Man said. "What happened after your friend . . . uh . . . distracted the guard?''

"Then the way was clear to the clinic—wait . . . no; I almost forgot the old nun.''

"The old nun?''

"Sister Rosamunda. She was sneaking along the hallway ahead of me.''

"What is this, a Mack Sennett comedy?''

"No. She went into the clinic ahead of me. Then I went in and was able to see what she was doing. But she never saw me. Do you know what she did?''

He had their attention.

"She took some bottles out of a cabinet after she unlocked it."

"She stole!" the First Man exclaimed. "An old nun stole! Is nothing sacred? What was it? Did you get a chance to check it out—Lourdes Water or something like that?"

"It was Terpin Hydrate Elixir . . . whatever that is."

"Whatever that is!" the Third Man exclaimed. "What did you do with your time in here anyway? They call that GI Gin. It's potent. Got lots of codeine in it. And alcohol. A few slugs of that and you're out. Either that nun has got one hell of a cold or she's bending the old elbow."

"You mean she's an alcoholic! An alcoholic old nun! Nothing is sacred," said the First Man.

"She has to be," the Third Man affirmed. "She's not picking up GI Gin with a prescription. She's stealing it. She's a lush. Just an old religious lush."

"Very interesting," the Fourth Man observed. "We'll have to keep that in mind. It may help us somehow. You never can tell. All right, then, after the nun, you made your . . . honest mistake. And that was all there was to it? There was no further incident?"

"None."

"All right, then. What we have is a failure . . . albeit an honest mistake. But no other harm done. We can go on from here."

"What about that newspaperwoman?" the First Man asked. "The one you said came to do the story on St. Vincent's?"

"I can't figure that out at all. I went out of my way to personally make sure she saw the clinic. And she did see it. And she saw the evil things that are going on there. And I know that she knew they shouldn't be going on in a Catholic hospital. And because it's such a little hospital and rumors get around pretty quickly, I know that she had a couple of meetings with Sister Eileen. But nothing came of it."

"Nothing?"

"Nothing. Well, not so far, anyway. It's probably too soon to tell for sure . . . but she was back the next day having lunch with the staff as if nothing had happened. I don't know why, but it looks to me as if she isn't going to do an investigative story on the clinic after all. Maybe Sister Eileen talked her out of it . . . although that seems hard to believe. But whatever the reason, it just doesn't seem that she's going to follow up on that situation."

"Unless we force the issue," the Fourth Man said pensively. "I've been spending some time in the library. They've got a good collection of old newspapers from around the country. I've been looking through them for hospital stories. You don't have to look far. The papers are running stories all the time about things going wrong in hospitals. If you put all these stories together, why, hospitals are simply filled with accidents."

"Something like ourselves," the First Man admitted.

"Speak for yourself, Rumdum," the Third Man said.

"Now, now," the Fourth Man cautioned, "let's not have any falling out. We've got to be united to be effective."

"Yes, you're right. It's like what I saw in the emergency room the other day. A man was brought in unconscious. They almost sent him up for X-rays. But at the last second, one doctor decided to give him some test. Then they gave him some medicine and he recovered. Like almost immediately. It was like a miracle. And if they'd sent him up for the X-rays, he would have died. Is that your idea?"

"Yes. The idea is that newspapers—and magazines, for that matter—feature prominently the mistakes, blunders, and accidents that happen in hospitals. They happen all the time. But even though there are many, many accidents, there are never too many, it seems, for the media to overlook.''

''I think I understand,'' the First Man said. ''Sometimes so many instances of a normally noteworthy occurrence take place that the news media tend to overlook the latest happening. Like there are so many murders in a city like Detroit or New York or Chicago, that not all of them get big headlines or are even reported. Whereas, when a murder occurs in someplace like Kalamazoo, that gets a lot of notoriety there.''

''That's it,'' the Fourth Man chimed in. ''But somehow, for some reason, when major blunders happen in hospitals, they always seem to get well publicized. I guess it's because on the one hand, you come to expect a certain level of violence in a big city. But hospitals are supposed to be places where, even if cures can't be worked all the time, at least you expect good care to be taken of the patients. So when the wrong fluid is injected in a spinal column or the wrong kind of anesthetic is used and the patient ends up as a vegetable, crippled, or dead, that's big news as far as the media are concerned.''

''Sort of like when a dog bites a man as opposed to when a man bites a dog,'' Whitaker added. ''But what has this to do with where we are now in our project?''

''Only to put it in perspective,'' the Fourth Man said. ''We had a good plan and we still have a good plan. All right, so we suffered a minor setback when somebody put the wrong thing in the right drawer. And so the lady reporter at St. Vincent's, for whatever her reason, seems to be avoiding a story that's right there in front of her. It's still a good plan. If we can make something happen at that hospital that is newsworthy, somebody in the media is going to pick it up and use it. And all we need to do is get one segment of the media to use it prominently and all the rest of the media will jump on board.

"Once we do that, the spotlight of investigation and publicity will be on St. Vincent's and the evil that's going on there will be exposed. Then the archdiocese will be forced to act. And then we will have achieved our mission.

"Now, what do you say? Let's get back in this and see what we can do. Any suggestions?"

"Well, yes," Whitaker said. "I have a few ideas. I've been reading up on this. But mostly I've been trying to overhear some of the doctors when they are talking over some of their problems. And from all this, I have a few ideas, one of which I'd like to try next. Want to hear it?"

"Yes, yes, of course." The Fourth Man was enthusiastic. Among other goals, he hoped to infuse his colleagues with a new sense of confidence.

"Would anyone like something to eat?" the First Man inquired.

"What!" the Third Man exclaimed. "You didn't do it again! Tell me you didn't do it again!"

"It's just a slice of baloney." The First Man removed his right hand from his trouser pocket. Clutched in his fist was what at one time had been a thick slice of baloney. It now resembled modeling clay squeezed into the shape of inverted brass knuckles. Also, it was beginning to lose much of its savory piquancy and take on the stench of sweaty prison clothing.

"God! How can you do that to food?" the Third Man demanded.

"Where did you get that?" the Fourth Man asked.

"The chow cart. There's never enough to keep from getting hungry between meals."

"You idiot!" the Third Man exclaimed. "We've got to get rid of that somehow. You try eating that and the guard will be on you in a minute. And the way it's beginning to smell, we're not going to keep it a secret much longer. You stupid bastard! This is just like the goddam cheese!"

"Cheese?" Whitaker asked. "You mean the cheese you hid in the heat duct last time?"

"That's it."

"What happened? I thought you hid that good enough."

"Not quite," the First Man explained. "At first, they thought they were looking for a dead animal. Then they found the cheese. I guess they knew it didn't get in the heat duct all by itself. So they looked some more."

"And it wasn't all that difficult an investigation," the Third Man continued. "Dumdum here couldn't get the odor out of his armpit."

"So," the First Man said, "they knew we had been sitting together in here. So they took good time away from all three of us."

"And now," the Third Man said, "this idiot comes in with a putrid piece of baloney. So what the hell are we going to do?"

"I'll take it," Whitaker volunteered. "I'll be leaving in a few minutes. They won't check me on the way out. I'll get it out of here."

"I hate to say this," the Third Man said, "but I guess we owe you one."

Keeping an eye on the guard, who had wandered slightly further away, and assisted by Whitaker, the First Man pried the baloney out of his fist. Whitaker then plunged the gook into his pocket without being discovered.

"Now, then, what is it you have in mind?" the Fourth Man asked.

"Okay." He was eager to explain his plan. "Get close."

The four huddled. Noting this, the guard returned to his vantage near their table.

After several minutes, the Third Man fairly shouted, "You're going to do *what?* That's insane!"

His outburst activated the guard, who strode to their table. "Okay, okay, okay, that's it. I told you no commotion, no commotion! Now break it up! Break it up! Let's go! This visit's over! Move it! Move it! Move it!''

They had no alternative. The three, still muttering, were herded to their cells while Bruce Whitaker and his contraband baloney returned to the streets, confident of his plan despite the incredulity of his colleagues.

Father Koesler studied his patient chart. It was run off each day and contained such information as the patient's name, room number, nature of illness, religion, and doctor's name. Other information was added as needed.

He noted that several patients had requested the Sacrament of Reconciliation. Odd. From his limited experience, as well as the briefing he'd received from the now-vacationing Father Thompson, he knew confession was rarely requested in this hospital. This was due partly to the fact that Catholics did not go to confession nearly as frequently as they once had, and partly to the fact that there just were not very many Catholic patients in St. Vincent's.

One of the confession requests had been penned in by a nurse's aide. The patient was on one of Sister Rosamunda's floors. Another oddity. Sister of course was not empowered to hear confessions. So when one of her patients asked for the sacrament, Sister routinely would communicate the request to the priest-chaplain. In this case, she had not.

He decided to look in on this patient first.

Alva Crawford was in Room 2214, Bed A, which meant she was near the window. Near the door was one Millie Power. Both patients were in their beds. Koesler's luck was holding; more often than not when he went to call on a patient, the bed was empty and the patient was anywhere from the bathroom to therapy to the operating room to wandering the halls.

"Hello." He approached the window bed. "Are you Mrs. Alva Crawford?" Always well to check; hospital lists were by no means infallible.

"Yes, sir, Reverend."

Odd again. If she wanted to confess she must be Catholic. But if she were Catholic, why was she calling him "Reverend"? Well, he would push on.

"Did you want to go to confession, Mrs. Crawford?"

"Uh . . . no, sir."

It was evident that the thought of confessing had not occurred to her in recent memory.

"It says on this list that you wanted to go to confession." As soon as he said it, he regretted it. He was asking her to explain something for which she had no responsibility whatever. Without waiting for her response, he continued, "Are you a Catholic, Mrs. Crawford?"

"No, Reverend, I can't say as I am."

"Ah-ha. Somebody has made a mistake." Stupid aide, he thought. Koesler glanced at Mrs. Crawford's bedstand. No sign of the familiar pink brochure given patients by the chaplains on their first visit. However, he glanced at her neighbor's bedstand and there it was, the welcoming brochure.

"Has Sister Rosamunda been in to see you, Mrs. Crawford?"

"Sister what?"

"Rosamunda," said Mrs. Power in the next bed. "No, she ain't been in for a day or so, Father."

Mrs. Crawford seemed thoroughly confused.

"Here . . ." Koesler took one of the brochures from his jacket pocket and handed it to her. "You can read this later, Mrs. Crawford. It explains a little bit about what we in pastoral care are up to. We aren't so much interested in your liver or gall bladder as just in you. We want to help any way we can. We'll be eager to be with you, to pray with you, or just talk, or just be with you. You'll also find some prayers on the back and inside of that brochure . . . see?" He took another brochure from his pocket and indicated the prayers. "There: *Morning Prayer, Evening Prayer, For This Hospital, For Doctors and Nurses, and Their Assistants*"—stupid ones as well, Koesler added silently. *"For Healing, For Relief From My Sickness, In Time of Distress, In Time of Discouragement, In Time of Great Suffering, Before an Operation—"*

"That's it."

"That's what?"

"A operation. I'm gonna have a operation."

"You are? When?"

"Tomorrow morning."

"Oh, my."

"I gotta swallow a tube."

"You have to what?"

"Swallow a tube. I don't like that much at all." She stroked her throat in anticipation of swallowing some foreign substance.

"I told you before it ain't so bad," Mrs. Power said. "You just go in there and do what they tell you. You ain't gonna have no trouble. You just do what they tell you and relax."

"I don't jes' know." Mrs. Crawford continued to stroke her throat. Her eyes showed there was real fear in her heart.

"I told you, child," Mrs. Power said, "you gonna be okay. You got Doctor Jesus with you!"

That stopped Koesler cold. He was unaware of a Dr. Jesus on staff. Then it occurred to him that the "doctor" was an outgrowth of Mrs. Power's beautiful faith. He consulted the patient chart once more and found Mrs.

Millie Power. She too was not a Catholic. While admitting he could easily be mistaken, Koesler supposed the average Catholic would not be on familiar enough terms with the Lord to call Him "Doctor Jesus." Too bad; Mrs. Power's was a touching faith.

"Says here on the chart, Mrs. Power," Koesler said, "that you've got pneumonia. That right?"

"That be right."

"How do you feel?"

"Some better. Some better. Coulda been lots worse though."

"How so?"

"Doctor was gonna put me in some kind of test group or somethin'. But just at the last moment, I 'membered I'm allergic to penicillin. So I ain't in the test. See: Doctor Jesus was with me." She nodded confidently.

"I'm sure He is. Well, Mrs. Crawford, since you're going for an operation tomorrow, either Sister Rosamunda or I will call on you tonight. Somebody from pastoral care always calls on a patient before an operation. It's nothing to worry about or to be concerned about. We just like to make sure that somebody's with you the night before surgery. Just to talk, maybe pray."

Before leaving the room, Koesler assured Mrs. Power he would also return to visit with her.

Outside the room he paused to think this through. When he'd agreed to be a substitute chaplain, he had not anticipated any problem such as this. But here it was. Sister Rosamunda was not doing her job. Probably was not her fault. But disregarding accountability, she still was not doing her job. This was Alva Crawford's second day in St. Vincent's and the nun had not yet visited. Thus in all probability, Sister was not aware that Mrs. Crawford faced surgery on the morrow. Among the duties the importance of which had been impressed upon him, high on the list was the necessity of visiting one's patient before surgery. What to do about this?

If he did nothing—by far the easier choice—it was likely the patient would be in and out of the hospital without having received the requisite visit from pastoral care. Not good, especially for a Catholic hospital.

On the other hand, what right had he, a mere substitute chaplain, to offer correction to a lady who had been in hospital work before he'd been ordained?

He checked his watch. If Sister Rosamunda's routine was on schedule, she should be just finishing up lunch now. He'd give it a try.

Sure enough, she was in the cafeteria and, fortunately, seated alone at a small table. Koesler got coffee and made his way over, greeting several employees as he went. He was pleased at the number of St. Vincent's personnel he'd become acquainted with in a relatively brief time.

"Mind if I join you, Sister?"

"Oh . . . oh." She had been deeply preoccupied. "Father Koesler. Yes, of course." She rearranged some dishes. It was no more than a welcoming gesture; there was not enough crockery on the table to cause Koesler any problem. Rosamunda, tiny and frail, ate very little. "How is your new career as hospital chaplain going?"

"Not so bad." Koesler wrapped both hands around the coffee mug. He wondered if this cafeteria ever became comfortably warm. "It kind of wears on you, though. I mean, this unremitting dealing with the sick and dying. I can see how you could burn out in this work."

"Oh, it's not as bad as all that. You get used to it. If you didn't, I'd have been in the loony bin long ago, *in nomine Domini*. Part of the saving grace is that far more often than not, the patients are happy to see you. After all, you're not going to plug another tube in them or take any more blood from them. If for no other reason, you are a pretty welcome sight. You just haven't given yourseif enough time.''

"Time. That's what you've given. Lots of time in hospitals. Lots of time in this hospital.''

"Lordy, yes.'' The hint of a smile crossed her face.

"The memories you must have!''

"The memories. Oh, yes, the memories. Funny thing, as the years go by, the memories of the distant past grow clearer. But I have some trouble remembering what happened yesterday.''

"Tell me some of them, Sister.''

"Oh, they're not all that interesting.''

"Try me.'' Koesler genuinely loved stories of the past from those who had lived them.

"Silly. Well, I remember all the way back to my first day on the job. I was only a novice then. Hadn't been in the convent little more than a year. But they put you to work in a jiffy back then.

"Well, I was assigned to give baths. And I tell you, the only thing that got me out on the floor with a basin and cloth was the vow of holy obedience. Lordy, I was embarrassed! I'd never seen an unclothed man before, let alone touched one. And, as it happened, my first patient was a hirsute creature, a bear of a man. He had hair on his chest like a shag rug.

"Well, I can't tell you how nervous I was. The only way I could get through it was to concentrate on not spilling the water basin. But in the process, I put so much soap on the poor man's chest that it got all matted in his hair. And this was long before there was a water faucet in each room. I had to go all the way down the hallway to get water. I think I spent most of that day getting water and coming back to try and get the soap out of his chest hair.''

Koesler was laughing.

"I suppose the only good thing to come out of that, as

far as me and my innocence were concerned, was that I never got beyond the man's chest."

"That was nice of God to protect your modesty." Koesler smiled. "More."

"I think about this sort of thing from time to time. But you know, most of the things we find funny now were not at all funny when they happened. For instance, I recall a time when the nurses had to provide most of the equipment they used. Very little of it was supplied by the hospital."

"I didn't know that. That must have been a terrible burden for the nurses. They don't make all that much even now. They must have made considerably less years ago. And then to have to buy equipment!"

"Yes. And—you may find this hard to believe—but back in those days most of the nurses used to sharpen their hypodermic needles by scraping them across the ternazzo floor."

Koesler winced as he smlled. "Nothing like giving the patients something genuine to complain about."

"As I was saying, it sounds odd and a bit humorous now. But back then it was pretty grim. Dreadful for the nurses and frightful for the patients. But the poor girls simply were unable to buy new needles all the time."

"And now in this plastic age, most everything is used once and then discarded." He shook his head. "Tell me some more."

"Oh, you've got better things to do than listen to an old biddy tell stories about long ago."

"I will never have anything more important to do."

"Well, I do remember a time—and not all that long ago—when the second floor of this building was reserved for black people. We called them Negroes then."

"Segregated! St. Vincent's was segregated?"

"Hard to believe, isn't it? But it did happen. I don't suppose there's any way to remember a time when just about everything in this country was segregated. And it all seemed right and proper. We've had the civil rights movement with us now for so many years. But that's the way it was. As far as I can remember, our black patients got the same kind of care and treatment as the whites, but they were all on the second floor.''

"Incredible."

"But true.

"Sometimes a very light-skinned black patient would be assigned to one of the other floors on admittance. We never asked people their race, you know, just looked at them. That was enough in most cases. But visitors would come. And that light-complexioned person would get a lot of dark-complexioned visitors. Then, without anyone's saying anything, the patient would be moved to the second floor.''

Koesler shook his head. "And now, it's rare to find a white patient here. Sister, you know you really ought to write these things down, get them published. The present and the future need to know the past. You could just turn your memory on and record these marvelous anecdotes for the rest of us. And for those who will follow us.''

"In nomine Domini, who's got time for that?''

"Well, you, for one. Now don't be offended, but it's no secret around here that you are more than eligible for retirement.''

Rosamunda's countenance changed swiftly and dramatically. Koesler was aware that he had skated onto thin ice.

"I just want you to know," he plunged ahead, "that I can understand your reluctance to go into retirement." He paused, hoping she would contribute something. She did not. "I'm sure you have no fear that retirement will only lead to consequent death as it does for some people. I'm sure you are not afraid of death. It isn't that, is it?''

Steely silence.

"I can remember when nuns did not retire. They died teaching school or nursing or whatever else they had been actively involved in. They didn't retire unless they were physically unable to put one foot in front of the other.

"I can also remember—and so can you—when priests didn't retire. They died giving absolution or hanging on until the end of Mass. It was a disgrace to retire." The last was said with deliberation.

It did the trick. Koesler could see the sudden spark in Rosamunda's eyes. That was it. She equated retirement with what it had been throughout most of her long career: disgrace. Was there some way he could dislodge her mental equating of retirement with disgrace? He waited to see if she would respond. Time passed. Though little more than a minute, it seemed much longer.

"Why are you doing this to me?" she said finally.

"Doing? I'm not doing anything to you, Sister. I'm trying to help you. That's all."

"It's none of your affair You have nothing to do with it. It's between me and Eileen. And that's bad enough. Eileen has all the power of the administration behind her. How can anyone expect me to fight all that and the rest of you too? It's unfair. It's just unfair!" Her lower lip trembled. It was as close as Koesler had come to seeing her break down and cry. It was about as close as anyone had come to that.

"Sister, I just called on one of your patients."

"How—" Koesler broke in before she could finish the sentence—"*dare you!*"

"It was a mistake that called me there. Some nurse's aide had noted that the patient had requested confession. So I called on her. Turned out she isn't Catholic. It also turned out that she's been here a couple of days and you haven't called on her. She's going for surgery tomorrow morning and it was even money you wouldn't be seeing her before the operation.''

"How can you . . .''

"Because it's been happening a lot lately. Others have been talking. Sister, no one wishes you any evil. Everyone here has the highest regard for you. I was just trying to help. There is no disgrace in retiring. I've suggested only one of many contributions you could make if you didn't have the pressure of this active life to weigh you down. All of us just want to help.''

"Then get out of my way. Stay out of my way. I am not going to retire. Things will be much clearer for all of you who 'just want to help' if you will only understand one simple fact: I am not going to retire!''

"Sister, as I understand it, you have no choice.''

"This is between Eileen and me. The rest of you stay out of it! Do you hear? Eileen may have the administration on her side. But I've got a tad more experience. I am not going to retire!''

She rose unsteadily and turned to leave. Abruptly, she turned back. Koesler thought it was as much to give herself time to regain her balance as it was to ask her final question. "Who is it who's going to surgery tomorrow?''

"Mrs. Alva Crawford . . . 2214-A.''

"I'll see her tonight!''

The implication clearly was that he was to stay out of her business entirely.

Koesler sipped at his lukewarm coffee. He had not anticipated the response he had triggered from Rosamunda. He shook his head sadly at the futility of it. There was no way she could stave off an inevitable retirement. She might, as she claimed, have a tad more experience. But Eileen, as her superior and with the rules on her side, held all the cards.

There was no doubting Rosamunda's determination. But

what could even that degree of determination do? How far would Rosamunda be willing to go in her battle to stay active? In her war with Eileen? As he drained the now tepid coffee, Koesler began to wonder about that. How far *would* Rosamunda go to stop Eileen? He did not like to consider the perimeter of those possibilities.

✛ ✛ ✛

Seated at another table in the refectory was Bruce Whitaker. He had carefully selected this table because it was adjacent to the table where two specific doctors were eating lunch. These doctors were select because they were conducting a study among the hospital patients. A study in which Whitaker was intensely interested.

A very recent addition to Whitaker's table was Ethel Laidlaw. This to Whitaker was the source of both positive and negative vectors. He was, of course, happy to see and be with Ethel. At the same time, it was most important that he be able to pay close attention to what these doctors were talking about. And of course Ethel would want to talk. Whitaker did not command the language to tell Ethel to be quiet. All in all, he felt, it was going to be a challenge to listen to both the doctors and Ethel.

"I've been thinking," Ethel began, "about your offer to help with my problem . . . you know, with Sister Eileen. I don't really think you have to go out of your way to help with this. I mean, there are other ways."

Ethel was holding a cup of very hot coffee near her mouth, absently blowing over its surface, attempting to cool it. But she was paying little attention to it. The cup had tipped over so slightly and the coffee began dripping ever so slowly into Ethel's lap. The old water torture with caffeine overtones.

"I think I may have a plan that would surprise you," Ethel continued. "It's just kind of hard to talk about it, especially with you. I don't understand it all that well myself. It's something that's going on in my head. Like maybe there are two persons there. One of them is the usual bonehead me. The other one seems much more clever. I guess I just don't know how to explain it very well . . . do you know what I'm talking about, Bruce?"

"What?"

Ethel began, again, to explain her conundrum, trying to find clearer language. All the while, Whitaker tried to catch the doctors' conversation.

"Are there really that many people in here with pneumonia, do you think?" said one doctor.

"Oh, yeah," said the other. "At least enough for the study. Don't need that many."

"What're you using?"

"One group gets penicillin, the other tobrimycin."

"What are the protocol numbers?"

"Ouch!" Ethel cried.

"Not now!" Whitaker warned.

"Whaddya mean, 'not now'?" Ethel almost shouted. "I burned myself with coffee. It's scalding. Look! It's been dripping in my lap. It hurts! Whaddya mean, 'not now'!"

"Sorry, Ethel." Whitaker strained to hear the doctors. Fortunately, the doctor who was to respond with the protocol numbers had taken a bite of food and was chewing. And fortunately, his social code did not countenance talking with a full mouth.

Thus, Ethel was well done complaining about the burn, the stain, and Whitaker's failure to offer solace when the doctor replied.

"Odds and evens. Odds get tobrimycin. Evens get penicillin."

"Sounds good to me. Got your ass well covered?"

"God, I hope so. We've checked out the stickers as carefully as possible."

"Check out the crew, too?"

"Yeah. Pretty good, at least for this place. There shouldn't be any slipups."

" 'samatter, you don't believe in Murphy's Law?"

"Oh, yeah, I believe in it like hell. I just think we're gonna get through this study in one piece."

"Well, good luck. Lemme know how it goes."

"Sure. Right."

The two doctors picked up their trays with the used crockery, deposited them, and left the cafeteria.

Whitaker hoped against hope that he could remember what he had just overheard. He would have a difficult enough time carrying out his plan even if he had all this information accurately recorded. It would be doomed if but one detail were incorrect.

But he would get it right this time and he would confound his colleagues back at Van's Can. They thought he couldn't do it. But with the help of Jesus, Mary, and Joseph, by God, he would!

The most crucial bit of information he had just learned was the protocol numbers. As it happened, it was the easiest to forget. He would jot the numbers on his paper napkin. And, he was pleased to submit, for this very necessity he had planned ahead. He removed a number two pencil from his breast pocket and pressed the point to the napkin. The point broke.

"Quick, Ethel, do you have a pen or a pencil?"

"What is this with a pen when I've been burned half to death?"

"Please, Ethel, I've got to write something down. It's an emergency."

"Oh, all right already." She offered him her pen. It was a fountain pen. One seldom saw such an instrument in these days of throwaway plastic ball-points.

Frequently fountain pens tend to leak. Ethel's did.

When Whitaker finished, the figures were barely legible. The rest of the napkin was saturated with blue ink.

Ethel had watched the process with interest. "Here," she said, offering her napkin. "Wipe your fingers."

He accepted her napkin and wiped vigorously. It didn't do much good. It never did, not since his days in parochial school, when, over the months, ink had gradually become the finish for his desk and chair.

"What's with that?" Ethel asked. " 'Odd tobrimycin, even penicillin' . . . what does that mean?"

"It's just a project I've got to do. It's not important."

"But you said it was an emergency."

Whitaker despaired of ever getting his hands clean with a paper napkin. He crushed it into a ball and dropped it on the table. Whence Ethel retrieved it and began dabbing at her coffee-stained white skirt, thus dying it a light blue. The blue ink dabs, together with the brown coffee stains, gave her uniform the appearance of a painful bruise.

"What was it you were saying, Ethel?"

"You should listen more careful, Bruce. It isn't like you not to listen."

"I'm sorry. I really am. But I just had to hear what those doctors were talking about."

"Whyever for?"

"It's just this project I've got. Now, please: What were you telling me?"

"Well, I was just telling you not to feel bad if you can't help me."

"If I can't help you!" Whitaker sounded offended.

"I mean with my job here and my problem with Sister Eileen."

"Oh, but Ethel, I *am* going to help you. That's why I had to pay such special attention to those doctors. They don't know it, but they're helping me help you. Help us."

"Bruce . . ." Ethel's brow was furrowed. "I don't understand you. I really don't."

"Ethel, you said that if Sister Eileen were gone from here, your job would be secure, didn't you?"

"Well, yes. It's Sister Eileen who's threatening me. If she weren't here, there'd be no one to fire me . . . far as I can see."

"Well, that's it. Just trust me and I'll get you through this."

"Gee, Bruce, I've never had anyone take care of me like you do. Not even my parents. It's a funny feeling . . . but I kind of like it."

It was a bit of a magic moment for them. They leaned closer across the table, both spilling their coffee. Fortunately, by now there was very little left to spill.

Ethel's nose wrinkled. "Bruce what is that smell?" She glanced under the table. "Did something die?"

Whitaker sniffed. He did not detect any particular odor. But then the sensory perception of smell does tend to neutralize itself over a period of time. "I don't get any smell, Ethel."

"Oh, yes, Bruce. If you don't mind me saying so, it seems to be you."

"Me?"

"You."

Whitaker sniffed again, more intently.

"I believe you may be right, Ethel." Gradually, he was remembering. He reached into his trouser pocket. It was there, all right. It blended into his hand and fingers the way the handle of a good golf club should. Very carefully he removed it, keeping it close to his side so onlookers couldn't see it. Ethel, of course could.

"Oh, my God, Bruce, what is it? Is that a fetus, Bruce? Oh, my God, Bruce, why would you carry a fetus around in your pocket? Oh, my God, Bruce, that is gross!"

213

"Quiet, Ethel. It's not a fetus." But Whitaker was studying the object as if it might be something akin to a fetus. "Ethel, do you know if penicillin can grow on baloney?"

"Baloney! Do you mean to tell me that is baloney?"

"Well, yes, as a matter of fact . . . at least it *was* baloney."

"Where in the world did you get it? And why would you carry baloney around in your pocket?" For the first time in their relationship, Ethel began to seriously wonder about Bruce. After all, she began to reason, how far can you trust someone who carries a slice of baloney around in his pants' pocket until the meat begins to grow a culture?

"Ethel, you'll just have to trust me on this. I did somebody a favor by taking this baloney. Honest. Then I forgot all about it until now. Honest, Ethel, it is just a fluke. Forgive me?"

Ethel thought about that one for a while. "Well . . . okay, I guess. But I still think this is a bit strange."

They continued to sit across from each other but the magic moment had been somewhat spoiled. Not unlike the baloney.

Ethel had to think things through once more. It was a new and wonderful feeling being protected and looked after by someone for the first time in her life. But when that someone carried dead baloney around in his pocket, the rapture becomes somewhat modified.

✦ ✦ ✦

"That is almost unbelievable: The entire riot was caused by inferior marijuana?" Inspector Walter Koznicki observed.

"Yup," Lieutenant Ned Harris replied. "One kid bought a bad joint from another kid. The trouble was the one kid was Hell's Kitchen and the other guy was Devil Drivers. And both gangs were at Cobo in force."

"So what began as a war between two gangs grew into a full-scale riot." Koznicki frowned. "It makes me wonder whether everything that goes wrong in this city is caused by drugs or dope."

"Kinda seems that way, don't it," Harris agreed. "Even muggers usually go through a pawnshop to support a habit. I guess some of the domestic disturbances are just bad blood between a couple or a triangle. But even some of them start when somebody is snorting . . . or drinking."

"What are the damages for the other night?"

Harris consulted his note pad. "Let's see . . . seventy-three injured—twelve still hospitalized—luckily no one killed."

Koznicki shook his head.

"And all over a lousy joint!" Harris added.

"Do the media have the complete story yet? Including the marijuana?"

"As far as I've been able to tell, so far only Cox of the *Free Press* has it."

Koznicki smiled. "Ah, yes, Cox of the *Free Press*."

"He got it about the same time we did, I think. So far, it's his exclusive."

"There is no reason to hold it any longer. You might as well hold a news conference. Mr. Cox will still have his scoop."

Harris was about to leave the office. He hesitated. "Is there something else, Walt? You've been sort of glum the last day or so."

Harris, tall, handsome, black, had moved through the Detroit Police Department virtually in Koznicki's shadow. Koznicki, almost ten years Harris's senior, had gone rather quickly from patrol to homicide, from sergeant to lieutenant to inspector. Harris had followed suit and everyone believed that one day he too would be an inspector. In the homicide department, Koznicki and Harris had been partners at one time. They remained close friends. They were sensitive to one another.

Koznicki waved a hand, as if brushing away Harris's concern. "It's nothing."

"Something."

"Oh, I've been a bit concerned about Father Koesler."

"Koesler! What's he been up to?"

The priest's involvement in several homicide investigations over the past few years had never set well with Harris. He was a strong believer that murder was a matter for professionals to investigate. There was no room for amateurs in something so serious.

The fact that Koesler would have agreed wholeheartedly with Harris made no difference. With Harris it was an emotional reaction. Intellectually, Harris would admit that the relatively few times Koesler had been involved in police business, he had been practically dragged in because he was a natural source for consultation on religious matters, or because he was simply there on the scene and thus involved. Intellectually, too, Harris would have had to admit that when drawn into an investigation, Koesler had proven helpful. Sometimes to the point of actually solving the case. And this, emotionally, was Harris's complaint.

If there were a reasonable aspect to Harris's standpoint, it would be that the department might be mesmerized by Koesler's luck and grow somewhat dependent on him. Down that road, Harris was certain, lay disaster. Thus he was not overjoyed when Walt Koznicki dropped Koesler's name.

"Is your Father Koesler ill or something?" Harris inquired with no noticeable concern.

"No; nothing like that. He is substituting as a chaplain in St. Vincent's Hospital."

"Right in our backyard," Harris commented, not happily. "But why should that give you concern? Nothing wrong with being a chaplain, is there? I mean, he's qualified; he is a priest, after all."

"No, no. It's just that he has a premonition that something bad is about to happen at St. Vincent's."

"A premonition! Really, Walt!"

"You do not know him as I do, Ned. Father is not one to cry wolf. And when it comes to an intuitive sense, he has been right more often than anyone else I know. So if he has a premonition of evil, I tend to pay attention."

"But, Walt, that's something like saying that things come to a conclusion at a mortuary. Things like that happen in a hospital. People are sick. People die. It happens whether Father Koesler is there or not."

"He is not concerned with the ordinary, expected occurrences of hospital routine. He is worried that something extraordinary might happen at St. Vincent's."

" 'Something extraordinary,' Walt? You're talking about murder, aren't you?"

"That was the ultimate concern."

"Even then—even if he's right—there's nothing we can do about it. We're not in the business of preventing homicide; we just investigate it."

"I am well aware of that. I am concerned mainly because if he is proven correct, he is there in the midst of it. He could be drawn into it innocently."

"There is always another possibility, Walt."

"What?"

"That he's wrong."

"I hope you are right."

"I have a premonition. It's that Father Koesler is wrong. And I'll match my premonition against his any day. Make you feel any better?"

Koznicki sighed deeply. He wanted to argue the point no more. "You win, Ned. All is well."

Sister Rosamunda was making her rounds. She was trying not to be bitter. It was not easy. Her bones seemed to ache clear through to the marrow. She was feeling her years and trying not to show it.

Put her on the shelf, would they? Well! We'll see about that!

She had checked the Crawford woman and her neighbor, Millie Power. All appeared normal there. Power's pneumonia seemed stabilized and Crawford was just scared, as well she might be, being operated on tomorrow. Rosamunda promised herself and Crawford a visit tonight to try to quiet and reassure the patient into a decent night's sleep.

The next patient on her list was an Alice Walker in 2218-A, who had been admitted earlier this day.

Rosamunda entered the room, her practiced eye catching all the essentials at a glance. The bed nearest the door was vacant. Too much of that going on at St. Vincent's. A hospital's financial situation is not helped by empty beds.

Obviously, Alice Walker was very elderly and very ill. She seemed to be sleeping, but you could never tell just by looking. Her wispy white hair was matted from perspiration. Her cheeks and eyes were sunken. She lay perfectly still. Only the merest periodic rise and fall of her chest indicated she was breathing.

There was nothing on her bedstand next to the window but a bare tray on which was a water pitcher and an empty glass. No card, no flower, no personal effect. Likely, Alice Walker's friends and relations were gone before her or were unable to visit her. Rosamunda had seen it hundreds of times. An old person, usually a woman, who had outlived her contemporaries. There is no one as alone as one who reaches the end of life without anyone left who cares. Well, Rosamunda would be the one who cared.

The nun made a conscious effort to see not a barely animated relic, but a total woman. She had been a child, a young woman, a mother, a grandmother. Once she had given life to others, cared for them. Now she was in desperate need of care for herself. Everyone she might have depended on was gone. If help came now, and that was not likely, it would have to come from some stranger.

Rosamunda stood at the bedside. She could tell the patient was resting and not in deep sleep.

"How do you feel, dear?" Rosamunda touched the woman's shoulder.

Alice Walker opened her eyes and seemed startled to see someone in traditional religious habit. "All right, I guess. Tired. Sister . . ."

"Rosamunda. We're about the same age; why don't you call me Rosey. Other people do, but mostly behind my back."

Alice Walker smiled weakly.

"What's ailing you, Alice?"

"Oh, gall bladder. Been acting up. I guess they're going to take it out. Another part of me in the grave ahead of time."

It was Rosamunda's turn to smile. "Cheer up, Sweetie, gall bladder's the *in* operation these days. All the swells have it. You're just being fashionable. Says here on the chart that you're a Catholic. Would you like Communion tomorrow morning?"

"That would be nice. Can I go to confession first?"

"Uh-huh. We've got a priest for that. I'll ask him to see you before Communion. I can bring you Communion but we've got to hunt up a priest to absolve you. Just as well! Give them something to do." It was said only partially in jest. She still smarted from what she considered Koesler's meddling. "In the meantime, let me leave this little brochure with you. Explains the pastoral care department. Got some handy prayers, too. Read it once if you get a chance. Then I'll be back later on and we'll have a nice chat."

"That would be good." Alice, sensing she had found a friend, was grateful.

Rosamumda was about to leave but hesitated. There was something . . . something unspoken, but something wrong. Her extensive experience suggested there was something more that needed attention. She returned to the bedside.

"Alice, something else is wrong, isn't it? Something besides your gall bladder."

"I'm an old lady. There's lots wrong with me."

"No, there's something you want to tell me about. What is it? Are you ashamed or embarrassed? Don't be. By now, you and I have heard everything."

"Well . . . there's my feet."

"Let's see." Rosamunda pulled the sheet and light blanket away from Alice Walker's feet. They appeared to be in a terminal state of trench foot. Rosamunda was startled, mostly that she had not detected the odor.

"It's hard to keep them warm in the wintertime," Alice Walker said apologetically.

"I know you're here for your gall bladder . . . but hasn't anyone done anything about your feet?"

"No, I guess not."

This was by no means a unique case. Not long before, Rosamunda had encountered a patient with horribly ulcerated legs, who was about to be discharged after a successful colon resection. It was one of the nastier by-products of the DRG—Diagnostic Related Group—approach to health care. The patient's care was limited in time and cost to that allotted by the government to colon resections. His time and money was used up. Any additional cost would have to be borne by the hospital. And that would not do.

Rosamunda had been unable to aid that patient; his discharge had been too imminent. So he had been forced to depart from the hospital with a repaired colon and bad legs. The same would not happen to this patient!

"The priest will be in to hear your confession, darling, and I will bring you Communion. And there will be a podiatrist in to see you and take care of those feet. You can depend on that!"

Alice Walker knew she could depend on it.

Try to put her on the shelf, would they! Well, thought Rosamunda, we'll just see about that!

It hadn't been that long since George Snell had been forced to promise a reformation. The three pledges he had made to his superior burned in his memory. But so far—to his amazement—he had kept them. He had arrived for patrol on time and had not left early. He had faithfully kept up the log of his tour of duty. And—by far the most difficult—he had kept moving when on patrol. He had not succumbed to any of the upholstered chairs or couches in any of the visiting parlors. He had not sacked out in any empty one-bed patient rooms. And, most sadly, he had not philandered with any of the many nubile nurses or aides.

In short, George Snell had kept his nose clean. On the one hand, he was rather proud of his—albeit short-term—achievement. On the other, he was concerned that he might be sinking into middle-class morality.

These and kindred thoughts buzzed through his brain as he began this evening's tour of duty.

Once again, he had begun on time; he had manfully walked on by any number of comfortable chairs and couches as well as the occasional empty bed.

"Good evening, Officer Snell," a crisply dressed nurse's aide greeted as they passed in the corridor.

There it was, thought Snell, in a nutshell. A pretty young thing, chipmunk cheeks, nice trim body, perky steatopygic bottom, long dark hair, and willing. God, was she willing! But he was pledged to walk on by. So he did.

Besides—he continued to develop the thought—why was she so instantly willing? Prior to the other night when he had been instrumental in saving the CEO from probable death, that aide would have walked by without even acknowledging his existence. It had happened too many times for him to doubt it.

So why was she now greeting him so brightly? Because now he was a hero. Suddenly, the security guards' image had prospered. Before his ostensibly heroic action, the entire service had been lightly regarded. Now the guards, and especially and naturally George Snell, were treated with a measure of respect. With that in mind, Snell found himself reluctant to exploit the situation.

That little aide back there, for example: Only a few evenings ago, she might not have greeted him as brightly, but with any effort at all he could have charmed her into bed long before his tour of duty was over. As it was now, he couldn't bring himself to take advantage of the circumstances. But then, as he had already admitted, he was becoming a victim of middle-class morality. March on! he commanded himself like the shining knight he envisioned himself to be.

Meanwhile, in the medical office into which a stolen key had admitted him, Bruce Whitaker had prepared and was gathering his stickers. All was ready. How proud of him his colleagues would be when he carried off this gambit. Yet he readily would admit that he was far more concerned with Ethel Laidlaw's reaction. Without doubt, he was about to become her hero. That was proving to be a dandy feeling. He had never before been anyone's hero.

And to be considered a champion by the object of one's love was particularly delicious.

He had, of course, some lingering doubt about the coming adventure. On the face of it, this was a complicated and ambitious project. But he had carefully prepared for it. If not for his lifelong and virtually uninterrupted history of screwing up, he would have felt considerably more assured. Yet he could not deny his history. So he began the adventure as cautiously, deliberately, and carefully as possible.

He departed the medical office with mixed feelings of apprehension and enthusiasm. He had planned to be nonchalant but he found he could not carry that off. Unconsciously reverting to form, he found himself slinking along the shadows of the corridor. Now, instead of heading for the main floor clinic, he was headed for the second floor.

Whitaker was seldom in the hospital at this time of evening. Volunteers ordinarily served during the day shifts. He found the milieu peculiar to this period between the close of visiting hours and lights-out. It reminded him of what choir vespers used to be. Something between the busy prayer hours of day and compline, the night prayer. For those patients who were not suffering, this was a restful period. Everything gradually slowed in preparation for sleep.

No one on the elevator. Good. He hadn't really expected anyone, but there was always the chance. Actually, every successful step he took was for him a pleasant phenomenon. He was almost beginning to permit himself the thought that he might succeed at this. Was it possible?

The door hissed open. The second floor and no one in sight. He walked quickly to the end of the hallway and peered around the corner. A miracle: No one was at the nurses' station! Of course that was as he had planned it.

At this time of evening, a reduced nursing staff was

usually busy bringing final medications and answering call bells. It was a good possibility that the station would be vacated. Whitaker just couldn't believe his luck. It was working!

He moved into the station, trying, despite his excitement, not to botch this just when everything seemed to be moving like clockwork.

Just as Whitaker began fingering through the medical charts, George Snell turned the corner at the far end of the corridor. Immediately, Snell spotted him. Whitaker was too far away for Snell to be able to identify him in any fashion. But something wasn't right. Snell was certain of that. He moved rapidly toward the station.

"You! Down there! What are you doing?" Snell spoke just loudly enough to be heard by the person in the nurses' station without disturbing the patients.

Whitaker heard the challenge. No doubt about it: The ball game was over. He had not planned for the eventuality of being discovered. It would not have mattered. Even if he had prepared some sort of explanation, Whitaker knew he would be too nervous and nonplussed to carry it off. And so he was. He stood frozen while his knees turned to pudding.

"Where ya goin', big fellah?" a sultry voice called out.

Snell froze in midstride. The voice was familiar. Familiar enough for him to turn and investigate. Aha! The terrific aide of the evening of his triumph . . . what was her name? Helen. Helen Brown. But what a time to show up! What a goddam time!

"Well, where are you going, anyway?"

"There's somebody . . ." Snell had no idea what to do next. He was the human embodiment of the donkey standing between two bales of hay.

"C'mere, big fellah," Helen Brown beckoned.

Snell had to give this situation serious, if hurried, thought.

He had no idea who was in the nurses' station. It could very possibly be a legitimate staffer. It probably was. Why would anybody else be there checking things out? Especially someone in a hospital frock?

Added to which, there was this willing young woman. And, added boon, she was the sole person in the world who knew he was no hero. She had been alone and very intimate with him when he had tumbled from the bed and flattened the CEO's assailant. With her, he would betray no trust . . . there was no trust to betray.

No contest. Time enough to find out more about whoever was in the station. For the moment, he would explore Helen Brown. It was kismet.

From his vantage under bright lights, Whitaker could not see clearly down the corridor, although he could see well enough to identify his challenger. He did not know the man's name, but he knew it was the guard who had almost apprehended him the other night.

What Whitaker found utterly incredible was that the guard had stopped halfway down the hall. Whitaker could not see Helen Brown standing in the shadows of a patient's room. All he could know was that, for whatever reason, the guard had halted and had apparently lost interest in him.

It was so unexpected and unlikely a development that Whitaker could take it only as an act of God. As far as he could figure things, he had been on God's side through thick and thin. But now God seemed to be on his side. Well, it was about time.

Whitaker returned to his endeavor with renewed confidence. For once, things were working out perfectly. Until now, he would not have described anything in his entire life as "perfect."

"Well, if it ain't Ms. Brown." Snell had turned his

complete attention to the task at hand. "Have somethin' in mind?"

"Seems to me we got some unfinished business from the other night. When we were so rudely interrupted you was about to show me some kind of movement."

"Maneuver," Snell corrected.

"Whatever."

"Well," Snell looked about, "not in the hallway."

"Follow me, big boy." Helen led the small procession down the hall in the direction whence Snell had come.

Snell followed gladly, focusing intently on the rhythmic undulation of her tight bottom.

Helen Brown entered Room 2218, tailed, almost literally, by George Snell. Almost at once, by a magical wave of her hand, Helen's clothing dropped on an empty chair. As wondrously expeditiously as Helen disrobed, Snell would have won that race, but he was momentarily distracted.

"Somebody's in here! There's a patient in the other bed," he protested.

There was. Even though the curtain had been pulled shut around the bed near the window, a soft light outlined the bed and its diminutive occupant. And there was the steady, muted sound of chewing.

"Don't you worry your head, big boy. That's just old Alice Walker. She's been in here off-and-on a hundred times maybe. Believe me, she don't know what's going on. She's just chewin' her crackers before she goes to sleep. Believe me, this room is the best shot we got tonight. Come on, big boy, I'm waitin' for your movement."

"Maneuver."

"Whatever."

George Snell decided to take his time. By his standards, it had been a long while since he had frolicked in the sack, an activity which showcased perhaps his greatest talent.

Having completed his disrobement, Snell observed Helen

Brown as she climbed onto the narrow hospital bed. Such confined quarters might have proven too constricting to the average practitioner of concupiscence. To Snell, it was no more than a small challenge inventively met.

When it came to women and sex, a single concept in Snell's lexicon, he was an omnivoluptuary. He lusted after them all. Each had her own peculiar attraction. Of course some were declared off limits by society due to the veneration of old age or the proximity of relationship. Snell was willing to go along with this. There were some conventions of middle-class morality that made some sort of sense. But George remained eager to accommodate all women not proscribed by society's mores.

However even an omnivoluptuary had his predilections. And among George's favorites was a zaftig frame such as that of Helen Brown. Which is why he derived particular joy and arousal from studying Helen in bed nude. The soft light from behind Alice Walker's curtain highlighted the curves, the hills and valleys, of Helen's tantalizing body. As far as Snell was concerned, the greatest declarative statement in the English language, whether or not the Ape Man ever said it, was, "Me Tarzan! You Jane!"

But enough of philosophy—to bed!

He clambered onto the bed and enveloped her body almost as completely as water in a pool.

"Do we start where we left off, big boy?"

"Oh, no. That's the piece of resistance. We're gonna start with the hors d'oeuvres."

"If they're as good as last time, that'll be fine with me."

Both George and Helen could testify that hors d'oeuvres could be better the second time around and their barely restrained moans and groans blended with Alice Walker's barely audible, rhythmic mastication.

In the nurses' station, Bruce Whitaker's hands trembled as he manipulated stickers on a medical chart.

Whitaker's amazing string of luck would, in an ordinary human, have engendered feelings of growing confidence. The ordinary human might well feel that this was his lucky day and be loath to go to sleep and end that day.

Not Whitaker. The longer his good fortune continued, the more he expected doom to strike at any moment.

It almost did.

He had almost completed his work when an aide came out of a nearby utility room and entered the nurses' station. Whitaker allowed himself only a furtive glance, but he didn't think he'd ever seen her before. That was probably true, he assured himself, since most of the staff worked the same shifts each day. And ordinarily, Whitaker was not active in the hospital at this hour.

As he pretended to study the chart he had been altering, he kept turning so that his back was to the aide. At every moment he expected her to notice his peculiar behavior and challenge him. Or even worse, to summon that guard who had disappeared somewhere.

Once challenged, he knew he would become a blithering idiot. Oh, God, he prayed, I don't know how you're going to get me out of this, but please, please, get me out of this.

As if in answer to his prayer, the aide left the station. He watched her out of the corner of his eye. She walked down the hall and into a patient's room. She did not reemerge. She stayed in. Miraculously, yes miraculously, she had paid no attention to him. His mission was still intact. And it was nearly completed.

He examined the stickers. They were not neatly placed, that he had to admit. The out-of-sync positioning of the stickers was attributable to his nervousness and consequent trembling hands.

And yet, as he checked the chart critically once more, it

looked quite normal. After all, genuine hospital personnel spent no time at all on producing a neat chart. They slapped things together in a perfunctory manner born of necessity. Yes, it looked better, more authentic, this way than if he'd been able to be precise.

His work was done. It looked to be a success. But, as he replaced the chart and departed, he was more than willing to give the entire credit to God, whose humble and unworthy instrument Bruce Whitaker was pleased to be.

Meanwhile, back in room 2218, two exhausted, perspiring bodies panted in Bed B. There was no sound but the heavy, satisfied breathing of George and Helen—and that of Alice Walker's methodical chewing.

"Oh, oh!" said Helen.

"Oh, oh!" said George.

"Oh, George! I've never . . . come . . . like that . . . before!"

"Matter of fact . . ." Snell thought on what he was about to admit. ". . . matter of fact . . . neither have I. Amazing!"

"You are something else, my man!"

"I know that. What I can't quite figure out is, so are you."

"We-ell, thanks . . . I guess."

"You're welcome."

"Give me just a couple of minutes to get my breath, then we can get dressed."

"Get dressed! We're only halfway through."

"Halfway! You've got to be kidding! I'll be lucky if I can walk!"

"Baby, you ain't seen nothin' yet!"

"Oh, God! You mean—"

"The Maneuver!"

"George, I don't know what you're talking about. But whatever it is, I think I'll break in half if you try it."

"Baby, you are about to find out what a climax is."

"George, you're out of your mind! You can't dish out any more just the same as I can't take any more. You're going to kill the both of us!"

"What a way to go!"

Snell raised himself on one elbow; he seemed to need more room, but was willing to go with what he had. He raised one arm high above his head and reached back as far as he could without falling out of the bed. With the other hand he began positioning Helen to receive him.

"George! George!" Helen was close to instant panic. "George! She stopped breathing! She stopped breathing! George, stop! We've got to help her! George! Alice stopped breathing! We've got to help her!"

George did not seem so inclined. "There are some things once you start 'em, there's no stoppin' 'em!"

"George!" Helen pushed as hard as she could.

By now it was becoming almost routine.

It was late at night. The bright overhead lights in the corridor should have been off, but they were on. A crowd of staff and patients had gathered. At the center of the group stood Guard George Snell and his superior, Chief Martin. There was much hubbub. People who could inch close enough tried to touch Snell or pat him on the back. All seemed very pleased, with the exception of Chief Martin, who was wearing his usual look of skepticism.

"So," Chief Martin began to recapitulate, "you just happened to be walking down this corridor at the right time. And what made you go into Mrs. Walker's room?"

"Well," said a modest George Snell, toeing the carpet, "she had stopped breathing."

"You heard her stop breathing." Martin used his most incredulous tone.

230

"Uh . . . no . . . 'course not. I heard her choking. That's it, I heard her choking."

"Then what?"

"Well, I looked around for some help. But all the nurses and aides were occupied, I guess." Snell glanced down at his side where Helen Brown stood, a smug smile on her face. For some unaccountable reason, Snell feared that Helen might mention how it was she was occupied. But she said nothing.

"So?" Chief Martin prompted.

"So there being no one else around, I entered the room and ascertained that she was indeed not breathing . . . uh . . . choking."

"So?"

"So then I picked her up out of bed and performed the Himmler Maneuver."

"Heimlich," Helen whispered.

"Heimlich!" Snell corrected himself. "And then this lady"—he gestured toward Helen Brown—"came in and . . ."

"I see," Chief Martin said. "How did you happen to know about the Heimlich Maneuver?"

"Uh . . . I read about it, I guess. Shoot, everybody knows that. It's all over the place. Information on how to do it."

"Then how is it that Mrs. Walker has bruises all over her side?" Chief Martin pressed.

"I guess she must have hit her side on the guardrail when I picked her up out of bed. I didn't have time to be very delicate, you know."

"What is this, Chief, the Inquisition?" one of the nurses challenged. "After all, Officer Snell just saved a woman's life. This is a time of celebration, not incrimination."

"All right! All right!" Chief Martin knew when he was creating a needlessly hostile crowd. And he knew when to retreat. "I just have to get the facts for my report. But you're right. Congratulations, Snell! Drop into my office before you leave in the morning and we can finish this report."

Snell might just as well have been revealed to be Superman in disguise. Patients and staff pushed forward to congratulate him. It was clear that everyone felt safer physically, emotionally, medically, and spiritually for having this shining knight on duty to protect them. If an election had been held at that moment, Snell would have been a shoo-in chief executive officer against whoever else might be running.

Only one person other than Snell knew the truth. But Helen Brown was not talking. If she had . . .

Helen Brown could not recall the exact moment when she became aware that something was wrong. It had to have been sometime between their initial torrid coupling and George's yet-to-be-demonstrated bravura performance. It must have been a reflex of her health-care training. There was a moment when that hypnotic chewing sound was supplanted by a small inoffensive strangling noise, followed by an ominous silence.

It was at that moment, as George was about to strike, when Helen realized that they had only a few seconds to act or a fatal calamity would occur in the neighboring bed.

She had been unable to convince George that this was an inopportune moment for his beau geste. So she had shoved him—hard. Taking into account their comparative size, a shove, no matter how vigorous, would have been fruitless had George not been in a state of precarious balance.

Balance upset, George had tumbled out of bed and hit the floor rolling. He struck Alice Walker's bed with considerable force. Enough force to, in effect, knock the bed right out from under Alice. The bed eventually hit the nearby wall. Alice, proving again that what goes up must come down, landed atop George—which was fortunate for Alice since George broke her fall. As it was, she collected a few bruises from the impact. If George had not been beneath her, the fall easily could have been fatal.

The masticated crackers that had matted and lodged in her throat became dislodged in the fall and she began breathing again.

But Helen had no way of knowing whether any serious damage had been done by the crackers or the fall. So she signaled code blue. By the time the resuscitation team reached Room 2218, Helen and George were fully, if untidily, clothed and Helen had somewhat breathlessly instructed George on the basics of the Heimlich Maneuver to which he would attribute Alice Walker's resuscitation.

Helen was able to run through her original and fictitious scenario with George while the code team checked Alice Walker and found that all was well, with the minor exception of the bruises.

By the time Chief Martin and the crowd had gathered, George had pretty well learned his lines and was letter-perfect—with the one flaw of not being able to remember the name Heimlich. But, as with most things in life, one need not be able to spell it if one can do it.

Beyond sotto-voce correcting George when it came to specifying the method used to revive Alice Walker, Helen had little to contribute. Thus, she had time to reflect on the incongruity that while she and George were bandying about the Heimlich Maneuver, she had yet to experience the storied Snell Maneuver.

She wondered if she ever would.

✦ ✦ ✦

One pair of eyes had followed Bruce Whitaker throughout this evening with keen interest.

233

God knows what is going on down the hall. But as long as everyone is occupied with that, I have a chance to see what he was up to.

Now, which chart was he working on? Ah, here it is. He didn't bother to push it back in place tightly. God, I can barely see, the pain in my head is so intense. Nothing to take for it either. Wait, give yourself a little time. There, it seems to be easing up a bit.

All right. He removed at least one sticker; that is obvious. He seems to have added one. But for what purpose? Let me think. He seems to be putting her on a program. But why? No, she can't be on the program! Not as long as . . . Ah, I see what he had in mind. Hmmpf; all he had to do was remove one more sticker . . . how could anyone be so stupid!

But the final question: What does he hope to accomplish by this? If this were to go through the way he has set it up—if he had done it correctly . . . why . . . yes—this would be a blunder so egregious that the hospital would have no way of covering it up. This would indeed make the news media.

First the attempted mutilation of IUDs. Now this. He does not seem capable of carrying it off. Yet, all unknowing, he seems to be trying to do just what I would wish. But he needs some help. Oh, yes, he certainly needs help. And I can give it. I will just take this other sticker off the chart.

Now, Bruce Whitaker, your plot will work. It may prove a costly price to pay, but we will be rid of that troublesome nun before she gets rid of me.

I have no idea why you are doing this, Bruce Whitaker, but you are playing right into my hands. And with you as my emissary, I now hold all the cards.

At long last, farewell, Sister Eileen!

234

✛ ✛ ✛

Pat Lennon lifted her glass of sherry in salute.

"Congratulations, Joe. You broke it."

Joe Cox inclined his head ever so slightly in acknowledgment. Then he frowned. "But, when you think of it, what a waste! All that destruction and all those injuries because somebody was peddling substandard joints."

Having accepted her toast and waited for her to take a sip of sherry, Cox tasted his Gibson. The smile returned. No water in the world, he thought, was as clear and inviting as vodka or gin.

They were dining at Joe Muer's, an extremely popular seafood restaurant within strolling distance of their Lafayette Towers apartment. The walk had been complicated this evening due to near-blizzard conditions. But they made the trek anyway.

They were celebrating Cox's reporting of the recent riot at Cobo Arena following a rock concert there. By now, of course, the rest of the media—the *News*, television, and radio—had the story. But Cox had gotten it first and had as yet exclusive access to the same essential source as the police had. The *Free Press* had copyrighted Cox's account. Thus the rest of the media were forced to play catch-up to the *Free Press*.

As Lennon popped open her napkin and spread it on her lap, the fragrance of her perfume wafted in Cox's direction. His smile widened. This was so much better than going out for drinks with the guys. No—Cox amended that—this was better than anything he had had in his entire life.

"What's next, Joe?"

"I don't know. Sort of between stories. But I'd better come up with one pretty damn quick or Nelson Kane is gonna nail me with one of those what-are-kids-doing-with-guns-in-school assignments."

"Oh, yes. Where the parents jump all over the school, while their kids bring the guns in from home."

"Exactly."

"That, by the way, is how I got on this hospital story."

"How?"

"Made it up so I wouldn't have to cover the Cobo Hall fracas."

Cox thought that over as he sipped his Gibson. "So," Cox said, "how's the hospital piece coming?"

"So-so. I'm not too enthused about it."

"Oh?"

"I can't quite put my finger on it. It's not working out the way I planned. It was going to be a puff piece that highlighted this unsinkable nun. It's still going in that direction. But I get the feeling that the story wants to take off on its own in another direction."

"The contraceptive angle?" Cox caught the waiter's eye and ordered another Gibson. Lennon passed.

"I'm not sure. But that has something to do with it. Right there—when I found out all that one Catholic hospital was doing that the Catholic Church forbids—the story wanted to go in that direction. But when I decided I wasn't going to subvert all the good that the hospital was trying to do just for a story . . . well, at that moment I started steering the piece in a direction it didn't want to go."

"I know the feeling. I've done it."

"But it's still going on. As I stick to my original theme, it seems as if I'm forcing the story in a direction it doesn't want to take."

"How so?"

"Well, for instance, I've been interviewing staff personnel for possible side-bars. And instead of getting corrobo-

236

rating material I'm collecting bad vibes. Nothing explicit, mind you, but bad vibes anyway."

"Like what?"

"I don't know if it's unequivocal enough to put into words. Vibes aren't admissable in court, you know; they're just an impression. Now, as far as I can figure it, this Sister Eileen is the next best thing to Mother Teresa. But I don't get that impression from all the people I've interviewed. Some, yes. Some, no. Why? I just don't exactly know how to react to it."

"You mean if she were a Mother Teresa, everybody'd love her?"

"Something like that. But there are at least three or four people at the hospital who definitely don't love her. Again, I can't get anything explicit from them. A couple are faced with compulsory retirement. A couple are on the verge of getting fired."

"Hey, that's the sort of thing that just doesn't endear employers to employees."

"Yeah, I know. But with these people there seems to be a feeling of personal bitterness. Like it's her fault they're old or not doing their jobs right. And then when she was attacked the other night—"

"What? Attacked! You didn't tell me—"

"I didn't learn about it until there wasn't much news value in it any more. It was all internal, an accident of sorts. A mental patient got loose from the psycho ward. He grabbed her in a hallway but some guard broke it up before any major damage was done. By the time I got the story, it was all over. The patient was back in his ward under restraints and Sister Eileen was back at work. You know what they say: Nothing is as dull as yesterday's news. Don't worry, Joe; I'm not trying to hide a legitimate story from you."

She knew him. That was precisely what he feared.

"Anyway," she continued, "when I heard about the attack, it sort of intensified the vibes I'd been getting all along. Like maybe Sister actually is in some sort of danger."

"I don't know, Pat. That's a big leap. People are retired and fired every day. I don't suppose many of them, even the retirees, feel good about it. But that's no reason to jump all over the boss. They may have a few harsh words. But in the end, they usually just fade away."

Their dinner was served.

"I suppose you're right." Pat finished her sherry. "In fact, just articulating the possibility makes me feel a lot better about it. The talking cure."

Cox squeezed lemon over his fish. "Have you noticed how warm it is in here? Maybe we can stay here all night. I'm not too eager to go back out in that blizzard. I never should have let you talk me into walking here."

"The walk'll do you good, lover. Besides, when we get home, I have a few ideas that may help us feel warm all over."

From that point, Cox did not exactly wolf down his dinner. But then neither did he dawdle.

9

MOST DAYS, FATHER KOESLER DID NOT EAT a large lunch. As a rule, he had cold cereal for breakfast, an extremely light midday meal, and a substantial dinner. He had read that this was not the healthiest of regimens. In fact, it was reportedly the reverse of the best. But he didn't care. All his life he had enjoyed anticipating good things. Indeed, it was part of his creed that anticipation, particularly since it lasted longer, was better than the attainment of whatever was coming.

He also believed there were exceptions to rules.

So this day he juggled a tray holding a cheeseburger, fries, vegetables, salad, milk, coffee, and a sliver of carrot cake. While trying to spill nothing, he searched for a place to sit in the now crowded cafeteria.

"Why don't you join us, Father? John Haroldson indicated an empty chair at the table where he was sitting with a young doctor.

Haroldson smiled broadly, emphasizing the creases and wrinkles of his lived-in face. Koesler, from experience, did not wholeheartedly trust hail fellows well met. But it would have been awkward to spurn the offer. Besides, there didn't appear to be any other open space at this moment. So he carefully set down his tray and joined them.

"Actually, you couldn't have timed this better, Father. Dr. Anderson here was telling me about a medical-moral decision he has to make. Why don't you ask the good Father, Larry?"

"First, I guess we'd better meet." Koesler introduced himself to the young doctor, who appeared none too eager to present his problem to the priest. Koesler wondered fleetingly why a doctor would bring a moral dilemma to the chief operating officer. An analogous mystery was why the doctor would hesitate in presenting the puzzle to a priest. But for the moment, Koesler decided to put these brainteasers on the back burner. He tried to look interested while holding together a cheeseburger that wanted to slide apart.

"Well, you see, Father," Anderson began, "the problem involves a woman who's had five C-section deliveries. Uh . . . that is, she's had five previous births by Caesarean section," he explained needlessly. "I delivered her latest child last year and advised her against getting pregnant again. You see, Father, her uterus is . . . uh . . . all worn out. It's been traumatized from all those sections. But she checked in yesterday, pregnant. She's got to have another section and it's going to be touch-and-go. So I was asking Mr. Haroldson whether it would be morally acceptable to do a hysterectomy on her, after the section."

Once again, Koesler wondered why the doctor had directed his indecision to the COO for resolution. Also, he had a strong suspicion that such a question would be posed only in a Catholic hospital. Not that other sectarian or public hospital personnel were unconcerned with medical

240

ethics, but Koesler supposed that in most other hospitals this would be a rather easily resolved consideration.

That there was a measure of difficulty here was directly attributable to the Catholic Church's traditional, as well as officially current, teaching on family planning. In Western civilization, the Catholic Church stood virtually alone in its total condemnation of almost all methods of contraception. The Church's ordinary magisterium held that there were but two methods of family planning: abstinence from intercourse, or the rhythm method. And to licitly practice rhythm, a couple must willingly consent to limit intercourse to a monthly infertile period; they must be able to do this without the danger of committing some related sins such as adultery or some form of "artificial" birth control; and they must have a positive—not selfish—reason to limit their family.

Koesler knew all this. And he was aware that he was, at best, rusty in this field. But he could see no booby traps in the conversation. So it was full speed ahead.

"As I recall," Koesler began, "this is one of those times when the moralist must depend on the medical expert. I mean, if a hysterectomy were performed on a woman with a perfectly healthy uterus, the purpose would seem to be clearly contraceptive. So Catholic theology would oppose that. In this case, I just don't know how 'abnormal' or unwell this particular womb may be. That would be up to the doctor, it would seem."

"That's the problem, as I see it, Father," Dr. Anderson said. "This is not a case of a diseased organ. There's no CA or anything like that. But this uterus has been so traumatized by past Caesareans that it is unreal to expect this organ to carry another pregnancy even to the point of viability. Another pregnancy can only lead to the death of the fetus and a serious threat to the mother's life. The womb will rupture. It's as simple as that."

Koesler meditatively chewed a morsel of cheeseburger. He was losing his zest for theological inquiry. He had overlooked how frequently moral questions lacked a black-and-white certainty. Most ethical matters, such as the present uterus that was about to give up the ghost, came in tones of gray uncertainty.

"Seems to me," Koesler swallowed most of the mouthful of cheeseburger, "it seems to me that we're dealing with, if not a diseased organ, at least one whose usefulness is gone. I mean, from what you say, Doctor, this woman's uterus can't sustain another fetal life. From all the cutting that's had to be done, it's worn out. So I think we could conclude that the organ has been rendered useless. And that, I would guess, might put it in the same category as an appendix. Whatever our appendix once did, it does no more—it's a useless organ that no longer serves any positive purpose. Except that it can become infected and be a threat to life. And I think the rule of thumb for surgeons is that should they encounter the appendix during any sort of surgery, they routinely remove it . . . don't they?"

Dr. Anderson nodded.

"Then I suppose the same can be said for this worn-out uterus. It can no longer serve any positive purpose. It's just a trauma waiting to happen. So I'd say that it would be morally acceptable the next time you see that womb to remove it." Koesler fingered some fries. He felt somewhat self-satisfied.

"That's pretty much the way I figured it, Father," Anderson said.

Koesler lost some of his smugness. "If that's the way you had it figured, what in the world was the purpose of asking my opinion?"

"Well, you see, Father, I just got done talking over that part of the decision with Mr. Haroldson here, just to make sure it would be okay to do the hysterectomy. But that was preliminary to the other more pertinent question I had just posed to Mr. Haroldson right before you came to the table.''

''And that was . . . ?''

''If it was okay to do the hysterectomy, then wouldn't it be preferable just to tie the woman's tubes? That way we would isolate the uterus. She would never get pregnant again and we would avoid major surgery in favor of very minor surgery.''

Koesler glanced at Haroldson, who was sitting back wearing a large smile as if waiting to see if the priest could guess the correct answer. Koesler hated to be put in this position. It was as if he'd been tricked. He'd settled a problem that had already been settled. For no accountable reason, he felt as if he had passed some juvenile test and now was being put through a similar, but higher-level exam.

''Apparently,'' said Koesler, ''you came down here to ask Mr. Haroldson's opinion. Why don't you do that?''

''Oh, no, Father,'' said the still-smiling Haroldson, ''you're the designated expert on theological matters. Why, young Dr. Anderson is in luck that you chanced to join us.''

I didn't ''chance'' to join you, Koesler thought. You invited me to join you, you curmudgeon.

Anderson seemed to be playing the role of monkey in the middle. By this time, he didn't much care which of them fielded the question.

Koesler inserted a single strand of fried potato in his mouth and thought. ''Tie the tubes, eh?'' he said. ''It makes sense to me. And it might make glorious sense to the poor woman.''

''Then you think it would be morally acceptable to perform a tubal ligation!'' Haroldson more challenged than questioned.

Koesler felt a moment of embarrassment as if he had given an incorrect answer in class. But he recovered quickly. "Well, yes. However you wish to figure it; a part for the whole, if you will. If it's acceptable to perform a hysterectomy, it seems equally, if not more, acceptable to perform a lesser operation for the same purpose. The idea is this woman shouldn't chance being pregnant again. Or, rather, that she can no longer depend on her womb to sustain a fetal life."

"You'd allow that even though there is nothing whatsoever wrong with the Fallopian tubes!" Once again, Haroldson put an audible exclamation mark at the end of what might have been an honest question.

"Yes, I think so. It serves the same purpose and certainly makes more sense than a hysterectomy. As the Doctor here has said, it's a trade of minor surgery for major. I think it's the obvious conclusion."

"And how would you justify that theologically, Father?" As time passed, Haroldson's questions became more clearly a series of challenges. The plaster-of-paris smile began to fade as well.

"Justify it? What are you driving at?"

"What principle in moral theology would justify your conclusion, is what I'm driving at. Sounds like situation ethics to me!" It was evident from Haroldson's inflection that he considered situation ethics a pejorative term.

Anderson glanced at his watch. Two things were certain: He had to get back to his hospital duties and his procedural dilemma had become a bone of contention between Haroldson and Koesler. "If you don't mind, I'll just get back to my rounds. I'll get back in touch with you both later and find out what you decided."

Anderson left the table. As far as Haroldson and Koesler were concerned it was as if the Doctor had never been there.

244

"Well, I'll admit that, while I gave the uterus business some 'theological' consideration, the opinion on the tubes was sort of off the top of my head. But it certainly did not spring from situation ethics. I'm afraid I can't subscribe to a school where all morality is weighed by an intention to do the 'loving' thing."

"Well," Haroldson said, "that's refreshing. But then, may I ask what theological consideration you used to justify the original hysterectomy?"

For some reason, Haroldson seemed determined to keep Koesler in a pupil-teacher position.

"I suppose," Koesler replied, "that would be the principle of the double effect."

"You mean," Haroldson corrected, "the principle of the indirect voluntary, of course."

Damn, thought Koesler; he's right. But he's also nit-picking. Indirect voluntary was but the generic term under which fell the principle of the double effect. In either case, one dealt with a consequence that was not directly willed. Specifically, in the double effect, one posited an action from which flowed two distinct effects, one of which was "evil." To be justified in traditional Catholic theology, the action must be good, or at least indifferent. The immediate consequence of the action must be good and the good must outweigh the evil of the secondary consequence, which, in turn, is not directly desired or willed but only permitted.

That, in a nutshell, was the principle of the indirect voluntary and its firstborn child, the principle of the double effect. And the insistence on a reference to the generic term was an indication to Koesler that Haroldson could be a difficult person with whom to do business.

"Yes," Koesler admitted with little grace, "you're right. It's the principle of the indirect voluntary."

"Exactly. The operation is not only warranted and good,

it will happen of necessity because of the Caesarean delivery. The first and immediate effect of the surgery will be the removal of a worn-out, tired, and ineffective organ. And that is good, and it outweighs the contraceptive effect, which is not directly willed, but only tolerated."

"Uh-huh." No doubt about it, Koesler was becoming testy.

"And you feel the same reasoning applies to a tubal ligation in this case?" Haroldson made it seem a rhetorical question to which Koesler was about to wrongly respond.

"Yes, I do," Koesler replied, giving, by Haroldson's standards, the wrong answer.

"Would you mind explaining that, Father?"

"Look, I'll admit we aren't dealing directly with the defective organ. But in performing the hysterectomy the surgeon's going to have to cut the Fallopian tubes anyway. So what's the difference? What's the difference if he cuts the tubes and then removes the defective uterus, or if he simply cuts the tubes, isolating the uterus, and leaves the organ there—to the great benefit of the patient?"

"The difference is, Father, that the surgeon is operating on a healthy organ and on a healthy organ alone. Thus making the action *in se mala*."

It had been a long time since Koesler had heard the term *evil in itself*, or totally evil.

"And besides that," Haroldson continued, "the Pope had something to say about this!"

"The Pope?"

"Yes, the Pope!"

"Which one?"

"Pius XII."

"That was a long time ago."

"Words for the ages."

"Well, what did he say?"

246

"That when someone halts ovulation to save a damaged uterus, that is direct sterilization and therefore illicit."

"He was talking about the prevention of ovulation. At most that would refer to the antovulent pill."

"Or to the Fallopian tubes that carry the ova."

"I don't think so. Besides, that opinion must go back to the forties or fifties."

"Father! That is—"

"I know, I know: the ordinary magisterium."

"Yes! The ordinary magisterium!"

"I don't suppose it would help to point out that the usual teaching function of the Church has developed and changed over the years . . . make that over the centuries."

"Father, since you are a part of this hospital, at least for the time being, maybe it would be good to know just what you believe. Just what theological school do you belong to? Vatican II? Vatican III? Vatican IV?"

Koesler laughed. "I believe about what you do, John, except not quite so rigidly."

"Not so rigidly! Then you are a situationalist."

"No. No, just someone who cannot help seeing some grays in moral theology."

"Grays?"

"John, the theology we grew up with . . . well . . . it was the theology of *The One, Holy, Catholic and Apostolic Church*. There was development going on, but ever so slowly. And John, I don't think it will ever be that way again." Haroldson was about to interpose an objection, but Koesler quickly continued. "Not that I am about to adopt every new thought just because it's new. But the theology we grew up with is based on a natural law ethic. It's an absolute and objective sort of morality. And, on the one hand, I think there's been considerable development in our understanding of the natural law. And, on the other, I think we can stand some mix of proportionalism where we weigh the proportion between good and evil, where the human person is the norm and each person is unique.

"Besides"—Koesler winked—"I'll bet I could dig up a probable opinion to support doing a tubal ligation to isolate that woman's uterus."

Haroldson shook his head. "I don't care. I'm just glad I've lived my life at a time when Church teaching was clear and objective and dependable. Today's young priests are creating their own Church. And they can have it."

"As hard as it probably is for you to believe this, I don't disagree with you all that much. But I've got to hand it to you, John; you have an excellent understanding of moral theology. Usually, when I get into a discussion with a layperson, the main problem is that we're not talking about the same thing. Usually, our disagreement rests with the layperson's misunderstanding of traditional theology. That certainly is not the case with you. You have an excellent grasp of systematic theology. I can't help wondering where you got it."

"It's nothing."

"I beg to differ. And you couldn't have picked it up in just any parochial school. Where?"

Haroldson sipped his coffee as if trying to decide whether to get into this. "The seminary."

"The seminary! I didn't know. Tell me about it. How far did you go?"

Haroldson smiled grimly, "From the very beginning to the very end."

"The very end! I don't understand: You weren't ordained a priest?"

"No."

"Then . . ."

Haroldson hesitated. "The thing is, you see, Father, I'm an ecclesiastical bastard."

Koesler was neither shocked nor surprised. There were

lots of ecclesiastical bastards around. This was not caused by an unmarried mother. It was a case of one's parents not having their marriage witnessed by a priest. And this was the result of one or both parents opting out of a Catholic wedding; or one or both parents had been previously married and not in possession of the required declaration of nullity for the previous marriage.

"And that," Haroldson continued, "is an impediment to Holy Orders."

"Well, yes. But a dispensation is possible. Now it's routine."

"Not then. Not when I was a seminarian. Oh, the dispensation from the impediment of illegitimacy was possible. But the petition for the dispensation was by no means routinely made. And in my case, the bishop simply decided not to petition. And that was that."

"But the bishop must have known the problem of illegitimacy was there. Why would he let you go all the way through the seminary if he wasn't going to ask for a dispensation?"

Haroldson shrugged. "I don't know. I've always thought that he let me complete my seminary education because it certainly couldn't hurt me even if I lived the rest of my life as a lay Catholic. In retrospect, I'd have to agree with that. And I suppose he spent some of his time during all those years praying for guidance. The answer to his prayers must have been not to process my case to Rome."

"My God!" Koesler was appalled. "All those years! You were no better than a puppet. And the bishop was playing puppeteer!"

"Oh, it wasn't that bad."

"Wasn't that bad! You spent nearly twelve years preparing for the priesthood. Early on, the bishop could have told you he wasn't going to do anything about an impediment that was no more than a Church law that could have

249

been suspended. If nothing else, you could have been freed to find a bishop who would have gone to bat for you.''

''You're building this up larger than life, Father. I wasn't blindfolded during all those years. I knew about the impediment and I knew the decision was entirely in the hands of the bishop. You see, for me, the bishop's decision in the matter was the will of God. I entered the seminary intent only on knowing whether the priesthood was, for me, God's will. As it turned out, it wasn't.''

Koesler looked at Haroldson as if for the first time. ''I admire your faith, I really do. But I think I would have to look well beyond the whim of a bishop for an expression of God's will.''

''For me, that was it. Besides, all those years of a fine liberal arts education paved the way for my premed.''

''You were premed!''

''Yes.''

''But you didn't complete it. You didn't become a doctor.''

''No, one more incomplete endeavor.''

''But why?''

''No money. Or, rather, I ran out of money. There were no government loans. Nor any other, for that matter, for someone of most modest means. But,'' Haroldson began arranging his tray, ''neither experience was a failure as far as I'm concerned. Since both of them led to this hospital. This,'' he said it fondly, ''this Catholic hospital. The seminary trained me in things Catholic. And medical school gave me a special preparation for the hospital. And this has been my life . . . my very life.''

Koesler noticed the slightest quiver at the corners of Haroldson's mouth. The priest was touched at this sign of emotion.

''And now,'' Haroldson continued, ''they expect me to

leave it. Just, one day soon, stay home instead of coming to where my life is. Just because a man reaches an arbitrary age, he is expected to die.''

Strange, thought Koesler, the similarity of reaction to retirement on the part of Haroldson and Sister Rosamunda. ''Oh, come now, John,'' Koesler said, ''that's painting it rather more bleakly than necessary, don't you think? Especially with your background, there must be any number of fulfilling things you could do. Teach, for instance.''

''That's what she said.''

''Who?''

''Sister Eileen.'' Haroldson almost spat the name. ''She doesn't understand. You don't understand. Nobody understands. A man can die when he's forced out of his life's purpose. Father, I'm fighting for my life!''

''John, I've known people who dreaded retirement every bit as much as you do. And they managed to live through it. Even thrive on it.''

''You don't understand. You just don't understand . . .'' Haroldson picked up his tray with its now-empty dishes and left.

Easily half of Koesler's lunch remained. It was cold and now unappetizing. That was all right, he thought. Selecting that much food had been an inprudent whim. It was just as well to leave half of it uneaten.

He sat for a few minutes pondering his conversation with Haroldson. Koesler had learned much. Perhaps it was true that every organization needed at least one hatchet man. And perhaps John Haroldson was that man on behalf of St. Vincent's Hospital.

On the other hand, it might be true that to understand was to forgive all.

✦ ✦ ✦

''Aren't you finished with this story yet?''

The peevish tone took Pat Lennon back to her youth when, as she liked to joke now, nuns were nuns and religious sisters were prone to admonish young Catholic students to "cast down your bold eyes!" But she was utterly unprepared for any harsh statement from Sister Eileen Monahan. So, Lennon was startled by the question.

"Why . . . yes, as a matter of fact," she replied, "I am almost finished. Another interview or two and I'll have all the information I need. Then there's writing it up for the magazine. But that's a rather flexible deadline. Was there some hurry, Sister? I wasn't aware of any."

"It just seems that it's taking an awful lot of time."

Lennon hesitated. "Is there something wrong, Sister?"

"Wrong?"

"You don't seem yourself."

Eileen pinched her brow just over the bridge of her nose. "I have been abrupt, haven't I? Sorry."

"No need to apologize. On the contrary, you've been most patient and cooperative. Everybody at St. Vincent's has been. Especially you. That's why I was surprised just now. It is perfectly reasonable for you to want me out of your way. But it seemed sort of . . . out of character for you."

Eileen smiled, it seemed in spite of herself. "Well, I'm glad we've managed to give you a good impression of St. Vincent's. All the more reason I feel ashamed I was short with you just then."

"Is there something . . ."

"No. No, I've been having some headaches and a little dizziness lately, that's all."

"Are you taking anything for it?"

"Some aspirin. A little Terpin Hydrate, but that's for a kind of constant congestion. It's probably just the onset of a cold. We've got the kind of weather for an annual

Michigan cold or flu. It's nothing to be concerned about. I'll be all right.''

"I don't know . . .''

"Oh, don't worry about me. I'll be okay. And even if I do get sick, I couldn't be in a more appropriate place, now, could I? Where better to get sick than in a hospital? And even if worst came to worst and I were to die—well, this is a Catholic hospital and I assure you, dear, I am well prepared. Now, let's get on with this interview. And take your time. There's no hurry.''

Eileen tried to smile, but involuntarily winced. It must be the headache pain again, thought Lennon. She was concerned for the nun. In a very short time, Pat had come to care greatly for Sister Eileen. Thus, when the nun brought up the subject of her own death, it sent a shiver through Pat.

She had a premonition of danger and evil. The feeling was associated with this hospital and converged on Sister Eileen Monahan. Eileen's articulating the possibility of her own death intensified Pat's apprehension.

She felt as if she should somehow protect this nun. But there was no way of doing it. As long as she remained in this hospital, Sister Eileen would be vulnerable to anyone here who wished her harm. And there was nothing anyone could do about it.

✣ ✣ ✣

"*Father in heaven, through this holy anointing grant Alice Walker comfort in her suffering. When she is afraid, give her courage; when afflicted, give her patience; when dejected, afford her hope; and when alone, assure her the help of your holy people. We ask this through Christ our Lord. Amen.*"

This was nice, Father Koesler reflected. For almost the

only time in his priestly career, he had the comparative leisure to minister properly to the sick.

In his early years as a priest, he was rarely called to a sickbed without its also being a deathbed. Back then, the sacrament was known as Extreme Unction—a last anointing. And, while the rite contained several prayers for a return to health, popularly it was looked upon as a one-way ticket to eternal life in the hereafter. So, although priests periodically instructed parishioners to inform their clergy when anyone became ill, generally, it was a useless plea. Catholics, by and large, continued to view Extreme Unction as a final statement that they tried to postpone as long as they possibly could. Thus, Koesler was accustomed to anointing people who were apparently dead.

Then came the Second Vatican Council and, among other things, liturgical renewal. And the sacrament that had been known as Extreme Unction was modified and given the more updated name of the Anointing of the Sick. However, by that time, most sick people died not at home but in hospitals, where they were ministered to not by their parish priest but by chaplains. And that was the role Koesler found himself playing now as he substituted for his classmate.

Of course this was a little more than Alice Walker had bargained for. All she had asked of Sister Rosamunda was confession. Indeed, Alice had confessed her few sins of impatience, anger, and borderline despair in the early portion of this rite. But Koesler correctly judged that a woman of Alice Walker's advanced years, facing major surgery, was entitled to the Anointing of the Sick. And, after her initial apprehension that this priest was trying to slide her into eternity with Extreme Unction, Alice admitted she felt consoled by this rite. Until now, she had never heard of the Anointing of the Sick.

254

But then, there were many interesting things going on in Catholicism of which even most Catholics were ignorant.

"*God of compassion,*" Koesler continued with a prescribed *Prayer Before Surgery,* "*our human weakness lays claim to your strength. We pray that through the skills of surgeons and nurses your healing gifts may be granted to Alice Walker. May your servant respond to your healing will and be reunited with us at your altar of praise. Grant this through Christ our Lord. Amen.*"

Koesler continued with the rite of Communion, then prayed the concluding blessing: "*May the God of all consolation bless you in every way and grant you hope all the days of your life. Amen.*

"*May God restore you to health and grant you salvation. Amen.*

"*May God fill your heart with peace and lead you to eternal life. Amen.*

"*May almighty God bless you, the Father, and the Son, and the Holy Spirit. Amen.*" Koesler's right hand traced the sign of the cross.

"Is that it?" Alice Walker asked.

"That's it," Koesler confirmed as he removed the stole from his shoulders.

"That was nice."

"Yes, I thought so too."

"I didn't think I was going to get all this when I asked Rosie—uh, Sister Rosamunda—for confession."

"I know. But I didn't think you'd mind the sacrament of Anointing too."

"Oh, I didn't. I was afraid to ask for more than confession. I was afraid you'd come and give me Extreme Unction. And that would have been it."

"It?"

"Yes. Then you'd've prayed me right into the next life."

Koesler smiled. "I wouldn't have done that. We need you too much right here."

There was a slight pause as Koesler folded the stole and gathered up the pyx that had contained the consecrated wafer.

"They didn't fool me, you know," Alice Walker said in a knowing tone.

"Huh? Who didn't fool you?"

"Those two last night."

"What two last night?"

"The two in the next bed."

Koesler glanced at the empty bed near the door. It was made up with customary hospital care. There was no doubt that it was not being used by any patient. He knew that Alice Walker was of advanced age and that she was ill. But he was not conversant with her mental state. For all he knew, she might have a touch of Alzheimer's. Or possibly she had been just hallucinating. In any case, no one was occupying 2218-B.

He decided to try a little reality therapy. "Mrs. Walker, there's nobody in the other bed in this room."

"There certainly was last night."

"There was?"

"Yes, two."

"Two? It's a single bed."

"Not when one is on top of the other."

"On top? Mrs. Walker, what happened last night?" Koesler was mystified. What did she *think* happened last night?

"Well, I was havin' my evening snack—graham crackers and milk—when I heard them. There was two of them. I couldn't see who they was right off. This curtain was pulled around my bed and the only light was this one at the head of my bed. They was whispering, but I could tell it was a man and a woman. At first they was just sparkin', but then they went into the act.''

"The act?''

"Yes, you know what I mean. What could I do? I couldn't stop 'em or cheer 'em on. Besides, they got through it rather rapid. So I just kep' eatin' my snack. But then they started in again. I never heard nothin' like it. I mean it wasn't ten minutes after they finished the act the first time when didn't they start all over again. Well, I tell you, nothin' surprises me much anymore. But that surprised me. And a bit of the snack went down my throat the wrong way and I started chokin'. The next thing I know, the man fell out of the bed and, I guess, rolled across the floor until he hit my bed. Wham!

"Well, my bed hit the wall and I pitched out of it and onto him on the floor. Knocked the morsel right out of my throat. Saved my life, I guess. But what a way to do it!

"Next thing I know, the nurse—'cause that's who I think it was—was gettin' herself and him dressed. They got me back in bed. I guess they didn't think I knew what was goin' on.

"Then all hell broke loose. people comin' in here makin' a fuss over me. Shoot, I was okay by then. And while they're makin' this fuss over me, this man—turns out he was a guard . . . at least he had a guard's uniform—is tellin' everybody this cockamamie story about how he heard me chokin' and came in and saved me. I mean, I've lived a long and eventful life, but that's the first time anything as weird as that ever happened to me.''

Koesler was unsure what to believe. It was a wild tale. A bit too wild, he thought, to have sprung out of whole cloth. Perhaps it was true.

"Have you told this to anyone else, Mrs. Walker?''

"No, just you.''

"Why didn't you tell somebody? The people who were in here last night? Or someone this morning?"

"Don't want to make any enemies. I'm goin' into surgery, you know. I want to have at least an even chance to come out of it okay."

"So why did you tell me?"

"I can trust you. God! If you can't trust a priest, who can you trust?"

"Well, what do you want me to do about it?"

"Whatever you want. I don't care. It ain't my responsibility anymore. If you tell, they can't blame me. It's your responsibility. Or if you don't tell anybody, that's okay too. I don't care anymore. It's your kettle of fish now."

Koesler shrugged. "Glad to be of help." He made ready to leave.

"One more thing," Alice Walker said.

"Yes?"

"Pray for me and my operation."

"I just did—in the sacrament of the Anointing of the Sick."

"I know. But keep it up. It couldn't hurt."

"Right."

Father Koesler made six consecutive calls on new patients on his floors, each of whom was otherwise occupied, either with tests, therapy, or being examined by doctors. Time, he decided, for a coffee break.

The cafeteria coffee had its usual severely strong character. So as usual he was more warming his hands from the cup than drinking it. The people who complained about his coffee-making should be made to sample this coffee, he thought. That would teach them to better appreciate his efforts.

While he sat by himself in the nearly empty cafeteria,

two nurses seated themselves at a neighboring table. Evidently, they were also on coffee break. They were actually sipping the coffee. Koesler wondered if it just took time to get used to its industrial strength.

The two nurses began chattering away, seemingly oblivious of Koesler's proximity.

In order to distract himself, Koesler weighed what he might do with the information he had been given by Alice Walker. It all came down to: to tell or not to tell.

Before Mrs. Walker's revelation, Koesler had heard something of the event. The version he'd heard was considerably less titillating than Alice Walker's account. He had overheard some talk of the rescue. But the emphasis was on the coincidence that a guard should be passing by a room at the exact moment a patient happened to be choking. Beyond that, there was some comment about the guard's being able to execute the Heimlich Hug. It was, Koesler had been led to believe, not so outstanding or newsworthy an event.

If one could rely on Mrs. Walker, there was a far more colorful aspect to this rescue now celebrated in the lore of this ancient hospital. Which were it known would undoubtedly trigger a couple of dismissals. Was it worth it to reveal the story and cause a couple of people to be fired?

Probably not, Koesler concluded. Security in this hospital was not the best, to say the least. It would not be improved with the revelation that one of the guards had been horizontal when he should have been vertical. Same for the nurse—or aide, whichever.

Peripherally, he noticed the two nurses changing position preliminary to leaving. "What's the hurry?" the blonde asked. She seemed to be down to the dregs of her coffee, but not ready to leave.

"I gotta get back," the brunette answered. "One of the gals in 2214 is having problems."

"Oh?"

"Yeah. No one can figure it out. Just took a bad turn. I promised to cut my break short and get back. I gotta go."

"Okay, okay. Hold your horses. I'll be right with you."

The two nurses departed, leaving Koesler wondering. Something about that room number . . . Ordinarily, there was no reason a particular room would strike any chord in his memory. But, for some reason, Room 2214 stood out. Of course it must have something to do with the patients in that room. But what?

So absorbed was he in trying to recall the patients of 2214 and why the memory should disquiet him so, that he was oblivious to the arrival of someone who seated herself at the table directly across from him. Thus, her greeting startled him.

"Father . . . Father!" Ethel Laidlaw felt as if she were awakening someone.

"Oh . . ." Koesler's attention came back to the scene. He smiled. "Hello. Sorry; I'm afraid I was distracted."

"It's okay," Ethel said. "Maybe I shouldn't have sat down here. I didn't have any appointment or anything like that. I just needed to talk to somebody. Probably a priest. And I kinda thought you might be the one who'd understand."

"Sure, that's fine. You certainly don't need an appointment. For the time being, I'm chaplain at this hospital and I am quite literally at your service. But I don't think we've been introduced."

"Oh, I'm sorry, Father. No, we haven't. I'm a nurse's aide here. I'm Ethel Laidlaw." Ethel offered her hand. As she did so, she knocked over the saltshaker, spilling salt on the table. "Oops," she said, "got to avoid bad luck." With that, she picked up the shaker as if to flip a little salt over her left shoulder. Instead, she lost her grip and the shaker sailed across the room, landing with a smack against the wall.

For some reason, it reminded Koesler of the biblical incident of the two disciples on their way to Emmaus on the original Easter Sunday. In their walk they were joined by Jesus but they did not perceive who He was. It was only during dinner at an inn, "at the breaking of the bread they recognized that it was the Lord." In this instance, it was the fiasco with a saltshaker that jogged Koesler's memory. This one was one of a matched pair. Koesler had watched the couple demolish a meal at least once. And he had been duly impressed with their clumsiness. Ethel's performance with the salt confirmed the image.

Clearly, she was embarrassed.

"Just an accident," Koesler assured her. "Nothing to be concerned about."

" 'Just an accident'!" Ethel mimicked reproachfully. "More like the story of my life. I wonder about that, Father: Do you suppose some people are born clumsy?"

"Oh, I don't know about that, Ethel. I suppose people have a greater or lesser degree of coordination. I don't guess it's any more than that. But that's not what you wanted to talk to me about, is it?"

"Not exactly, Father, but it's got something to do with it. Actually, it's a kind of complicated problem. I don't know exactly how to tell you."

"Well, let's start at the present. What's the problem right now?"

"The problem right now is I could get fired. In fact I probably will unless something happens."

"The unemployment rate in this town being what it is, that could be a pretty serious problem. What makes you think you may be fired?"

Ethel shrugged. "Like that saltshaker. I break things. A lot."

"That many?"

"I guess so. It's kind of hard for me to tell exactly. I've

been doing this sort of thing all my life. But, whatever, Sister Eileen said she'd have to fire me if it didn't stop. Well, Father, I mean it can't stop. I'll probably find some way of falling out of my coffin and knocking over all the flowers. That is, if anybody sends flowers."

"Well, Ethel, if you can't help being clumsy, you can't help it. If that's the way you are, it's not your fault. But maybe you're just working in the wrong job."

"The wrong job?"

"Yes." It was an opening for one of Koesler's anecdotes. "Did you ever hear about the guy who went to New York to get a job? He got in a cab and said to the driver, 'T-T-T-Take me to N-N-N-NBC in a hurry.' You see, he stuttered very badly.

"So, to make conversation, the cabbie asked, 'What do you want to go to NBC for?' And the guy says, 'I'm going to an au-au-au-audition for a j-j-j-job as an a-a-a-announcer.' When they reach NBC, the guy says to the cabbie, 'W-W-Wait for me.'

"After a while the guy comes back and gets into the cab. The cabbie says, 'So, did you get the job?' And the guy says, 'N-N-N-No; they're p-p-p-prejudiced against C-C-C-Catholics.' "

Ethel laughed. "That's funny. But, if you don't mind, what's it got to do with me?"

"Just this, Ethel: There seem to be an outstanding number of things in a hospital that are breakable. Test tubes come to mind; thermometers; breakfast, lunch, and dinner dishes; all the things that are used to carry specimens and medications around the hospital—the list just goes on and on. Almost everywhere you look in the hospital; there's something breakable. Doesn't it seem to you that this is not the best place to work for someone who . . . uh . . . has a problem with awkwardness?"

"I suppose. But I gotta work."

"Well, then, not at a restaurant either. All those dishes. Maybe a drygoods store. Something with a lot of cloth."

"It doesn't matter, Father. I think I've tried them all. There's no place where you can't spill things, break them, damage them, rip them, and on and on. When I got this job here at St. Vincent's, I decided this was it. This was where it was going to come together. I would work here till I retire. And now I'm on the verge of being fired."

"Well, we all have to alter our goals every once in a while, you know."

"There's something else."

"There is?"

"It's a fella. My first real fella, would you believe that? Yeah, I guess you would."

"Not really. . ." Koesler attempted to dismiss her disclaimer.

"Sure you would. Anybody would. I mean, look at me. I know you're a priest and all that, but you've got to have at least looked at girls. Marilyn Monroe I ain't. Not really bad looking, but no raving beauty either. Just barely good enough so that a few fellas have asked me out down through the ages. But once we get out on the date and I spill and break enough things, that's it! One-date Ethel. Until now. Now I got a fella and I think this one's gonna take."

Koesler felt himself desperately hoping that Ethel was right about this upswing in her love life. "Well, that sounds great. Just what the doctor ordered, as it were. If this works out—and you sound pretty confident—this job isn't all that important. So what if you lose it? Your fella can bring home the bacon and you can gracefully retire and become a homemaker." Koesler knew that by current standards this scenario reeked of male chauvinism. But for her benefit he was trying to conjure up a padded cell with as few breakables as possible.

"But see, Father, that's sort of the good news and the bad news."

"Oh?"

"The good news is I think I got a man and I think I really love him and I think he really loves me. But the bad news is he's as clumsy as me. That's why we get along so good. We wouldn't even think about complaining about each other. It's more like looking in a mirror.

"Besides, I think he's so nice he might not dump me even if he wasn't as clumsy as me. But the thing is, he is. And he's gonna spend the rest of his life going from one lousy job to another. He ain't got much of a job now. In fact, it's a worse job than any that I've ever had. But even with all that, he still is a volunteer here at the hospital . . . ain't that something?"

"That certainly is something." Koesler got the image of two people slowly sinking in quicksand and being clumsy about it to boot.

"That's why my original promise to myself is so important, Father. I got to keep this job. I got to prove to myself and the rest of the world that I can hold this job. It may be Bruce who stays home and keeps house. That's fine by me. I don't mind working outside the home. But I gotta keep this job, Father; I gotta!"

Koesler was impressed. He had met very few who were more determined than this young lady. Nor few who were more doomed to failure.

"All of which," Koesler said, "gets us down to the question that occurred to me when you first began speaking to me. Why are you telling me all this?"

"Because I thought you could help. Ain't that what priests are supposed to do—help?"

For an instant, Koesler wondered if it had all begun in the early forties when Bing Crosby became Father Chuck O'Malley in *Going My Way?* The fictional O'Malley did, indeed, go around helping. There was nothing he set his hand or heart to that wasn't helped or fixed. Everything from the local Dead End Kids to the parish mortgage.

The movie was released two years after Koesler entered the seminary high school, so he hadn't been intimately familiar with what priests could or could not fix before The Groaner became a clergyman. But Koesler's many years of experience since his own ordination indicated that priests were by no means able to solve everything. That sort of magic was reserved to the world of fiction. And this was one of those cases whose solution was simply beyond his power.

"You're right, Ethel: Priests are supposed to help. And I want to help you. But how can I?"

"Well, I thought you maybe would talk to Sister Eileen. Maybe talk her out of firing me. You could do that, couldn't you?"

"Sure, I could talk to Sister. But this is her hospital, not mine. I can plead your case—and I will—but she's the boss. Besides, I'm here only temporarily. Don't you know the regular chaplain, Father Thompson? He'd be an even better go-between than I. He's here full-time. This is his job. He'd be more familiar with the way this hospital runs. He knows Sister Eileen better than I do. I'm not trying to pass the buck . . . really I'm not. I'm just trying to get you the best help I can."

Ethel's shoulders dropped in an attitude of resignation. "Father Thompson's a nice guy. He just ain't here when I need him. By the time he comes back from vacation, Sister will have fired me. I just feel it." There was a moment of silence, then Ethel spoke again. "It's okay, Father. You talk to Sister and do what you can and I'll appreciate it. But I gotta do something on my own. I gotta hold on to this job. That's all there is to it. No matter what

I got to do I got to hang on to this job. No matter what."
She began massaging her forehead.

Koesler was concerned. "Is there something wrong,
Ethel? Don't you feel well?"

"Oh, it's okay, Father. Just a headache. I been getting
lots of them lately. I don't know. Maybe it's the stress.
It's okay."

"Ethel, I really think it's a big mistake for you to put all
your eggs in one basket. Particularly this basket. There are
undoubtedly lots of jobs you could do well. Tell you what,
I'll even help you find one."

"No, thanks, Father. I've gone as far as I'm gonna go.
This is where the searching stops. I gotta make it in this
job. I gotta make Bruce proud of me. I gotta hold the job
for the two of us. And this is the one. It's gotta be, no
matter what. No matter what."

Ethel rose from her chair a bit unsteadily. The chair
tipped and fell.

Koesler half-rose as if to help, but she waved him away.
"It's okay, Father. I'm okay." She picked it up with a
"See?" and carefully slid it in place, hitting Koesler on
the knee.

Koesler seated himself and watched her as she left the
cafeteria. What chance did she have? None that he could
think of. He would keep his word and talk to Sister Eileen
in Ethel's behalf. But he was certain it would do little
good. Even if he could dissuade Eileen from letting Ethel
go just now, she would go on causing havoc all around
here. Eventually, she would have to go.

He only wished she were not sticking so single-mindedly
to this specific position. Even with her penchant for clumsiness, she probably could wander from one job to another
until money from something like Social Security would
rescue her.

A vast pity, too, he thought, that she intended to marry

practically a cloned klutz. She might have married someone who could have cared for her and removed her from what had become her enemy—the job market. Pity A great pity.

Koesler now was virtually alone in the cafeteria.

What was it that nurse had said: something about a patient in trouble. Something she had said had struck a chord in him. The room number, that was it. Twenty-two something—what was it? Oh, 2214. Yes, that was it.

Fortunately, he had his patient chart at his side. Number 2214 . . . who was in that room? Alva Crawford and Millie Power. He remembered them now. Alva had been his wild-goose chase. The lady who might have wanted to go to confession if she had been a Catholic. And the other one, Millie Power, had, as he recalled, pneumonia. She was the one who claimed Dr. Jesus as her physician.

Koesler wondered which of the ladies was in trouble: Millie, who had seemed to be recovering nicely from a bout with pneumonia; or Alva, who probably had had her operation during which she would have to swallow a dreaded tube. On the face of it, Koesler guessed the crisis patient must be Alva.

He was wrong, as he discovered upon entering Room 2214. There was a great deal of activity going on around Millie Power's bed, while Alva Crawford intently watched her small-screen TV. Evidently, Alva considered this problem to be none of her business and she was not about to get involved.

Nevertheless, Koesler approached Alva's bedside. Actually, if he were going to move at all in that small room, the only direction open to him was toward Alva's bed. Reluctantly, she took her eyes from the television and glanced at him briefly.

"What happened, Alva?" Koesler asked softly. He did

not wish to disturb the consultation that was being stage-whispered around Millie's bed.

"She got sick." Alva nodded toward Millie.

"Do you know what's wrong?"

Alva shook her head. "I guess they don't either."

"Oh."

Alva returned her attention to soap-opera time. Koesler remained standing near the head of her bed. It was the only place in the room whence he could have a clear vision of Millie.

She certainly looked gravely ill. She appeared to be unconscious. At least her eyes were closed as her head moved slowly from side to side on the firm white pillow. Then Koesler noticed her hands. They were restless, moving up and down her arms, seeming to scratch endlessly. He could hear only snatches of the conversation going on around her bedside.

"Did you change her medication in any way?" The speaker appeared to be a doctor. The telltale stethoscope. But more than that, the imperious attitude one occasionally finds in a doctor. He was angry. Obviously, his patient was not doing well and it was up to him to discover the reason.

"No, Dr. Wilson," said the brunette that Koesler had noticed earlier in the cafeteria.

"I don't understand it," Wilson whispered. "I don't understand it at all. Her blood pressure has dropped out the bottom. I don't understand. There's no reason for this to be happening."

No one responded. Perhaps, Koesler thought, no one else could understand it either. At least none of them offered any possible solution. Wilson whispered something to the others. It sounded like he was giving instructions. But Koesler could barely hear the doctor, and the little he could make out was, to him, unintelligible medicalese.

When Wilson finished, all the medical personnel left the room.

Koesler approached Millie. Clearly she was in great distress. He tried to touch one of her hands, but Millie shook him off and continued her ceaseless scratching.

Koesler strongly suspected she could hear him. He began slowly and loudly to recite the Twenty-Third, his favorite Psalm. *"The Lord is my shepherd, I shall not want . . ."*

He thought she seemed more calm. Her expression appeared to have relaxed somewhat.

". . . And I shall dwell in the house of the Lord for years to come."

He paused. She lost the little serenity she seemed to have gained. He took out the small booklet, *Pastoral Care of the Sick,* and turned to a *Blessing for the Sick.*

"All praise and glory is yours, Lord our God, for you have called us to serve you in love. Bless Millie so that she may bear this illness in union with your Son's obedient suffering. Restore her to health, and lead her in glory. We ask this through Christ our Lord. Amen."

He looked long at the suffering woman whose affliction remained undiagnosed. Silently, Koesler commended her to the care of her personally selected physician, Dr. Jesus.

Peculiar how quickly the fortunes of life could change, thought Koesler, as he walked slowly up the corridor to the nurses' station. It was just yesterday that Millie was, to the nonmedical eye at least, in fairly good condition. Indeed, it was Millie who had gone out of her way to assure her roommate, Alva, that an operation would go well. Now Alva, who seemed well, had, as promised, successfully undergone her operation and was divorcing herself from Millie's predicament.

At the nurses' station, Koesler shuffled through the patient lists trying to organize the order of his visits so he would not be constantly doubling back and forth. As he did so, he became aware of someone very nearby talking, but not to him. He looked up to see the same two nurses whom he'd recently observed in the cafeteria. They were again conversing and once more disregarding his presence.

". . . Just the same, it's not fair. How can he blame you for something that isn't your fault? As a matter of fact, it's probably his fault."

"Maybe he's just frustrated. After all, she was doing just fine yesterday."

"That happens. I've seen it a zillion times. When you've had as much experience as I have you'll know the signs."

"Come on, now, I didn't pass boards yesterday. I tell you this one's different. It's like she came in with one problem and overnight she came down with an entirely new and different illness."

"Even that. I've seen that, too."

"Maybe you're right. But then, why was Dr. Wilson so bugged? He certainly must have encountered this before. I mean if you have—"

"Malpractice. They're all running scared of malpractice suits."

"You think she could sue?"

"If she survives, sure. If not, watch out for the relatives. How bad is she anyway?"

"Pretty bad. Blood pressure dangerously low. Looks as if she's about to slip into a coma. Keeps scratching herself. Why would she be itchy? She certainly wasn't yesterday."

The blonde grew thoughtful. "Blood pressure dropping, and itching. Hmmm . . . I don't know. Sounds like an allergic reaction to something. There was a patient here, oh, about four or five years ago, who had the same kind of reaction. I know the doctor had a hard time of it. At first he couldn't . . ."

Koesler stopped listening. He was distracted by a memory. What was it the blonde nurse just said? She knew a patient who had had "an allergic reaction to something" and, as a result had ended up with about the same sort of symptoms as Millie Power.

Why did that ring a bell? Hadn't Millie told him something to that effect? Something that had happened to her after she was admitted to the hospital. Somebody had asked her something. If she would be in some kind of test program. And she was about to agree to it when she remembered that she was allergic to penicillin. So they had taken her out of the program. Was it possible? It didn't seem likely. But it certainly seemed possible.

"Excuse me . . ." He spoke up, interrupting the two nurses, who looked at him somewhat startled. "Excuse me," he was speaking to the blonde nurse, "but did you just say something about a patient who had an allergic reaction or something . . . and that it produced symptoms something like what Millie Power has?"

The blonde nodded. It was obvious from the roman collar beneath his hospital jacket that he was with the pastoral care department. Her expression was a blend of "What's it to you?" and "Where did you come from?"

"Well," Koesler said almost apologetically, "I was just wondering: When I first visited with Millie, she mentioned that shortly after she was admitted, a doctor asked her to be a part of some hospital experiment. And she was about to say yes when she remembered that she had an allergy to penicillin. And she would have been given penicillin if she had been in the experiment. Do you suppose there could have been some mix-up and she got included in the test? And that what she's got now could be a reaction to the penicillin?"

With a look of great incredulity, the brunette slowly

extracted Millie Power's chart from the file drawer, carefully opened it, and studied it.

"Well . . . I'll be damned," the brunette said. After a brief pause, she added, "Oh, excuse me, Father."

10

"IT WAS ALL A MATTER OF TIM-ing"

"Timing!"

"Yes," affirmed Whitaker. "The timing was off just a bit."

"Bah!" said the Third Man. "That's like a weather forecaster saying that if only the day had lasted forty-eight hours, his prediction of rain would have come true."

"No, it isn't."

"Hear him out," said the Fourth Man.

"Everything worked!" Whitaker said in a tone of incredulity. "It worked just as I had it planned. They gave her the penicillin routinely, without asking any questions or informing anyone else. Just because her chart indicated she was in that study group, they gave her the penicillin. And she had her allergic reaction to it. She got sick and she was getting sicker as time went on."

"So what was wrong with the timing?" the First Man demanded.

"I'm getting to that. I was watching her very carefully. I was waiting for her to get sick enough so that they would really worry about her dying. Then I was going to get a note to that reporter—Lennon—and inform her of what was going on. That a patient was dying because the hospital messed up her chart and, even though she told them she was allergic to it, they were giving her penicillin for her pneumonia. Once the reporter got involved in saving the woman from the hospital's mistake, she would have to report what's going on there. And just as soon as the media started getting in there, the lid would come off."

"He's right, you know," the Fourth Man said. "When a Catholic hospital refuses to follow the clear teachings of the Catholic Church, that's news. All we have to do is show them what's going on."

"Oh, yeah?" the First Man said. "If that's so, then why didn't that reporter write up the hospital's policy on birth control? She knew about it. You led her to it. Or so you said!"

"I did lead her to it! And she did see what was going on! And after that . . . I don't know!"

"Quiet down," the Fourth Man cautioned, "or that guard will come over and break up our meeting."

"I don't know," Whitaker repeated in a more restrained tone. "I really don't. Somebody told me she was working on a feature story on the hospital. But I don't know; if she changed her mind and was going to do a story on the immoral birth control, she would have just done it. Don't you think?"

"All I can think of is that the nun must have charmed her, or scared her, or something. But I'm positive Lennon could not look the other way if I could have handed her the story of how the hospital was killing one of its patients. And we would have had it all—the story would have been out and Lennon would have stopped the experiment before it had gone too far and killed the patient!''

''Okay,'' the Third Man said, ''if, as you claim, you finally did something right, what happened? What threw your goddam timing off?''

''Watch your language!'' the Fourth Man cautioned. ''There's no need to take the Lord's name in vain!''

The Third Man shrugged. ''What threw your timing off?''

''That priest! Koesler!''

''What! How?''

''Somehow he found out what was going on. I don't know how. But he told one of the nurses that the patient was allergic to penicillin. The only thing I can figure is that the woman herself must have told him. It's the only way he could have known. Just lucky!''

''Was he 'just lucky' when he saw through our plot to even the score with those seminary professors a few years ago? Was it just luck that put us in here?'' the Third Man challenged.

''You're right,'' the First Man said. ''You're absolutely right. Koesler is a clear and present danger to us. He's going to ruin our plan again.''

''Unless we do something about it!'' The Third Man's meaning was evident.

''Now, wait a minute!'' Whitaker said.

''Yes, wait a minute!'' the Fourth Man agreed.

''Why not?'' the Third Man pressed. ''We are just trying to do God's holy will and Koesler keeps getting in our way.''

''He's a priest!'' Whitaker protested.

''So? What was it, you know, Peter O'Toole said—Will no one rid me of this troublesome priest?''

''Yes,'' Whitaker said, ''and they went out and killed Thomas à Becket. And he became a saint.''

"That was different. Henry was wrong. And we are doing God's work. I only brought that up to show that it's possible to at least think about killing a priest."

"The whole thing makes me shudder," Whitaker complained. "We are doing God's will. We're not trying to kill anybody."

"We may have to."

"I don't want to think about it."

"Let's just put that notion on the back burner," the Fourth Man said. "What we must consider is where, if anywhere, we are going from here."

"I've got another idea," Whitaker volunteered.

"No!" the First Man said.

"Not again," the Third Man said.

"Let's hear him out," the Fourth Man said.

"I've been keeping my eyes and ears open and I've got a plan. A very good plan. What would you say if I told you I could shut down the operating room?"

"I'd say you couldn't do it," said the Third Man.

"I'd say so what?" the First Man said.

"So what," Whitaker replied, "is just this: The operating room is the hub of the hospital. It's where the hospital makes most of its money. If the operating room closes down, there is no possible way the hospital can avoid tons of publicity. It's like a baseball team trying to play without any pitchers. I guarantee you, once the operating room closes, there will be reporters, radio, and TV crews all over the place. From that point on, it will be easy to get them interested in 'other things' that are going on in that supposedly Catholic institution."

"So," the Third Man evidently was not convinced, "how can you do that?"

"Leave it to me."

"Ha!" the Third Man commented.

276

"We have no one else," the Fourth Man said. "We must leave it to you. We put our trust in you."

"Thanks. I won't fail you. And . . . I have this feeling. I mean there are a couple of portents that seem to indicate that things have turned around for us . . . that things are looking up."

"What are they, Bruce?" The Fourth Man said. "God knows, we certainly could use a favorable sign or two."

"Well, for one thing, there was that control-group experiment at the hospital."

"You mean when you got the patient to be given penicillin when she was allergic to it?"

"Yes. I overheard some of the hospital personnel talking about it, several times, as a matter of fact. They kept talking about how not only did she have the wrong protocol number that would include her in the experiment, but she also did not have any sticker on her chart that indicated she was allergic to the medicine.

"So I remember very clearly removing the number they gave her when she was admitted and substituting the number that would put her in the experiment. But I don't remember pulling off the sticker that said she shouldn't be given penicillin.'

"How could you—"

"That's just it—I must have. There was no other way it could have worked. I take that as a sign—a sign that things are turning around for us. It was a miracle, I guess, how that sticker disappeared from the lady's chart. It must have been a miracle. I didn't take the sticker off—and yet, I did. What else could anyone call it?"

"Dumb luck," the Third Man said.

"Maybe he's right,' the Fourth Man said. "Anyway, Bruce, you said there were a couple of portents that augured well for us. What else beside the disappearance of the telltale sticker?'

"Well, this very meeting right now. We've been talking for a long time and nothing's gone wrong. Not one of us has had an accident or done anything to attract the guard's attention or anything like that. Now I ask you: Doesn't that bode well?"

"Maybe. But I still think we've got to keep our options open on Father Koesler. He may have to be eliminated."

"I don't even want to think about that," said Whitaker.

"Don't think about it,' the Fourth Man reassured. "As I said before, we'll put that on the back burner. We may have to consider it, but, for the moment, let's just put all our chips on Bruce's plan. We're behind you, Bruce."

"Wait a minute!" The Third Man looked searchingly at the First Man. "Did you take anything from the Big Top again?"

"No. . . ." The First Man hesitated.

"How about the chow cart?"

"No, absolutely not."

"Then what's that bulge under your shirt?"

"Nothing."

"Something. Obviously something."

"Well, maybe I took a little something out of the Big Top."

"You're going to do it to us again, aren't you, dummy!"

"I'm not doing anything to you guys. It's just that I get hungry. It's just for me and don't worry about it. I can take care of myself. No one is going to catch me at this. I am going to get away with this, just watch."

And it's likely he would have gotten away with it if he hadn't, as he walked past the guard, folded his arms so tightly across his chest that one end of the loaf protruded from the open collar of his shirt. No guard could miss that. And this one didn't.

✛ ✛ ✛

"Let me understand this," Sister Eileen addressed her somewhat apprehensive secretary, "a patient entered St. Vincent's with a mild case of pneumonia. Her prognosis was good. There were no known complications."

Dolly nodded.

"Somehow she was put in a test group that was to be given penicillin, even though she had stated that she was allergic to the drug."

Dolly nodded.

"The admissions clerk's records show she was given the correct protocol number that would have excluded her from the test group. Yet, that is not the number that was found on her chart. The number on her chart automatically placed her in the study and insured that she would receive the penicillin."

Dolly nodded.

"We have on record that someone remembers seeing the allergy-warning sticker on her chart. Yet the sticker seems to have just disappeared somewhere along the way."

Dolly nodded.

"She was given penicillin and we almost killed her. Is all that a fairly accurate history of this patient?"

"Yes, Sister."

Eileen leaned forward, resting her elbows on the desk. She massaged her temples with her fingertips. "Why wasn't I told about this immediately?"

"Because"—Dolly shifted her weight; she'd been standing quite a while—"Mr. Haroldson took immediate charge of the investigation. He told everyone you were not feeling well and you were not to be disturbed. But after I thought about it for a while it seemed to me you'd want to know no matter how you felt."

"I feel fine!" Eileen snapped, though she did not appear well. The unrelenting headache had left her pale and in obvious pain.

"Yes, Sister."

"On top of it all, the patient might actually have died if Father Koesler had not remembered a conversation wherein she had mentioned her allergy to penicillin."

"Well, that's probably true, Sister. Except that the doctors told Mr. Haroldson that they would probably have identified the allergic condition if her symptoms had continued much longer. And Mr. Haroldson says that's probably true."

Eileen thought about that for a few moments. "All right, so she probably would not have died. The fact remains, we made her a very sick person."

Dolly nodded.

"I suppose we ought to prepare for a malpractice suit."

"I don't think so, Sister."

"No?" Eileen was surprised.

"No. It seems Mrs. Power is a very religious woman. According to Father Koesler, she tends to put herself in the hands of God. Father mentioned that she refers to God as 'Dr. Jesus.' Anyway, everything that happens to her is fate—"

"Or providence."

"Yes. So the bad period she just went through—"

"Was God's will . . . is that it?"

"That's it."

"It seems I've been getting a lot of 'good news-bad news' packages lately." Her frown intensified. "Whatever else happens, we've got to get to the bottom of this. We've got to find the responsible party or parties and take appropriate action. This particular calamity seems to have had a relatively happy ending, but there is no doubt it could have been a disaster. We've got to find out who's responsible for this. Dolly, please tell Mr. Haroldson to see me about this at his earliest convenience."

"Yes, Sister." Dolly exited.

Eileen continued to massage her temples. Something was wrong; no doubt about that. Never before had she had such a persistent and intense headache. But now was not the time to be sick. So she would not be. She could not be. She had to stay on top of this mess.

Thanks to the remarkable faith of Millie Power, there would be no outside repercussions. But there might have been. There could have been. A malpractice suit could have caused such an increase in their insurance premiums that St. Vincent's simply could not have afforded it. With no insurance coverage, St. Vincent's would have been forced, at long last, to close its doors for good and all. And if the unaffordable insurance had not done the job, the media coverage would have accomplished the same.

Cardinal Boyle could be counted on to look the other way as St. Vincent's fudged on Catholic teaching in order to be relevant to its community. But massive media coverage could not be overlooked. Sister Eileen could not guess how the hierarchy would react to a media exposé of St. Vincent's. And she didn't want to find out.

In either eventuality—litigation or publicity—St. Vincent's seemed the loser.

Pat Lennon riffled through her notepad. She appeared to be studying the contents. Actually, her attention was some distance from the city room of the *Detroit News*. She was thinking about St. Vincent's. She was supposed to be doing a story on St. Vincent's. But there wasn't much connection between her notes on St. Vincent's and her musings about St. Vincent's.

She had completed all the research needed for the *Michigan Magazine* article. She had gathered all the background information and done all the interviews. The facts were scattered throughout her notebook. All she had to do was put them together. But rather than collating the material, she was woolgathering.

It was unlike Pat Lennon. She was a professional who could be depended upon. Editors had become used to giving her an assignment and then not having to be concerned about it again. Lennon would bring it in acceptably and on time. While time on a piece for the Sunday magazine was somewhat more leisurely measured than for the regular daily deadline, she was admittedly procrastinating. She had the data. All she had to do was write it up.

But she was distracted by something she could not quite define. Call it a sixth sense, or intuition, or perhaps a hunch. There was some impending danger at St. Vincent's Hospital. She had felt it during some of her interviews, notably with John Haroldson and Dr. Lee Kim. There was some unrest among certain of the nursing staff. Even Sister Rosamunda seemed to be holding something back. And Lennon had anticipated nothing but the stereotypical sweet little old nun.

Then there was Sister Eileen herself. Somehow she seemed to be the cynosure of the hostility Lennon had uncovered. Pat was also concerned about Eileen's present state. The crippling headache from which the nun was suffering seemed to make her more vulnerable.

Yet there was nothing Lennon could do about a premonition, or intuition, or a hunch. Staff reporters dealt in facts, events, reality, not in emotional reaction, no matter how strong it might be.

She sighed. Enough of this! Speculation was the purview of columnists and editorialists. She was a pawn in the chess game of journalism. Let's turn this story out! She switched on the CRT.

"Lennon!" It was Bob Ankenazy.

She looked up and reflexively turned off the word processor.

"All hell's broken loose at Van's Can. A full-scale riot! The prisoners have barricaded themselves in the central dining area—the . . . uh . . . Big Top. The riot's less than half an hour old. We've got three people on the scene. We need a rewrite and you're it! Get on the phone—line three. The story's coming in right now."

This, she thought, is more like it. A breaking news story you can sink your teeth into. Nothing speculative or conjectural about this: X-number of prisoners have rioted, X-number of prison guards have been taken hostage, X-number of law enforcement officers will be gathering, armed with everything short of nuclear weapons. There will be X-number of prisoner demands. Eventually, X-number of public officials—mayor, police chief, maybe governor—will assemble.

The first need: Fill in the Xs. Then do a more complete, insightful job of it than either radio or TV, which will reach the public hours before the print medium will be able to tell the story. And, as rewrite, she would quarterback.

For no more than an instant, she thought of Joe Cox. Undoubtedly, he would be covering this for the *Free Press*. She wondered whether he would be on the scene, where he would want to be, or if he would be, as she was, working from the city room. She had no more luxury than an instant to give to Cox. She put on a headset and activated line three.

"Bill Dunnigan," the voice identified.

As the story unfolded, Lennon pictured Dunnigan at the scene. Blond, mild-mannered, wearing granny glasses behind which soft blue eyes usually seemed wide with surprise. Dunnigan was the sort of reporter who could be depended on to bring in a careful story faithful to facts. Dunnigan was a professional in the best sense of the term.

"That you, Pat?"

"Uh-huh."

"Good. What we've got here is an insurrection—a riot. Occurred at 12:25 P.M. in the central dining area—the Big Top, as the prisoners call it. That's upper case B and T. Five guards—all male—have been taken hostage. So far, no one's been hurt. None of the guards was armed. So the prisoners have no weapons except the tools and kitchen utensils they managed to appropriate. That would include screwdrivers, knives, and saws. Of course, to the hostages these things can be both frightening and threatening.

"Actually, the riot just got under way. So there isn't much more to tell just yet. We know there will be demands made. But so far, we have no intimation of what they'll be."

"Is the entire prison population involved—all the inmates?" Lennon was feeding Dunnigan's information into the CRT.

"No. Just the ones who were in the Big Top at that time. That would exclude those inmates restricted to their cells, the ones in solitary, and the ones in the 'dog ward' —the most violent ones."

Lennon liked that. Readers would relish getting acquainted with prison jargon like the "dog ward."

"No," Dunnigan continued, "not everybody. Maybe from 85 to 90 percent of the inmates are in on it. There's talk that the prisoners themselves want to exclude three of their fellow inmates from the riot. None of us can figure that out yet. The word is that these three are born losers, considered jinxes by the others. If this is true, those three jerks must be the crap de la crap. It may make a good side-bar. I'll get into that later. Right now, we're waiting for the mayor, who's supposed to be on his way over. I'll be back to you."

The connection went dead. Concise, factual, interesting, current, with a possible side-bar—everything you'd need to begin an important, breaking news story. Lennon had

284

no sooner completed feeding the CRT when the phone rang again.

"Pfeiffer. This you, Lennon?"

Pat shook her head. Mark Pfeiffer was close to being the antithesis of Bill Dunnigan. Where Dunnigan was careful, factual, inclined to understatement, Pfeiffer was careless, and often inaccurate, with a massive ego—built up to defend an equally massive inferiority complex—that crowded out all consideration of others. Pfeiffer's creed seemed to be: He that doth not tooteth his own horn the same shall not get tooted. Finally, Dunnigan was respected and liked by his peers, while Pfeiffer was neither respected nor generally liked.

"Yes, "Lennon responded wearily.

"Listen, this place is a madhouse. Everyone's running around like their ass is on fire. Which reminds me, what are you doing tonight, Honey?"

Silence. Lennon knew of several *News* staffers who would willingly contribute to Pfeiffer's severance pay just to get rid of him.

"Okay." Pfeiffer was undaunted by Lennon's stony silence. "We'll pursue that and you later. Back to the dull stuff. Right now, nobody knows nothing. Seems some inmates got steamed and rioted at lunchtime. Nobody knows for sure whether they're armed, but I'd lay you five-to-one they probably broke into the arsenal and got guns. Now that I think of it, I'd lay you for free gratis."

Silence. Come to think of it, she'd contribute to a fund to have Pfeiffer castrated. Thank God for staffers like Dunnigan. From long experience as well as just the tone of his voice, she could tell Pfeiffer didn't know what he was talking about. If she hadn't had Dunnigan, she would have had nothing. She certainly wasn't going to share a by-line with a nincompoop like Pfeiffer.

"Wait a minute, Sweetie," Pfeiffer continued, "the

mayor just got here. He's being surrounded by the TV and radio creeps, and he's got his usual entourage of bodyguards. But I'll get to him. I'll be right back with you, Honeypot.''

Not if I can holp it, thought Lennon. The problem was, for this story she could not help it. She would have to listen to him, but she didn't have to use anything he called in. And she was fairly certain she would use nothing of his. It wouldn't make any difference. He wouldn't recognize that—despite having his by-line with the others on the story—nothing that he had called in had been used. Lennon would have to rely on the dependable Bill Dunnigan and whoever the third reporter might prove to be.

The phone rang.

''Dunnigan. Pat?''

''Yeah.''

''The mayor's here. Says it's too early to comment; he'll have to hear the demands before he can make a statement. The governor's on his way. But right now, Mayor Cobb is the authority of record. It's his jurisdiction and he's not one to slough it off.

''Pat, this is gonna be a step-by-step procedure. We're going to have to take one comment at a time. So stay with me and I'll give you the developments as they happen. One thing: From everything I've been able to gather so far, this place is going to be shut up tight as a drum even after the riot's been settled. It'll be a long, long time before any of these guys get another visitor from the outside world.''

Father Koesler wondered why it had taken him so long to find the doctors' lounge. It was an almost perfect place to wait for the bereaved when there had been a death in emergency or the operating room. The lounge was comfortable, some unseen hand kept the coffee brewing, and it was near the "quiet room" in that area of the hospital where the chaplain and the bereaved would meet.

Koesler was, indeed, waiting for just such an event. An elderly man had suffered a heart attack while shoveling snow. He was dead on arrival at St. Vincent's emergency room. His next-of-kin had been contacted. Koesler was awaiting them.

In the lounge with Koesler were the members of an OR team, consisting of two surgeons—one of whom was Dr. Lee Kim—an anesthetist, a scrub nurse, and a circulating nurse. They had informed Koesler that they were waiting for a "hand." Someone had put a hand through a pane of glass and, judging by Dr. Kim's blood-spattered tunic, the wrist had bled quite a bit. One of the nurses commented on Kim's stained tunic.

"Wrists bleed," the principal surgeon observed laconically. He introduced himself to Koesler as Dr. James Meyer.

"She really did a job on herself," said Kim, who had treated the patient in the emergency room, thus the blood. "Wrist is almost completely severed."

"Oh. God!" Meyer said, "that means three or four hours."

Both nurses winced. The anesthetist showed no emotion.

"I was home," Meyer said. "We were just getting ready to go skiing at Pine Knob when the damn call came."

"Yeah." The anesthetist smiled. "You said good-bye to me in OR."

"Well, hello again."

"You keep referring to the patient as a 'wrist,' " Koesler addressed him.

"That is all we will see," Kim said. The rest of her will be draped. All that will be exposed will be her wrist. You get used to that after awhile. All you deal with in OR are appendages of one sort or another.''

The nurses' expressions seemed to register a silent protest.

"Do you know what happened to her?'' Koesler asked.

Kim shook his head.

"Didn't you talk to her?'' Koesler could not imagine treating a conscious injured person without inquiring what had happened.

"I used to ask people what happened,'' Kim said, "but it was always the same story. Nothing unexpected. Just walking down the street. Just washing a window. Just opening a door. When the glass broke, or the piano fell, or my boyfriend shot me. Always the same. So, I stopped asking.''

Koesler thought that an odd explanation.

"What's the status?'' Meyer asked.

"I put a pressure pack on it,'' Kim said.

"What time is the hand scheduled?'' Meyer asked.

"Four-thirty,'' a nurse replied.

The principal surgeon consulted his watch and sighed. "It'll go right through dinner.''

The intercom squawked. Koesler was not expecting the voice nor was he attuned to it. He needed a short period to grasp part of what he'd heard and put it together.

There had been an announcement of a trauma. About that he was sure. A trauma case had just entered the emergency room. A motorcyclist had been hit by a car. There were multiple head injuries. There was more to the announcement, but that was all Koesler was able to decipher. He thought that must be the substance of the matter.

Dr. Kim said something. It might have been in his own language. It sounded like an expletive. Koesler didn't understand it, but he recognized the tone. The others registered emotions from disgust to disappointment.

"What's the matter?'' Koesler asked of anyone.

"The head will take precedence over the hand," Dr. Meyer explained.

"They'll have to call in another team," the anesthetist said.

"Looks like we could be here till midnight," one of the nurses said.

There followed a lively discussion ranging from laws that would compel cyclists to wear helmets to the general danger of riding on anything so unprotected.

"Danger or not," Kim said, "that is what I want."

"What's that?" Meyer asked.

"A bike. A big one. With horses to spare."

Koesler was slightly surprised. He never associated the notion of doctors with their wanting anything. His concept was too generalized to be all-encompassing, but Koesler subconsciously thought doctors could buy anything they wanted. Evidently, Dr. Kim could not. Not yet. A big expensive motorcycle must be part of his planned upward mobility. The plan that Dr. Scott had described.

"I've got a friend with a bike like that," Meyers said, "who wants me to go along on a ride all the way out to the West Coast. A nut."

"Sounds terrific," Kim said. "If you do not want to go, you might tell your friend that there is another doctor at St. Vincent's who is willing to go along with him."

"Who said anything about a 'him'?"

Kim smiled. "Even better."

The phone rang. Kim picked it up. "Yes, the cyclist . . .? He what . . .?

"You could not, eh . . .?

"Well, that is terrific news! Very good! Magnificent!" Kim hung up and turned to his team. He obviously considered himself the bearer of good news. "The cyclist is dead. He arrested in ER and they could not stabilize him. The hand is coming down now."

For just a moment, revulsion passed across the faces of the two nurses. Neither Meyer nor the anesthetist displayed any emotion.

"Will we do this with a local or are you going to put her out?" Meyer asked.

"She'll be asleep," the anesthetist replied.

A medical student appeared at the door of the lounge. "Your family is here, Father," he announced.

"Thanks." Koesler rose and left the lounge for the quiet room that in a few minutes would not be very quiet. He was shocked at Dr. Kim's reaction to the death of the cyclist. Koesler could not imagine exulting over the death of anyone, much less a stranger whose care would be the cause of nothing more than an inconvenience.

During his time as temporary chaplain at St. Vincent's, Koesler had met many other Oriental doctors on the hospital's staff. He had never encountered a shred of indifference to human life from any of them. Before coming to St. Vincent's, he had shared the Occidental prejudice which hold that Orientals had a lesser value for life. That prejudice had been shaken when a Philippine parishioner had reminded Koesler that, to date, only Americans had dropped a nuclear bomb, that it was the Occidental allies who had leveled much of Germany with bombs of just about every description, and it was the United States that nearly destroyed Vietnam and Cambodia.

Considerations like that could shake one's faith in convenient prejudices.

And, as far as St. Vincent's was concerned, there was no hint of a lack of respect for life among either Occidentals or Orientals.

With the major exception of Dr. Lee Kim.

Until now, Koesler had only heard-tell of Dr. Kim's reputedly casual approach to human feelings and life. Now,

Koesler felt he had experienced at least the semblance of such an attitude.

Of course it was possible that Kim's reaction to the death of a patient might have been a poor joke or perhaps an aberrant response. But given his reported history, this probably was Kim's real personality.

If this were true, Koesler wondered further about Kim's attitude toward Sister Eileen. If Kim, indeed, had precious little regard for human life, and if Sister Eileen posed a serious challenge to all Kim desired, what might be Kim's intent with regard to Eileen? Could he be a threat? To her life?

Koesler had no answer to these questions. At the moment, they were no more than hypothetical. But how long could such a dangerous hypothesis go unchallenged? Koesler had no answer to this question either. Nor had he any more time to spend on such speculation. He was nearing the quiet room and a very vocal group was impatiently awaiting.

George Snell, nonpareil guard of St. Vincent's Hospital, assessed his situation.

On the plus side: He didn't have to patrol the ill-lit corridors. All he needed to do for this entire night shift was sit in the command center and watch the closed-circuit monitors. It was a promotion, with a promised raise in the near future. And he was out of harm's way.

Actually, he never thought of St. Vincent's Hospital in terms of danger. He was a very large man. And he was imbued with the false confidence of the big man who feels he can handle any challenge. He had never been thrown by a small person who was skilled in the martial arts. He had never even given any consideration to that possibility.

On the negative side: He didn't have to patrol the ill-lit corridors. Thus he would have no opportunity to find empty rooms with empty beds and a growing list of willing nurses and aides to help fill them. This was the one and only negative factor. But given Snell's proclivity for rambunctious sex, it was nearly enough to offset all the positive factors.

Upon further thought, he would add one more drawback. It was dull.

He tilted his chair back and propped his feet on the desk. He scanned the four monitors. One was out of order. Well, he thought, three out of four ain't bad. The three functioning screens revealed little. The areas they covered were, by and large, not sufficiently illuminated to avoid obscuring shadows. Some system, thought Snell; if thieves wanted to clean out St. Vincent's, nighttime, with a skeleton staff and monitors that were either inadequate or nonfunctioning, would be the time to do it.

Fortunately, there was a commercial television set in the room. It was a miniature set, identical to those provided the patients. The set might be small but the picture was in color and it provided just the distraction that Snell would need to get him through the night.

WKBD-TV, Channel 50, was carrying a rerun of an old "Barney Miller" episode. Snell had seen practically every "Miller" show repeatedly. He now was able to anticipate most of the dialogue. From the first few frames of tonight's program, Snell instantly recalled the entire plot. Wojo's girlfriend bakes a batch of cookies. Wojo brings the cookies to the squad room where Sergeants Harris and Yamana eat a goodly supply and then begin to react. Eventually, Barney wants to know what's happening. A bemused Harris diagnoses that the cookies have been laced with hashish.

Snell could hardly wait for Harris to say he thought there was hash in the cookies. ". . . from the way that I feel . . ." Then Yamana would continue the thought in song: ". . . when that bell starts to peal. Why, it's almost like being in love."

Great episode. Snell had always thought Barney Miller was the coolest dude. He intended this as a compliment from one law-enforcement officer to another, of course.

Before beginning his own evening program, Bruce Whitaker took the time to check out the command center. He was overjoyed to find George Snell ensconced there and completely absorbed by a TV program.

This Bruce took to be a further sign of divine providence. Snell had appeared to be his nemesis. Twice, when Whitaker was on his way toward that ill-fated mission to mutilate the IUDs and while he was altering the pneumonia patient's chart, he had almost been apprehended by the same guard—George Snell.

But increasingly, Whitaker was becoming convinced that God was prospering his objective.

There was no question that the IUD caper had been botched. But how could anyone have expected him to know the difference between an intrauterine device and curtain hooks when he'd never even seen an IUD and the curtain hooks were in the drawer reserved for IUDs?

On the positive side—and for Whitaker a very definite plus—he hadn't been caught. That was definitely providential.

God's protective hand had been even more in evidence in his second attempt, Whitaker thought. While he was altering that woman's chart, Snell had had him dead-to-rights. All the guard had to do after calling out to him was simply walk the rest of the way down that corridor and Whitaker would have been apprehended red-handed.

But something miraculous had happened: The guard had disappeared somewhere. Figure the odds on something like that! So, Whitaker had been able to finish his work. And even though for the life of him, Whitaker could not remember removing the allergy sticker from the chart, that plan had worked. God was indeed good.

Or at least the plan would have worked if that priest hadn't interfered. If only the woman had been given the penicillin a bit longer! When she had gotten near death, Whitaker would have seen to it that the news media got the story, and the hospital and all of its immoral deeds would have been exposed for all to see. Then the archdiocese would have been forced to act. . . .

But now he was on the right trail. He knew it. He sensed it. The very fact that his nemesis, Guard Snell, would not be out roaming the halls was an added and very welcome sign that God was with him. God wills it! The battle cry of the Crusades—those of yore as well as this present one.

After checking out the command center, such as it was, Whitaker made his way through the empty corridors en route to the operating room area.

At least Whitaker *thought* the halls were empty. He saw no one as he kept to the shadowy walls. But someone was there. Someone following him. Someone who had stalked him in the past. But the one keeping vigil was even more careful than Whitaker to remain undetected.

Cautiously, Whitaker eased open the door to the operating room area. A soft, indirect light illuminated the area just enough so that anyone unfamiliar with the territory might avoid running into anything. That is, if he—or she—were careful.

At least one possible major block was missing. No one was in the area. Of course there was no elective surgery at this late hour, but there was no emergency surgery either.

Whitaker had the place to himself. Or so he thought. Aware of his penchant for clumsiness, he moved very slowly and carefully. As he moved, he noted that he was colliding with nothing, upsetting nothing, making no noise whatever. This he again interpreted to mean that God was with him.

Whitaker now stood in the doorway of Operating Room One. By now, his eyes had adjusted to the dim light. He looked around the room. It was an old hospital and an old room. But the equipment was about as up-to-date as St. Vincent's tight budget could afford. It had long been the hospital's policy that while they must scrimp on some facilities and functions, OR was given a prime budget position.

Whitaker allowed himself a moment of awe at the many complex machines as well as the thorough sterility of the place.

But he knew what he had to do. He'd gone out of his way both to remain undetected and, at the same time, to listen in on conversations of personnel in the anesthesia department. He had also spent considerable time in the medical library. All this research led him to the head of the operating table, the area where the nurse anesthetist would function.

It was easy to find the container of nitrous oxide. The canister was clearly labeled. Deliberately, Whitaker turned the handle, releasing the gas. That was really all he had to do—just let the gas escape.

He then repeated this same procedure in the other operating rooms.

Tomorrow, when the anesthetists attempted to anesthetize their first patients, an inadequate supply of nitrous oxide would be delivered. The patients would be near death. The anesthetists would notice this and "bag" the patients, manually delivering life-saving oxygen. But the operations would have to be canceled. And no one would know why the patients had arrested. Without knowing the cause of this life-treatening situation, they would have to close down the operating rooms—the chief money-making section of the hospital.

If shutting down the operating rooms for unexplainable reasons didn't qualify as a good news story . . . well, he certainly missed his guess. And once the news people were in here, he'd make certain they became interested in more than the operating rooms.

And that was the scenario according to Bruce Whitaker!

Having done the deed, he moved most cautiously out, taking extreme care to upset nothing. In this, he succeeded. God was good!

The eyes that had watched intently as Whitaker had busied himself in the operating rooms now watched him leave. It was not difficult to remain undetected, shielded by the dim light, the shadows, and the huge machines. Particularly if one were familiar with the area.

Once Whitaker was gone, allowing a few minutes more to make sure he would not return, the figure moved out of the shadows to the head of the operating table.

What in the world was he doing? Ah, yes, I see. The nitrous oxide. The handle has been turned. The container is empty. He bled the oxide. But why? What must he think that will do?

Does he think that will somehow hinder the operation procedure? Why else would he have done it? How typical of him!

But why would he . . .? Of course; he plans that the shutdown of the OR will bring the notoriety he wants. Yes, of course. Not a bad idea. If only he could have carried it off!

Well, perhaps I can improve on his plan. Let us see. Whatever is done must be bigger than this and much more attention-getting. Bigger and unavoidably catching every-one's attention . . .

Of course!

Here, in the maintenance closet, there should be . . . yes . . . a screwdriver and a file. Good.

A tank of nitrogen gas, under enormous pressure. It looks like . . . what?—a torpedo. And it can become one. It rests on its three-wheeled cart. If I loosen the cotter pins of the wheel on one side . . . there. Now, if I file through the cap until it is hanging by a thread . . .

There.

Now I have but to leave it resting against this outer wall. Now it is a bomb waiting to explode. My inept friend would have been so pleased with himself if he had thought of this. Never mind. As long as it accomplishes our pur-pose. And it will.

Before leaving the operating room, the mysterious fig-ure dropped rubber gloves into a waste container. A pre-caution Bruce Whitaker had not thought to take.

11

" ' . . . *SINCERELY YOURS, ET CE-*
tera.*' And Dolly make sure that letter gets in tomorrow
morning's mail. It's important that the Cardinal has ad-
vance notice that I won't be able to attend next week's
vicariate meeting."

"Yes, Sister." Dolly had filled many notebook pages
with Sister Eileen's dictated letters. Ordinarily, instead of
asking Dolly to stay late, Sister would have used the tape
recorder. But tonight, it was as if Eileen were doing
something akin to making out her last will and testament.
She had caught up on all her correspondence, which was
unusual for her. Odder still, she had cleared her calendar
for the foreseeable future, canceling appointments and ap-
pearances. Dolly could not understand it. But she was not
the type to question superiors.

Eileen gently massaged her forehead. She was not sure
what was causing the pain. But if she could not shake it
soon, she would be forced to let one of the doctors see if
he could find anything. Meanwhile, she was so sure she

was going to be incapacitated for at least some time, that she had kept Dolly overtime to finish the letters and clear the calendar. And now both were completed.

"Oh, and Dolly, as soon as you can, get someone from maintenance to change the locks on the cabinets and drawers in the pharmacy. And tell them to make sure only the pharmacists have the new keys. Then tell the pharmacists that it is my express order that they let no one else use their keys. No one, no matter who."

"Yes, Sister."

"That'll be all for tonight, Dolly. You'd better get home and get some sleep. There's a heavy snowfall predicted for the early morning hours. If you can't get in on time, don't worry. Just make sure sometime tomorrow you get those letters out. And that notice to maintenance and the pharmacists. That's important. And Dolly: Thanks."

"You're most welcome, Sister." Dolly exited into the outer office, where she put her notes together. She expected she would indeed be late arriving for work in the morning and she wanted everything lined up so she could get it all finished tomorrow. A feat she would accomplish only if there were no unforeseen obstacles.

She dialed the superintendent of maintenance and told him of Eileen's order. Dolly knew Joe to be conscientious; he would not be upset at being called at home. Joe would, she knew, be in at the crack of dawn or earlier no matter how bad the weather became. And he would see to it that the parking area and the approaches to the hospital were cleared of snow.

Now that the pharmacy matter was taken care of, there was just the paperwork to do tomorrow. Dolly bundled herself warmly and made certain she had car keys in hand.

She was about to leave when she heard a small cry and a thud.

Dolly hurried to Sister Eileen's door. She knocked. When there was no answer, she timidly opened the door and peered in.

Sister Eileen was sprawled on the floor. Clearly, she was, at best, unconscious.

Dolly experienced a moment of panic. But, with no one in the immediate vicinity to call on for help, she quickly pulled herself together and dialed emergency.

Dr. Fred Scott was told about the headaches Sister Eileen had been suffering. He knew she had been assaulted the other evening. Putting the two together, he ordered a CAT scan, which revealed what he suspected: Sister Eileen had a subdural hematoma.

Under the best of circumstances, this would be serious. But Eileen was in her late sixties and undoubtedly had been suffering from this condition for up to forty-eight hours. On top of which, she was a nun. Thus, particularly in a Catholic hospital, a Very Important Person. And on top of that, she was chief executive officer. Thus, anywhere, she was a Very, Very Important Person.

Nevertheless, standard protocol was followed.

Dr. Robert Rollins was the neurosurgeon on call. So he was called. But he did not answer. it was not immediately known why he did not answer. Not until the next morning, during the incredible confusion that was to come, was it learned there was nothing wrong with Dr. Rollins's beeper. The trouble was that Dr. Rollins was not wearing his beeper during the time it was beeping. Indeed, Dr. Rollins was not wearing anything.

Dr. Rollins was attending one of the seasonal parties by

300

which Detroiters try to defeat the post-New Year's doldrums. For no discernible reason, Dr. Rollins simply assumed he would not be called while he was on-call. Thus, he entered into the high spirits of the party. So Dr. Rollins's beeper, along with all his clothing, was two rooms removed from the bedroom wherein the doctor and several others were cavorting.

Trying to get Dr. Rollins to respond to his call consumed considerable valuable time. Mostly because the patient was a Very, Very Important Person, a halt was called to the futile efforts to raise Dr. Rollins and the decision was made to contact the first available and qualified neurosurgeon.

Of course it took more time to rouse another neurosurgeon. Then it took more time for the neurosurgeon to dig out and drive down to the hospital. The gently, but steadily, falling snow made the almost deserted streets resemble a picture postcard. But it also made driving slow and treacherous.

Bruce Whitaker had worn white coveralls for his tour of the operating room area. He did so because whites, if not the scrub uniform, were required in that section of the hospital. In the event he had encountered anyone, he would not have been stopped for being out of uniform. As it happened, he had, as far as he knew, come through the venture unscathed. But it never hurt to be careful, as he was learning.

As was the custom, he had donned the white paper coveralls over his street clothes. He was now having considerable trouble getting the overalls off. He had perspired generously and the garment clung to his sweatladen clothing. It did not occur to him that, particularly since whites routinely were discarded like wastepaper, he could simply rip them off. As he struggled to work the coveralls down over his hips, he heard the locker-room door open. He stood absolutely still. The perspiration began again.

"Anyone here?" a small voice inquired.

Whitaker's surprise at hearing a female voice in the men's locker room caused him to topple backward over the low wooden bench. The crash was substantial.

"Who's there?" the small voice asked.

Whitaker, scrunched in the corner, contemplated the folly of overconfidence. Everything had been going swimmingly! Now he would be discovered.

Tentatively, Ethel Laidlaw peered around the corner of the lockers. It was impossible to identify who it was wrapped like a pretzel. "Who is it?"

"Ethel?"

"Bruce?"

"Ethel!"

"Bruce!"

"Ethel, help me."

The plea was redundant. Ethel was already unwinding him.

"How did you ever get tangled up like this?"

"What are you doing here?"

"One thing at a time." Ethel finally got Bruce into a redeemable position, then ripped off the remainder of the coveralls and threw them in the basket.

Whitaker adjusted his toupee, which had slipped to a devil-may-care angle. "What are you doing here?"

"Looking for you."

"Me!"

"I knew you were here somewhere."

"How did you . . .?"

"Oh, Bruce. You want to help me so much. I just knew

you'd be here somewhere trying to help me. I just wasn't sure where I'd find you.''

Still and all, it seemed odd to Whitaker that in the entire hospital, Ethel would have stumbled upon the men's locker room to search. But this was not the best time to sit around wondering. "We've got to get out of here.''

"Gee, I think that might be the worst thing we could do right now.''

"What?''

"This is a bad time—I mean a bad time to leave. It's too late to just walk out as if we were part of one of the shifts going off duty. And it's too early to leave completely unnoticed. Some of the patients get restless about this time and the nurses and the guards are pretty active now. We'd better wait awhile.''

This did not fit into his plan at all. Whitaker was becoming a bit panicky. "Where can we hide?''

"Sometimes the best place to hide is right out in the open.''

"What?''

Ethel removed something from the pocket of her uniform. "Here, take this stethoscope and hang the earpieces around your neck.'' She fixed the medical instrument on him. "Like this. Now, put on your white jacket. See, now you're a doctor. And I'm your nurse. This way, as long as we don't get too close to anyone, and especially if we don't meet anybody who knows you, we'll be able to go anywhere in the hospital until the early hours of the morning. Then we can slip out.''

"You really think so?''

"Uh-huh.''

"Just with this stethoscope?''

"When you see someone, particularly a man, in a white coat with a stethoscope, who do you think he is?''

"A doctor."

Ethel nodded. "And so does everyone else. Come on, let's go."

"Huh?"

"One thing's for sure: We don't want to stay in here. We're pinned down. And for sure I don't want to be caught in the men's locker room."

"Where'll we go?"

"Just walk the main floor, maybe the basement. We don't want to be near the patients. One of them might need a real doctor. Then we'd be in real trouble."

So Whitaker in his white jacket and stethoscope left the locker room with Ethel. The two walked together, slowly but purposefully.

George Snell saw Bruce and Ethel on one of the monitors. They were not of even passing interest to Snell. Just two more figures moving across grainy screens. Besides, Snell was far more involved in what was being shown on commercial TV. And that, as the night or early morning wore on, became more and more select. He was down to mostly test patterns and two UHF channels showing ancient movies. But he kept switching around. One never knew when a given channel might start programming for a new day.

Meanwhile, Bruce and Ethel pretty much maintained their pacing, occasionally resting against an unoccupied booth or station.

"Bruce, I been thinking. We've gotten kind of close, you and me. I mean, we have, haven't we?"

"Yeah, Ethel, I think so. I hope so."

"And you been going out of your way to try and help me with this problem that I got with Sister Eileen."

"Oh, Ethel, it's more than your problem. See, the thing about Sister Eileen, it's bigger than just you and me. I've been meaning to talk to you about that. But it's not time yet. It's too early. At least I think it's too early. But, after tomorrow . . ." Whitaker checked his watch. "Actually, in just a few hours at most . . ."

"That's okay, Bruce. The thing I was gettin' at is . . . well, we're gettin' kinda close, and I think I really like you a lot. But we don't really know each other very good. You don't know anything about my life . . . I mean before we met. And I don't know anything about yours."

"I guess you're right. Is it important to you? I mean, it's not all that important to me. The most important thing for me is that we like each other a lot. Maybe we even love each other."

"I think we do, too, Bruce. But it's important we know more about each other just so's we don't go into this like blind."

"Oh . . ."

"I'll go first. I was the fifth of five children—all girls. I never figured out whether Pa kept trying for a boy and didn't get one and gave up, or whether I wasn't intended at all. All I know is I wasn't terribly wanted. So I had a kind of miserable childhood. I went to parochial school and I was smart enough, but . . . clumsy? I broke everything but the rules. And 'cause the nuns were always yelling at me for being uncoordinated, I didn't do as good in school as I might have. See? There's a good example for you: I know it should be 'I didn't do as *well* in school . . .' But why should I speak correctly when I can't keep a ham sandwich together? I'm so clumsy that I just naturally act dumb. The two go together."

"Gee, Ethel . . ."

"Wait! So I entered a convent but I didn't last past being a postulant. By then I had gummed up so many things the mother house hasn't been the same to this day.

"Since then, I've been pretty much on my own trying to find jobs and—even harder—trying to held onto them after I get them. And that sort of takes us up to the present, where I'm trying like mad to hold onto this job. While the big boss is doing her best to fire me. And what chance do I have in a fight like that!

"So that's what I am, Bruce: a loser. I've been a loser all my life and there ain't nothin' that indicates things are about to change. That's what you got, Bruce, a loser."

"Ethel! You think *you're* a loser! I'll tell you about a loser! I was an only child. And I went to parochial school too. And I was as awkward and clumsy as you even thought about. Only I wasn't as smart as you. So when I went to the seminary, I guess I don't have to tell you I didn't last long.

"Back then, particularly, there were lots of guys in the seminary. And the professors demanded that you put out. They demanded, oh, accomplishment. I gotta confess to you, I've been bitter about that ever since.

"And this is the part that turned out bad: I got in with some other guys and afterward we tried to get even with some of the professors that were in the seminary when we were students. Well, these other guys are easy as clumsy as I am. They won't admit it, but they are. And, well, being the kind of klutzes we are, we didn't actually do all that much damage to the priest-professors. But we did enough so that we all got prison terms. I'm out now on parole. The other guys are still in."

"You mean you actually tried to kill priests? Catholic priests?"

"To be honest, yes."

"But why?"

"Because we were doing God's will."

Ethel shook her head. "Do you do this sort of thing very often?"

"Oh, good grief, no. But I gotta be honest with you: We're doing it now."

"Now?"

"Yeah. See, I'm embarrassed about this, Ethel, but I've been giving you the impression that I've been working on your case, trying to do something about Sister Eileen, so she won't fire you. Which is true, as far as it goes. But what I'm really doing—or what we're doing, 'cause the other guys still in prison are in on this too—is we're trying to get the public eye on this hospital so the Church authorities will have to crack down on all the immorality going on in this place."

"Immorality?"

"Birth control and illicit operations and like that."

All the while Bruce was explaining himself, Ethel's eyes continued to widen in disbelief.

"You mean . . .? So that's what you've been up to. I had no idea . . ."

"You mean you knew what I was doing?"

Ethel nodded. "But I didn't know why."

"Now you know, Ethel. I hope you don't try to talk me out of it."

Ethel shook her head.

'But," Bruce continued, "with my luck, eventually they are going to catch me and I will probably end up going back to jail. And, Ethel, I know I haven't got any right to ask you, but if I do have to go back to jail, I mean, would you wait for me?" Bruce hurried on, not giving Ethel an opportunity to respond. "I know I shouldn't ask you this. I've got no right to ask you. So I shouldn't ask you. Forget I asked you."

"Don't be silly! Who else have I got to wait for but you? Oh, Bruce, I didn't mean for it to sound like that. Truly, I think you're wonderful. And I don't care if you did do all this as part of some kind of conspiracy. You did it for me, too. I know you did.''

"You're right, Ethel; I did. And I'm proud of that part of it . . . well, I'm proud of all of it. No matter what price I'll have to pay, it was God's will.''

"God's will. That's important for you, isn't it, Bruce?''

"It's the most important thing in the world. But''—Bruce studied the floor, unwilling to meet Ethel's gaze—"you are right up there now, Ethel. You and God's will! The most important things in the world for me.''

"Are you saying you love me, Bruce?''

Bruce nodded sheepishly,

"And I love you too, Bruce.''

Bruce grinned.

"Bruce, do you think that some relationships are made in heaven?''

"I never thought about it much until now. But, uh-huh.''

"I think that's what happened to us, Bruce. You going to the seminary, me to the convent. Both of us being clumsy as a pair of oxes. Meeting each other here in the hospital. Joining together in more things than even you know about. Bruce, we were meant for each other. . . what do you think?''

"I think you're right, Ethel.''

"But with our luck, it will be years before we can get together. One or another or both of us might go to jail and God knows when we'd get out, if ever.''

"You, Ethel! What—?''

"Never mind, Bruce. We got to get together—now. It's God's will.''

"God's will?''

"God's will! But . . . where?'' Ethel thought about that. "I think I know. Come on.''

Ethel led Bruce through the corridors in a much more

decisive manner than before when they were wending their way around with no more purpose than to pass time.

They encountered no one. But, unknown to them, George Snell again noticed them on one of the monitors. He was slightly surprised to see what appeared to be a doctor and a nurse hurrying so rapidly, so early in the morning. But that was the way with hospitals. Emergencies could not be scheduled to happen only during business hours. By definition, emergencies could occur at any time. So, he turned from the monitor to the commercial TV set.

Only one channel was telecasting. And Snell wasn't very interested in the offering. After all, how many times could one be expected to watch Laurence Olivier in *Wuthering Heights?* Shakespeare was all well and good, thought Snell, but not this early in the morning.

However, given the choice between grainy monitors showing mostly empty corridors, and something—anything—commerical, Snell knew what his selection would be. But, just for luck, periodically he would run the selector switch through the gamut of stations, just in case there might be something, anything, else besides Shakespeare. One never could tell.

"Where are we going?" Bruce Whitaker was nearing hyperventilation.

"To the chapel," Ethel said over her shoulder without slowing a step.

"The chapel! The chapel's not on the basement floor."

"Not the main chapel; the studio chapel that the chaplain uses to send services and Sunday Mass through the hospital."

Bruce tried to concentrate on slowing his heartbeat. "Why should we go there?"

"Because it's the emptiest place in the whole hospital."

"Oh." It seemed to be working. His heartbeat seemed to stabilize, but certainly not at a normal rate.

There was an empty gurney in the hallway. Ethel pushed it into a room in which there was no light whatsoever. Bruce followed her, but stopped just inside the door. He could see nothing in the room. The only illumination was the dim light coming through the door which had been left ajar. Then the door closed. Ethel had closed it. All was black. This was not helping his heartbeat.

"Come here, Bruce."

"Where?"

"Home in on my voice. Come here. That's better. Now, kiss me . . . longer . . . like you meant it . . . that's better."

"Wait a minute."

"What's the matter?"

"You're unbuttoning my shirt."

"I sort of hoped you'd do the same for me."

"Do you think that is all right?"

"It's God's will."

"Never in my life did I want to do God's will more. But do we have to do it in the dark?"

"Oh, you want light." Given Ethel's self-image, she would have preferred the darkness. "Wait a minute. I think there's a light switch over here near the door . . . there!"

"Wow!" Bruce shielded his eyes. "That's bright! Does it have to be that bright?"

"That's the only light there is in this room. This is where they broadcast the services and Mass on closed-circuit television. I guess the light has to be bright."

There was no reason that Ethel should have known that she had turned on not only the klieg lights, but also the TV camera. What was transpiring in the studio chapel was being carried, closed-circuit, throughout the hospital on Channel 13.

As fate would have it, only one person in the hospital was watching television at that early morning hour.

Out of sheer boredom with *Wuthering Heights* and on the off chance that something, anything, had begun on another channel, George Snell turned the selector switch once again. Realistically expecting nothing, he flipped past Channel 13; paused, then returned to it. He was unacquainted with that channel since he religiously never watched the Mass or services. But, with relief, he noted there was, indeed, something going on over Channel 13. As far as he was concerned, whatever it was would probably beat out *Wuthering Heights*.

"Well, now, what could this be?" Particularly when alone, Snell was known to talk to himself. "This don't look like one of them big-screen movies. Only two people. And no set to speak of. Just bare walls, far as I can see. A table of some sort off in the background. Some sort of small cart. That's it? That ain't much.

"Hey, wait a minute! What're they doin'? They're takin' off each other's clothes! This must be one of them cable channels. You'd never get this sorta thing on a network station. Well, well, well, this is gonna beat hell out of that *Wuthering Heights*. To hell with Shakespeare!"

He settled back in his chair, keeping his eyes on the screen. Shortly, he edged forward slightly.

"I don't know whether they're actin' this way on purpose, but those two ain't very good at this. Hell, he can't even get her clothes off." He reflected. "I don't know; maybe it's better this way. Most skinflicks, people are dressed one minute and naked the next. But, glory, glory, they sure are makin' a production out of gettin' undressed."

Although Snell had seen his share of pornographic films, he always found them stimulating. To him, sex was a sport for all seasons, for spectators and participants alike. There were those who acknowledged him, and rightly so, to be an expert. Thus, when he viewed a skinflick, it was as an epicurean critic.

"They sure as hell need somethin' bigger than that little cot. Only experts could function on somethin' that small," Snell commented. "Amateurs! You'd think at least they could get pros. How did those two rubes ever get cast for a flick like this? It's come to a sorry state. That's all I can say. A sorry state!"

"Is it over? Did we do it?" Bruce Whitaker was perspiring mightily. He wasn't sure what had happened, but he felt rather indescribably good about it.

"I think so," Ethel said. "At least from what I've read about it, I think we did it. Did it feel good to you?"

"I think so. It all happened so fast. I don't think I was thinking about anything at all. How about you?"

"I guess I didn't feel anything. Maybe I'm not supposed to. I've heard women say they got nothing out of it. Maybe this is what they mean."

"Oh, it couldn't be that way. God would not be so unfair. If a man is supposed to get something out of it, certainly a woman should too. But what?"

Ethel pondered that for awhile. "I've been thinking," she announced. "I mean, some of the things I've read said that something like this could happen."

"Something like this?"

"Yes. The first time. The books warn that the first time can be disastrous."

"Disastrous!" As time passed, Bruce was feeling better and better. "I would hardly say it was a disaster!"

"That's right, don't you see? So, if the books are right, it should get better the second time."

"What do the books say?"

"That the first time is liable to be too rapid and the

secret is in slowing everything down, which can be better done the second time. Particularly if the second time immediately follows upon the first time. I think I'm quoting exactly. It also says that when we are able to go slowly, we might become more imaginative. At least we are supposed to open ourselves to our imaginations.''

"Are you quite sure this is God's will?''

"Oh, yes, quite certain.'

"Then"—Bruce's smile was beatific—"God's will be done!"

"There they go again," said George Snell, who had come close to turning back to *Wuthering Heights* just as Bruce and Ethel once more launched themselves onto the Seas of Providence. "I don't know about those two. I don't think they've got much of a future in this sort of thing." He shook his head. "Skinflicks have come a long way from the days when nobody was sure just how far you could go and what you could get away with. Nowadays, the flicks have got porno pros, young people with great bods. I don't know if those two could have made it even in the old days. They definitely have not taken care of their bodies. Shame. Nobody ought to neglect their bodies like that.''

He looked at the screen a bit more sharply. "Wait, that's not bad! Wonder what happened to that technique the first time around? Maybe that was a teaser. Musta been. They're beginning to look like pros. And looka that! How many times in a flick like this does the broad look like she's really enjoyin' it?

"And look at the guy! I don't believe it—he's going to . . . God, even I—wait a minute! Wait a minute! Wait a minute! He's going to . . . he couldn't be . . . he's not . . . he is! Holy glory . . . it's the . . . he's gonna . . . he's gonna . . . IT'S THE SNELL MANEUVER!"

313

George Snell was standing, the chair tipped over behind him. He felt as if his copyright had been violated. He felt as if he'd been violated.

"Oh, Bruce," Ethel sighed.

"Ethel," Bruce whispered.

It was just at that moment the explosion occurred.

"What in hell was that!" Snell cried.

Bruce and Ethel were dumped from the gurney.

It was only later, much later, that Snell reflected that the two people he had thought were part of a movie also experienced the explosion at the same instant he did.

And it was only later, much later, that it occurred to him that he recognized both those people who he had thought were actors.

12

CHAOS. IN WHAT HAD BEEN AN ORDERLY, neat, sterile operating room.

The police technicians had been at their job for hours. Some, particularly the photographers, had completed their work. All the technicians, as well as the investigating detectives, had treated—and were continuing to treat—the crime area with the reverence reserved for the only witness that was guaranteed truthful: the evidence at the scene.

Photographs had been taken from almost every angle. Surfaces had been dusted for prints. Detectives were questioning anyone and everyone who was or might in any way be involved in this case.

A hospital maintenance crew was putting a temporary patch over a huge hole in the outside wall. Since their work was not yet completed, the room was not that much warmer than the 29 degrees Fahrenheit that downtown Detroit was experiencing.

Uniformed police from the Third (downtown) Precinct were barring entry to inquisitive gawkers while permitting access to legitimate hospital personnel. Thus, among those present in OR One were John Haroldson, Dr. Lee Kim, Sister Rosamunda, and Dr. Fred Scott. Among the gawkers persistent enough to remain at the very edge of OR One were Ethel Laidlaw and Bruce Whitaker.

Channels 2 and 7, the CBS and ABC affiliates respectively, had completed their filming and departed. But not before Bruce Whitaker had tried his best to interest them in other aspects of the hospital. All, as it turned out, to no avail.

Gerald Harrington, the smooth, imposing black reporter for Channel 4, the NBC affiliate, was almost ready for his stand-up report. He needed to gather only a bit more information. His crew was setting up camera and sungun.

By far the most imposing figure in the room was Inspector Walter Koznicki. Imposing, not in any vehement or aggressive manner. If anything, he would more accurately be described as reticent and almost shy. But his bulk was considerable and his demeanor commanding.

Koznicki had been on the scene almost from the very beginning. As it happened, he had been serving his tour of duty in what the police call Code 2400, which consisted of a driver and an inspector ready to take charge immediately in any emergency. And what had occurred at St. Vincent's clearly qualified as both a police emergency and a media event.

At this moment, Koznicki was addressing a biomedical engineering technician, one Frank Reese. Reese had been over the details many times, but this was the first time with the Inspector.

"I am well aware that you have answered these questions before, Mr. Reese," Koznicki said, "but I am sure you will be kind enough to go over the matter one more time with me. And I have asked Dr. Scott to fill in the details so that we will have a complete picture of what took place."

This benovelent invitation coming as it did from Koznicki was equivalent to a command performance.

"Dr. Scott, you will begin?"

"Well, it was late last night, maybe ten-thirty or eleven o'clock, when Sister Eileen was taken to emergency. She was comatose. She had been complaining of headaches and she had been the victim of an assault earlier—though she gave every evidence of having come through that with no ill effects. But sometimes . . .

"In any case, I ordered a CAT scan, which revealed a subdural hematoma—in layman's language, the blood was squishing her brain.

"I scheduled her for surgery stat. But we had the devil's own time trying to locate the neurosurgeon on call. By the time we located another one and he got down here and we got ready, it was nearly four in the morning.

"Sister was prepped and placed on the table. Oh, yeah, then something odd happened. Bill started the anesthetic, but the gauge indicated he wasn't getting any nitrous oxide in the mix. So he checked the tank and it was empty. As a matter of fact, the valve was open. Someone—I can't think why—had bled the tank."

"Let me interrupt, Doctor," said Koznicki. "If that had been the only thing to go wrong with the procedure, what would have been the effect?"

"Not very much, really. If the patient had been awake, she just wouldn't have gone to sleep as expected. No matter what, the anesthetist would have found the problem, just as he did in this case. Then, all he had to do was get a full tank of nitrous oxide and hook it in."

"I see. Strange. Please continue, Doctor."

"As soon as Bill replaced the oxide, we got started. Sister had already been prepped, of course, so all that was left as a preliminary was to drill into her skull. For that, we needed the nitrogen. That was in the large tank standing near the wall. The circulating nurse went to get it and then, well, all hell broke loose."

"Could you be more specific, Doctor?"

"Oh, sure. Well, she'd just begun wheeling it to the table when it seemed to tip over and fall off the dolly. The tank seemed to rip loose. Then it just took off—it simply took off, like a jet plane. There was this enormous whoosh and the tank shot across the floor and exploded right through the wall there. I guess it ended up where you found it, lodged in the motor of a police car that was parked just outside the hospital.

"And that's about it. We were all so shocked, I think the whole team just stood there looking at the hole in the wall. I don't know how long we did that. It probably seemed longer than it was. But when we finally came to, well, there was work to be done. We got Sister into another OR and did the job. I must admit we were pretty shook. But we got the job done." He paused. "Funny thing, though: the nitrous oxide tank in there was empty too; Bill had to hook up another one."

"And Sister?"

"She came out of it fine. She's in ICU, of course, but the prognosis is very good."

"Thank God.

"Now, Mr. Reese: What happened to the tank of nitrogen to cause it to act as it did. An accident?"

"No way! The manufacturer is well aware of the danger of gas under a lot of pressure, and so are we. So all of us take a lot of precautions."

"Enough precautions to avoid anything like this happening?"

"Absolutely."

"Go on, Mr. Reese."

"Well, I brought another tank in to demonstrate what happened. I showed the other officers." Reese looked meaningfully at Koznicki to ascertain if the previous explanation would suffice. It would not, Koznicki's steadfast demeanor made clear. Reese proceeded. "You see this little three-wheeled cart. It's called an H-Tank carrier. 'H' refers to the size. It's one of the largest tanks.

"What happened, to begin with, was that whoever did this loosened the cotter pins in the outside wheel. What that did was to guarantee that when somebody started to pull it, the wheel would come off the carrier and the whole assembly would tip over. Still nothing much would happen, 'cause the tank is strapped to the carrier, but most of all the valve assembly and the pressure regulators are firmly affixed to the tank.

"But what this guy did was he filed almost completely through the base of the cylinder valve. And that's not something added to the basic tank, like the regulator; the cylinder valve is part of the tank itself.

"So, you see, the guy fixed the carrier so it would tip over. Then he fixed the valve so it would tear loose from the tank. At that point, about two-hundred pounds of nitrogen per square inch tried to get out of the tank all at once. Wasn't nothin' gonna hold it back. It became a kind of unguided missile. And the rest of it you see. The hole in the wall and a wrecked engine in the police car."

"I see," Koznicki said. "That was a very clear presentation, Mr. Reese, and understandable even to the nontechnician such as myself."

"I'm getting practice."

Koznicki overlooked the sarcasm. "I have just one or two questions. You say the nitrogen tank, once it was torn loose, became an 'unguided' missile. Do you mean, literally, there was no way of telling in which direction it would travel? It could just as easily have injured, perhaps very seriously, someone in this room as it could have gone harmlessly through the wall? Conceivably, might it have been intended for someone in this room? Perhaps the patient who was about to undergo surgery?''

"I see what you mean: Could it have gone crazy like a deflating balloon? Maybe. A lot depended on how it broke free of the valve. But if you're counting percentages, odds are it would have acted just as it did. Since it was stationed against the outside wall, the nurse would have started to pull it toward the table so the drill could be hooked up. It would have tipped over on the way to the table. And it would have broken off the valve cap while it was pointed toward the outside wall. So, as long as the break was clean—and the guy filed it down close enough to practically insure that the break would be clean—it was pretty well programmed to go through that wall, just like it did.''

"I see. Very well. My final question, Mr. Reese, is: You keep referring to the one who was responsible for this as 'the guy.' Is there any reason you can think of that it had to be a man?''

Reese thought for a moment. ''No, now that you bring it up. It didn't require any special strength. Anybody—man or woman—could have loosened the wheel. And filing the valve didn't need strength as much as just patience, stick-to-itiveness. Anybody could have filed it down. He—or she—would just have had to stay with it awhile.''

"Very good. Thank you, Mr. Reese.''

Koznicki wandered across the room to gaze at the hole that was being crudely patched. And to wonder at the mind that had converted a tank of nitrogen gas into a torpedo that might easily have killed someone, if not in that room, then on the street outside.

✦ ✦ ✦

". . . that's it. A wild and woolly way to begin the day. We'll be bringing you further developments in this story as they happen. From old St. Vincent's Hospital in downtown Detroit, this is Gerald Harrington, Channel 4 News, reporting."

The sungun faded and the TV team began to pack up. This was the first story of this day. It was not likely to be the last.

"Mr. Harrington! Mr. Harrington!"

Gerald Harrington thought he heard someone call his name. He wasn't sure. The voice, while it seemed insistent, was barely audible over all the sounds in the still-crowded operating room.

"Mr. Harrington! Mr. Harrington!"

Harrington spotted him. A small, roundish man wearing perhaps the world's worst toupee and standing behind the tape placed by the police to keep the crowd back. Harrington crossed to the man. "Hi, there. What can I do for you?"

"This isn't the whole story," Bruce Whitaker said.

"Not the whole story? What do you mean, Buddy?" Harrington was interested. Any competent newsperson would have been.

"There are things going on in this hospital. Illicit things." Whitaker could not resist a conspiratorial tone.

"Illicit things?"

"Yes. In the clinic. You can see for yourself. I'll show you. Birth control. Devices. Instructions. Tubal ligations. You can see for yourself. I'll take you there."

Harrington was pressed for time. He was by no means averse to following news leads, but he had to make judgments on which ones to pursue. This one gave every appearance of being both a wrong turn and a dead end. It was not just that the informant seemed to be a run-of-the-mill crazy; as far as Harrington was concerned, the man was speaking nonsense.

"Okay, Buddy. Maybe I'll check those things out later. Meanwhile, keep a good thought."

As Harrington prepared to leave, the sound man looked at him inquiringly. Harrington's exaggerated expression told him that it was one more of the city's many neurotics. The sound man nodded and the team departed.

Damn, thought Whitaker, this is my golden opportunity. I don't know how that explosion happened, but it was a godsend. Maybe literally. The news media are here in force. And I haven't able to lead anybody to the real story. Maybe I'm coming on too strong. But how else can I do it? We never thought of this part when we were planning. You need a PR person for this sort of thing. What am I going to do?

"Hey, you!"

"Me?" Whitaker was taken by surprise.

"Yeah, you. I heard you talking to that TV guy before. I'm Pfeiffer, *Detroit News*." He showed no identification, but he had a note pad, which was enough authentication for Whitaker. "You got something on this story?"

"Yes, as a matter of fact." How to handle this? Imagine: a real reporter who wanted to hear the real story! God was good!

"Name?"

"Bruce Whitaker."

"Doctor? You a doctor here?"

"No. I'm a volunteer."

"Then what's with the stethoscope?"

"Oh, my . . ." In the confusion he had forgotten the stethoscope. "Never mind that. I need it in my job." Whitaker hoped the bluff would work.

Pfeiffer looked a bit skeptical, but forged on toward a

possible new development in this bizarre incident. "Okay. What've you got?"

Not so pointblank now, Whitaker cautioned himself. "There's a reason behind this explosion."

"You mean you know who did it?" Pfeiffer was immediately excited.

"Well, not exactly. Almost."

"Whaddya mean 'almost'! How could you know 'almost' who did it! Have you got both oars in the water?"

"Let me tell you what's behind all this, then you'll know what I mean."

Pfeiffer closed his note pad and pocketed his pen. He would give this nut at most three more minutes to babble on. And that only because the reporter was feeling unusually generous today.

"Inspector?" A Third Precinct detective approached Koznicki.

"Yes?" Koznicki had been absently following the patching of the wall while recalling his conversation with Father Koesler. Unfortunately, this was his day off from the hospital. He had missed all the excitement. Koznicki would bring his friend up to date tomorrow.

"Inspector . . ." The detective drew very near so he would not have to speak loudly. "We got lucky."

"Oh? How so?"

"We got a full ten prints off that nitrous oxide tank, and identical prints off one oxide tank in each of the other rooms. They'd all been bled. Undoubtedly by the guy whose prints were on the tanks and also on the valves."

"Very good."

"And we got an ID."

"So soon?"

"Well, we had both hands. And we didn't have to look far: He's on parole from Van's Can."

"What does his rap-sheet show?"

"Attempted murder."

"Hmmm. Name?"

"Whitaker. Bruce Whitaker."

Koznicki reflected. "Rings no bells. Where do we find him?"

"See that guy over there in the white coat talking to Pfeiffer?"

Koznicki followed the direction of the detective's inclined head, then nodded.

"That's our guy."

Koznicki shook his head in disbelief. "Take him."

The detective nodded to his partner. They closed in.

"Bruce Whitaker?"

"Y . . . Y . . . Yes?"

"You are under arrest for malicious destruction of property, violation of parole, endangerment to life, and a few more things we'll think of as time passes." The detective took a card from his wallet as his partner handcuffed Whitaker. "You have the right to remain silent. . . ."

"You!" Pfeiffer was astonished. "You? You did this? My crazy did this? How lucky can I get? Now, you were saying . . ."

All for nothing! They will never believe him. All for nothing! What a waste! I have accomplished nothing. I should have done it myself from the beginning. It must be done. And I must do it! I must do it quickly now!

13

IT WAS ONE OF THOSE DAYS WHEN Detroiters felt lucky to get where they were going. It had snowed off and on, with varying intensity, for the better part of two days, accumulating an additional five inches.

Because he had traveled Ford Road, the Ford and Lodge Expressways, all priority-plowed thoroughfares, Father Koesler had actually arrived early at St. Vincent's. So it was with a sense of unhurried relaxation that be was able to enjoy coffee and a Danish with Inspector Koznicki in the cafeteria.

Since yesterday had been Koesler's day off, he had missed all the excitement. He'd read the first sketchy details in last evening's *Detroit News* in a story carrying Mark Pfeiffer's by-line. TV news had had film on both the six and eleven o'clock news. He hadn't yet had an opportunity to read this morning's *Free Press*.

But all of these gaps in his news-information education were more than filled in by the presence of essentially an eyewitness to the event. By now, Koznicki had told Koesler, step-by-step, what had happened almost twenty-four hours ago not far from where they now sat.

"What a coincidence," Koesler observed, "that you should be called in on this case."

"That is indeed what it was—a coincidence. I just happened to be the officer on duty that night."

"I haven't as yet been able to get a very clear picture of what happened. The account in the *News* seemed sort of garbled. One of those stories that a reporter gets as a sort of exclusive, but while he's got it first, he doesn't know exactly where it's going."

"A very perceptive observation, Father. Mr. Pfeiffer happened to be actually interviewing our suspect as he was arrested. Another coincidence, and a very serendipitous one for Mr. Pfeiffer."

"I should say. Then about all I got from the TV news was a glimpse at the pandemonium here, then a brief look at the suspect covering his face as he was taken in."

"I gather you haven't read today's *Free Press* or the morning edition of the *News?* They have rather more complete accounts of the matter."

"Haven't had a chance yet. What was the guy's name? Whit-something . . . Whitman?"

"Whitaker. Bruce Whitaker."

"Hmmm. Why does that name ring a bell?"

Koznicki smiled. "In time you would remember. But you must recall some four years ago, four very conservative Catholic men tried to take vengeance against their former seminary professors? And they were not too successful, although they came close? Well, it is typical of this man that, on the one hand he would not think to use an alias, and that, on the other, no one would remember him anyway."

"Yes, yes, yes, I remember. Of course! The gang of four! Good grief, they could scarcely tie their shoes! That's why he looked familiar.'' He shook his head. ''Bruce Whitaker did all that damage? It hardly seems possible. I mean, with his penchant for failure . . .''

Koznicki frowned. ''Well, he does claim he did not do it.''

''But you have evidence?''

''Tanks containing nitrous oxide were emptied in each of the operating rooms. His fingerprints were found on each tank. His were the only prints of unauthorized personnel we found in that area.''

''That's interesting. So he seems to have emptied the nitrous oxide tanks. I'm not familiar with that. What's nitrous oxide used for?''

''It is one of the gases that is used as part of a mixture in anesthesia.''

''And if there isn't any nitrous oxide?''

''The patient does not go to sleep—at least not as rapidly or deeply as the anesthetist would expect.''

''Hmmm. So, emptying the tanks . . . that wouldn't seem to accomplish much. Sounds like it's right in the ball park for those guys. What was he trying to do anyway?''

Koznicki shook his head. ''He claims he was trying to call attention to the hospital to reveal its immoral deeds. But, at that point, he becomes quite incoherent.''

''Strange.'' The rationale made no sense to Koesler. But then he did not consider any of the hospital's policies immoral. ''At any rate, he certainly got everyone's attention.'' He looked at Koznicki questioningly. ''But then, you said he claims he didn't do it.''

Again Koznicki frowned. ''He is an odd person and this is an odd case.''

''Oh?''

''He freely confesses that he bled the nitrous oxide tanks—which affected virtually nothing. But he denies tampering with an extremely dangerous tank that might have injured or even killed someone—anyone, in this case—and which did become a media event."

"Excuse me, Inspector, but that doesn't sound very odd to me. It seems kind of understandable that someone would admit doing something harmless yet deny responsibility for a serious crime . . . no?"

"As far as that goes, Father. But Mr. Whitaker goes on to confess and deny things he has not been charged with. Some things which are—well, incredible."

"Such as?"

"Do not feel inappropriate should you laugh at this Father; everyone else has. He claims that he mutilated a shipment of curtain hooks, mistaking them to be—can you imagine—intrauterine devices!" Koznici barely suppressed a snort.

Koesler started to laugh, then suddenly stopped. "Wait a minute! That explains it. I was here in this cafeteria when a woman brought in a box of curtain hooks that had been damaged. The presumption was that it was the manufacturer's fault. But if I remember correctly, the lady said she had stored them in the compartment reserved for IUDs."

"You mean—"

"It makes some sort of crazy sense now. Apparently, he went looking for the IUDs, but didn't know what they looked like. He found the hooks in the drawer with an IUD label on it." He shook his head. "I must admit, if you didn't know what an IUD was, these hooks might just pass for IUDs. But . . ." His brow furrowed. ". . . why would he want to mutilate IUDs?"

Koznicki tapped an index finger methodically on the table. "If he was telling the truth, at least about his reason for bleeding the nitrous oxide tanks, he wanted to call attention to the hospital—for whatever reason."

"Mutilating IUDs seems a pretty roundabout way of doing that, although I guess it could work. Of course no

328

doctor would put a mutilated IUD in a patient. But if one were to assume that a woman was fitted with something like that, you could be certain she'd be hurt. She'd probably see another doctor, then a lawyer. Next, she'd be talking to reporters.''

Koznicki looked intently at his coffee, with a bemused expression. "You know, Father, I never thought I would hear a rational explanation for, on the one hand, mistaking curtain hooks for IUDs, and, on the other, mutilating the hooks. But I believe you may have hit upon it.''

"It does sound like his method of operation, doesn't it? Like the MO of all four of those guys. But you would have found this out anyway, Inspector. In your investigation you would have discovered the mutilated curtain hooks that had been stored in the wrong drawer.''

"That is true. But it is a happy coincidence that you happened to be there when the damage was reported. It has saved us much time. I wonder if I would be tempting fate to test you on Mr. Whitaker's second bizarre confession?''

"I would really be surprised if it worked. But go ahead, Inspector. What was it?''

"Well, this confession was as unsolicited as was his admission that he had mutilated curtain hooks. He claims that several nights ago he altered a patient's chart, putting a woman into a test program she should have been excluded from because she was allergic to the medication used in the program.''

Koesler's eyes widened.

"In addition,'' Koznicki continued, "he claims that his scheme worked even though he is certain he omitted an essential part of the plan. He says he forgot to remove from the chart a sticker which informed medical personnel that the patient was allergic to the medication being used in the test.

"And the reason he forgot to remove the sticker was

because he had been observed by a security guard who—
and Mr. Whitaker can offer no explanation for this—neither
stopped him nor apprehended him. The guard, Mr. Whitaker
claims, merely challenged him from a distance down the
hallway and then, could anyone believe it, disappeared.''
The Inspector looked more bemused than ever. "In all my
years in the department, I have never encountered anyone
like Mr. Whitaker.''

Koesler was silent for a few moments. Then, "You
know, Inspector, strange as it seems, I think I can put that
one together.''

It was Koznicki's turn to look surprised.

"I remember the mix-up when a patient got the wrong
medication,'' Koesler began. "It must be the same case.
The patient had pneumonia and was given penicillin but
she was allergic to it and had a bad reaction . . . right?''

"That is what he claimed. Indeed it is.''

"I remember that very well because I talked to the
woman shortly after she was admitted. She told me she
had been asked to be part of that test, but she told them
she was allergic to penicillin, so she'd been excluded. I
had no more to do with her—she was on Sister Rosamunda's
floor—until I overheard some nurses discussing her deteri-
orating condition. Then I remembered her allergy and
pointed it out.

"Everyone thought it was an accident, one of those
foul-ups that are forever happening in hospitals. Fortunately for St. Vincent's, the patient had a faith in God so
strong that she attributed everything that happened to her
as coming from God—even what seemed to be a near-fatal
blunder in a hospital.

"But you undoubtedly would have uncovered that incident also in your investigation. Just as you would have
found the mutilated curtain hooks. And it's always possible that Whitaker was aware of these incidents, just as I

was, and was confessing to them for God-knows-what reason.'' Koesler looked to Koznicki for some reason.

"Well, under this hypothesis, he might have been building a basis for some sort of insanity plea. Or he may just be one of those compulsive people we meet from time to time who must confess to every crime imaginable.''

"Okay,'' Koesler agreed, "but what may be unique about what Whitaker told you was the part about the security guard who challenged him from a distance down the corridor and then seemingly disappeared. If that part is true, then it would add a lot of credence to his overall story, wouldn't it?''

"Yes, but how could it be true?''

"There's a patient named . . . let me see, I'm sure she's still here.'' Koesler checked the current patient list he'd picked up earlier. "Yes, here she is: Alice Walker. I was sure she'd still be here. Sister Rosamunda made sure she'd stay here long enough to have her infected feet taken care of.

"Okay, on the night in question, the night that Whitaker claims he altered a patient's chart and was challenged by a vanishing guard, this Alice Walker's life was saved by what had to be that same guard.

"The official story had it that Mrs. Walker was having a before-bedtime snack when she started to strangle on some crackers. At that point, or so the guard claims, he happened to be passing her room when he heard choking noises. He claims he came to her rescue and with the Heimlich Maneuver saved her life. That's the story the guard told and the story that went around the hospital.

"However, the next morning, I heard Mrs. Walker's confession and brought her Communion. And, after Communion, she told me quite a different story of what had taken place.

"According to Mrs. Walker—and I have no reason to

doubt her—the guard did not 'just happen' to be passing her room when she began coughing. He had been *in* her room a considerable time. He was . . . um . . . carousing in the other bed with someone, a nurse or an aide, Mrs. Walker couldn't be sure. The curtain had been pulled around her bed.

"Anyway, at about the time she began choking, the guard didn't apply any Heimlich Hug. He fell out of bed, rolled across the floor, hit her bed, knocking her out of it; she fell on top of him and that dislodged the food that had been stuck in her windpipe."

Koznicki could not help himself. He began to laugh. It was several minutes before he was able to compose himself.

Somehow, when Alice Walker told the story, Koesler had not found it all that funny. Now, as he recounted it to Koznicki, it seemed ludicrous. Only gradually, inspired by the Inspector's example, was Koesler able to get control of himself.

"And she has told no one but you?" Koznicki asked, finally.

"As far as I know. You see, Mrs. Walker is on the same floor as the pneumonia patient . . . uh . . . Millie Power. So it makes sense. Bruce Whitaker could have been tampering with Mrs. Power's chart when he was discovered by the security guard who challenged him. Now, what could possibly distract the guard from checking out the person who was fooling with some patient's chart?"

"I see. Yes, that does make sense. It is possible, then, that Mr. Whitaker has been telling us the truth. You say that this Mrs. Walker is still in the hospital. So her statement can be taken officially. It will be a simple matter to locate and speak to the guard. Now, then, let us get to the bottom of this."

✝ ✝ ✝

Mrs. Walker's statement was taken. And, as Koznicki suggested, it was a relatively simple matter to summon George Snell from his bed, which he had entered only a short time previously after finishing his tour of night duty.

Koznicki had set up temporary headquarters in an empty room adjacent to Dolly's office. Thus, one room removed from Sister Eileen's office, he was in the hospital's central location. The Inspector was indeed determined to get to the bottom of this, and quickly.

George Snell was interrogated in the presence of Father Koesler and Snell's supervisor. On his way back to the hospital, Snell had pondered how he would respond. He knew of Inspector Koznicki and understood the futility of any attempt to fool the Inspector. Snell decided that he would answer all direct questions truthfully. But he would not expand on any answers he gave nor would he volunteer any information.

The questioning quite promptly got down to the night Bruce Whitaker claimed to have been in the process of altering Millie Power's medical chart when he was briefly interrupted by a security guard. According to the log for that evening, the guard had to have been Snell or no one. Either it was Snell, or Whitaker had invented the story.

Snell remembered the incident clearly. Yes, there had been someone in the nurses' station who seemed not to belong there. Yes, he had challenged the man.

Why had Snell not followed up on his verbal and long-distance challenge? Snell weighed that one momentarily. He was not particularly adept at extemporaneous lying. He knew that. All in all, he considered the truth would serve best here. And, after all, he *had* determined to be truthful.

Yes, he had been distracted by someone. No, not a nurse; a nurse's aide. Honest to God it had not been his idea in the first place.

It took a while before Snell was able to convince

Koznicki—and even longer to convince the supervisor—
that this impromptu roll in the hay had been the aide's
idea. Yes, they had used the empty bed in Alice Walker's
room. Snell had thought she was out of it. At least the aide
had assured him the patient wouldn't know what was
going on.

No, Snell had not heard the patient choking. The aide
heard it. Well, no, he hadn't exactly fallen out of bed. He
had been attempting . . . well . . . maybe it would be just
as accurate to say he had fallen out of bed. And yes, the
rest of it happened about the way Mrs. Walker had recounted it.

In fact, that's why Snell had been convinced the aide
was right about the patient's not knowing what was going
on. Mrs. Walker had not contradicted any of their story
about how Snell had just been passing by when he heard
her choking and had performed the—he still had difficulty
with the term—yes, the Heimlich Maneuver.

Now, the essential question: Was the man Snell had
challenged Bruce Whitaker?

Snell studied the mug shots Koznicki offred. The four
photos were equally divided between Whitaker with and
without toupee.

"Yeah, that's the guy." Snell tapped the pictures of
Whitaker covered. But, even more startling, he recognized
Whitaker sans toupee as one of the two performers on the
television channel Snell had assumed was porno cable.
That was the bastard who had successfully executed the
one and only Snell Maneuver! For that occasion, Whitaker
had been wearing nothing, including his rug.

However, Snell kept this latter information to himself.
At this point, he did not care what else Whitaker had done
or what the police had charged him with. As far as Snell
was concerned, Whitaker's sin that cried to heaven for
vengeance was his carrying off the Snell Maneuver with-

out a license. Or impersonating George Snell during the execution of the Snell Maneuver. Or something like that.

No, Snell told Koznicki nothing about the TV caper. No volunteered information. Besides, this was a matter of honor, a score that must be settled privately between the two of them. As near as Snell could figure it, this matter had the same sort of enormity as when one man stole another man's horse in the Old West.

After advising him to remain available for further questioning, Koznicki dismissed both Snell and his supervisor. The Inspector then summoned the detectives who had been interrogating hospital personnel. Father Koesler's observations having lent credence to Whitaker's claims, Koznicki had called in several detectives from the Third Precinct as well as three from Squad Seven of his own homicide division. Lieutenant Ned Harris of Homicide was coordinating the investigation and now reported to Koznicki.

Once again, Harris made no attempt to mask his distaste at having to check out leads from this priest—the perennial amateur. However, to be fair—and when it came to police work Harris was nothing if not objective—Koesler's leads had checked out.

There had been a shipment of curtain hooks that had been mutilated. And, according to the housekeeping department, the manufacturer remained adamant that no one in his company would have done such a thing. The manufacturer insisted there had been nothing wrong with the hooks on shipment. Whatever was done to them had to have been done after receipt by the hospital. At that point, the matter had remained inexplicable. No one could guess why anyone would mutilate curtain hooks.

One mystery apparently solved.

Everyone on the second floor remembered very clearly the mix-up of Millie Power's chart. A mix-up that, had it not been caught, could have cost her life. As a matter of fact, by direct and insistent order of the CEO, an intense in-house investigation was even now being conducted to determine how and why that chart had been altered.

Another mystery apparently solved.

Koesler of course had been certain that the police investigation would bear out his eyewitness observations. So, while Lieutenant Harris was, item by item, filling Koznicki in on what the detectives had uncovered, Koesler was off in his own world of speculation.

In his mind's eye, he saw Sister Eileen being wheeled into the operating room on a gurney. He assumed that her head would have been shaved for the operation. She would be completely helpless. In Koesler's scenario—the only one that made sense to him—the carrier wheel had broken away earlier than was planned. Whoever had tampered with the carrier and the gas tank must have intended for the wheel to give way during the operation. It made no sense to Koesler that the wheel was intended to come off the cart before the operation.

Thus, the way the plan must have been conceived, the nitrogen tank would be delivered to the operating table. Then, during the operation, as doctors and nurses moved about the table, the tank would be jostled frequently. Not too much of that sort of bumping would be needed before the weakened wheel would collapse, tearing the valve from the tank and, in the ensuing turmoil, the neurosurgeon would inadvertently drive the drill into Sister's brain. And that, finally, would be that.

Then Koesler tried to reverse the movie in his mind. He tried to visualize the person who would do such a thing. Who might actually plot Sister Eileen's murder?

He had several candidates. Four, to be exact.

First to come to mind was Ethel Laidlaw. First, because she was least likely. And least likely because she was such a klutz herself. It was ludicrous to imagine that Ethel

336

might follow behind Whitaker to correct his mistakes. To mix a metaphor, it would be a case of the blind leading the blind.

But, wait a minute! Whitaker's first name was Bruce. And that was the name Ethel had mentioned as her new boyfriend and possible spouse. It must be the same person. With that relationship in mind, mightn't she be the one who conclusively altered the chart and programmed the nitrogen tank?

No. Impossible. Whatever Ethel's possible motivation, she had as good a chance as Whitaker of getting things right. Which was no chance at all.

Next in the least likely category, as far as Koesler was concerned, would be Sister Rosamunda. Of the four people he had in mind, Rosamunda probably had the strongest motive for wanting Eileen out of the way. Rosamunda's fear of a forced retirement was almost pathological. For her, there were no gray areas in retirement. Everything was black and bleak. She seemed to envision it as a sort of burial alive.

But, while her fear of the fate Eileen was forcing upon her was morbid, Rosamunda gave no indication that she was insane. And some form of insanity would have to be present before a dedicated religious woman would seriously consider murder. It was unimaginable that Rosamunda could have plotted the death of anyone, let alone that of another religious.

In considering John Haroldson as a possible suspect, Koesler slipped away from the "least likely" category. The priest hated to consider anyone capable of premeditated murder, but someone was guilty. And of those he knew as prime suspects, Haroldson had to be seriously considered. His motive was practically identical with Sister Rosamunda's. Each of them saw Sister Eileen as the one responsible for condemning them to retirement.

And where retirement for Rosamunda was a living death, for Haroldson, it seemingly spelled death itself. He did not consider himself capable of continued life if he were separated from the hospital for which he lived.

Added to that was his festering resentment over the fact that Eileen held the post that he coveted. And, according to Haroldson's lights, the position of chief executive officer should, by rights, be his. His background in theology, medicine, and business qualified him as CEO to a far greater degree than Eileen. As far as he was concerned, she had gotten the job for one reason alone: She was a member of the religious community that operated this and other institutions in this section of the country. So blinded was Haroldson that he simply could not appreciate the abilities and achievements that perfectly qualified Eileen as CEO.

But, thought Koesler, even with all this perceived provocation—murder? He wondered about that. The likelihood of Haroldson's plotting murder paled when Koesler compared him with the one who topped Koesler's list of suspects.

Like the others, particularly Rosamunda and Haroldson, Dr. Lee Kim had a strong motive for wanting Sister Eileen out of the way. She had been on the very verge of dismissing him from St. Vincent's staff. Few words could adequately describe how much he feared that.

As a doctor, he could have had a good life in his native South Korea. But nowhere near as good a life as he might have garnered here in this land of near limitless opportunity. He was a young man with long life promised him. He had plans for that long life. He anticipated an ever-improving lifestyle. He would make very worthwhile the sacrifice of leaving his homeland to set up shop in this foreign country. Kim could virtually taste the luxury and affluence of his future.

338

But at this stage of his life, very low on the rungs of the ladder he planned to climb, one person stood in his way. More than stood in his way; Sister Eileen threatened to throw him from the ladder entirely and permanently. If she moved against him, it was possible he might be forced to leave this country of his dreams. Conceivably, he might even find it difficult to set up practice in his homeland now. In sum, Dr. Kim had the very real prospect of losing not only everything he had, but all he hoped to have.

In addition, there was that attitude of Kim's that so disturbed Koesler.

Death certainly was no stranger to doctors. Of all vocations, doctors dealt with death more than almost anyone. Surgeons, moreover, not infrequently were helpless to prevent death even during their ministrations. Koesler had suffered only momentary shock when hearing surgeons refer to a part for the whole—as in operating on a "hand" or a "head." But Koesler had not been prepared for Dr. Kim's elation that a "head" had expired in emergency . . . so that no extra time would have to be expended for the "hand."

Of all four of Koesler's suspects, Kim was, by far, the most likely. He had a motive, arguably the strongest of the four. He certainly had the means. The operating room would be to him like a second home. And of the four, Kim seemed most at home with death and most casual in his attitude toward it.

There was one person he hadn't considered. Now that he thought about it—and he hadn't before—Dr. Fred Scott was certainly suspectable, particularly from an opportunity standpoint. He was certainly as conversant with hospital procedures as any of the others. Although he and Koesler had established a rapport, Koesler was conscious that it was always possible that Scott's befriending him could have an ulterior motive. And Scott was not a creampuff;

he had the grit and the spine—and the stick-to-itiveness—to carry him along any path he chose, without looking back or suffering second thoughts.

Yes, Koesler concluded reluctantly, Scott would have to be included.

But what would his motive be? There was the rub. As far as Koesler could figure, there was none. Scott was good at his work, happy at his work, and seemed to have come to terms with the contradictions of life at St. Vincent's. Indeed, rather than wishing ill to Sister Eileen, he was one of her staunchest champions.

No, on second thought, Koesler decided, at least for the moment, to cross Scott off his list of possible suspects. Which left Dr. Kim as the leading nominee. And as Koesler once more retraced his rationale, he nodded to himself. Yes, that was it.

The priest emerged from his reverie far more assured than he had entered it. He returned his attention to what was going on in the room just as Lieutenant Harris completed his summary of what the investigation had revealed.

"So," Koznicki said, "what we have here is a suspect who may be telling us the whole truth, the entire story. Or he may not. But at least with the corroboration of some of the bizarre ingredients of his confession, the likelihood that he speaks truth grows.

"If what Mr. Whitaker says is true, then he had proceeded in a most roundabout way to attempt to focus media attention on this hospital for the purpose of exposing what he believes to be, in the context of Catholic medical moral ethics, immoral. But all he has managed to do is to come up with such an incredible, confused, ridiculous story that, to this point, the media are having a field day making a fool of our bumbling suspect.

"On the other hand, if what Mr. Whitaker claims is true, there is someone else in this hospital, who, for whatever reason, has been following our suspect, correcting his mistakes, improving on his schemes. But"—Koznicki spread his hands palms up—"who? And why?"

During Koznicki's summation, Father Koesler had been fidgeting in his chair, like an eager schoolboy who knows the answer.

And now, like a benevolent schoolmaster, Koznicki recognized him. "I believe Father Koesler may have something to add at this point."

Koesler, well aware that he was among police professionals and not one of them, spoke as deferentially as possible. "I am almost embarrassed to say anything about this matter. And I wouldn't, except that . . . well, I've been part of this hospital's personnel for a little while, even if only on a temporary basis. So I got to know many of the people here. And it's just my familiarity with the situation here that prompts me to speak."

Lieutenant Harris looked heavenward. He was convinced the priest had nothing of substance to say. He just wished Koesler would get on with it.

Even Koesler was aware that this was becoming awkward. Everyone in the room knew he was out of his depth. There was no need to belabor the point.

"What I'm getting at," Koesler finally explained, "is that I think I know who tried to kill Sister Eileen."

There was a brief, uncomfortable silence.

Harris cleared his throat. Was there a hint of a smirk playing at the corners of his mouth? "Nobody tried to kill Sister Eileen," he stated.

"But . . ." Koesler was bewildered. ". . . but she was the patient being operated on. It's perfectly possible—probable—that the tank was supposed to explode while the operation was in progress."

"Immaterial," Harris said.

"But—" Koesler felt his face redden.

"You see, Father," Harris's tone was that of an adult explaining something simple to a child. "At the time the tank was tampered with, there was no way of knowing who would be the first patient in that room. No way of knowing, even, if the first patient would need the use of the nitrogen tank.

"Sister Eileen collapsed and was taken immediately to the operating room from emergency. The tank had to have been tampered with before she was brought in as a patient in need of emergency treatment. Whoever sabotaged that tank could not have known that Sister Eileen was going to be operated on, let alone that she would be first and that the nitrogen tank would be needed for her.

"So," Harris concluded rather pleasantly, "nobody was trying to kill Sister Eileen."

In the brief silence that followed, Koesler considered how many kinds of fool he was.

Before be lapsed into another contemplative state, he heard Inspector Koznicki say, "As I was saying, if Mr. Whitaker is telling the whole truth—and, to be perfectly honest, I now believe he is—then there must be someone else in this hospital following him around remedying his mistakes. But who? And why?"

"I'm not that ready to believe Whitaker," said Harris, "though if, as you say, there is someone else, I suppose he or she would be trying to accomplish the same thing as Whitaker.

"But I can't think of why anybody would want to, or who would be doing it.

"Personally, I think Whitaker did it all and now is doing nothing more original than trying to alibi out of it by blaming some nonexistent person for picking up some loose ends that were never there in the first place."

Harris quickly was tiring of this case. He wanted to get

342

back to homicide cases, which were what he was being paid to work on. God knows there were more than enough homicides in Detroit to work on. The only reason Harris and the other homicide detectives were here was because Inspector Koznicki had called them in. And the only reason Koznicki had entered this case was the coincidence that he'd been the inspector on Code 2400 the night all this had happened.

As the officers discussed the possibilities in the hypothesis that there had been a second person involved, Koesler's mind had taken another tack suggested by something Harris had said.

All right, thought Koesler, if Sister Eileen was not the target in the operating room, why would someone bother to improve on the bumbling Whitaker's ineffectual plan? Why would someone complete the alteration of a medical chart to actually accomplish what Whitaker intended? Why indeed?

Unless . . . unless the two were in basic agreement. Both wanted to create a media event. And why? Because both wanted the same thing: the exposure of the medical moral practices of St. Vincent's Hospital. And who might that second person be? Someone who would for some reason be attracted to and in agreement with either Whitaker's ultimate goal . . . or a side-effect of that goal.

And that would be . . .

Of course!

Koesler stood abruptly. "Excuse me." He had no idea what was being discussed at the moment, nor who was speaking. He knew only that there was urgency in getting to the bottom of this conundrum.

One thing was certain: With his movement and the tone of his voice, he had everyone's attention.

"Uh, excuse me, but I think I have it now." There was no time for further preamble. "If you don't mind, I'll just outline my reasoning. If I'm correct, I think it may be important to take some action quickly or something terrible may happen. But first, let me sketch what I believe did happen.

"Bruce Whitaker came to this hospital with one purpose: to create a media event that would focus attention on St. Vincent's. And through that coverage, he hoped to expose certain practices, which, as a matter of fact, are not in strict accord with official Catholic teaching.

"I was made aware of these practices, and I must say that, on the one hand, given this hospital's purpose and other circumstances, I do not disagree with what's being done here.

"On the other hand, there has been some fudging with official Catholic teaching. There is a tendency in this archdiocese, particularly when it comes to the core city of Detroit, to look the other way when it comes to certain, one might describe them as fringe, precepts of Catholic morals and dogma.

"But if the news media were to headline the fact that a Catholic hospital is in violation of Catholic teaching and law—a rather newsworthy story, I think you'll agree—the archdiocesan authorities obviously could overlook the violations no more.

"Okay, so that's the objective of Bruce Whitaker. The problem is that Bruce Whitaker has trouble tying his shoelaces and combing his hair. His attempts at creating a media event are, in chronological order, the mutilation of curtain hooks; the alteration of a patient's medical chart—an alteration which is so imperfect it will accomplish nothing—and finally, the emptying of a gas tank that, when the absence of its contents is noticed, will simply be replaced.

"Next, apparently, someone becomes aware of Whitaker, sees what he is doing, and correctly surmises why he is doing these things. Now I know this sounds a bit tenuous,

344

but believe me, it is amazing the leap of comprehension that can occur in two like minds . . . particularly two similarly fervid minds. In any event, it does not take this person long to observe Whitaker's, uh . . . difficulties in trying to accomplish his goal. So this person begins surreptitiously to fulfill what Whitaker has attempted so ineptly.

"This person follows Whitaker to Millie Power's chart, sees that the alteration as it stands will do nothing; Whitaker has merely attempted to put the patient in the test program by changing her protocol number. Which means she would routinely receive penicillin to which she is allergic.

"But Whitaker has neglected to remove the notation signifying that Mrs. Power is, indeed, allergic to the drug. That dichotomy would, of course have been noticed by the staff, a check would have been made, and she would never have been given the drug. So the person removes the allergy notation. Now Whitaker's plan will go forward.

"But, quite by accident, I learned of Mrs. Power's allergy and also that she had been given the penicillin. So that scheme goes by the board.

"Then Mr. Whitaker plans on shutting down the operating room, which closure undoubtedly would have drawn in the media. But his plan, as usual, is destined to fail. Until this mysterious person intervenes. As a result, we have a good-sized hole in the wall and the local media are here in force.

"I think the conclusion is inescapable: This person and Whitaker have an identical objective: to draw the media into the operation of this hospital.

"As far as Whitaker is concerned, once the archdiocese is forced to act, St. Vincent's will no longer be allowed to overlook the letter of Catholic teaching. And that is all he wanted to accomplish.

"Now, I believe that his anonymous conspirator, while he shares Whitaker's objective—to draw the media into the affairs of this hospital—had a somewhat different reason for wanting all this exposure.

"Four people here very much wanted Sister Eileen out of the picture. Two of them, Dr. Lee Kim and Ethel Laidlaw, a nurse's aide, face imminent dismissal. The other two, Sister Rosamunda and John Haroldson, face a forced and most distasteful retirement.

"If Sister Eileen were to be removed from St. Vincent's, the worries of each of these four people would be over. There are a couple of ways that could happen.

"Sister Eileen might die. She might, indeed, be murdered. That would be the simplest, most direct way of getting her off the scene.

"Or in a slightly more circuitous way, she could be removed from her position here. And that could be accomplished in one of two ways. Her religious order could do it. But, in fact, her order had consistently backed and supported her.

"Or the archbishop could depose her. And if enough pressure were exerted, the archbishop might have no other choice.

"So you see, I think we are not necessarily looking for someone who wanted to murder Sister Eileen," Koesler nodded to Lieutenant Harris, "but, I think, we are very definitely looking for someone who needed to have her removed from office. The person who has been repairing Bruce Whitaker's blunders is in accord with Whitaker's objective, although not for Whitaker's reasons.

"There is also one more outstanding area of agreement between the two: the method of operation.

"As I said before, there were a couple of ways of getting rid of Sister Eileen. The most direct was murder. Many people have been murdered with far less motivation than that held by the four people I've mentioned.

"The other way was the extremely circuitous method

used by Whitaker . . . whose chief goal was not to get rid of Sister Eileen, but to force the archdiocese to act on what he saw as evil.

"As soon as Lieutenant Harris reminded me that in the operating room no one was trying to kill Sister, it dawned on me that we were looking for someone who, far more than being in agreement with Whitaker's objective, was as one with Whitaker's method of operation.

"Whitaker did not want to kill anyone. He kept doing things that would have multiple effects. He wanted to mutilate IUDs, he planned on making a sick person a little more ill, he plotted to close down an essential hospital function. Each of these plans was intended to have a side effect: the creation of a media event for the purpose of getting St. Vincent's in alignment with official Church teaching.

"Well, not too long ago I had lunch here with a gentleman who was actually lecturing me about the same sort of philosophy. He even corrected me when I referred to the method as the principle of double effect, which is its more popular identification. He insisted on calling it the principle of the indirect voluntary, which is more technically correct.

"This person, John Haroldson, was extremely comfortable with the indirect voluntary. For instance: A surgeon operates, a good or indifferent action; the first effect—and the one desired—is the health of the patient; a secondary, only tolerated, effect is the removal of an ectopic pregnancy.

"Or one alters a patient's chart, perhaps an indifferent action; the desired effect is that this will draw in the media who will be instrumental in returning the hospital to orthodoxy as well as removing Sister Eileen from the scene; the only tolerated effect is that the sick person becomes a little more ill before an intervention is made and the patient is saved.

347

"Although Mr. Whitaker would seem to be a very traditional Catholic, he probably would be hard pressed to explain either the indirect voluntary or the double effect. But, as it happens, what he was trying to do very closely resembled the indirect voluntary.

"Someone like John Haroldson would easily recognize the comparison. It was natural that the scheme would appeal to him. And very understandable that, to accomplish his own goal of ridding himself of Sister Eileen, he would find Whitaker's scheme particularly appropriate.

"Now, the special problem that presents itself is, as Inspector Koznicki has mentioned, that the whole scheme has not worked. Because of John Haroldson's expertise, both as theologian and medical student, the media event did occur. But, to date, no one has been able to take Mr. Whitaker seriously. After all this, the plan has failed. And, as far as Mr. Haroldson is concerned, it matters little that St. Vincent's is still doing business as usual. What matters to him most is that Sister Eileen is still in place as CEO.

"Haroldson's tenure here at St. Vincent's grows shorter and more tenuous by the day. But I think that is less significant to him than the frustration he must feel now that what must have been his last-ditch plan to unseat Sister Eileen is in shambles. I'm just afraid that now he may be tempted to do something . . . uh . . . drastic.''

Koesler halted. There was nothing more to say. He had presented his theory, explained it, and drawn his conclusion. Either these officers would, in the face of his previous blunder, stretch credulity and believe him, or they would not. He looked about. The expressions reflected everything from the friendly faith of Inspector Koznicki to the hostile skepticism of Lieutenant Harris, and all points between.

"I think," Koznicki said at length, "that in view of what Father has expressed, and as a matter of precaution—"

He was interrupted by a series of hysterical shrieks coming from nearby.

Led by Koznicki and Harris, Koesler and the officers rushed from the room in search of the source of the sound. The screams were coming not from the adjoining office but from the one adjoining that.

It was Sister Eileen's office. It was her secretary, Dolly, who was screaming.

Koznicki, unexpectedly agile for his size, was first to enter Sister's office. He saw Dolly standing near the large executive desk. At sight of him, she ceased screaming, but stood badly trembling.

Koznicki followed her riveted gaze to the knees and feet of a prostrate figure half hidden by the desk. It was a nun; he could see the white habit extending to sensible black shoes.

As one of the officers steadied Dolly, Koznicki crossed behind the desk and knelt beside the still figure of Sister Rosamunda. Father Koesler eased his way through the now crowded office and knelt on the other side of Sister's body.

Koznicki felt for an artery in Sister's neck. There was no pulse. He shook his head. A small bottle lay on the floor a few inches from Sister's outstretched hand. It was empty, or nearly so. Only a few drops remained.

Koznicki read the label: "Elixir Terpin Hydrate." He sniffed at the bottle. "Nothing I can identify. But poison, I assume." He looked intently at Dolly and by sheer force of his will drew her gaze. "These questions are important, so please compose yourself." He waited a moment until he could tell that she was in greater control of herself. "All right. Now, where is Sister Eileen?"

"In there." Dolly pointed to the rear door that led to Eileen's living-and-bedroom suite.

Koznicki jerked his head toward the door. Instantly,

Lieutenant Harris entered the inner suite after a perfunctory knock on the door.

"Why is Sister Eileen back in her suite so soon after major surgery?" Koznicki asked.

"She was doing so well," Dolly explained in a low tone. Though she seemed composed, the tremolo in her voice betrayed her continuing anxiety. "Of course she was taken to ICU after her operation. But she recovered remarkably well. And she asked . . . well, she demanded to be returned to her own room instead of one of the regular hospital rooms. And she is CEO, you know . . . ."

"Of course."

Harris reentered the office "She's okay. Just sleeping."

"She's been heavily medicated," Dolly added.

"Did you know Sister Rosamunda was in here?" Koznicki asked.

"No, I didn't. I knew Sister Eileen was here, of course. But I didn't know Sister Rosamunda was. She must have come in before I came on duty."

"Dolly . . ." Father Koesler looked up from his kneeling position; although she was quite obviously dead, he had given the nun conditional absolution. " . . . has John Haroldson been in here since you came on duty?"

"Why, yes . . . just a short while ago. But . . . you don't think that he—oh, my God! You can't think that he—"

"Show us to his office, Father. Quickly." Koznicki was off his knees and pushing Father Koesler out the door.

All told, there were only six officers and one priest. But because they were all large men, the number seemed larger.

Almost as one they stormed through John Haroldson's

outer office. His secretary was not there. With no preliminaries they burst into his inner office.

Haroldson looked up from his desk. He had been writing. His expression was grave; his visage seemed drained as if he were about to faint.

"Mr. Haroldson . . ." Koznicki began.

Haroldson held up a restraining hand. Everyone stopped in his tracks. For several moments Haroldson continued to write. Then he laid his pen to one side.

He picked up several sheets of paper and offered them to the Inspector. "I believe this is what you want."

Koznicki did not move to accept the papers. "Before I accept or read what you have written, I will ask Lieutenant Harris to apprise you of your rights." He nodded to Harris.

Lieutenant Harris took a card from his wallet and began reading the Miranda Warning. Harris of course knew the warning by rote. But reading it was accepted police procedure. Thus, if a defense attorney were to ask an arresting officer how he could be certain he had given the required warning, the officer could honestly respond, "I read it to him."

The scene resembled a tableau. No one moved as Harris delivered the text. Haroldson continued to extend his papers toward Koznicki, who made no move to accept them. Until the warning was completed.

Then Koznicki asked, "Do you understand what has been read to you, Mr. Haroldson?"

Haroldson nodded and shook the papers insistently.

Koznicki took them, put on his reading glasses and began to peruse the neat, precise script.

Sister! Can you hear me? Can you hear me even though you are dead?

"Mr. Haroldson, Koznicki looked up from the paper, "is this part of something like your diary?"

"Continue reading," Haroldson replied. "All that you want will be there."

I am the one who killed you. But you must know that. By now, you must know all the answers.

It was a mistake. It was a mistake ever to have set myself on this course. But that is of little consolation to you. It is too late for consolation. And I must confess I am sorry. But what good does that do you? It is too late for sorrow.

You are dead and this unbearable pain in my head goes on.

It was all so useless.

With all my heart I wish I could change the course of these events. I wish I could change what has already happened. But of course no one can do that. No one can bring you back to life.

If I were to tell this story to someone—and I may very well be forced to do so—where would I start?

I suppose I would start where so many hospital stories begin. In the emergency room . . .

Haroldson's account went on to tell of how he had been in the background of the emergency room mostly to monitor the new substitute chaplain's work. While there, Haroldson had noticed this odd character, a volunteer also trying to keep in the background.

Later, in his regular perambulations through the hospital, Haroldson became more aware of this uncoordinated dolt who managed to botch nearly everything he attempted.

Haroldson was about to dismiss the man he had identified as Bruce Whitaker. Even as a volunteer he was costing the hospital far more than he was worth.

And then came the incident of the mutilated curtain hooks. There was no reason for it. The most intriguing feature of the fiasco was that the hooks had been stored in the IUD drawer. He also noted that at a nearby cafeteria table, Whitaker seemed in a state of panicky confusion when the housekeeper presented the curtain hooks.

It had been simple for Haroldson to check out Whitaker. His name was on file as a volunteer. With Haroldson's civic contacts, he easily learned of Whitaker's background, his trial and conviction, and present parole. Haroldson recalled well the crime spree waged by Whitaker and his three arch-conservative friends. Armed with that background information, it was not all that difficult to surmise what Whitaker might be up to now.

Haroldson, at that point, made Whitaker a prime subject for surveillance. Gradually, Haroldson ascertained Whitaker's scheme: to create a media event that would bring to light St. Vincent's casual approach to authentic Catholic medical-moral ethics.

Well then, the hospital's ethical standards were those of Sister Eileen. Whitaker's objective was to force Church authorities to crack down on the hospital's moral aberrations. If that were to happen, Eileen surely would go. She would not compromise her own beliefs. She was not that sort of person. If Whitaker was successful then not only his goal, but Haroldson's too, would be achieved. Eileen would be forced out before she could pressure Haroldson into retirement.

What's more, Whitaker was not trying to seriously harm anyone. Thus Haroldson would be able to oversee Whitaker's foredoomed endeavors and amend them. All the while, by the principle of the indirect voluntary, Haroldson would be guilty of no sin. At least as far as his own conscience was concerned.

After a while, the revelation went on, it got to be a sort of contest for Haroldson. Surmising what Whitaker's next ploy would be. Remaining undetected while following him. Trying to figure out what Whitaker was attempting to do when he did it. And finally, correcting Whitaker's pitiful blunders.

Haroldson chronicled the alteration of Millie Power's chart and how he removed the sticker that denoted her allergy to penicillin. A sticker that Whitaker unaccountably did not remove. Haroldson surmised that Whitaker's plans included blowing the whistle before the patient lapsed into a terminal condition. If, typically, Whitaker had fumbled that too, he, Haroldson, would have seen to it.

And it would have worked had not the priest accidentally come upon the scene.

Finally, the statement told of the episode in OR. His disgust at Whitaker's feeble attempt to cause a breakdown in OR procedure. Of course it was a good idea; any hospital would be in the news should its OR shut down. But nitrous oxide tanks! The man was a functional idiot.

So, with the sabotaged nitrogen tank Haroldson at last had his media event. An event which Whitaker managed to move from the front page to the comic page. And, as the affair, along with the alleged perpetrator, became a farce, Haroldson's last hope evaporated.

I cannot express how deep was my depression, how complete my sense of frustration. I had banked everything on being able to manipulate Whitaker to achieve my goal. When that failed, I failed.

That is why, in a moment of utter despondency, I poisoned the medication. I knew that Eileen would need it in the earliest stages of her convalescence. If I could not effect her removal from my beloved hospital, I wanted her dead.

It did not take me long to repent my completely un-Christian action. Just long enough for you to come upon the poisoned expectorant and consume it. When I returned to Eileen's office and found you dead, I knew all was ended. Unwittingly, I have taken an innocent life. And for that I must pay. It is God's law and I accept it.

I pray only that God will grant me time for penance, penitence and repentance so that in time I may become worthy to join you, with all the angels and saints in Paradise.

Koznicki finished reading. The statement was more a letter to the deceased Sister Rosamunda than a confession. But it was sufficient for his purposes. He had Haroldson sign the document.

Momentarily, Koznicki wondered whether an attorney might use this statement to begin building a defense of insanity. It was no more than a passing thought. Guilt was the decision of the courts. Koznicki had his perpetrator. As far as he was concerned, the case was closed.

But there were other concerns that needed resolution before all the loose ends were tied.

14

JOE COX TOUCHED HIS CHAM-
pagne glass against the one Pat Lennon held. They made a
pleasant, bell-like sound.

"To the victor . . ." Cox did not bother completing the
quotation.

"It was hardly a battle." Lennon sipped her champagne.

"I suppose that's true. Once you got into it, the battle
was over." Cox closed one eye and squinted at the champagne. There are those who may be able to tell something
of the quality of champagne by the coloration. Cox was
not among them. Not unlike duffers who line up a putt the
way they see the pros do it on TV. Except that the
amateurs have no idea of what they are doing.

Lennon smiled. As she consulted the menu, her smile
faded. "Joe, did you get a load of these prices?"

"Impressive, aren't they? But it's not as bad as it looks;
don't forget we'll get a great rate of exchange."

They were dining in Canada at the Windsor Hilton,
almost directly across the Detroit River from the Renais-

sance Center and downtown Detroit. Among Detroit's distinctions, it is the only major U.S. city from which one travels south to Canada. And many, many Detroiters do.

Windsor, easily accessible by tunnel or bridge, is a pleasant place to visit. Depending on monetary fluctuations, Canada can prove to be a country in which one can exchange U. S. currency advantageously. And, especially in a place such as the Windsor Hilton, Detroiters like to contemplate their own skyline with such highlights as Tiger Stadium, Cobo Hall, Ford Auditorium, and the monster complex of the Ren Cen that blots out much more that might have been viewed.

"Did you notice," Lennon observed, "that one side of the menu is in French and the other in English?"

"Yeah. I caught onto the English just before I almost asked you for a running translation."

Returning the compliment, Lennon raised her glass to Cox. "And here's to you, Joe, and the remarkable restraint you showed when the 'Nitrogen Bomb' story broke."

Cox grew serious. "I gotta admit that was a tough decision. Whitaker opened Pandora's box when he started spouting off about Catholic morality and the ordinary magisterium and the rest of that gobbledygook. If anybody besides Pfeiffer had written that original story, the lid probably would have come off right there. But one thing you gotta say for Whitaker and Pfeiffer: They deserve each other."

"Still, you knew what Whitaker was trying to say. You knew about St. Vincent's clinic, the birth control, the ligations."

"Yeah, I knew. But the only way I knew—what the story really was—was from you. If you hadn't told me what you found out, I'd never have been able to make head-or-tails out of what Pfeiffer wrote."

"Still, Joe, it was remarkable restraint."

"Well, I don't want to muddle up what we've got. It's our agreement. I'm not gonna bust that up. Besides, the story did break once Haroldson tried to stiff Eileen and got Rosamunda instead."

Lennon shook her head in sympathy. "Poor Haroldson. Poor Rosamunda."

"I guess. But Haroldson opened up the gates for you. It's funny, how in this competition between the *Freep* and the *News* that, especially with local stories, one of the papers will get an edge and the other one just can never catch up. It certainly happened with St. Vincent's. Once it broke, no one could catch you."

"Pound for pound, Joe, you did a great job, as usual. But you're right: It was my story . . . only because I was on the damn thing before it got to be a story. I was doing, in effect, a self-assigned puffpiece on St. Vincent's. So I had the background on all the principals before they became principals. I guess it just went from a backgrounder in the magazine to a who's who on page one."

"Virtue is its own reward," Cox said. "You had the story while you were doing your initial research and you gave it up out of principle. It would have been a first-class rotten break for someone to take it from you."

"Maybe. But if somebody else had got it . . . well, that's life."

The waitress took their orders. After which they silently sipped more champagne.

Pat contemplated the massive concrete and steel of Detroit. "You know, Joe, we're lucky."

"Ummm."

"I mean, our jobs . . . our lifestyle . . . us."

"Hey, is this a preamble to another try at getting me to go to church?"

Pat snorted. "If you ever darkened a church door, they'd have to reconsecrate the place."

358

Cox covered Pat's hand with his. "You're right; we are lucky." He lifted his glass and squinted at Lennon through the remaining champagne. "Here's looking at you, kid."

"How's it going, Sister?" Dr. Fred Scott asked.

"Oh, I'm a little wobbly. But not bad for an old lady."

Under her modified veil, Sister Eileen wore a wig while her own hair was growing back. The thought had occurred to her that in the not-so-distant good old days she wouldn't have had to worry about her hair. The traditional habit would have covered everything.

"You sure you should be up and about?" Scott sat opposite the nun in her office. He had just taken her blood pressure, which was a little high, but understandably so.

"Not much help for it, Fred. So much going on since John . . . well . . ."

"Yeah, everything did pretty much hit the fan. How'd your meeting with the bishop today go?"

Eileen glanced sharply at him. "You knew about that!"

Scott shrugged. "Small hospital."

"Hmmm. Depends on whose side you're on. As far as my side goes, not well."

"How bad?"

Eileen winced. It was difficult to tell whether it was from the occasional pain she still felt or the memory of her episcopal visit.

Scott leaned forward. "You all right?"

"Yes . . . yes. I'm okay. It still hurts once in a while, but not as often. I guess the thought of this afternoon doesn't help."

"You see Cardinal Boyle."

"No. That was last week when we went over my options."

"Oh?"

"Even in this 'small hospital' you didn't hear about that?

"Well, it was one of those things that had to happen after all this publicity. I can't really blame His Eminence. I have a hunch he was aware of what we were doing here about family planning and the like. But he was able to pretend he didn't know, until just about everybody in the country found out. The poor man! He couldn't really approve of what we were doing—even though he could understand why we were doing it. But in the glare of all that publicity neither he nor I could dodge the issue."

"Which was?"

"That we were going to have to make some kind of public response. All I could tell him was that I was, in conscience, unable to change the philosophy and interpretation of theology under which we operate. He said he'd take my answer under advisement. And that culminated with my meeting today with Auxiliary Bishop Ratigan. I met with him and our Mother General, Sister Claire Cecile."

"And?"

"Bishop Ratigan was nice enough. But he had a job to do. He explained that if this had happened a few years ago, Cardinal Boyle would have resorted to his former custom of appointing a 'blue-ribbon committee' to study the matter. And they would have studied it until hell froze over or until the media forgot about it. Whichever happened first.

"But now . . . with the climate in Rome . . . well, there was no getting around it. We had to face up to conforming to the Church's magisterium. I was to enforce the letter of the law or I had to step down. I told him that left me no alternative."

"Sister?"

"The next part has got to be just between you and me, even though this is a 'small hospital.' " She forced a smile. "St. Vincent's is going to close."

"No!"

"I'm afraid so. Sister Claire Cecile said the Board had anticipated this sort of dilemma and had voted that, with my departure, St. Vincent's would be closed. The only reason they've been sustaining it, in the face of serious financial loss, was because I insisted I could make it work.

"But even to keep the poor old place alive, I can't compromise my principles. St. Vincent's conforming to the letter of Church teaching would have no meaning here in any case. So John Haroldson got at least part of what he wanted. I will be gone. But so will St. Vincent's . . . and at what cost!"

There followed several moments of silence. Scott reflected that the closing, as shocking as it was, also solved Dr. Lee Kim's problem. Under the circumstances, Kim would have no problem transferring to another hospital. And wherever he went, it would be a step or more upward.

"And how about you, Sister? What will you do?"

"Oh, Sisters don't join the unemployment line. Not even old ladies like me. I talked to Sister Claire Cecile about it. Well, we've talked before about what might come after St. Vincent's—if that ever happened.

"I'm going to be in charge of a new health-care program for our senior Sisters. Right now, there's little rhyme or reason to the various scattered houses that care for our elderly and ill. The program needs to be pulled together and coordinated. Without lots of young Sisters out in the field to bring in money, we're financially pinched as never before. It's a good program and I'm eager to get into it. It's . . . it's the program Sister Rosamunda ould have been a part of. But . . .

"Poor Sister Rosamunda." Eileen shook her head sadly. "A classic case of being in the wrong place at the wrong time. She went to the pharmacy to get a supply of Terpin Hydrate . . . the poor dear probably couldn't sleep a wink . . . all that pressure. She didn't know I had ordered all the locks changed just so she wouldn't be able to lean on that crutch anymore.

"And when she couldn't get the pharmacist to give her the new key—again at my order—she knew where she could find a bottle. Everyone who knew me well was aware that I needed it for this postnasal-drip problem. If she hadn't taken the poisoned bottle, I might have. Or John might have retrieved it. Poor Sister: in the wrong place at the wrong time.

"Well, God writes straight with crooked lines. I guess it was time for me to move on."

"And St. Vincent's?"

"Yes, I suppose. Even time for St. Vincent's to . . ." There was a catch in Eileen's voice. ". . . to close its doors for good."

"One thing, Sister."

"What's that?"

"Don't ever play poker."

✦ ✦ ✦

"I can't say this hasn't been fun, big fella. But don't you think we ought to get outta bed?"

"Why?" George Snell was deeply depressed.

"Why?" Helen Brown echoed. "Because call lights will be going on and the nurse is gonna wonder why she's runnin' her ass off when there's an aide someplace on the floor."

"That's just it," Snell observed, "you ain't exactly been 'on the floor' for quite a spell now. You been off the floor, as it were."

362

"I know, big fella, and that's why I gotta get back on duty. All somebody's gotta do is look in this room and our collective ass'll be in a sling."

"What difference does it make?"

"What difference! The difference between gettin' a paycheck and standin' in line waitin' for charity. If it trickles down this far."

"It don't make much difference. This place is gonna close down anyhow."

"This hospital?"

"What else?"

"How do you know that?"

"Small place. Rumors travel fast."

"Rumor! That's all it is."

"No. It's gonna close."

"Is that what's gettin' you down? Just 'cause this place closes don't mean there won't be any more jobs anywhere."

"Yeah? Like where?"

"Like lots of places. You keep forgettin': You're a hero!"

"That's right, ain't it?"

Happily for George Snell, he had not been compelled to testify in the case of Bruce Whitaker. So the knowledge that his "heroics" were no more than a series of accidents did not go beyond the police and Father Koesler.

"But wait a minute!" Snell sat upright. "You know I ain't no hero. You were with me both times I was suppose to've saved somebody. You know!"

"Yeah, I know, big fella. But I ain't likely to tell. Far as I can see, if this place closes, we'll just move along. They always need aides—that's me. And they always need heroes—that's you. By and large, we oughta be able to spend a good part of our lives in the sack."

"Worse luck for you." Snell lay back in the narrow

bed. Instinctively, he wrapped one long arm around Helen Brown, absently caressing her bottom.

"What do you mean, worse luck for me? You're a lot of fun, big fella. Oh, yes, a lot of fun. You have given me some of the very best lays I have ever had in my whole life. And that includes tonight. And this is an unsolicited testimonial."

"Yeah." Snell grinned, then quickly grew serious. "But there's more. At least there should be."

"More! You're kidd—oh, yeah, that's right. Both times you became a 'hero' you were about to do something 'more.' But you never got around to it. Now what in hell you could do more beats me."

"Well, it looks like you're gonna have to take it on faith. But there was somethin' more. It was one of a kind. And now," he choked back what sounded like a sob, "it's gone. Gone. Gone."

"When did it leave? Oh, what the hell we talkin' about, anyway?"

"It left after I saw somethin' on TV I'll never forget the rest of my life. And we're talking about a . . . oh . . . somethin' like a maneuver."

"That maneuver again! Look, man, I still don't know exactly what you're talkin' about. But I know you certainly know how to satisfy a person. I truly don't think I could stand any more from you than what you already done. Besides, big fella, two can play at that." Helen Brown shifted so that she was roughly one-quarter of the way on top of Snell.

"What? What you gettin' at?"

"Just this, big fella, You're not the only one who's got some fancy maneuvers."

"Wait a minute!" Helen Brown was doing things that made George Snell grin broadly. "Wait a minute! I'm kind of tired."

"That's okay, big fella. You know what the helpful cow said to the tired farmer."

"No! Hoo! Ha!"

"She said, 'You just hang on; I'll jump up and down.' "

"Oh, God!" Snell shouted in spite of the danger. "To hell with the Snell Maneuver!"

"How does it feel to be home?" Inspector Koznicki sipped his Frangelico, the after-dinner liqueur supplied from the extremely limited stores of St. Anselm's rectory.

"Great. It always feels good to get home. But the time spent at St. Vincent's was good. I learned a lot," Father Koesler said.

Koznicki licked his lips. The liqueur had a pleasant nutty taste. "That is important to you, is it not, Father? That you are always learning."

Koesler smiled. "Don't mention something like that to the few professors of mine who are still living. As a matter of fact, don't mention it to any of my peers. Both groups would laugh you to scorn.

"But, yes, as one born out of due time I have become intrigued with learning as much as I can about nearly everything. And in that context, St. Vincent's Hospital— soon to be of happy memory—was a genuine learning experience."

"You are referring to the health-care facility itself or to that most unfortunate episode?"

"Both. Interesting people. Interesting experience. With a very sad ending, no matter how you look at it."

"We have not seen much of each other since the death of Sister Rosamunda and then the trial."

"I guess we've just been busy. I had so much to catch up on here in the parish. It's always a bit of a surprise to be confronted with all that accumulates over just a few weeks. Not the mail; I stayed pretty much up on that. No, it's the decisions that everyone was kind enough to leave to me. Then, of course, you've been occupied. You're always busy."

"Life goes on."

"And so does death, and murder. And that's why you're so busy."

Koznicki smiled and sipped at the liqueur.

"I've been meaning to ask you, Inspector: Whatever happened to Bruce Whitaker? He seems to have just dropped out of sight."

"Oh, yes, Mr. Whitaker. He has moved to California . . . the Los Angeles area. He is married now, you know. . . that nurse's aide who also was one of your suspects."

"Ethel Laidlaw. That's great. But don't remind me of 'my' suspects. That was when I thought there was a plot afoot to murder Sister Eileen. As it turned out, harming Eileen was almost an afterthought."

"Sometimes one gets a feeling."

"That's what it was, Inspector, a feeling. There was indeed a good bit of animosity in the atmosphere. There really was a lot of ill feeling toward Eileen coming from Dr. Kim, John Haroldson, Sister Rosamunda, and Ethel. Except that it wasn't a murderous anger . . . at least in retrospect it seems not to have been homicidal. That is until the whole scheme fell apart. Then poor John, I feel, just took leave of his senses.

"I guess we'll never really know, since all that conflict is resolved now."

"But you got on the right track."

"Only when Lieutenant Harris pointed out that in the OR no one could have been trying to kill Eileen since no one could have known she would be a surgical patient, let alone that the nitrogen tank would be needed for her. It was more like a paramecium finding its way. Or a mouse successfully negotiating a maze. When I realized we weren't looking specifically for someone intent on murder, I simply moved one notch over and tried to imagine someone whose moral approach to things might match the MO exhibited by Bruce Whitaker and his friends.

"That's when I remembered my conversation with John Haroldson. Of everyone I knew in the hospital, he was the only one whose natural law approach to morality, specifically the indirect voluntary, came very close to what Whitaker was actually doing.

"I must say, though, Inspector, there is nothing intrinsically wrong with the principle of the indirect voluntary or double effect. It is a very legitimate theological school of thought. But, like everything else, if it gets twisted by a sick mind—as happened with John Haroldson—it can become pathological. And so it did.

"But, back to Bruce Whitaker. From the news broadcasts and papers, I was never clear on what happened to him. Is it true that no charges were brought against him. . . even after all he did at St. Vincent's?"

"I do not blame you for being less than enlightened by the news accounts. After that initial incoherent story in the *News*, it was almost impossible to get anything clearly until, of course, Mr. Haroldson became perpetrator of record. And that, by the way, is largely what saved Mr. Whitaker from a serious problem."

Koznicki paused to take another small sip of Frangelico. It was his plan to make this small snifter of liqueur last until the coffee Koesler had made would be cold and, thus, for more than one reason, undrinkable. Koesler's coffee was legendary.

"You see, Father, the prime difficulty in this case always is this business of Mr. Whitaker's mistaking curtain hooks for intrauterine devices. Everyone knows it must be a crime of some sort. It is just difficult, after that, to remain serious about the whole affair.

"I remember very well when presenting this case, the prosecuting attorney said, with a straight face, 'We are talking about first-degree, premeditated mutilation of curtain hooks, right?'

"You see, it was difficult to be serious after that.

"But the statutes did reveal that malicious destruction of property under $100 valuation is a misdemeanor. Over $100 is a felony. Since the hooks were worth less than $100, we had no more than a misdemeanor.

"The only real problem Mr. Whitaker faced was the alteration of a patient's chart. The technical charge would have been 'assault with intent to do great bodily harm.' But since the real harm was done when Mr. Haroldson amended the chart's alteration, and adding the overall considerations in this case, the decision was made not to charge Mr. Whitaker as long as he made restitution and promised to stop harassing the Catholic Church.

"When the authorities were finished with Mr. Whitaker, I can assure you he was one deeply impressed young man. Then, his parole and the new probation were transferred to California along with Mr. Whitaker."

"But," Koesler interjected, "what about what Whitaker did in the operating room? I mean, with the nitrous oxide?"

"In effect, the prosecutor's opinion was that he had done nothing. Oh, possibly he had created a nuisance for which he would be banned from the hospital. But then, no hospital would ever want his services again.

"On the other hand, the charge against Mr. Haroldson was most serious. Placing an explosive with intent to destroy and causing damage to property is punishable with twenty-four years in the state prison. But that sentence, as you know, pales when compared with life imprisonment for murder in the first degree."

368

"Yes, I know those sentences were imposed on Haroldson. But I wondered about first-degree murder. After all, he did repent and intended to retrieve the poisoned medication. Except that Rosamunda got there first. And he never intended to do any harm to Rosamunda in the first place."

"Well, his repentance may or may not have something to do with his moral guilt. It has nothing to do with his guilt in criminal law. Neither does the fact that he got the wrong person. It is called transferred intent. If a man wants to shoot Inspector Koznicki and the bullet hits Father Koesler instead, he is not innocent of murder because he killed the wrong man."

"Poor John!" Koesler noticed that Koznicki's coffee was not only untouched, it by now appeared quite cold. "Oh, Inspector, may I hot-up your coffee?"

"Oh, no; no, please! I must be going very soon."

"As you wish. You know, I intend to visit John at Jackson sometime soon. It's such a pity: Here he will be locked up with real criminals probably for the rest of his life. And he could be enjoying a trouble-free retirement."

"But that is the point, is it not, Father: that he felt he could not enjoy a trouble-free retirement. That is what led him into this much troubled retirement."

"Well, I must be going. It is getting late."

Koesler retrieved Koznicki's coat and hat from the closet. "Oh, I meant to ask you, Inspector: What was the poison John used?"

"Isopto Carpine. An eye medication, highly toxic.

"He got it from the hospital pharmacy. He tried to use his own key, but the locks had been changed by then. As chief operating officer, he was about the only one in the hospital who could countermand Sister Eileen's order.

"Of course, with his having done so—he was not thinking very clearly at this point—it would have been easy to trace the drug back to him. However, we did not need to do so as he was in a most confessing mood."

The high that had been sustaining Koesler took a sudden dip. "I'm afraid I did not contribute much to help you. You were on the verge of the solution yourself."

"Not at all, Father. You discovered the vital link between the crimes we knew of, largely defective though they were, and the crimes we were trying to solve."

"But if I had been more perceptive and quicker, I might have been able to prevent Rosamunda's death."

"Possibly. But if you had, Sister now would have been forced into that retirement which she so dreaded. And even if you had discovered the link sooner, Mr. Haroldson would still be serving the twenty-four-year sentence for tampering with the nitrogen tank. And, at his age, the difference between twenty-four years, even with good time, and life may be negligible.

"Besides, I am quite convinced that you very probably saved Mr. Haroldson from suicide."

"You think so?"

"I am quite certain. So, as they say, God writes . . ."

". . . straight with crooked lines."

"Exactly. Well, thank you, Father, for the lovely meal and, as usual, for good companionship."

"Not at all, Inspector. You sure you wouldn't like a little hot coffee before you go out into the cold?"

For a moment, Inspector Koznicki toyed with the idea of telling his friend the truth about the execrableness of his coffee. Almost, but not quite. It was late and he wanted to get home.

"I think not, Father. Thank you just the same." And the Inspector departed.

Koesler closed the door and reflected. It was odd. As often as he dined at other people's homes or in restaurants, everyone usually had more than one cup of coffee. Sometimes several cups. Yet he could not recall anyone's ever having more than one cup of his coffee. Often, the first cup was never finished.

It was a mystery he simply could not solve.

"Do you still love me?"

"Of course I do; don't be silly."

"I wouldn't blame you if you didn't."

"How can you say a thing like that?"

"You know!"

"Ethel, I love you. With the exception of my mother and Holy Mother Church, you're the only one I've ever loved. Now, it's late. Why don't we just go to sleep. I've got a busy day tomorrow."

"That's it, Bruce!"

"What's it, Ethel?"

"Your busy days."

"Ethel, do you remember just a few weeks ago? Your hospital was going out of business and you were about to be unemployed with absolutely no prospects for another job."

"I remember."

"And I was in a holding cell charged with a misdemeanor and a felony. And I couldn't afford a lawyer. And I had failed miserably in my mission. The only reason the mission finally worked is because somebody much smarter was following me around doing things right. And I couldn't even get in touch with my three friends in Van's Can because they were being held incommunicado because of the riot there.

"And because we've started a new life and they would never understand, I will probably never see them again. And it was only because of a miracle and a sympathetic judge that the charges against me were dropped. And, finally, it was only through the grace of God and your faith in me that I got this job out here.''

"So what are you driving at, Bruce?"

"What I'm driving at, Ethel, is that you and I just ought to be real grateful for what we've got and not ask any questions . . . see?"

"I'm not sure."

"Look. I could be in jail. You could be on the outside waiting for me, maybe for a lot of years. Or we could both be free and both be out of a job and lucky just to live in some godforsaken barn like the Back Porch Theatre attic . . . see?"

"I don't know. Maybe. I gotta admit I like your title . . . associate director. And the corporation is certainly high class. Gosh, the Center for Id Expression runs lots of big ads in lots of expensive magazines. And the Maharidian Maker Shalal Hash Bash is a great boss. At least he's been very generous so far.

"But Bruce, I can't help being jealous . . . what wife could?"

"Ethel, I'd be the first to admit that I am not all that wise in the ways of the world. But I gotta think that most wives would be very happy if their husbands brought home $33,000 a year plus incentives. That's not hay.''

"Maybe so, but most wives' husbands aren't sex therapists.''

"Somebody's got to do it.''

"I suppose. But—it's only natural—I still get jealous of all those women who have you all day long.''

"Ethel, what can I do? Before I met you I proved beyond the shadow of a doubt that I could do nothing. Not anything. And then, in one magic moment, on a cart in a chapel in a Catholic hospital I discovered a talent that— well, let's face it, Ethel: the chapel, the Catholic hospital, the way we are destined to do God's will—it's a talent that's got to be God-given.''

Ethel smiled in spite of her fears. "That *was* a magic moment, wasn't it, Bruce?"

"Yeah, it was. I never did anything right before in my life. But that moment! There was something about that hospital. It was like the power was flowing out of someone else—God, I guess—and flowing into me. Right after I experienced my reaction and felt your response, I knew this was a God-given gift and it had to be used for the betterment of mankind.''

"Womankind.''

"Whatever. Anyway, it felt kind of funny making a demonstration tape and sending it to the Maharidian. But since I was doing it with you, it wasn't so bad.''

"And it was on the strength of that tape that you were hired.''

"That's true, Ethel. But in no time now I've worked my way up here at the Id Center to be the number-one surrogate. You should be proud.''

"I am. But I'm jealous too.''

"Don't be. I'm doing it for the greater honor and glory of God—like the Jesuits say—AMDG. Besides—now don't you go telling this to anyone; it might ruin me—''

"Okay.''

"I don't get any pleasure from it.''

"You don't get any—! How can that be?''

"I save all my pleasure for you.''

"You do?''

"Absolutely.''

"Oh, Bruce. That makes me so happy. I'm even happier now that the Maharidian has named it—you know, the thing—after you.''

"Uh-huh. The Whitaker Maneuver! Can we go to sleep now, Ethel?''

"Sure, Bruce."

"Bruce?"

"What, Ethel?"

"Could we do it just once? It helps me go to sleep real good."

"Ethel!"

"Please."

"Oh, okay. Give me a moment."

"Are you ready yet?"

"Wait a minute."

"Yet?"

"Um-hmm."

"Now?"

"Oh!"

"Bruce, I think you're ready."

"It's God's will!"

"God's will be done!"

About the Author

William X. Kienzle, author of seven bestselling mysteries, was ordained into the priesthood in 1954 and spent twenty years as a parish priest. For twelve years he was editor-in-chief of the *Michigan Catholic*. After leaving the priesthood, he became editor of *MPLS* magazine in Minneapolis and later moved to Texas, where he was director of the Center for Contemplative Studies at the University of Dallas. Kienzle and his wife, Javan, presently live in Detroit, where he enjoys playing the piano as a diversion from his writing.

Attention Mystery and Suspense Fans

Do you want to complete your collection of mystery and suspense stories by some of your favorite authors? John D. MacDonald, Helen MacInnes, Dick Francis, Amanda Cross, Ruth Rendell, Alistar MacLean, Erle Stanley Gardner, Cornell Woolrich, among many others, are included in Ballantine/Fawcett's new Mystery Brochure.

For your FREE Mystery Brochure, fill in the coupon below and mail it to: